ACKNOWL[...]

The following people have been en[...] of this book.

The ball dancers of Black Leather Wings, Poppy Z. Brite, Anne and Drew Campbell, Scott Knell and David Christensen of Casa Larue Investments, M. Christian, Doctor Beth, Cléo Dubois, Jesse Fishhook, Michael Thomas Ford, Richard Labonté, Fakir Musafar, Ian Philips, Carol Queen, Kirk Read, Matt Rice, Thomas Roche, Michael Rowe, Martha Silverspring, Vikki Sinnott, Jezi Strong, Tristan Taormino, Glenn Turner, J.W., and Greg Wharton.

However, all sins of omission and commission are my own. Readers who would like more details about the Christian conquest of pagan Europe can turn to Prudence Jones and Nigel Pennick's excellent book, *A History of Pagan Europe* (Routledge, 1995). The 14th-century activity of armed orders of Christian crusaders against pagans in Old Prussia are also documented in *A Distant Mirror: The Calamitous 14th Century*, Barbara W. Tuchman (Ballantine Books, 1978). Although some of the background of my characters is loosely based upon this information, this is a work of fiction, and none of the individuals or organizations in this book are intended to represent actual persons or entities.

PUBLICATION CREDITS

Portions of this book have appeared previously (in a slightly different form) as short stories, as indicated below.

"The Angel at the Top of My Tree," *Best Lesbian Erotica 1996*, Tristan Taormino, ed. (Cleis Press, 1996).

"Parting Is Such Sweet Sorrow," *Sons of Darkness: Tales of Men, Blood and Immortality*, Michael Rowe and Thomas S. Roche, eds. (Cleis Press, 1996). Excerpted in *Canadian Male*, Nov./Dec. 1996, pp. 22-27.

"The Wolf Is My Shepherd, I Shall Not Want," *Switch Hitters*, Carol Queen and Lawrence Schimel, eds. (Cleis Press, 1996). Translated into Dutch and reprinted in *Wilde Jongens*, Kyra Andriese, ed. (Prometheus, 1997).

"I'm Not Well, but I'm Better," *Love in Vein Two: Eighteen More Original Tales of Vampire Erotica*, Poppy Z. Brite, ed. (Harper Paperbacks, 1997).

"Take one erotic master; open up a vein of eternal yearning. Look into the heart of horror, and find its greatest intimacy: the infinite thirst for blood and love in the hands of Patrick Califia's *Mortal Companion*."
—Susie Bright, editor of *The Best American Erotica* series

"Patrick Califia has crafted a lush and passionate tale of bloodlust, ennui, and immortality, fairly crackling with the erotic energy and gender bending that only lurk sedately beneath the surfaces of tamer vampire novels. This is Anne Rice on ecstasy, with all the stops pulled out!"
—Caitlin R. Kiernan, author of *Threshold* and *Low Red Moon*

"Patrick Califia straps in readers for a wild ride. It's all here: love, passion, seduction, violence and revenge, laced with vampires, spliced with vanilla-to-dark-chocolate sex, cut with B&D, S/M, straight, gay, lesbian and outré eroticism that will delight. *Mortal Companion* is well-written, highly charged, funny, sexy, and tender—loved the talking cats! What a pansexual adventure!"
—Nancy Kilpatrick/Amarantha Knight, author of *The goth Bible*, *The Power of the Blood* series, and *The Darker Passions* series

"*Mortal Companion* is like a big slice of Sacher torte: rich, sweet, dark, complex, and memorably delicious. Patrick Califia has mixed the Byronic hero, Gothic romance, and the BDSM subculture to create a sensual, fast-moving, perverse, and intelligent novel that delighted me from beginning to end. In smoldering pagan leatherbear Ulric Jäger, the novel's passionate protagonist, Califia has contributed a character of great depth and originality to vampire literature, a hero whose adventures I relished mightily and a kindred soul whose future exploits I hungrily anticipate."
—Jeff Mann, author of *Bones Washed with Wine*, *Edge*, and *Devoured*

"Patrick Califia has been one of the bravest, most articulate, and most original voices in alternative literature for longer than many of today's writers have been plying their craft. His masterful touch and authoritative voice are immediately apparent in this new novel, and can only serve to further burnish his literary crown, adding the fantasy field to his many other conquests."
—Michael Rowe, editor of the *Queer Fear* anthology series

Mortal Companion:
An Erotic Tale of
Love and Vengeance

Mortal Companion:
An Erotic Tale of
Love and Vengeance

PATRICK CALIFIA

suspect thoughts press
www.suspectthoughtspress.com

Copyright © 2004 by Patrick Califia

Author photograph by Mark I. Chester
Cover image and design by Shane Luitjens/Torquere Creative
Book design by Greg Wharton/Suspect Thoughts Press
Print Management by Jackie Cuneo/Little Jackie Paper

First Edition: May 2004
ISBN 0-9710846-9-6

Library of Congress Cataloging-in-Publication Data

Califia-Rice, Patrick, 1954-
  Mortal companion / Patrick Califia.
      p. cm.
  ISBN 0-9710846-9-6 (pbk.)
  1. Vampires--Fiction. 2. Loneliness--Fiction. 3. Brothers and sisters--Fiction. I. Title.
PS3553.A3987M67 2004
813'.54--dc22

                            2004001196

Suspect Thoughts Press
2215-R Market Street, PMB #544
San Francisco, CA 94114-1612
www.suspectthoughtspress.com

Suspect Thoughts Press is a terrible infant hell-bent to publish challenging, provocative, stimulating, and dangerous books by contemporary authors and poets exploring social, political, queer, spiritual, and sexual themes.

DEDICATION

This book is for my chosen family,
bound to me with leather and blood.

IN MEMORIAM

To the memory of
Magical Mystical Mister Mephistopheles
Many Toes of the Thunderfoot Clan.

Dear Purrfessor,
May Golden-Eyed Bast the Ever Merciful and Merry
cherish you with tinfoil balls, fried chicken, and ripe avocados
until I can join you in Her temple of many armchairs
and sing your songs again.
I was never happier than when I slept
with your big gray self at the foot of my bed.

Mortal Companion

TABLE OF CONTENTS

DRAMATIS PERSONAE
(In Alphabetical Order)

Adulfa Jäger	Ulric's vampiric and vengeful half-sister
Alain Tremblay	a Cajun leatherman, briefly Ulric's lover
Albert Ching	owner and proprietor of the Heavenly Golden Palace of Sleeping Dragon Dreams, an opium den circa 1890
Alice and Moe, Chloe, Curtis, Evan, Fortescu, Fortunata Noir, Fox and Lynyrd, Horace, Isabeau, Janice, Jonathan Steel, Madison, and Pipe	mortal members of the Jäger Family
Amy Ross	a therapist who specializes in dual relationships
Billy	a troublesome bartender
Bridget Marie	Mary Beth's fellow student and best friend
Davy	a former hustler and homeless youth, now Patrick Kelly's dog
Evelyn Harkness, Ellen Bauer, Linda Treat, Jocelyn Dewars, and Eddy Silverstein	Amy Ross' former clients. RIP.
Sir Frederic	Hilbert's second in command
Harvey	Alain's business partner and ex-lover
Henri	a coach driver
Sir Hilbert	Head of the Germanic Knights of the Holy Sepulcher

Jamie	a shopworn girl
Kip	Alain's fuck buddy
Lilith	(née Mary Beth Wolcott), Ulric's mortal companion
Luna, Anastasia, Charley, and Hecate	Ulric's vampire cats and bodyguards
Modeen Jefferson	Mary Beth's fellow student
Monica Bradshaw	one of Adulfa's more deserving and terpsichorean victims
Mordecai	Rhys' bandmate and keeper of the keyboard
Father O'Donahue	a priest with an evil secret
Olav	the brother of Ulric's mother; today we would call him a father figure
Patrick Kelly	a corrupt vice cop (see "The Cop and His Choir Boy," *No Mercy*, Alyson Publications, 2000)
Poison and Bo	an Asian stripper and her butch girlfriend (see "What Girls Are Made Of," *Melting Point*, Alyson Publications, 1993)
Rhys	a homeless punk musician who catches Adulfa's eye
Madame Rousseau	manageress of the Café Jolie
Rowan Silverhair	The Eldest of the Boar People of Red Springs Village
Tabitha	a Parisienne with a burning passion for Adulfa
Ulric Jäger	a vampire

CHAPTER 1
Why Stone Lions Roar

There is no loneliness like that of the vampire.

Caesar in the midst of his assailants, the cosmonaut whose malfunctioning space capsule is falling into the sun, the sailor marooned on a desert island, are still sustained by a sense of their oneness with humanity. The nun who has taken to her cell for a life of silent prayer may have turned her face to God alone, but this only emphasizes her apartness from the divine; her mortality. The condemned man who walks to his own execution is shackled to his jailers, and he knows he will have witnesses who will flinch (or rejoice) to see him encounter the noose, electric chair, or poisoned needle. His crimes were committed against creatures like himself.

But the vampire is reminded each evening that those who most resemble him are in fact of a different order entirely. Survival in this Christian millennium depends on maintaining that distinction— physically, psychologically, and spiritually. Nor can one vampire solace another. They are as much each other's enemies as they are a danger to their prey; competitors held apart by an inborn antagonism toward one another. It is nature's way of distributing them evenly across their hunting ranges, keeping a territory free for each one's private use and grim stewardship.

Ulric had endured that loneliness for so many centuries that he was very nearly bored to death by his own suffering. He was fair enough to look at, for he had been changed just as the slenderness of youth had turned into the bulkier physique of a full-grown man. His long black hair was thick and curly, and his face was intelligent, masculine, and full of an unvoiced grief that drew both men and women whose hearts were also heavy. His loneliness was a scar that encumbered his psyche, a second skin of rigidity and tingling numbness that came between him and the world. Fate had left him with only one reliable pleasure, and he could not deny that it was as wild a thrill as sex or narcotics. But deep in his heart he knew that he was close to the point where even that addiction would fail to goad him on through one more cycle of sleep, fevered hunting and livid feeding, and another resentful dawn that robbed him of his senses. So he had become a wanderer, a derelict, so accustomed to isolation and the failure of happiness that he was not even searching for a reason to live. Rather, he was avoiding a confrontation with his own feelings, refusing to add up the score of his worth and then deliberately put himself in the way of either joy or harm. Let chance decide what happened to him now; he willed himself to be like a storm of pollen carried unresisting on the summer wind. Except that he was utterly sterile: as often as he was planted in the earth, no germination could be wrung from his ancient husk; there was nothing in him that could inspire new life into reaching for the sun.

On this particular twilight, Ulric awakened to the taste of earth and moldering leaves. He was breathing through a plastic tube that had been held in place all day by the rictus of his insensible mouth. Knowing better than to open his eyes, he made the graceful swimming motions that would demolish the thin lid of his shallow grave. He surfaced in the warm darkness of a Midwestern summer night. His makeshift snorkel (was it part of a vacuum cleaner?) was stashed away in his pants pocket. As he lay in his cradle of earth, which retained some of the warmth of the now-vanished sunlight, his ears were soothed by the rustle of leaves in the evening breeze. He had camped in a small copse of trees one hundred yards away from the tracks of the freight train that had brought him here. Rivulets of green scents poured over his face and were drawn up to be sampled and relished. In an instant, he built an accurate and evolving image of the world around him, as if he were calling roll and getting an answer from every squirrel, thistle, bird, and twig.

A cloud of fireflies sailed past, unaware of their own beauty. The tiny outbursts of iridescence were almost painful to his eyes. Ulric's vision was sharpened like all of his other senses by the keen hunger that had driven him back to consciousness. But his appetite gave a priority to other, potentially more gratifying sensory impressions—the stench of cough syrup and unwashed mortal flesh, and the sonorous peal of a drunkard's snore. Some poor unlucky hobo had passed out by the ashes of Ulric's campfire, not even an arm's length from where he had dug his solitary niche.

Each morning before he slept, Ulric imagined that the next time the hunger electrified him, he would resist it. And every time he woke, he realized he had forgotten how hard it hit him, as if he had been changed into some predatory animal that had no second thoughts about killing when its stomach collapsed from hunger. Instinct does not take no for an answer.

Ulric grinned at the crescent moon, who seemed to dip her horn to toast him. "Someday it will be me," he whispered, "but not tonight. I will live for one more day." Then he rolled over and took the life that fate had stretched out beside him. It was not a particularly brave or even coherent life, so there was no struggle; but rich or poor, every mortal possessed a kind of wealth. They were brimful of the scarlet brandy that Ulric rose up each night afire to quaff. He took and took until the captive heart stopped drumming, his hands warming as the body they gripped grew cold. He felt a brief stab of sorrow, not for the stranger's death, but for the fact that Ulric had not mourned his victim's passing. What he felt, more than anything, was envy. It might even be rage. If he had to drag his feet through one more span of dark hours, carrying a heart made of dry bone, it was only fair that someone else should not take one more weaving, dirty-faced, obsequious step.

Barely holding shame at bay, Ulric stood, wiping his mouth, feeling a little drunk. With thoughtful fingers, he groomed his long black hair and short, neat beard, discarding crumbs of bark and loam. He checked his earlobes to make sure the gold circles still swung there. Then it was a simple matter to deepen his nest, digging it out with an empty tin can, and tip the depleted and withered body into the trench. Already rumors of a serial killer had traveled across the country and back again as frightened drifters shifted their train-jumping routes, looking for safety. But hoboes did not talk to cops, and cops did not care much if tramps died. By the time anybody official was put on the trail, it was very possible all the evidence would be gone, eaten by the earth, which was more voracious than any vampire. Bodies did not last long once their previous owners had ceased twitching in Ulric's embrace. It was as if contact with his immortality made them even more ephemeral, hastening their dissolution.

Ulric danced on top of the grave to make everything flat and tidy, but knew that a good dog—or an indifferent sheriff, for that matter— could easily find buried forensic treasure there. He did not care; it was his innate sense of orderliness that made him take these precautions, not a fear of being caught. Soldiers and policemen had apprehended him before, and it was a simple enough matter to go into their minds and change them. But he did not like rearranging mortal memory and opinion. It was difficult to wash away the soiled feeling of rummaging about in someone else's stained emotional laundry. Interrogations and such were time-consuming. "I may be immortal," Ulric told a particularly splendid beech tree, "but I have no time to waste."

What bluster! Now that he had chosen to prolong his comfort for another twenty-four hours, what was he to do with the next five minutes? He spun in a full circle to survey earth and sky, doubting that what was left of the wild green world would offer him an omen.

Ulric had taken to the rails some months ago, at the tail end of winter. For a split second, he considered returning to his house in San Francisco, which was being guarded by his feline companions, who grew increasingly irate about his long absence. Something irked him about that prospect, though he loved his house and the unnatural cats who kept it safe. He was looking for...something. And struggling to remain tolerant of his own restlessness, because he knew he was as likely to succeed in his quest as the knights who sought out the Holy Grail. But he might at least win through to a state of exhaustion that could be substituted for peace. In that depleted state, some hare might cross his path and briefly divert him. What else was left to him but a series of detours?

Suddenly revolted by a memory of the vagrant's unshaved neck and the musty smell of his thrift store apparel, Ulric strolled toward the sound of running water. His wolf's eyes guided him easily through the dark. At the edge of the river, he simply kept on walking, laughing a little at the picture of insouciance he made, until he was up to his neck in cold water. The wet riverbed stones shifted beneath his feet, and he enjoyed the challenge of picking his way across them. It was important to enjoy these little pleasures as much as possible. That was why he had settled, for the last hundred years or so, in this country, this place they called America as if it were synonymous with the entire continent. Things changed rapidly here—technology, language, music, fashion. There was always something new to learn. His books, investments, art, music, and pets were only the facsimile of a life, but Ulric clung to it. He had more experience than most with death, and thus perhaps had more reason to fear it.

In the middle of the river, he allowed himself to be submerged completely and floated for several long minutes, sluicing out his mouth, suddenly desperate to feel clean. Perhaps if he could have swallowed the icy water, at least diluted the murderous burden that weighed down his belly. But he knew better than to try, just as he knew no tears would come to relieve his grief. The sickness in the old man's lungs would have given him a more painful death than the deadly trance that Ulric had spun for the victim as he had pinned him to the ground in a parody of love. But who knew exactly when that death would have come? And who knew what the vagrant himself would have chosen, or what value he might have placed on the remaining span of his natural life, even if those days were to be harsh ones full of poverty, sickness, and aimless wandering? From the outside, it might look as if he was just stumbling from one makeshift campfire and over-the-counter buzz to another opportunity to curse, jostle his fellows, and eat something he had salvaged from the garbage or stolen. But maybe this was not someone whose highest aspiration was a can of malt liquor or lining up to rape a smaller, more naïve man. There were philanthropists in rags, saints in madhouses.

Stop it, Ulric finally told himself. *I am no assassin on a grassy knoll; I cull the herd of mankind. I am a part of All-That-Is, a child of this injured earth. And so I take what I must to live.*

Once out of the river, Ulric felt disinclined to return to the junction and snag an outgoing freighter. He shook himself briskly, expelling water and sorrow, and set out for the town. He did not know which town, it did not particularly matter. As he walked, the warm summer breezes dried his thin shirt and trousers. The wet would make his long, black hair break into a mass of curls. He had not checked himself for blood stains. There were none. If centuries of feasting on the living cannot teach you decent table manners, what good is being undead?

When humanity clusters together, certain smells and sounds are predictably present, even at night. Ulric did not think this was a city, it was just a small town. Still, he wrinkled his nose. This far inland, the breeze carried no trace of the ocean. But he could pick up the scent of wheat, corn, and alfalfa in the fields the road parted. Pieces of claptrap rusty farm machinery slept here and there among the fruitful furrows. A little hut or two would not be amiss, here in the tranquility and order of the farmland. The crops were different—taller, more regimented—than the grains and vegetables he had once harvested with his own folk. Why didn't people limit their numbers and spread themselves out instead of concentrating their habitations, like a boil coming to a head?

The wind carried his scent to a small herd of black-and-white dairy cows, who threw their heads up in fear and moved to the far side of their pasture. When he thought of the little, shaggy, sharp-horned brown cows he had herded as a boy, these slab-sided beasts looked as impersonal as milk cans. They had been bred to fit the machine that stole nourishment from them. It was a disturbing thought.

The asphalt road turned without apology or warning into Main Street, lined with houses, each with a yard, and then there was a park with a gazebo. A band probably played there on the Fourth of July while children waved sparklers and parents packed up the remains of fried-chicken picnics. There would be fireworks and teenagers slipping off to meet one another in the disreputable shadows under the bleachers.

Ulric walked at a steady pace, swinging his arms, calmed a little by the presence of these small-town, orderly lives, these people who thought they knew everything that was important to know about each other and the world they lived in. Sometimes it drove him mad to walk alongside this complacency and intimacy. Sometimes he could not bear it, and he had to run riot, smash their serenity and smug assumptions, show them the terrible grin of the bone beneath their stupid faces. Sometimes he just could not go near it at all, and lived in what remained of the wilderness, drinking the blood of animals until the rank unsatisfying taste of it drove him once more in to the company of the species that had exiled him.

Past the park were more houses. Ulric kept to the main road, sparing a few cautious glances for dogs that might be on the loose. Dogs were sometimes inconvenient, and he did not enjoy dispatching them. Soon enough the houses gave way to the town square. Two Greco-Roman buildings—a town hall, he suspected, which no doubt also contained the county jail, and a library—faced each other with a plaza between them. The grassy square was bordered with maple trees. In its center was a large fountain. Its other two sides were occupied by incongruous modern office buildings that did not go up more than four stories.

The stone lions that flanked the library's steps drew him forward. He stood across the street from the marble facade of the pretentious and dumpy little building and admired the frothy manes and apparently unwarranted snarls of its leonine guardians. Such a display of bravado on a balmy evening! Ulric smiled and toyed with one of his gold earrings. He knew a lot about the ways men displayed their ferocity toward one another. It amused him. He thought vaguely about sculpting, wondering if it held the germ of a reason to go on living. His other attempts to launch the ship of artistry had foundered upon the rocky shoals of his lack of talent. They say practice makes perfect, but he had never found that to be true. "Those who can't, collect," he said aloud, and wondered if he was talking too much to himself to be considered sane.

One of his senses tingled: the nameless one in the roof of his mouth that recognized the presence of a warm-blooded creature. Then she came out of the door of the library, posed between the lions to lock it up, and turned to descend the stairs that divided them. Her clothes were ill-fitting, a plain white blouse and a black skirt, and she wore scuffed pumps with flat heels. But he could discern the royal curves of her body within the cheap outfit. When she paused to regard him, Ulric's unnatural heart seemed to stop pumping the rich blood he had stolen. He had discovered the white offering cup of a lily, held aloft on its green stem in the middle of an onion field.

If only there was one person who took delight in who he was, who could look at him and understand how he lived, accept how he spent his nights without screaming and going mad or struggling to escape. How he craved the simple boon of mortal companionship. Of course, there was one person who knew the entire story of his life. But she was a fearsome entity, and it troubled him to invoke her memory. He prayed that the gods might keep her busy with her own affairs, ideally upon another continent. To be in the presence of his half-sister, Adulfa, was to be in terrible pain.

Ulric had been born in 1339. Though he did his best to make sense of the twenty-first century, the meaning of such verities as "man" and "woman" had changed so much in five hundred years that he often felt he hunted in a horde of mad things, caricatures of the real human beings he remembered as his mother, mother's brother, shield-friends, lovers and members of his tribe. These dear ones were slaughtered when the Germanic Knights of the Holy Sepulcher, returning from a failed crusade to seize Jerusalem, declared a holy war against the pagans who occupied the land that the Pope in Avignon had given them, land that would eventually be claimed by Germany and Poland. Those ancient and beloved faces were still more real to him than the living bodies he took into his strong arms each night. Sharpening his teeth upon his victims' throats, Ulric felt them to be phantoms.

How other vampires coped with this anomie, he did not know and had no way to discover. The only other vampire he knew for a certainty existed (other than a few trifling young ones he had taken to clear his own territory and walk without hunger for a few days) was Adulfa. Fair as he was dark, and tall enough to look him in the eye, that Valkyrie nourished a hatred of him as fierce as that she felt for the Christian crusaders who thundered into their village and took the children of murdered pagans as slaves to serve their jealous, womanless god.

Adulfa had never wanted to be one of the wise women who might aspire to immortality. She was a warrior, blooded even before Ulric. With great glee, she had chosen a brief life of risk and adventure. She liked to race her horses, steal cattle, fight and drink, and sleep with the wives of jealous men. She had no patience for the poky life of the elders, who must memorize genealogy and tribal lore, study the stars and the weather, become wise about the human heart. To find herself unwillingly made a member of that tedious class, even though the Eldest and the people they served no longer existed, was a humiliation she would never allow him to forget. Sooner or later, she would come up with a way to make him pay. *Just one more reason*, Ulric thought, *to keep moving.*

The fact that he had not wanted to be immortal either counted for nothing in Adulfa's eyes. But to have his life prolonged by the gift of another's blood was not a fate he had ever envisioned for himself. Men were rarely elevated to the ranks of the Eldest anyway. Only old women were thought to have the strength of character that was necessary to control the blood-hunger. Sir Hilbert, Templar of the Germanic Knights, had killed Rowan Silverhair with his own hands, to shame the soldiers in his party who might still be afraid to break the ancient taboo on shedding a woman's blood. Ulric thought that Hilbert killed women with the same zeal that other men hunted game for their table. To prove himself beyond all pagan notions of morality, Hilbert had cut out Rowan's heart and eaten it, and cursed himself more effectively than the Eldest had done. He later forced what he saw as a taint on to Ulric, whom he also forced into his bed. The bewildered and transformed young man was hooded and caged, left without blood for a fortnight, and of course fell upon the first warm-blooded thing that was thrust into his cell. When he realized who slumped bloodless in his arms, Ulric made the hasty decision to bring Adulfa into the ranks of the immortals rather than kill her as Hilbert intended. Their escape from the knights' fortress and subsequent parting of their ways was a long story that Ulric refused to revisit as he stared at the fascinating woman who hid behind a humdrum facade.

Adulfa's ice blue eyes would always regard him with contempt. She had never forgiven Ulric for that violation or for the sexual intrusion that accompanied it. Ulric was not sure he would ever forgive himself. Men were welcome to gamble with Adulfa or become her shield-friends for a raid, but they were never invited to share her bed, no matter how rowdy or handsome they might be. She would hear no mitigating excuses — the strength of the new hunger that he could not control; the desire to save her life. From time to time, she visited him. Though he had made her, she was able to compel him to remain in her presence; tolerate the agony of her nearness. She was a woman, after all, and everyone knew women were more powerful than men in magical or spiritual matters. She visited him to tell him he would live until she had devised the perfect punishment.

Ulric supposed it must be this desire for revenge that filled her with the ambition to survive life eternal. He himself had no such daemon. He had tried many times to ease the torture of the years — acquiring wealth, knowledge, beautiful possessions. But despite all that he remained a man at heart and wanted what every proper man needs to have as a reason for living: the passion and pride, recognition and acceptance in his lover's eyes.

It had been so long since he had even been able to hope for the sweet pain of love that he had let himself go. For months now, he had wandered aimlessly, hitching rides on freight trains, burying himself in the dirt if he was caught outside at dawn, keeping company with bands of bums who were beginning to realize someone — or some *thing* — was hunting them, thinning their undernourished, grubby, and ethanol-marinated ranks.

All this history flashed through his mind as *she* paused at the top of the granite stairs. Ulric knew she could see him perfectly under the hazy cone of the streetlight. He had been very tall in his own age, and he stood straight while she regarded his unruly mane and pirate's beard. He almost felt her eyes taking note of his earrings, as if someone had flicked them with an index finger. Strangers must not turn up often here, and he did not look like a respectable citizen, but she was not afraid of him.

His eavesdropping powers had already leapt involuntarily toward this woman. He *must* know her — he felt he had known her all his life. Ulric quickly discovered that there were not very many things that frightened this little librarian. She knew that the police chief owned a brothel located in a trailer park just outside the town limits. She knew that one of the women on the city council had murdered her elderly and ailing husband. She knew that a local clergyman had molested his only daughter until she went away to college. And she knew that the tailor at Murray's Suit Shack had AIDS. She accepted these facts the same way she accepted gravity or tornadoes. She knew the truth about other people because she was willing to see them as they actually were. The woman reminded him of his last lover, Alain, who had a gay man's disrespect for the complacent assumptions of heterosexual society.

Ulric also got a sense of the way her clear-sightedness had influenced the web of life in this little town. The clergyman's daughter had been able to leave high school a year early and go to a university several states away on scholarship, thanks to information provided by the librarian. Books about appropriate topics found their way into the hands that needed them — a nervous newlywed, a teenager who thought he should have been born a girl, a man whose alcoholic wife was battering him. A few words exchanged as she stamped a book had changed more than one life here. And while she had been the town's librarian, not a single book had been banned. She kept her own little corner of the world cosmopolitan and open-mineded.

It took Ulric only seconds to sample the gestalt of her. And while her history unreeled for his enjoyment, she displayed herself to him in another way. She reached up and took the pins out of her hair and shook it down. Ulric made an involuntary movement toward her as the long brown waves fell past her hips. Why did she dye it and hide its natural golden color? This wanton gesture, he knew, was not done to entice him. She did this every night when she got off work, and she was not going to alter her routine just because he stood in the street below her. He relished the vicarious sensation of her relief as the tight pins stopped tormenting her scalp, and the weight of all that glossy hair was redistributed, let loose in the gently rising wind. She took off her glasses and stuck them in her purse. Why hide her face with those fake lenses? Her vision was perfect. He found himself falling head over heels for this fanatic, this closeted intellectual, this strange woman who deliberately made herself look dowdy and nearsighted so she could win her townsmen's trust and funnel them ideas that would otherwise seem heretical.

She tilted her face a little as if to catch the freshening breeze, then unbuttoned the top button of her blouse, as if she were alone in her own sitting room, not standing at the top of a flight of stairs while a strange man watched. Ulric's eyes stroked her collarbones, and wanted more. She came down the stairs as regal and secure as a bride on her wedding day, and crossed the street to brush past him. "Good evening," she said, then walked on, apparently giving him not another thought.

Ulric wanted to howl. His body strained toward her. But he would not let himself slip the leash. For another fact had entered his consciousness: This woman was almost as lonely as he was—and a virgin.

The antlered priests who would have once shouldered this awesome responsibility were all gone. Even the dust they had become was gone. But somehow, all the proprieties appropriate to the situation would have to be observed. Ulric viewed this duty gingerly, then embraced it as carefully and completely as he longed to embrace the woman herself. He had a fond memory of an older woman who had initiated him. It had been at Beltane. Several tribes had come together for trade and celebration. The strange priestess had been so kind to his impetuous young body, careful to make him think well of himself while teaching him a thing or two that would keep him from making a fool of himself with a younger woman who was perhaps not so patient. It was a good memory, one he had not savored for a long time, and it carried a little healing with it.

Ulric took careful note of the door that the librarian entered. So this was the place she called home. It was a small, run-down apartment building, a big box that had been divided into smaller boxes that must chafe the people who inhabited them. He went past it, then circled back to her block and made his way through an alley until he stood in the small parking lot behind the brick building. She lived on the second story in a one-bedroom apartment that had a lovely maple tree outside the bedroom window. Once all her lights were extinguished, it was easy for Ulric to climb the tree and perch only a few feet from where she slept. She was naked under her blankets. The fact that she was so available and yet so inaccessible tore at his heart. How could he breach the gulf that lay between them?

He mentally tiptoed toward her, trying to catch a whiff of her unconscious mind. He saw a series of brightly colored shapes tumbling and twisting. It was a pretty picture, abstract and relaxing, and then he realized it was accompanied by music. His sweetheart did not know she was composing music in her sleep. He set a part of his mind to memorizing the melody. Of all the arts, this was the most ephemeral. But he came from a people who memorized volumes of their own history, traditions, legends, and songs. His lover-to-be's compositions were safer in his memory than they would have been on a tape recorder.

Materializing in her dream might alarm her. She would recognize him from the street and wonder why he was so significant that he turned up there. Time enough for that later, when she became accustomed to his presence without seeing his face. He sent a thought along her bare arms and let it creep down her back. She sighed and settled more deeply into sleep. The lady liked a light, tickling touch then. *Well and good.* Ulric settled himself into a marathon of moth kisses, caressing her all over with butterfly wings and the eyelashes of little fairies. She smiled in her sleep at this picture. "There's no such thing as fairies," she told him sleepily.

"Oh, I think you're wrong. Can't you feel them kissing you?" he replied. First Ulric brought her back up in a flush of goosebumps, then he moved to her buttocks and thighs. That seemed to disturb her a bit, so he drifted lower down her body, not wanting to awaken her. Ah, her calves, the slender feminine muscles, so lean and fine. Her feet, shapely, arched high, made to dance or dig their heels into his lower back. He stroked her feet and ankles. She shivered with bliss. Ulric had learned more patience and yet more with each of his centuries. He gave her the kind of prolonged whole-body pleasure that women dream of receiving from their male lovers but hardly ever get. His hands studied her skin, massaged her muscles, and ran through her hair like a man who had five years to get a doctorate in touching her. As his first instructor had said, laughing wickedly, "If you want to heat a woman's little goddess, you must touch her everywhere else. Pretend her sex does not exist until she brings it to your attention."

Ulric kept at it, moving from one part of her body to another, until the moon sank and he was afraid he might be caught out-of-doors by the rising sun. Loving her had aroused him until he felt ready to burst with need. Perhaps that was what made him bold. In her dreams, he appeared suddenly, and she greeted him happily, instantly recognizing him as the source of all this pleasure. He knelt at the foot of her bed, parted her thighs, spread her inner lips, and left one long burning kiss upon her clitoris. With his lips cupped around the sensitive bud of her sex, he breathed in and out, applying just enough pressure, barely jiggling it until she cried out and came in his mouth. The artful and sensuous stranger touched her wetness, dipping his fingers in it like a priest reaching for holy water. He left a streak of it along the inside of one of her thighs, and went away, licking his own fingers, leaving her wanting more.

It was hard to leave the treasure of this virgin body, the body of a woman he had thrown himself into loving, with his heart on his sleeve and his cock in his hand. But his skin was burning, and the dawn-anxiety was mounting. So Ulric renewed the see-me-not and climbed down from the tree outside her bedroom window. He must find shelter quickly, and make a home for himself in this little town. As the men of his tribe had always done, he had gone to live with a strange people in order to woo his sweetheart.

The graveyard was not far away. Ulric broke into a crypt that smelled abandoned and made a place for himself among the quiet brown bones and addled mice. He would stay here for a while. He had so much to teach her about herself, so much to learn about how to love her. The courtship had just begun. The joy he had gotten from this imaginary seduction was so powerful that the torpor of day seized him without engendering its usual stab of panic. For the first time, he smiled as death's weaker companion held him still.

When Mary Beth woke up, she was in a lovely mood that could not be explained by the day of the week (Wednesday) or the weather (unseasonably hot). Still, she showered, dressed, and ate breakfast in an efficient state of good humor, humming a tune without being able to remember the words that went with it.

It wasn't until she got to the steps of the library that she remembered her dream, that long and shameless inspection by the kind and knowledgeable hands of a faceless stranger. She felt her face grow hot as she recalled his fingers sliding beneath the sheet, making free with her arms, back, and neck, her legs and feet. She had rolled over in her sleep and then he had lingered over her breasts. They still tingled from those impudent touches, smoothing and tweaking her—

Taking a deep breath, she resolved to climb the stairs and think of nothing but the day's work ahead of her: mending the complete set of the Oz books, which suffered mightily at the hands of the children who loved them. She was not responsible for the content, however bawdy, of a dream.

But when she topped the stairs and took out her keys, she inhaled sharply because there *had* been a face to go with the sly hands. A face framed with a short black beard and long, curly dark hair. A man with two big gold earrings, absurd things like a child's Halloween costume accessory. He had put his mouth—oh, those red lips, pressed deep inside the dark private place, and the moist shudder that welcomed him! Talk about kissing on your first date! He'd gone way past first base, all the way to the rings of Saturn.

She grabbed the brass door handle to support herself. It was as if that burning, obscene kiss was being performed anew, making her knees shake. These were the feelings she dreaded, the voluptuous temptation she had organized her life to avoid. She had told herself that sex was overrated, something that most women would gladly give up in exchange for more affection. It was apparently pleasurable for men, but their need for sex allowed them to rationalize coercing other people (women...children) into providing it. The best you could probably hope for, she believed, was that you would find a man who was decent, if clueless, who wouldn't want sex very often, and wouldn't make it hurt. She could see why some women had sex with their husbands or lovers in that sort of situation. It was the marital version of the maternal duty to breast-feed an infant. Beneath all her disappointment and self-denial was a deep sense of injustice and rage, that nature had fashioned women's bodies to make them vulnerable to forced penetration, childbirth, subordination to the needs of others.

But the pleasure in her dream had not been an altruistic one; there was no mild sense of self-satisfaction because she had been generous to someone else. His pleasure, his genitals, had been completely absent from her consciousness. Instead, her own flesh had asserted itself in a way she had not even imagined was possible. Could it be that a woman's sex would demand to be served, as imperious as a hard-on? She could feel the physical changes that occurred to bring her to a place where she could not—would not—hesitate to take what she needed from his mouth. This knowledge, though deeply enjoyable, was also very unwelcome. She wanted to—what? Tell him to stop, ask him why, beg for more?

This was no random dream about some character cobbled together by her imagination. Her unconscious had summoned a real person to provoke a shocking transformation. It was the man she had seen last night, the one who had looked her up and down on the library steps at quitting time—damn him. But this wasn't his fault. It was hers. He must have affected her even more than she knew. If she had not wanted him, surely he would not have resurfaced in the privacy of her own slumber.

It troubled her to be so susceptible to a man's physical charm. There was no room in her life for sexual or romantic entanglements. It was not part of her plan. By now, the handsome stranger was no doubt hundreds of miles away. He was just some vagabond, passing through. She had seen too much of human cruelty to believe in the blissful communion between male and female that cluttered up her shelves with Harlequin Romances and their silly sisters. In her experience, men didn't even like women, most of the time. They just tolerated them and made use of them. If a man got too close, all he'd leave you with was nausea and terrible private pain. And the man did not exist who could be trusted with her deepest desires, those fantasies she could not scrub out of her psyche.

She braced herself, looked forward, and passed through the carved wooden doors. They were, as always, an effort to get moving. Mary Beth felt a little better inside the library. It was always cool in here, thanks to the thick stone walls. Everything important was here—all human knowledge neatly arranged for easy retrieval. This was her sanctuary, a temple to learning and reason. There was safety in tomes of nonfiction. Even fiction was safer than real life.

But try as she might, she could not sink into a trance of hard work. Mending and reshelving books, exchanging pleasantries with the patrons, stamping the volumes being checked out just seemed irritating. The day dragged like a severed arm trying to crawl out of the desert. She forced herself to stay an extra hour anyway, dusting things that the janitor would take care of, dreading her empty apartment. The new biography of Genet that waited on her bedside table no longer seemed like a tempting treat.

Eventually, she was so tired that she had to admit it was time to close the library and go home. The smells of old paper deteriorating in its own acid, mildewed leather book covers, dust, and library paste, which usually seemed rather pleasant, were giving her a headache. After locking the heavy front doors, she felt a wave of giddiness, then turned to face the street. Her lips were trembling.

He was not there.

Furious with herself for the sinking feeling of disappointment in her stomach, she took a tight grip on her ugly plastic handbag and stalked home. Each step hit the ground so smartly that she would not have been surprised to see a cobweb of hairline cracks in the sidewalk beneath her goddamned sensible shoes. Once inside her sterile, silent, and empty apartment, she threw those shoes in the closet, dropped her clothes—all of them!—on the bathroom floor, and defiantly walked naked into the kitchen. There, she threw a box of frozen pasta primavera into the microwave and slammed the door. She resisted the temptation to nuke it on high for ten minutes and make it blow up. Cleaning processed shrimp and cheese sauce off the walls of the little magic box would be too big a chore.

She forced herself to eat dinner slowly, making each mouthful last much longer than its defrosted flavor deserved. It really was time to start cooking for herself again. Then she sat in her only comfortable chair and made herself read at least a chapter of the new book. After the first few pages, she gave up on trying to make sense of it. Instead of rereading the same paragraph over and over, she just let herself glance at the words, then turn to the next page after a suitable interval had passed. When she reached the last of the chapter, she sighed and stuck her bookmark back at its beginning. Not one fact or insight had made it off the page and into her brain. Genet who? What was that, a new brand of foaming bathroom cleanser?

Mary Beth looked at the bed, thinking of getting into it, and blushed painfully hard. She averted her eyes from the yellow chenille spread as if it were an exhibitionist in a shopping mall, and went instead to her dresser, a mahogany behemoth that had belonged to the grandmother whose name she carried. After digging through its eight deep drawers and four shallow ones, she found a long flannel nightgown that had been wedged underneath a stack of panties that did not really fit and some embroidered handkerchiefs that were too scratchy to actually put to her nose. She pulled it over her head and instantly felt better. She had girded her loins, to get biblical about it, with the ancient armor of her sex.

Nevertheless, before she could lie down, Mary Beth went into the kitchen and fortified herself with a healthy slug of brandy, drunk straight out of the bottle. She'd already brushed her teeth after dinner, so she slid into bed with the hot fruity shout of its taste in her mouth. The fragment of a childhood prayer ran through her mind, but she was asleep before she could turn "Now I lay me down..." into a complete sentence. A god who did not rescue a suffering child was unlikely to help a grown woman writhing from a wet dream.

At first her sleep was clear and dreamless, and she thought perhaps she had escaped. Then she was wandering in the garden of dancing shapes, where there was always such wonderful music, and telling herself (as she did every night) that she *must* remember this place when she woke up, it was so beautiful.

Ulric, perched outside her window, was reading the account of her day from the surface of her mind. He felt a little guilty at her upset, but it was flattering to have made such a big impression. Why was she convinced that she'd be in terrible danger if someone found out what aroused her? The information was closely guarded. He would have to loosen her up a bit before she would let go of control at that deep level.

So he began as he had last night, tickling her. This time he used the shapes from her own dream, letting them collide with her body, roll over it, or melt and run down it. Slowly, too slowly to alarm her, the touches became more specific, and by the time she felt his hands again, she was too excited to be afraid. He used her hands to draw the sheet off her own body, and was amused to find the flannel nightgown that shrouded her. Like garlic and crosses, mirrors and running water, flannel had no vampire-repelling properties. He inched the nightgown up just enough to expose her thighs, and ran his imaginary hand across their surface, trying to persuade her to part them and ease his way. He wanted to taste her again.

Without waking, she tried to pull the nightdress back down around her ankles. Sensual persuasion was not going to work. Ulric had another trick up his sleeve. He simply began to raise her body temperature. By the time her sweat was pouring freely, Mary Beth had forgotten all about her fear of his touch, and sat up in her sleep to take it off over her head. She laid down again and kicked the blanket to the floor.

Ulric put one imaginary hand upon her thighs and the other upon her breasts. He understood that she thought her thighs were too fat and her breasts too large. In fact, she wore a sports bra that was a size too small to try to flatten her chest. Her curves were, in his opinion, deliciously feminine. Not at all like Adulfa's boyish flanks. Her nipples were as big as silver dollars, and when he stimulated them with a feeling of wetness and light pinching, they crinkled up until they were the size of the ball of his thumb. He wanted to put them in his mouth so bad it made his head hurt. How rapidly he had gone from being sated by an erotic dream to aching for the reality of contact with her flesh!

Ulric had been steadily smoothing her thighs, and he sensed that she was on the brink of allowing her knees to separate, but some mental or emotional resistance prevented her. So he went deeper, to the place where she kept her self-denial, and gently untied a strand or two of what looked to be a very large knot. Suddenly the knot fell apart, as if Alexander the Great's sword had cleaved it in two. And Ulric saw what she was afraid of.

"Darling, is that all?" he whispered inside her head. The monotheists, those damned People of the Book, had made such a mess out of sex. Why should it trouble anyone to want a lover to tie them up? In the springtime forests of his youth, you could not throw a rock without hitting some lad or lass who was trussed to a tree and being tantalized by one or more of their suitors. He understood that she was afraid of what such a desire might lead to—the world had become that dangerous. But if you had never had sex, wasn't it perfectly natural to want someone else to show you how to do it, to take charge of you and take responsibility for you? He would never order her to do something that did not please her to begin with. And if she discovered that she wanted him to bite or spank her, or give her to another man while he watched, or act out any of a hundred other scenarios, well, what of it? These things varied as much as the colors of the leaves in fall, for exactly the same reason.

"It's such a simple thing to give you," he said in the most reassuring tone he could muster. "Is this what you wanted?"

Imaginary cold steel bracelets went around both of Mary Beth's wrists, and her hands were inexorably drawn above her head. Her breasts broke out in a fine rash, a sex flush. Heavier and thicker manacles seemed to be weighing down her ankles, which were gradually dragged apart. She was stretched out upon the surface of her bed, held in a tight and inescapable position of complete availability. Yet still she dreamed, hanging on to unconsciousness like a life preserver. A scandalous dream would be much easier to live with than contact with the real man who she was coming to understand lurked just outside her window.

"Do you want me to come in to you?" Ulric asked. He was going too fast, but it had been so long since his body was awakened to desire that he was losing touch with yesterday's plan to seduce her a half-inch at a time.

Mary Beth could not tell if she was awake, but she could not claim to be sleeping, either. A raffish man was poised on her windowsill, sitting in the tree outside like an elven prince gone bad. He wanted her, but his desire resembled nothing that she had seen any other man display. He delighted in her pleasure, not his own. As wonderful as he made her feel, he also terrified her, because by putting the focus on her responses, he exposed much more than her body. She struggled with the bonds that his stronger insight and will had imposed upon her. Part of her knew the fetters were not real, and she was both angered and frightened by his power. She knew that he could do much worse things, and did not like relying on his charity or compassion. But the struggle only increased her arousal. She was on the brink of sobbing, she was so keyed up and frustrated. And she was on the brink of waking up.

"I love you," he said simply, showing her his open hands, no weapons. "May I approach? Touch you?" he asked again.

This time, she bit her lip and whispered, "Yes," then tossed her head and cursed herself. It was the kind of decision that changes the course of a lifetime, and she knew it, and had said yes anyway.

Moving carefully over the thin branches, Ulric opened her window and climbed into her room. He remembered at the last minute to throw a see-me-not behind himself, so no one would call the police to report a burglary. He broke a small limber switch from the tree, whispering an apology to it. His lady love whimpered when she saw him and vainly tried to get her mouth to form the word, "No."

"No what?" he asked kindly. "No, don't look? But I already have. No, don't stop? But I haven't begun."

He ran the tip of the switch across her breasts. How was it possible for her nipples to get even more rigid? Then he moved it back and forth across her thighs, a bow calling notes from the tension of violin strings. "I'm not going to hurt you," he reassured her, and read the relief as well as the disappointment on her face. "Much," he added, and brought the little switch down hard upon her lovely round thighs.

There was a muffled scream. He repeated the gesture two more times, then drew a line from her clit down, with his index finger. He painted the abundant moisture on her cheek. "I'm sorry you hate it," he teased, and laid the switch upon her breasts.

This time, she did protest audibly. "Then hold still," he warned her, and began to touch her cunt in earnest. She swore she could read his fingerprints, so keen was the pressure of his fingers upon her. Her ambivalence melted and poured out to welcome him. He hissed, smelling her surrender before he even felt it. His damnably inquisitive fingertips circled the well that was the source of this abundant lubrication. "Do you know what it means that you're all wet?" he asked. She shook her head, and he tapped her nipples lightly with the switch, to warn her not to lie. "It means you need me to put my cock in you," he said, deliberately using a coarse tone of voice. Her legs shook, and he lashed her for moving. She had a red welt across her nipples, and he wanted to lick them. "But you're very tight," he went on. "You've never had a man before, have you?" She blushed and shook her head. "The first time you get fucked it might hurt," he said. "Probably will hurt a good deal. And I don't like that kind of pain, darling, so let me prepare you."

He slowly slid one finger into her, pressing up to find the sensitive roof of her sheath. She was pulling hard on her imaginary bonds, whether to escape or get closer, neither of them knew. He relished the smooth muscles inside her body, the place where he hoped she would eventually receive and entertain him well.

"Do you remember this?" he asked, and bent his head to her clit. He took it between her lips, and she rocked beneath his tongue. Carefully, impulsively, he built her tension up and up, working clit and hole in concert until she was shivering and pleading. She tasted salty and smelled like rut, and her hips moved with a grace that promised Ulric long hours of sport between her legs when she was ready to join completely with him. He knew his beard was chafing her a bit, but it simply made her want him more. Still, he was careful not to make her too sore. She was already going to be upset tomorrow by how far she had gone with him tonight.

"I'm not going to make you ask for it yet," he said, and increased the speed and pressure of tongue-tip and fingers just enough to make her come. He kept going during the orgasm, wanting her to enjoy every possible hot contraction and rush of sensation. She turned her face as her pleasure peaked, trying to hide her loss of control. He had done this for her, he was the first, he had found a way to set her little goddess free. Oh, gods, he was lost, crazy in love with her.

"But I am going to make you say thank you," Ulric said evenly, hands quiet on her beautiful body. She thanked him with tears in her eyes. Thus are the habits of sexual ownership acquired, he knew, and mentally thanked his own teachers.

"Sleep tight," Ulric whispered, drawing the covers back up over her. She tossed from side to side underneath them, already longing for a second climax, another encounter with his mouth and hands. "Here's this instead," he said, undoing his trousers. "You can't touch it yet. But just look at it. Look." Knowing tonight's play was not for his own gratification, Ulric had been tempted to skimp on feeding so he could get to her house more quickly. But something had told him to be prepared. So he had killed his victim, to make sure he got enough blood to make his cock full and lively.

Her head came up off the pillow. She could smell his body, but it was a clean, invigorating smell, not something dirty or guilty. His cock curved slightly up, and it was bigger than the only other one she had seen. She wondered if his chest was furry, and blushed to find herself speculating about his naked body. The head of his cock was as red as the mouth of the channel that it fit. He desired her. He would not stop pursuing her until she knew everything that he wished to teach her. Was that doom, or was it a blessing?

"Do you want it in your mouth?" he asked, stroking himself. The lewd bond between them was stretched too far, and it broke. She turned her head and would not answer him. Ulric gathered from the steel gate that came down in her head that this might be one thing she would never enjoy doing for him. Well, that was a pity, but fortunately there was never any shortage of good cocksuckers in the world, despite 2,000 years of Christian preaching against sodomy. He concealed his sex, not without significant regret, and resolved to bring their hearts into concord again before he left.

"I will know if you are telling me the truth or not," he reminded her, and stepped back toward the window. "I've done nothing tonight that you did not enjoy, have I?"

"No," she whispered finally.

"Please tell me I've made you happy," he begged, with genuine anguish in his voice.

Mary Beth surprised herself by saying, "I never knew what happiness was until I felt your hands upon me."

Ulric nodded, feeling he had not done too badly for a mere warrior, someone with no priestly insight into the feminine mysteries. "Good night, then, my love," he whispered tenderly, and went out the same way he had arrived.

He sat outside for another hour, watching her restless sleep. The imaginary bonds had disappeared when the window dropped shut behind him, but she kept her hands above her head and her feet apart until she was in the deepest current of the ocean of sleep. Toward dawn, just when he had to steal away, she came to enough to touch herself and feel the luxurious wetness that had gathered there. Ulric departed with an image of Mary Beth touching her clit, rearranging her labia, trying to reproduce the way his tongue had felt upon her.

Next time he would start there and teach her how to pleasure herself. That would give her more control over her sexual feelings and make her less defensive. Ulric wanted this woman to trust him, and before she could really do that, she would have to understand herself better and relax enough to trust her own core erotic fantasies. He had no fear of losing his allure to self-induced orgasms. She would probably learn quickly how to give herself intense climaxes. But women were not, bless the moon above, like men. The more she came, the more she would want. And as long as one of the things she wanted was him, he would be more than content. He would be enraptured.

All this contemplation about masturbation became more personal when he returned to his haven from the daylight. It had been several decades since he had bothered to pleasure himself. But once back in the crypt, Ulric thought he should put the erection he'd killed for to good use; so he pumped it alone in the dark, further disturbing the wild mice and swallows that tenanted his lair. In less than twenty strokes, he came with a jolt that crunched up his stomach muscles and made his balls shudder. It was good, so good, but weird. *By now I should stop trying to solve the Strange Case of the Missing Ejaculate*, he thought as his eyes grew heavy. Ulric had gotten off just a split second before he went into hibernation. Even dead to the world, it hurt his heart to be away from her, outside of her. He imagined his frustrated desire would rise off of his body like steam while he lay insensible.

CHAPTER 2
What Kind of Miracle Are You?

There is no loneliness like that of the human being, trapped between the animals (whose instincts presumably tell them everything they need to know) and a faceless god of infinite power who coldly refuses to protect or rescue us. *Or maybe*, Mary Beth thought, *it's just me.* Everyone else seemed to know how to meld into the herd of *Homo sapiens.* Had she been left on this planet by a UFO? Was she a changeling traded for a human child by the fairies? Were her real parents traveling with a band of gypsies?

She had grown up in a large East Coast city in a Roman Catholic family that occupied a neighborhood that had been predominantly Irish for three generations prior to her own. She was twelve years old before she even realized that her family did live in a large city, so rarely did they leave the ten-square blocks of their enclave. Her mother had to take her to a large department store downtown to buy new school uniforms, and Mary Beth could tell by her mother's body language that she mistrusted and disapproved of the other subway riders whose skin color or accents betrayed a different origin. She was instinctively drawn to an overheard conversation in Spanish, the veil worn by a Muslim mother with a small child, the contents of an elderly Chinese woman's grocery bag, the music that played from a boombox on the floor between two young black men's feet, and covertly studied these marvels.

Her mother frowned and pulled her close, hurting her, as they hurried off the train and up the street to the store. "Quit your daydreaming, we don't have all day," her mother said, flicking her on the ear. When Mary Beth put her hand up to the sting and looked at her mother with tears in her eyes, she said, "Don't you start blubbering on me like a baby. If you can't act like a lady, I'll take you straight home, and you can go to your first day of school in your petticoat. We'll see what the nuns have to say about that."

She didn't know how to tell her mother that she might as well go to school in her slip, for all the difference it would make. Without knowing how or why, she stood out from the other girls. Nuns would swoop down on her and make her hold her hand out to be swatted with a metal ruler because, they scolded, she had given them a proud look. The other girls stopped talking when she came near their tables in the cafeteria, and would not slide over to make room for her. She was always neat and clean, she got good grades, she wanted to be liked. But adults and girls her own age were always telling her to get her nose out of her book. Even though her mother spoke with tight-lipped disapproval about certain girls in the neighborhood who wore lipstick and short skirts and dated Italian boys, Mary Beth thought her mother might have been happier with her if she had been a little wilder—either that, or a little more religious. Wild girls got pregnant, and after a lot of yelling and screaming, their boyfriends married them, and they grew up to be wives and mothers; virtuous girls grew up to be nuns. What Mary Beth was to become, everyone seemed to sense, was neither of these things.

Her only friend was a girl who had been born with a cleft palate, Bridget Marie. The surgery to repair this problem was not expert, nor was it complete, so her speech was awkward, and she had a facial scar that doomed her to be a pariah. The two of them had little in common other than their outcast status. Mary Beth was too bookish for Bridget Marie, who tucked magazines full of pictures of pop music idols in her textbooks so she could moon over some boy singer when she was supposed to be studying. But they could at least sit next to one another to eat their brown-bagged sandwiches (the cool girls had metal lunch boxes) and walk around the perimeter of the playground with one another, brushing off the taunts and the occasional volleyball that the other girls would toss at them.

They were both in a communion class with Father O'Donahue. He was a strict man with a straight spine and not much of a sense of humor. He wanted them to come to class each week having memorized the designated passages so they could recite them back to him verbatim when he posed the questions in their books. Mary Beth had almost gotten herself kicked out of school when she had asked a question about what happened in the Garden of Eden. "If Lucifer was cast out of heaven for promising God that he would save mankind without free will, why does he get Adam and Eve to eat the forbidden fruit? Because then they know the difference between good and evil and they have free will. And why was it a sin for them to suddenly understand that they were naked, and be ashamed? Didn't God want them to be ashamed?"

Father O'Donahue took her by the pigtails, marched her to the head of the class, and took his pointer to her backside. It was only after he had beaten her so hard that she could barely endure returning to her seat that he told her never to speak of nakedness again. "It's a carnal indulgence," he told her severely, "and very nearly as bad as taking the name of our Lord himself in vain." The priest furthermore told her that it was not becoming for her to read the Bible. "You've overreached yourself," he said emphatically. "Everything you need to know about God's holy word is right here between these covers," he said, thumping the communion handbook on top of his desk.

He was what Modeen Jefferson, the only black girl in the entire school, called "a right bastard" for the rest of the day. Modeen had a British accent. Her father worked for the Jamaican embassy. The priest ignored Modeen and her accent but always picked on Bridget Marie for her poor pronunciation. But that day he took the unusual step of keeping her after class, so she wasn't able to take recess with Mary Beth. She wasn't in school at all the next day, and the day after that Mary Beth asked her if she was sick. Bridget Marie just shook her head. She didn't want to talk about it. "My mother said I had to come back," was all she would say. After that week, Father O'Donahue detained the disabled girl more frequently. Her attendance became spotty. "If you're ditching school," Mary Beth said, "I wish you'd take me with you."

"I'm not doing this to have fun!" Bridget Marie said loudly, then she looked around to make sure no one had heard her. They were doing their usual laps around the playground.

"Well, what's up?" Mary Beth asked, feeling an unusual spate of curiosity about her lukewarm friend. "Aren't you afraid you're going to flunk out? Or are you really sick all the time?"

"I just can't stand to be here. This place makes me sick. What a bunch of hypocrites they all are."

"The nuns?" Mary Beth was scandalized. "Father O'Donahue? They've got a spiritual vocation. They've dedicated their lives to God's service. How can you say that about them?"

"If you ever stopped doing homework for five seconds, you'd see what really goes on around here," Bridget Marie said furiously. She stooped to pick up some gravel from the playground and began throwing it through the openings in the wire mesh fence around the school lot. Buses were parked on the street, and some of the small stones hit their yellow sides and windows.

"Hey, stop that!" Mary Beth stage-whispered. "You'll get us both in trouble."

"Yeah," Bridget Marie slurred. "You'd hate that, wouldn't you? To be in trouble. But I don't care because I already am." Then she dropped all of the gravel and sank to the ground. With her knees on the asphalt, she covered her face in her hands and wept. Mary Beth dragged her upright and they both ran between the dodgeball pole and the hopscotch grid, to a corner of the building where nobody was hanging out because the nuns had recently caught four girls smoking there. She took a tissue out of her shoulder bag and made Bridget Marie take it.

"Tell me what's wrong," she insisted, sounding much more like a grown up than she felt.

"Why? You can't do anything about it!" The girl lifted her furious, tear-stained face to her companion-in-exile and looked ready to take all of her wrath out on her.

"I will do something about it," Mary Beth promised. "Tell me. Look, you're really upset. You have to tell somebody."

"All right, Miss I-Can-Do-Anything. You pushy, prissy bitch.

Acting like you like me. Everybody knows you don't. Nobody likes me. That's probably why Father O'Donahue thinks he can do what he does to me. Because nobody will believe me and nobody will stop him."

Mary Beth had a twofold response. Part of her was shocked, but a more honest (if slightly repressed) part of her, the part of her that had seen some of the drunken or just plain unsightly behavior that went on beneath the veneer of Catholic rectitude, knew what her friend was going to say and dreaded hearing it spoken out loud. She didn't say anything, just waited to see if the other girl would make good on her threat.

"He's doing me, all right? He makes me suck his dick. First he starts touching me. He puts his hands under my skirt. He feels around down there and talks about how dirty it is, and asks me if I touch myself, and he hurts me to teach me not to do that. He talks to me about original sin and how woman is the undoing of man and he says all this crazy stuff about how he's only human and it's really my fault for giving him a boner, and then he makes me blow him. Do you know that it smells like mothballs under there, under his creepy old black robe? Then he slaps me and tells me I should say five Hail Marys and ten Our Fathers and sends me away. He says if I ever tell anybody they will never believe me because he's a priest and I'm just a stupid little slut who's going to grow up to be a whore and go to hell for making men commit the sins of adultery and fornication. He isn't even nice to me! He just uses me like I'm some kind of dirty old rag. I hate him. I hate him. And I hate you!"

Each sentence of this tirade was spoken loudly and more quickly than the last until she finished in a shrill scream that made the hairs on Mary Beth's arms stand up. It was like hearing the fateful cry of a banshee.

Bridget Marie tried to run away, and for a time, Mary Beth managed to hold on to her, to try to comfort her. But the smaller girl was insanely strong, and broke away. She ran into the school, calling for the nuns. "I need to see the nurse," Mary Beth heard her say when she ran after her and stood at the double doors that opened into the front hallway. "I'm sick. I want my mother and I want to go home."

Feeling deeply ashamed of the way she had exploited her sister-in-unpopularity, goaded by her accusations, Mary Beth went home that night and cornered her mother with unwonted persistence. She told her, as plainly as she dared, that another girl at school was being molested by the priest. Her mother demanded the name of that girl, then began to shake her. The beating that she got made Father O'Donahue's work with the pointer seem as painful as jumping rope. Her mother even washed her mouth out with soap, then made her kneel in the corner on her rosary beads, pressing a medal of St. Jude between her forehead and the wall, because only St. Jude could save a hopeless case like herself from the pit of infamy that had claimed her. Her mother made two phone calls, one to Bridget Marie's mother and another to the school, to tell them about her daughter's terrible lies.

The school threatened to expel both girls. As the rest of the year dragged on, Mary Beth thought it would have been better if they had done so. Because Bridget Marie never forgave her for "snitching." Her former friend made friends with the smokers, who now hung out in the attic above the auditorium, by bringing them airplane-sized bottles of liquor stolen from her parents' bar. Instead of being Mary Beth's companion, she became one of her worst detractors. Mary Beth hardly dared speak in class or on the playground because Bridget Marie would round on her, saying snidely, "Is that your latest lie?"

Oddly enough, Father O'Donahue was transferred to another school. The communion class was taken over by the principal, who let the girls know how much she resented being taken away from her other, much more important duties. That was the only thing that Mary Beth had to cling to, because it was an admission that she had told the truth, even though everyone—including the priest's victim—was full of derision and denial.

This was a turning point that shaped the rest of her life. While she did everything she could outwardly to make herself bland and devoid of interest, inside of herself she became a collector of injustice. Instead of being driven away from books, she became even more devoted to them. She knew that not everything in books was true, but she came to believe that every truth was written down in a book somewhere.

She was especially alert, now, to all the topics that her teachers and her parents said were off-limits—especially sex. How did this thing between men and women really work? What she saw frightened and dismayed her. It was pretty easy to see what men got out of sex. But they weren't grateful for the pleasure that women gave them. They usually did just what the priest had done to her former friend. They got sex by being deceitful or intimidating. If they couldn't have it, they complained and sulked. Once they got it, they crowed and called the woman a slut and a whore. The only place a woman was able to have sex without being blamed for it was if she was married. But she paid for it another way then, by repeated pregnancies and the endless chores of raising babies and keeping house. Were there any husbands who didn't cheat on their wives or browbeat or strike them? She couldn't find evidence of many. So why open yourself to that possibility? The few boys who asked her out on dates found her to be polite but immovable on the topic of sex. There wasn't going to be any. Ever.

She decided that Bridget Marie's disavowal of their relationship was not important. This was a girl like herself, with very little power. Who knew what had happened to her when her mother got that phone call? There were things worse than a mouthful of soap and holes in your knees the size of rosary beads. The important thing was that the truth had gotten out. The priest had been sent away, though she suspected that he was only going to harm someone else, wherever he had gone. But if knowledge was placed in the right hands, there was at least the possibility that things would get better. She knew by the time she turned thirteen what she would study and become. And she believed that her chances of being left alone to distribute dangerous information would improve if she was a mousy, not very attractive spinster. In dowdiness would lie her strength. It was, in an odd way, a secular equivalent of becoming the bride of Christ.

But alongside this powerful worldview and logical plan there was another, more messy reality. No matter how unworthy and dangerous men might be, Mary Beth secretly longed for erotic rapport with them. To her shame and even horror, the desires that played like dirty movies in her imagination were not pastel daydreams about finding her soulmate. Where had these squalid images of bondage, degradation, and pain come from? She secretly collected comic books that had a few precious pages of drawings of people who had been tied up. When she realized that you could find lascivious paperbacks in a certain section of bookstores, she would buy a title by "Anonymous," read it in one day, committing as much of it as she could to memory, then throw it away on her way home. She could hardly say the word "spanking," it made her blush so hard. When she stroked herself, all she could think about were situations in which men forced women to have sex with them. In her fantasies, the women had orgasms, but in a way that just made the whole thing even more upsetting. She didn't want to submit to a man, any man. She wanted to run her own life. She wanted to be free. Why then did she go into pet shops and look longingly at the dog collars? Why had she bought a plain men's leather belt at a thrift store? If the world was a sick place, full of abuse, the sickness was in her as well. Whenever she gave in to one of these fantasies and made herself come, she was ashamed of her own weakness and felt soiled.

As time went by, she became a little more philosophical about the nature of her inner erotic world. These tableaus were not real, after all; they didn't hurt anybody. She sensed that to deny herself all pleasure would make the path she had chosen too hard to follow. It was safe to fantasize; she couldn't change the things that turned her on.

And as an adult, handling the steamier romance novels that were popular among the library patrons, and looking through the closed collection that was not made available to the public, Mary Beth learned that she was not the only woman (or man) who dreamed of being held down and taken. She even gathered that there were people who openly talked about doing these things and deliberately elaborated upon them.

Now there was a piece of dangerous knowledge! She held that information in her head like an unplanted seed, not yet ready to plant it and see what it might become.

And now, here was a man, a stranger who seemed to know all of her secrets. What did it mean to have submitted to him? Was this the beginning of the end? She was genuinely frightened. Could she trust him? She obviously couldn't trust herself. How far would they go? If he wanted to maim or kill her, would she be able to stop him? How could she be in love with the enemy, with a man who took power over her sex so easily? And what on earth would she do if he left her? She was surrounded by thorns and hard questions, but all she wanted to do was place her lips upon the rose-petal softness of his lips, and place his hands once more upon her breasts, then abandon herself to his mercy.

Every night, Ulric came to his love and introduced her to yet another pleasure. He licked her asshole. He tied her to chairs, in the doorway, on the bed, kneeling on the floor. He decorated her nipples with fancy silver clips that made them burn and tingle. He gagged her with a wet knotted bandanna. He penetrated her with toys, some of which vibrated. He used ice cubes and melting candle wax and his fingernails and teeth and strong limbs to wake up her skin. He spanked her and told her that she would have everything she had ever wanted, and much much more. He kept her turned on and hungry, sure that eventually this need would turn into love. Until then, he would not feed his aching erection into the little mouth of her soft muff, even though she had lost all shame about begging to be filled and fucked with his long, clever fingers.

If the only thing he offered her was sex, Mary Beth thought she could have summoned the willpower to banish him. But he also brought her food, special things she had never tasted before; he brought her music and listened to it with her, even discussed it with her; he read poetry to her. He washed and dried and brushed her hair, gave her pedicures, told her awful limericks and filled her little apartment with flowers. *He cleaned her house.* He made himself her friend and confidant as well as her lover. He approved of everything about her, believed in her utterly, wanted nothing but her happiness.

Mary Beth tried everything she could think of to escape from being corrupted by this depraved spirit. She seriously considered telling the parish priest about it and asking for an exorcism, but the things she knew about *his* sex life made it hard to view him as a holy man. During the day, she alternated between fantasizing about Ulric (he had told her his name), berating herself for being a wanton slut, looking up the phone numbers of psychiatrists in a nearby city who could medicate this psychosis out of existence, and coasting in a numb state of panic and denial. This couldn't be happening. Why was this happening? What did he want? It seemed that he simply wanted to love her and minister to the new needs of her increasingly sensitive body. How could that be? Why would he be so generous? She was paranoid, ashamed, distracted, and on fire. She resisted him as if her very life were at stake. Each climax was experienced on a burnt field of battle.

After a particularly adversarial evening, she went to bed full of self-reproach and grumpiness. Ulric had looked so sad when she refused to wrap her hand around his cock and bring him off. After all the gifts he'd given her senses, this was a mean-spirited and selfish thing to do. And dishonest as well. Because she knew that if she had really sent him away, sincerely told him that his suit was unwelcome and he should move on, he would take his broken heart elsewhere, and trouble her no more. She had been getting the goodies without admitting that she wanted them. It was time to face up to her own part in this drama, and let him know she needed him, much as she feared where he was taking her.

But that night, he stayed away.

By midnight, Mary Beth had cried herself to sleep. She woke up twice after that, expecting to hear him tapping on the window or feel rope coiling itself about her breasts. But there was no sign of him. Was he hurt? Injured? She could not imagine what could do him damage. It was clear that he was no human being in the ordinary sense of the word. Her body, spoiled by his expert fondling and solicitous humiliation, was experiencing the pain of deprivation. She tried and failed to make herself come. She wanted him. She needed him. And he was not there.

When dawn came, it was as unwelcome as a funeral. Nothing, she realized, could be more cruel than this, his absence from her life. Somehow, she dressed herself and went to work. She was tearful and exhausted, but closing the library for an entire day was unthinkable. There were schoolchildren who needed to write papers, Mrs. Greenwich's genealogy club, the old man who always came in this time of year to look at seed and bulb catalogs, the dead-broke newlyweds who rented videos and checked out books they could read to one another. People relied on her. She could not let them down, even though she was experiencing a bitter disappointment.

Later in the afternoon, she took a trolley of valuable donated books back to the stacks. Here were the books that were not in general circulation. Either they were too rare or too scandalous (and in either case, prone to being stolen). She locked the door of this section behind her and began tidying up, neatly placing a recently expired citizen and bibliophile's first editions where they belonged. It was hard to keep her tears from landing on the books, where they might very well ruin a valuable cover or folio. Her lower back ached, and she straightened up long enough to rub both of her fists into its hollow. Then she sidled down another row of books, looking for the proper place to put an oversized 1815 atlas of the world. She thought guiltily that perhaps it should be in a museum.

"Put that down," Ulric said, and pressed her back against a wall of leather spines and gold ink. He made the atlas go away. Then he kissed her. She could not figure out how he managed to get through a locked door. And she had never seen him during daylight before. She had assumed he was a nocturnal creature, like a lemur or a bat. His mustache and beard were scratchy against her face, but his lips were unbelievably soft, and his tongue slid into her with passionate delicacy. She wrapped her arms around him and cried like a baby. "Don't ever leave me again," she wept. "I love you. I don't know how or why you came to me, but I love you. Don't ever leave me again."

"Do you want us to be together?" he asked, drawing far enough away from her to look into her eyes. She nodded, and his green eyes reflected his happiness and desire. "There are things you should know about me," he warned her. "Let me tell you now, before we go any further."

"No," she said, laying her finger across his lips. "I don't care who you are. I don't care if you're a, a car thief or a murderer. Or even a lawyer. Just take me, come into me, I need you, I need to feel you inside of me."

She found her own hands at the fly of his leather pants, drawing the zipper down. It was easy to find his sex inside his clothing, because it was reaching for her. She felt as if she had always known how to caress him, as if she had always relished the silky sliding skin, the firm core of his cock. Her thumb moved over the spongy head of his erection, and he buried his face in the crook of her neck, groaning. His hands slid underneath her buttocks, beneath her skirt. She heard her panties tear. Ulric lifted her up, effortlessly, as if she weighed no more than a page torn from Genesis. She suppressed a moment of panic and allowed herself to relax into the strength of his arms, the strength of his desire. He had proved again and again that his need was synonymous with her pleasure.

And inside, she felt so empty. How could it be that a single night without his touch had driven her to this great hunger? He was rubbing his cock against her sex, teasing her, looking for the opening. She began to come just from thinking about how it would feel, sliding in all the way. Inch by inch, he put himself there, asking her for permission to advance each step of the way. Where did he find the self-control to fuck her with only the first two inches of his cock, to hold himself back for all the time it took to allow her to open and plead for yet another inch?

Despite all his patience, when he finally slid home, she felt a twinge, and cried out. Something inside shifted, gave way, and complained as it was vanquished. Ulric comforted her with his mouth, kissing her while she gave voice to her pain. Taking her hurt into himself. Soothing it with his gallant body. Taking her along on the ride to nowhere, any place, it did not matter what the destination was because they were going there together. They hammered into each other, faster and faster, would his arms never tire? She came between earth and heaven, held against his chest, filled with his flesh, a different sort of orgasm than any she had experienced before.

For a moment, there was quiet. Then he started moving again. "I don't think I can—" she said.

"Hush," he replied. "You know you are able. Want me. Want me, my love. You are a new woman now. You are Lilith, who would not lie beneath Adam. You are the first woman. You are the goddess who took demon lovers and talked back to Jehovah. I name you Lilith. I baptize you in that name." To himself, he said: *I will not sink my teeth into you. I will not use you that way.*

A new fire had indeed been kindled between her legs. Sure that she would regret this erotic combat tomorrow, Lilith willingly joined her body to Ulric's, wondering if she could ever have enough of him. "How can you do this?" she asked. "What kind of miracle are you?"

Then he bit her.

He drank her blood.

She let him.

She came from the movement of his cock within her still-tight sheath, and from the penetration of his fangs and the movement of his mouth upon the wound, drawing her into his own body. Ulric had not been able to restrain his need to taste her blood any more than he had been able to hold back his cock when it felt the soft folds of the opening between her inner lips.

She shared a portion of her finite life with his potentially infinite one.

His body was racked by the twin pleasures of blood-drinking and sex, and so overcome was Ulric that he held her too tight, forgetting his own strength, and fucked her too hard, and took perhaps a little too much blood. And Lilith held him, and loved him for being able to forget himself with her.

She knew now. She knew what sort of miracle he was.

And realized that she had known all along.

CHAPTER 3
The Poison Stream of Memory

"You're a vampire," she said. Then laughed at the absurdity of it all. It was a sentence out of a B movie, some cheap and camp silver screen rip-off of Bram Stoker's Victorian masterpiece. "I don't want to think about this. I want to hold onto the man who took my virginity and have him pet my hair and tell me I'm beautiful and he loves me. No, this can't be!"

Ulric touched the ball of his thumb to her tears and licked them off, then used his handkerchief to blot her face. Lilith was not appeased. "Nobody carries handkerchiefs anymore," she wept. "Why can't you be like everybody else and carry a stupid plastic pocket pack of Kleenex?"

Ulric took her in his arms, despite a little struggle, and insisted on smoothing her hair. "You are beautiful, you know," he said, and meant it. The sincerity of his words cut through her hysteria. "I began to carry handkerchiefs around with me when I had a lady who might need them," he added.

"Ah ha!" she accused, lifting up her face, still crying. "You knew that you'd make me cry. You're wicked through and through."

"That may be true," he admitted, squeezing her, still savoring the double bloodletting, with mouth and cock, that she had given him. "Lilith—"

"Don't call me that," she interrupted. "Don't make me the den mother of all your little demons. I refuse to be Satan's soccer mom."

"Lover," he substituted, then began again. "You've given me such a gift. I had to travel to another city to find a vampire that I could kill to give me the strength to endure the daylight. Even after that, I had to come here in my animal form so that the sunlight would not burn me alive. But with the power of your maidenhead fresh upon me, my love, we can do something that I rarely have the power to enjoy. Walk with me. Come walk with me in the woods. By the Lady of the Mountain and the Lord of the Animals, you do not understand how much magic is in you. There is no Satan. The only evil comes from love denied."

"I can't go with you," she said, trying to extricate her ridiculous spectacles from his jacket pocket. He would not let her take them and hide her beautiful face with such a self-destructive lie. "I am supposed to be at work."

"Bullshit," he said firmly. "I bet this place owes you at least five years of vacation days and sick days put together. You are coming with me."

And that was how the town librarian was seen leaving her granite sanctuary with a gypsy man or a hippy, a man at any rate who was clearly not a farmer, insurance salesman, or shopkeeper. He was carrying her in his arms, furthermore, and she had kicked off her shoes, and her hair was loose and wanton. Who knew that brown bun could come down into such abundant waves of feminine glory? Who knew that her two naked white feet would be as beautiful as lilies, or that her laugh would make anyone who heard it smile and blush involuntarily? The two of them were carrying on like high school kids, and they embraced as freely as...well, as freely as nobody should. Premarital sex was just the beginning of their misdeeds, the town gossips were sure.

Ulric took her up to the crypt where he rested during the day. It was an old cemetery, and woods had been allowed to continue to grow up all around it. The ground was too rocky and hilly for farming and had not yet been cleared for a housing development. He had not planned to tell her that the graveyard was his home, but when they passed the place, he could tell by the way she looked at the marble tombstones and vaults that she was imagining him inside a coffin, a fetid corpse bloated with blood, pillowed by dirt salvaged from the Old Country.

"I don't have to sleep in a coffin, you know," he said.

"I don't want to hear about it."

"And I don't have to rest on dirt from my homeland. Like all of us, I draw sustenance from the earth, that's true. But no more than you or any living being. People tend to avoid graveyards, and the crypts are made out of stone and cement, so light does not intrude. Coffins are preferred by some of us for the same reason. And not all of us realize we can spend our bright hours of repose wherever we please. Christianity has made even driving the devil's SUV no fun at all. I suppose it's all about guilt, really, and ignorance. Belief is a powerful thing. If you believe the sight of a cross will cause you agony, it does. I've sometimes wondered what would frighten a Mormon vampire. A seagull, perhaps, with a cricket in its beak."

As a disenchanted and lapsed Catholic, Lilith had read enough about world religion to know what he was talking about. She laughed, partly at his joke and partly at her own fruitless search for meaning beyond the material world.

Because his lady love's feet were bare, Ulric carried her up the hill. As he continued to bear her weight, with no sign of being strained or tired, she gradually relaxed in his arms. He dared intrude enough upon her anatomy to ease the pain within her recently opened body, and was rewarded by a more peaceful expression upon her tear-stained face. He put her on her feet on a grassy patch by the bank of a small brook. There were a couple of large boulders that they could sit on. She took her place on one of them and eased her feet into the chilly water. "I love somebody who's dead," she told the babbling stream.

He reached for her, decided it was a bad time to touch her again, and let his hands fall to his side. "Lilith, I walk, I breathe, I see, I feel—how am I dead?"

"Well, if you're not dead you should be."

"Do you really think that?"

"No. No, because then we would never have met. But I can't believe—I mean, this is like a myth or a horror story. It can't be real."

"There was a time when you would have taken the existence of people like me for granted."

"Oh, and when was that?" She heard the mean tone of her own voice and regretted it but did not know how to apologize without making it sound like she had accepted the situation. She did not want to injure him, but her emotions were running so high, she could barely hold herself still. She wanted to flee and run through the woods like a deer until she found a thicket where she could lie down and hide herself forever. She had done what she vowed as a child to never do—trust a man, want him, allow him into her heart and cunt. It felt as if her worst fears about the dangers of love and desire were coming true.

"When I was growing up. Before I was changed. About six hundred years ago."

"You're *that* old?"

"If only in my folly." Ulric fell silent and regarded the miracle of the world around him. He could hear birds, and see the wind making free with each tender leaf of the trees above them. There were water-skating insects on the pool just upstream, and trout lurked along its banks in daytime somnolence. They would rouse again at dusk to feed when clouds of flying insects plagued the glen. He could hunt here, make a shelter, have the necessities of life. When nature was allowed to set her own table, everyone was provided for, even human beings. But that way of life was very nearly gone for good, and he must follow the source of his daily nourishment into the crowded and poisonous places they had constructed on top of the corpse of the green world. The Lady of the Mountains could only look on appalled as they refused her gifts. The domain of the Lord of the Animals had been clear-cut, so that only a few pockets of haven for his winged and four-footed subjects remained. Trees could no longer carry a message around the world, just as the skein of whale song had been torn apart by the engines of men's ships.

Lilith watched him as he watched the play of gold and green light within the foliage of the trees, and followed the flight of a dragonfly. The peaceful look of concentration on his face, the way he squinted at the sun, his darting green eyes that sought out the source of a bird's song, these things more than anything he could say convinced her of his humanity. He seemed at home here, the way she imagined an Indian would be before white men came and ruined the land.

"Tell me," she said simply.

"Tell you?"

"You know what I want. The story. Out with it. Who, what, when, where. The Tale of Ulric and How He Became Immortal. Okay?"

"If I could touch your face," he said hesitantly, "I could show you instead. Please, I would rather not have to search for words while I am forced to relive these memories. But if you would just re-experience them with me..."

"This is hard for you?" She seemed surprised.

"Yes. Of course it is. I had never planned to become one of the elders of my people. I wasn't smart enough and even if I had been, I was too young to make such a big decision. I just wanted to sell my sheep and make enough money to buy a filly that would replace our old horse when she grew up, and a bracelet for my mother. That was all I was thinking about the day that my world changed."

"Elders, what's this about elders?" It was a hokey word, even if Ulric used it with sincere reverence.

"Lilith, we never used the word 'vampire.' It hadn't been invented yet. And we weren't afraid of our blood-drinkers. We cherished them. The Boar People always had at least one immortal with us, staying at each village in turn. The blood that we gave them was a small price to pay for their knowledge. They knew everything. Our songs and stories, the appropriate ritual for each holiday, the cycles of the moon and the stars, our ancestry, how to treat diseases, what the weather would be like. With all the wisdom of our people stored in the best among us, the kindest and the most intelligent, we thought we were well-armed to deal with any eventuality. But...we were wrong. And we paid the price for being on the wrong side when the world changed. Lady and Lord, it has changed so much, and not for the better."

"Show me," Lilith said, and took his hands, cupping them to her face.

It was a crisp fall day, late afternoon. The trees (so many trees!) had turned yellow and red, orange and brown, which brought out the dark green of the pines that clustered higher up the slopes of the mountains. Ulric was on foot, leading a gelding with a wise face and bad knees, laden down with such gear as he thought the steady old horse could carry. He walked with the aid of a staff, which he also used to signal the two dogs who flanked him to keep the herd of sheep gathered together. It was a small flock, but the animals were heavy with wool, like little storm clouds on thin legs. They were pure black animals, too, with long-tufted wool that would be easy to spin and not require any dyeing. Shearing them tomorrow was going to be a pleasant change from bringing them down from the mountain pastures, at least for the first hour or so.

A cranky old ewe in the front of the herd tried to evade the dogs, but one of them snapped at her, and she went their way, with a rude noise of protest to register her displeasure. With the dogs circling the milling herd, Ulric picked his way to the pasture fence and opened a gate. There was another skirmish with the ewe, but Ulric added his efforts to those of the dogs, and she popped into the enclosure. The rest of the animals followed her in such a rush that Ulric was afraid some of them would be injured. The gate was not wide enough to accommodate all of them at once. Somehow the sheep sorted themselves out, and by the time he latched the gate they were cropping grass and looking at him as if he were an idiot for staying on the other side of the fence.

Ulric went toward the smell of baking bread and stew. His mother was in the cooking shed, a lean-to built against the side of the cottage. It was almost time to move cooking indoors, and use the lean-to for an auxiliary shelter for winter's stores of split logs. She was already eating. Ulric was happy to see his uncle dipping into a bowl of stew with her. Olav was a good man who had taken his responsibilities seriously, teaching his sister's son to become a man whose word meant something.

His mother was already making noises about Ulric finding himself a wife and leaving the village, but Ulric was in no hurry. He loved his mother, and Adulfa was no help to her. His older sister (who probably had a different father than Ulric, as if it mattered) had taken to the raiding life to win her fortune, make dangerous enemies to bolster her honor, and capture the amorous attention of women who loved a bold heart. She never slept in the same place twice, it was said, usually with some fondness and admiration.

There had been talk last Beltane of going to visit a village where several of Ulric's neighbors had kin. It was on the far edge of the Boar People's territory, mostly occupied by Deer People. Beyond that were people who said they worshiped only one god, even though there were three of him. It was better to avoid them; the men treated the women badly, and both men and women were hostile to anyone who followed the spirits of the earth.

A holiday in somebody else's town was a good place to find a wife. You wanted to check out her family and friends before you joined her household. If all he found was a blanket-friend with a quick smile and supple thighs, that would be enough compensation for the journey.

The three of them washed their dinner down with cider and then went inside the cottage to find their beds. Ulric's mother slept downstairs near the hearth. During the day, her bed was used as a place to sit near the fire. When winter came, Ulric would probably bring his pallet down from the loft and huddle closer to her, for the sake of the warmth that came from the fire. Tonight, Ulric and his uncle climbed a pole with chipped-out steps and swung themselves into the loft where there was a mattress stuffed with straw that was almost big enough for both of them. The dogs circled uneasily downstairs, whining to be taken up into the loft, but when Ulric and Olav ignored them, they trotted over to his mother and curled up under her bed. By dawn, they would both be sleeping with her, Ulric knew. His mother swore you should never let a dog get up on the bed, but the rules apparently changed when her eyes were closed.

It was the dogs who woke them when the fire arrows hit the thatch of the hut. They were barking furiously, louder than Ulric had ever heard them sound off before. Up in the attic, it was already hard to breathe. Ulric woke up choking, his eyes stinging. He fell more than climbed down and shook his mother awake. "Fire!" he cried, and she threw herself upright and wrapped a blanket around her body. Olav was behind them, urging the dogs out the door. None of them knew exactly what was happening or why. None of their nearby neighbors had been antagonized recently enough to want to raid their village. A wayward bolt of lighting could set things blaze, but there had been no thunderstorms that night.

Lilith was so immersed in the body memories that Ulric was sending her that she felt sick to her stomach when that reality wavered and skipped over something. All she knew was that his mother and uncle were dead. She struggled to get him to go back, to let her see what had been done to them, but he refused. She could hear arrows—saw a dog leaping in front of his mother—Lilith retreated from the raw knot of his grief, feeling like a coward.

When next she merged with him and the story resumed, she was in his body, his hands bound behind him and his neck in a rope, tied to the saddle of a man who rode on horseback in front of him. The man wore armor. There were many men wearing armor. Their shields were decorated with the Christian cross. He was running and he knew if he fell he would be dragged to his death. He ran over rocks and more rocks, ran with no air in his lungs and no more strength in his legs. By the time the riders got to the center of his little town, they had taken more prisoners, and burned more houses. There had been no more than twenty homes here, built in a rough sort of circle around an ancient oak tree, where the villagers of Red Springs had built their shrine to house visiting elders.

It was there that his captors met up with others in the same band, and a man who was apparently their leader. He had a shield painted with a device Ulric had never seen before—a lion trampling on a crescent moon. The lion had a cross in one uplifted paw, but it was the strange Christian cross, with the vertical bar longer than the horizontal one, unbalanced, like the soldiers who attacked them. Village men were forcibly separated from the churning crowd of panicked women and children. There was screaming and pleas for mercy, and some resisted and were cut down with the knights' longswords and axes.

"Sir Hilbert, what shall we do with this rabble?" one knight called.

"Bring the young men with us," he said. "Kill the old people, and the women and children."

There was a strange hesitation among his followers. Men spat and crossed themselves. Did they understand that an evil fate pursued a man who had the blood of a woman on his hands? The Night Mare and her keening sisters would come for them with her noose, woven from the strands of Fate itself, and throw them across the withers of her flesh-eating steed. Who knew how many deaths these furies could force such cowards to endure? "We can sell the women and spawn too," one knight dared protest. Sir Hilbert roared at them, "Damn your insubordination! After all we've been through in the Holy Land, you hesitate to shed the blood of these pagans? They are infidels as surely as the Moors who took the sepulcher of our Lord Jesus hostage and defiled it. The Pope himself has given us these lands for our demesne. But first it has to be cleansed of the heathens who worship false gods."

When Hilbert drew a breath, no doubt to continue bellowing in the same vein, a small elderly woman came out of the oak tree shrine that was also her home. It was in the shape of a beehive, built of woven willow withes and sealed with clay and straw. This was where the Eldest and her chosen attendants lived. Perhaps because she was so small and elderly, it created a strange moment of silence when she hobbled out of her dwelling and confronted the roaring man in mail. The Eldest was hardly ever seen during daylight hours, and she wore a cape that concealed her skin from the sun.

"You have invaded the land of the Boar People. We do not know you, and we have never harmed you. What evil are you working upon my children?" she asked in her dry and blunt voice. Ulric had seen grown men shake in their boots rather than face her questions.

"That is none of your affair, hag."

Even though they were frightened to death, the villagers responded to his rudeness with shouts of indignation. "That is our Eldest!" some said. "Granny!" others cried. "Rowan Silverhair! Save us."

"If I have to show you cravens the way it is done, so be it," Sir Hilbert said, and lifted his greatsword in both hands. With one clean blow, he knocked off the old woman's head. Her blood covered him in one great gout. "She dies like any Turkish harem slut," he crowed. Not content with this, he drew his knife and cut out her heart, and before them all, held it upon the point of his dagger and worried a chunk out of it with his teeth. When they saw the Christian knight devouring the heart of their elder, utter despair fell upon Ulric's people. If such a horrible thing could befall Rowan Silverhair, the powers of land, air, water, and fire were not going to save them. They had been abandoned by the Queen of the Glaciers and the King with Tusks of Gold.

The soldiers were shamed (or frightened) into killing the women and children, every last one. The age or sex of their victims mattered not at all. They fell upon them, weapons rising and falling, with shouts of "For Saint Gregor! A lion! A lion!" Ulric and Lilith held one another's hands in a death grip as they both wept to see such a piteous sight. The only comfort that Ulric had was that his sister was not among those slaughtered. She had been out hunting that day, he supposed, and escaped these wicked men. He felt ashamed of himself to care so much about one person when dead bodies covered the ground and the stench of death hung thick upon the air, as if the wind could never whisk it away.

He was chained in a long coffle to the other young men in the village. When the knights ran out of manacles and chains, they used rope. All around them, houses were burning and livestock was being slaughtered. The waste was appalling. Some of Hilbert's knights even grumbled that supplies were being wasted that could have been put to better use. One man tried to lash a small chest to his saddle, but Hilbert slew him from behind, nearly cutting him in half with his greatsword. "Take his horse and mount up," he told the man's squire, and after that, there was no looting. The crops in the fields were put to the torch as well, perhaps to ensure that the Red Springs people would know their home was gone. Hilbert seemed to be everywhere, spurring his horse savagely, rearing above the chaos to shout encouragement to his vandals. He did not even bother to wipe the blood from his face.

Seemingly lost to all humanity, the knights were roughly herding their prisoners together, preparing to take them away. Then they ran again, and Ulric spared Lilith the entire horror of it. There were brief stops but no food and scant water for the prisoners. By the time they arrived at the castle, six of his boyhood friends had died. Their bodies were left in the open air for the scavengers, and to his shame he had no moisture left in his body to cry for them, and no breath to say the rites for the dead.

He learned many things after he arrived at the castle and was untied and thrown along with everyone else into the castle dungeons. He learned that he was now the property of the Germanic Knights of the Holy Sepulcher. This order of warrior priests had gone to a foreign land called Palestine to take back the tomb of their god, except that their god was not dead, he had come back to life. (So why did he care what happened to his tomb?) Even though they had not succeeded in this task, they had become very wealthy in Palestine, and on their return, the

French Pope had sent them here with a land grant. The only condition was that they convert every occupant of their territory to Christianity.

A man in a black robe came by, sprinkled them all with water, choked them with a thick cloud of cheap incense, and declared them to be Christians. The soldiers' priest was very strange. He made the sign of the four quarters, but not the circle of life. Anyone who refused baptism did not get bread or water, and was beaten. Necklaces with emblems of the boar were cut from their necks. Ulric said nothing when he lost the symbol that linked his village to the people who lived in several other hamlets. The conquerors could do what they liked to his body, but his soul would never belong to this alien and lonely god. Jesus ruled alone with no divine woman to share her wisdom with him or marry him to the land. Could anything make less sense than that?

The other thing that Ulric learned was that all of them were to be sold to the janissaries, who were another order of warrior priests, except that these warriors served the Ottomans, who were the Germanic Knights' enemies. The janissaries would geld them, because they were all eunuchs, which supposedly made them more faithful to the service of their sultan. If he weren't so frightened, Ulric would have scoffed. Had the world gone mad? Who would love or serve a leader who had deprived him of his manhood? What sort of king was stupid enough to believe such a thing?

When guards interrupted the prisoners' sleep one night, it took Ulric several moments to realize that Hilbert was standing behind them. He knew that he should hate this man and spit on him or lunge at him and try to strangle him or break his head open on the ground. But hunger and shock had deprived him of his warrior fire. He was not ready to die. The guards were motioning for each prisoner to come up to the front of the cell and present himself for Hilbert's examination. Ulric took his turn quietly. He did not spit at the destroyer of his people. The most that he could do was will himself to not pose before him, to not make himself look stronger or more attractive. He could not swear that he had avoided these things, however, because he did not want to be sold as a slave to the janissaries. What use he had made of his manhood left him very fond of that root.

Hilbert picked Ulric. The guards had to come into the cell to remove him at knifepoint. But he was not actively fighting them; he was just sluggish with disbelief. He was so tired, wretched, weak. What could he do unarmed against two guards with swords? They prodded him forward, and he wanted to look back—say farewell—but the words stuck in his throat. He was afraid his friends would curse him for a coward and a traitor, and he could not think of anything he might say that could ease their suffering. The torch light hurt his eyes as he climbed the stairs, even though it was a dim and inconstant light. One level at a time, he was taken to a fate he feared almost as much as castration and slavery as a mercenary in a foreign land. And he was hungry, wobbling at the knees, lurching even when the guards had not pushed him.

The room they eventually reached was drafty and ill-lit, but Ulric thought it was infinitely preferable to the cells below. He was handed over to an older man who wore a long tabard over his monk's robe. It was decorated with the arms of the Germanic Knights—a lion tramping on a crescent moon, with a cross in its uplifted paw.

Assessing Ulric as no threat, he dismissed the guards and offered him a basin of water. It would be cold, no doubt. He missed the hot mineral springs that gave his village its name, and was sorely tempted to just drink the water. Then he reminded himself that he was unlikely to have an opportunity to bathe again, because the Germanic Knights apparently believed there was something evil about keeping clean.

Humbled, Ulric gratefully sponged himself off and donned a simple wool robe much like the one his keeper, Sir Frederic, wore. The garment settled around his neck, irritating the red line around his throat where a guard had snapped the cord of his boar pendant and stolen the beaded leather bag that contained his umbilical cord and other sacred totems. If Ulric died now, how would his mother find him to bring him safely to the blessed isles? Then he was offered a place upon a bench near the fireplace and given a piece of bread and a bowl of soup. Ulric forced himself to eat slowly, afraid he could not keep the precious food in his belly if he ate as quickly as his hunger demanded. The gray-haired knight said little to him, but Ulric sensed he was uneasy. What could discompose a man who did not flinch at genocide? *Perhaps,* Ulric thought, *I will not struggle if Hilbert intends to kill me.*

As soon as he was finished with the simple meal, Ulric's enemy took him through other rooms and up more stairs. Few people were about. It was night outside, he saw through arrow slits and narrow windows they passed. The stars were still there: the sun trying to spy on what her sister-wife, the moon, was doing with their husband, through the blanket the moon had thrown over herself and the earth. What small things it had taken to make him glad to see the stars again—a crude bath, a little food, a clean robe. A sense of how precious life was briefly eased his pain and fear. Then Frederic stopped at a heavy wooden door reinforced with iron straps. "I will be waiting without," he said, opening it. "I will pray for you," he added.

Ulric proceeded into Sir Hilbert's room, and found himself alone with the man who had wiped out his peaceful life, had his mother and mother's brother killed. This man's soldiers had shot his wise and useful dogs full of arrows and left his precious herd of sheep rotting in their pen, bleeding in the dirt, of no use to anyone but the vultures and wolves. If wolves would even dare to venture where these madmen had rampaged!

The commander did not look well. The fire in his room burned high, but he shook like an old man who feels death's cold fingers counting his bones. Hilbert was pale, too, and clearly in pain. Ulric knew what was happening. Hilbert had consumed the flesh and blood of the Eldest. He was changing into something more than human, but he was doing it without the rituals and soothing herbs that made this ordeal bearable and meaningful. No one was singing to him, and he was not held securely on the breast of another elder, being fed by her. Hilbert had not studied to deserve this honor. He had not apprenticed himself to one of the beloved immortals, proved himself to be a fit repository of tribal lore. There was nothing in his head but superstitious nonsense. The man was so stupid he thought his Nazarene was the only god who had hung from a tree. He was full of pride, violence, rage —

And lust.

"Come here," Hilbert said, and beckoned him near. Ulric reluctantly approached him. He would not cringe in the presence of this lunatic. Nor could he attack him now. Hilbert would be strong, despite his ague, and very difficult to kill.

"What did that filthy witch do to me?" Hilbert demanded, gasping like a newly arrived messenger. He reached out and took Ulric by the wrist. Ulric tried to evade him, but Hilbert was too quick. He dragged Ulric close enough to smell his besieged flesh, which stank like burning blood. His fingers were hot to the touch.

Was today a good day to die? Perhaps. "You did it to yourself," Ulric said, hoping his voice sounded more confident than he felt.

Closer and closer Hilbert compelled him to come. His long dark hair was damp with acrid sweat, his gray eyes cloudy. "I slew a demon," Hilbert hissed. "An abomination. 'Thou shalt not suffer a witch to live.'"

"What we kill becomes a part of us," Ulric said as Hilbert ripped the robe he had just put on down the middle. As the cloth parted, the pagan captive turned to flee, but his feet were tangled in the ruined cloth, and Hilbert caught him easily and forced him toward the bed.

"She has bewitched me. And you will tell me how to lift this curse. I am a soldier pledged to the service of our savior, a hero of the glorious crusade against the Turk, and I will not be sullied by some pox-ridden succubus! You will wipe the taint of that rebellious daughter of Eve, the mother of whores, from me, or I will do the same thing to you that I did to her."

As Ulric landed face first upon the bed, he weirdly observed that he was tired indeed and would have been comfortable beyond measure to seek slumber upon this wool-stuffed mattress and pile of linen sheets and furs. He had taken pleasure with other men before. Who had not?

But it was a friendly exchange between two randy young bodies. It was easy enough to oblige another youth who was bored with his own hand, especially with someone else's fingers wrapped around your shaft, milking all the cream out of it. But Hilbert was on top of him, holding him down, and his cock was pressed between the cheeks of Ulric's ass. Ulric had never been penetrated by another man, or done this to another. That act was reserved as tribute for the priests of the Lord of the Animals, during the year-and-a-day when they lived as women to prove their devotion to their ecstatic, shape-shifting god. (Some, admittedly, let their time in women's apparel go on for longer than that, but that was between them and the Lord. And there were exceptions, of course — men with no religious vocation who still fancied a hard fuck. Everybody liked to wear the skirt sometimes.)

Forced sex was offensive to Ulric's every instinct. Pleasure was holy, the moment when men and women became almost divine, but if it was not mutual, it was wrong, an offense against all the deities. So Ulric struggled to throw off his attacker. He fought so hard that he thought his muscles or tendons might snap. The threat of being raped was bad enough, but somehow his own violation had become symbolic of the destruction of his tribe, his religion, his family, everything that had given him a sense of belonging and shelter and meaning in the green world. He could not escape Hilbert's hold, but for a few moments he dared hope that the horrible creature on his back would be unable to carry out his intentions. The knight's penis was limp as a drowning worm.

Then the breath upon Ulric's neck became hotter, more frenzied. He felt the edge of teeth approach his skin, but could no longer throw his abused body against Hilbert's weight. Again there was that dreadful sense of wrongness. Giving life to the eldest was a delirious honor. This was just brutal, pain and humiliation. Hilbert's teeth pierced him. He fed on Ulric as if he were a rare joint of mutton. And as his cock stiffened with the blood he had stolen, he plunged into the weeping heathen, intentionally hurting him, using his cock as a weapon. From the names that Hilbert called him, Ulric realized that the knight thought it was a great sin for men to have sex with one another, but that the one who got fucked was somehow to blame. These soldier-priests were so crazy that they not only denied themselves the sensual company of women, but believed they should not have any release with one another. Ulric had the dizzying experience of being simultaneously amused, physically torn and bleeding, and overflowing with hatred.

Hilbert threw him away, and Ulric barely had the presence of mind to wrap his arms around his head to protect it when he collided with the head of the bed. A tapestry hung there, but it did little to prevent a cold, wet draft from seeping into the room. He heard Hilbert stand up, and watched him warily, saw his own blood staining the knight's mustache and beard. Hilbert poured wine into a cup and made as if to drink it. "That won't do you any good," Ulric told him. The man had demanded to know what had been done to him. "You can only drink blood now. And you'll need it every day. You already know you can't go out during the day, don't you?"

"No wine?" Hilbert shouted, and threw the cup across the room. A spray of red dotted the clean robe that he had donned when he got out of bed. His discarded and soiled garment remained in the bed with Ulric, rumpled as the boy's pride. "You children of Satan have made me into a fiend. I am the devil's get now, and all the money in the treasury of my order will not buy me an indulgence for this. Will it?" He stormed over to the bed and lifted Ulric by his neck. "Will it?" he demanded.

"No," Ulric said, though he had no idea what Hilbert was talking about, buying an indulgence. He still could not stretch his mind around the concept of sin, because most of the sins the priests talked about were just normal human needs, and even in his limited opportunity to observe them, he saw the Christians doing everything the pagans did, albeit in secret. Look at Hilbert, who was obviously born to love men and serve the Lord of the Animals. The fact that you didn't want to have sex with women didn't mean you had to hate them. How could you, when you partook of so much of their nature? When he was much younger, a priest of the Lord of the Animals should have seen Hilbert's nature and brought him a scarf or a belt with some bells upon it and a brightly colored skirt. He would have learned some of the songs, danced with the older priests, and opened his heart to see if the god would take him.

But now it was too late. If there had ever been any gentleness or capacity for yielding and flirtation in Hilbert, it had been beaten out of him. Now he was just a monster, and no animal or god would come to him in his dreams and give him their teachings or warn him to change his ways. Eagle, deer, boar, rabbit, serpent, and salmon had all turned their faces from him. And he did not know enough to be terrified of that isolation. No man was born to endure the loneliness of thinking only his own thoughts, feeling for nothing but himself. Those who could not learn how to hear the conversation of the earth and sky, or eavesdrop upon the wind and water, would go insane. Hilbert was proof of that.

These thoughts had brought Ulric back to his center and returned to him some of his strength. So when Hilbert attacked him again, thinking to rape him on his back, Ulric fought him with renewed strength, and managed to get his hands on the knight's throat. Hilbert pried his hands off, but not before the captive pagan warrior dug his fingernails into the skin between the rapist's neck and shoulder and cut open the skin. "Damn you," Hilbert said, then apparently decided to make the sentence a literal one. Because he forced Ulric's mouth open and jammed it against his neck. Ulric could not breathe. So he did what instinct told him to do—he bit and clawed at the man who smothered him, trying to get away. Although he could tell his teeth were causing Hilbert a great deal of pain, the knight just laughed and held him in place until Ulric passed out. It was long enough to guarantee that the doom which haunted Hilbert would fall upon his victim as well. Hilbert completed the second rape with his victim unconscious, and then carried him across the room, and sat him up against the wall. A set of irons had been installed there, and so he used these to restrain the shepherd whose flock he had wasted.

Hilbert buried himself in his furs, feeling much better now that he had stolen blood and virtue from his prisoner, and sank into hibernation with a wolfish grin on his bearded face. Taming this boy would be very entertaining. "*Vengeance is mine, sayeth the Lord,*" Hilbert thought, feeling vindicated rather than chastened by the scripture.

Outside the door, Frederic crossed himself and went to find the officer of the watch. He posted a guard outside of Hilbert's room, just in case he was wrong and their general awoke from his unnatural slumber. Once he had seen to the day's routine, Frederic went to take a little rest himself. He was not happy about Hilbert's nocturnal schedule, but he had seen his leader preoccupied with a boy before. Once Hilbert was done chastising the heathen, the prisoner would perhaps be more amenable to setting aside his wickedness and pursuing the path of righteousness.

In Sir Frederic's eyes, the many battles that Hilbert had fought in the Holy Land had built up so much treasure in heaven for the order and its leader that no sin he committed while off duty could sully his soul. Even if he had seen Hilbert sucking blood from Ulric's body, Frederic might not have been dismayed. The pagans who occupied this land were vermin, and the faster they were eliminated, the more quickly the order could consolidate their holdings and profit from them. Hilbert was a soldier. He had done worse things, usually with the heat of battle as an excuse. The rites of the ungodly were infinitely more disgusting, and heretics could not be treated harshly enough.

Why, then, did Sir Frederic feel a chilly wind blowing down his own neck every time he had to stay up after dark and consult with his general?

Ulric regained consciousness slowly, and when he opened his eyes, the world was a flurry of brightly colored sparks, flying up as if from a fire. Spirals and fountains of light moved in front of his face, screening him from the real world. These lovely visions slowly faded, and he was forced to experience the pain in his rectum and all over the rest of his body. His mouth was so clotted and caked with blood that he found it hard to swallow. When something leaped upon him, even though it was much smaller than Hilbert, he could not repress a yell. But then he saw the creature and felt much more sorry for it than he did for himself. It was a rabbit whose ears had been cut off. It had only little triangular flaps where its long, floppy ears should be. And it was licking him, which wasn't like a rabbit at all, even a tame one. It didn't have big front teeth, and it didn't wiggle its nose. Then he saw that it had a long, thin tail, which it twitched, and he realized it was something he had never seen before. It was the color of sand, brindled gold and brown and black, and its eyes were amber.

He tried to pet the not-rabbit, but could not reach it. His hands were manacled above his head. But it seemed happy to sit in his lap and lick the blood from his chest. After it had cleaned him off, it cleaned itself, licking its paws and buzzing like a bee. Then it turned around twice, like a dog, and went to sleep. Ulric knew there was something about the blood that should have upset him, but his body and soul collaborated to send him back into unconsciousness.

Lilith had moved closer to Ulric and put her arms around him. She had drawn him down from his seat on the boulder, and now they were sitting on the springy greenery and gravel at its feet. She had swept a clear place for each of them and was encouraging him to lean back against her. She felt the rough gray stone at her back, supporting them both. His eyes were closed, his hands in his lap, his breathing shallow. She had interrupted his reverie by opening her own eyes and taking his fingertips away from her face. She kissed him on the neck, the cheek, the eyelids.

"Sweetheart," she whispered. "No one can hurt you here. Come back to me. Don't stay in that terrible place."

When Ulric opened his eyes, there was so much tender concern in her face that he could not bring himself to retort that the person who could hurt him more than anyone else was there. "I'm sorry," he said instead. "Was it too much?"

"Yes. But no," she said firmly. "If you could bear it, I will too. I want to know everything about you."

"There's more. I should show you. It's important." But he could not summon enough energy to insist.

"Not now," she said, putting her fingertips over his lips. "Look, we're going to get to watch a sunset together. Who knows when we'll ever get to do this again?"

They joined in silent appreciation of the red- and pink-streaked sky. She squeezed his broad shoulders gently, then nuzzled his neck. Ulric accepted her attention, needing the comfort and grounding of her embrace. She turned his head and kissed him. Her assertiveness awoke his more vulnerable passions. Her tongue in his mouth set off warning bells, but she was careful of his fangs. He was surprised when she did not stop with a kiss. She deftly unbuttoned his shirt and her small hands wafted between the fabric and his skin. She stroked his chest from collarbone to belly and asked, "Does it feel nicer when I move in the direction that the hair grows?"

"I think it does," he replied, distracted by her left hand plucking at his right nipple. She cupped his pectoral muscle with her hand and worried the nipple away from its base so she could twirl it and twist it. Then she petted his chest some more. "Does your fur make it hard to feel what I'm doing?" she asked shyly.

Oh, sensible librarian, researching the male body, looking for a footnote to verify her findings. When had he been asked such questions about his own body? *Never*, he thought. The last person who had touched him so intimately was another man who probably assumed that Ulric's body responded to touch the same way that his own did. Besides, the sexual heat between himself and Alain was doomed to be as brief as it was intense; there had been no time for foreplay or conversational explorations of one another's likes and dislikes.

"I—uh—I think it makes my skin more sensitive, not less," Ulric replied as his lover straddled him, swept his shirt back off his shoulders, and kissed him slowly and thoroughly. His reflex was to reach for her, but her hands were on his upper arms, pressing them in, and she was pushing at his sleeves. Ulric reclaimed the use of his own arms long enough to shed the shirt and tuck it behind his head as she bore him to the ground.

"Put your arms over your head and keep them there," she said. Her voice was soft but clear, and he obeyed—but asked, "Who are you?" He wanted to make sure that he had really heard a note of command, her first shy attempt to wield erotic power over him.

"Your lady," she replied after only the briefest of pauses. She was surprised to feel what seemed to be a whole new persona consolidate and occupy her body.

"Yes, my lady," he acquiesced, and lazily extended his hands as far away from his body as he could, arching himself for her inspection. Does every man consciously try to make his muscles stand out when the one he desires draws near?

She ran her fingertips along the hollows beneath his arms and down his flanks. Then she stretched out upon him, and the feeling of her clothed torso on his naked skin was oddly exciting. Ulric happily gave himself up to the fantasy that she was his protector and sovereign, and was prepared to offer her his best.

Mary Beth could feel herself becoming Lilith, the free and happily licentious creature that Ulric had called into being. She hiked up her skirts and rocked her pelvis into him, and experienced a strange desire to spread his legs and slide her cock into him. It was as if that male organ had been grafted onto her self-image, like a phantom limb. He could feel the hermaphrodite nature of her thrusts and opened his mouth to her kisses, altering his posture subtly to receive her aggression.

In her imagination, Mary Beth had been raped at least once a day. Like all women, she flashed upon the possibility of being victimized by random sexual predators at all sorts of times—leaving the house to go to work (even in broad daylight), walking into a deserted parking garage, leaving a grocery store after dark, awakening in the night to an unfamiliar noise in her apartment. Ulric's rape had taken place hundreds and hundreds of years ago, but she had just experienced it. Wasn't it odd that she felt closer to him, knowing he had been used this way? Another woman might have seen him as unmanned by violence. But it made her feel safer with him. A barrier that normally separated men from women had gone down between them. He understood one of her core fears.

But if she was going to offer him reassurance, shouldn't it be done by inviting him to ravish her, to prove he was still potent? Instead, Lilith took his clothes off, wanting to see him naked under the fading sun. And she touched him everywhere, with hands and lips, until he was quivering with the joyous tension of sexual readiness. The squalor and despair of being violated by the man he hated had been chased away by her caresses. She banished evil from his flesh: he was a pure and handsome receptacle for her stormiest needs.

His cock stood firm as the mast of a ship, but she still could not quite bring herself to put it in her mouth. She wrapped one hand around it and eased his foreskin up, down, rotated her hand and then just her cupped fingertips around the head of his cock. Her mouth was fastened on one nipple and then the other. As his breath quickened, she gradually increased the speed with which she stroked him and the firmness of her grip. He gasped, "If you keep on doing that, I'll come."

"Not yet," she said, and put two of her fingers into his mouth. He looked at her with his eyebrows cocked up in a question. Was she getting her fingers wet for the same reason he would have if he put his fingers in her mouth?

Lilith unbuttoned her blouse and unhooked her bra. She dragged her naked breasts down his body, and as she moved, he adjusted his thighs to make a gap where she could sit. The touch of her nipples ruffling the fur of his chest was tantalizing. He longed to reach for her breasts and tweak and tongue her nipples. But his hands remained where she had ordered them to be. Then she got his attention back to his own body. Her hand was wrapped around the base of his cock and balls. Two fingers nestled against his anus.

"I won't ever hurt you," she said, and wormed her fingers into the center of his hole. Who would have guessed she could gain entry so quickly sliding on nothing but spit? Hard to keep that or any other sensible thought in his mind as she pressed on his prostate, stroking it as she jacked him off with exquisite slowness. Arms still above his head, Ulric felt his heart and body make another decision to let go, to accept the gift of sensation she was offering him.

He was smooth inside, and Lilith loved fucking him. She was putting her love into him, filling him up with it, and once more banishing his hurt and shame. He was stretched out beneath her, staring into her brown eyes, paying attention to nothing but what her will declared he should experience.

"Lady!" he cried when her attentions were especially effective.

"Yes," she said. "Here I am."

"Don't leave me."

"Sssh. Don't worry about that now. What do you want?"

"I want you to keep on doing that, even though I can't stand it. Will you ever let me—"

"Not yet."

"Please!"

"Be quiet."

She teased him until he could no longer form words to beg for relief. When his stomach was rigid from the effort of holding back his peak, and his nipples stood out like brown caramel kisses, she said, "Come for me now."

A wave of power rode into her as he gave himself up. She could feel everything that happened to him because she had one hand around his rod and three of her long fingers buried as far as possible into his ass. Nuances of physical events that she could never have perceived if his cock had been inside her unfolded and amazed her. She could feel his balls trying to tug themselves out of her grip so they could unload. When he came, the contractions shook him inside as well as all along his cock. And by manipulating his prostate, she prolonged and heightened his pleasure until he screamed for mercy. What he gave her, of himself, was as hot and aromatic as a fire made with dry branches from a pine tree.

Lilith wrapped her legs around one of his thighs and ground her clit into his hip. The imaginary cock that had so abruptly appeared, attached to her loins, was back. As she imagined opening him with the rounded head of her phallus, the pressure of his hip bone upon her vulva built and built. After he came and collapsed, panting and sweaty, she kept on riding him, and was suddenly possessed with the desire to wrap her hands around his throat. He allowed even this, and held his breath for her. That sent a thrill between her legs that inspired her to say, "Don't you dare breathe until I come."

Under her sway, he willed himself to obey. With eyes that had gone shrewd and cruel, she watched his struggle to deny himself air. Lilith became more and more excited. He felt as if she were fucking him, not with her fingers, but with a long, slender, gently arched cock that tickled the internal root of his dick. When she finally came, he was seeing patches of black, but he also was shaken by the sensation of being filled with her essence, as if she had pumped him full of cum. He tasted musk and cinnamon, a love potion worthy of a maenad.

"Breathe," she said, letting go of his throat. "Hold me," she added, lying down upon him. He embraced her with one arm and succeeded in convincing her to let him stroke her wet inner lips and rouse her again with his fingertips. His thumb on her clit and other fingers buried in her, Ulric held her tight and fucked her once, twice, a third time. It was as if he had a cunt between his legs that needed what Lilith needed and told him what to do. She was within his aura as he was within hers. They were like one person, for he felt what she did, and she knew what he was thinking, coming from the stimulation of knowing how he felt while touching her as well as the actual sensation of his hand working her clit and hole. It was good to be Lilith. She was wise, free, strong, and whole. Completely a woman, yet more powerful than any woman in living memory had been allowed to be.

"Lady," Ulric said, stroking her hair. "Goddess. You are my wild Lady of the Mountain."

"You are my wild one, my divine sweetheart and Lord of the Animal in both of us."

"You realize we're married now," he said.

"What?"

"Well—we've made love outside, in the sight of goddess and god, and they've accepted our offering by lending us their divinity. Where I come from, my girl, that means you're hitched."

"We'll see what the justice of the peace has to say about that," she retorted. "Can I change the subject? I'm cold. I want to go home."

"The whole night is still before us. Let me take you home," he said gallantly.

She objected when he picked her up. "You can't walk all the way to my house carrying me," she said.

"I'm not going to walk," he explained.

When Lilith found out that this meant they were going to fly, she only screamed once or twice. On takeoff and on landing. She pressed her face into his chest so nobody could hear. Still, when she led him into the front door of her building and up to her apartment, she had the feeling that every other inhabitant knew she had come home, and she was not alone. The cat was so far out of the bag that it was practically standing on her foot and saying, "Meow." After five years of successfully passing as the least interesting person in town, she had become more interesting than front-page news. The bat guano had hit the fan.

CHAPTER 4
I'm Not Well, but I'm Better

Adulfa, dressed in her customary black leather and red silk, was the last to arrive. The room was too small for the six (now seven) women it held. There were some perfectly nice leather-covered sofas and chairs, but everyone had propped themselves up on large pillows on the floor. It was not Adulfa's way to lounge about. So she walked through the middle of the circle, picked a spot exactly opposite the therapist, and folded herself neatly into a cross-legged position on the carpeted floor. She did not look to the left or to the right to acknowledge the women who moved sideways, sliding awkwardly on their butts, to make space for her. Nor did she give the therapist a deferential smile or an explanation for her five minutes' worth of tardiness.

It would have been easy to spot who the therapist was, even if Adulfa had not been studying Amy Ross for the last month and a half. For one thing, she sat inside a slightly larger zone of empty space than anyone else in the circle. This gave her room to make expressive gestures with her hands, without the risk of bumping elbows with one of her clients. She looked prosperous—feminine, yet professional. Her dark brown hair turned under at the edge of her jawline, and she had barely enhanced her eyebrows, lips, and cheekbones with discreet shades of makeup. She wore a strand of carnelian and onyx beads, a lacy Victorian blouse, and a broomstick skirt of organic cotton whose rich rosy clay color was imparted by vegetable dyes. She had taken off her Italian sandals and placed them neatly, toes to the wall, behind herself.

Now Amy cleared her throat and began to talk. The women in the group looked at the floor and played with their hair. They seemed to wish desperately to be anywhere except trapped within this small room with its taupe carpet, the huge framed print of a fulsome Georgia O'Keefe flower, the handblown glass vases on the mantelpiece of the empty fireplace, the earth-and-sky hues of the dreamcatcher that hung on the back of the door.

Adulfa had buzzed her hair that morning, and by now it had grown out to half an inch of stubble the color of corn silk. She did not touch it, feeling no need to rearrange herself for scrutiny. She noticed then that all the other women in the group had taken off their shoes, in imitation of the therapist. So she stretched her legs out in front of herself, which gave Amy an excellent view of her riding boots. Adulfa had tucked her full-cut leather pants into the top of them. She looked like a Cossack on her way to Nordstrom's.

Adulfa felt someone else's eyes upon her, and tracked the stranger's gaze to the knife hilt that protruded slightly from the top of the right boot. Not that she needed it; her teeth were growing sharper by the minute, honed by boredom if nothing else. But Adulfa loved the drama of knives, their flashing beauty, the way they instantly reflected light and terror. It was Rhys who had seen it, of course. She was good at figuring out how other people could damage her. Adulfa idly made her forget about the knife.

The droning introduction to the group was finally over. The therapist had presented her credentials as an experienced healer for the trauma of childhood sexual abuse. This was a group for survivors, she had emphasized, a group for those who had the courage to heal. She promised that the work would be successful, if they had the faith and strength to persevere. It was vitally important to conjure up the past and its misery, so that it could be reexperienced in a safe context, and all the anger and fear vented, the old business finished. Then normal life could begin. A better body image, self-esteem, healthy relationships, healthy sexuality, were some of the fruits that could spill from Amy's cornucopia, if they were worthy. Were there any questions?

Adulfa, who needed to worry very little about her health, thought that vigor was probably a fine quality for a prey animal to possess, but the power of speech was wasted in such cases. Bored as a cat just waking up from a nap, she yawned, taking a good long time to properly stretch her jaws. But wait, someone was daring to ask a question. This was the woman on Adulfa's right, a voluptuous femme dyke in her early forties who worked as a travel agent. Her curls shook as she stammered, "How much longer, I mean, in the groups that you've led in the past, I know you can't really be specific but to just give us a general idea, how long have other groups lasted before you felt like people were, um, well, I guess you shouldn't say *cured*, but...?"

Amy gave her a smile full of pity that made the hair on the back of Adulfa's neck stand up in a silent shout of rage. "Well, we are doing depth work here," she temporized. "Incest is a serious trauma. It has long-term, wide-ranging consequences. We must be prepared to put in as much time as is necessary to address it."

The woman on Adulfa's left, a young musician with a mostly shaved scalp and an off-center, sapphire-colored mandarin braid, spoke out then. "That means we're never going to get well, doesn't it?" she said flatly. This was Rhys, not quite twenty-one. She wore her alien skeleton fresh and raw on the outside of her skin, having spent almost as much time getting tattooed as she would have spent in prison for manslaughter. Adulfa liked girls with tattoos, although she had to admit it was as risky as picking a bottle of wine just because it had a pretty label.

Amy acted as if she had not heard that comment. "I think we should go around the circle. Each woman should tell us what name she'd like used in the group and a little bit of the history that brought her here." And there was another one of those smiles that Adulfa hated, a coy smile, like a cat who knows her sister is waiting by the mouse's back door. Amy turned her head and sprayed the entire circle with that smile, except that when her gaze crossed Adulfa, two tiny creases sprang up between her eyebrows, little lines of concern. Adulfa was amused. Dissent had sprung from either side of her. Without saying a word, she had been identified as a troublemaker.

She exerted her will slightly, and the woman on her right began to talk. Adulfa did not listen to the details. She was more interested in the flavor of being that emanated from each woman. Mortals had that strange effect upon her senses, as if each was a dish that her mind had to sample before she could sink her teeth into them. It made walking through a crowd a real challenge; sometimes there was just too much data, and it made her feel crazy. Automatically, to keep herself alert, she paged through the past of each woman as she spoke, separating truth from fiction, belief from actual event.

The travel agent had an alcoholic father and a mother who insisted on staying married to him. She believed that her father had molested her, but in fact, it was her mother who had crept into her room late at night and put her hand where it did not belong.

The next woman was a graduate student who was having trouble finishing her thesis. She had short, naturally red hair and a lean, athletic body. After two years of therapy, she had come to believe that the only explanation for her fractured relationships, uneven sex life, and confusion about her future was a history of incest. In fact, Adulfa found, nothing of the sort had happened. But that would not be a problem in Amy's group. Amy was a certified hypnotherapist. She could give you the past that your misery demanded.

And so it went around the circle, until it came time for Rhys to speak. Adulfa did her the rare courtesy of turning to look at her. She had so much enjoyed listening to her band play in a warehouse that weekend. It was thrilling to take blood in a thrash pit, right in front of the victim's friends. She had not even bothered to cast a see-me-not over herself that night. Of course, Rhys did not remember her. Adulfa frequently found it convenient to be overlooked by her conquests, until the appropriate moment came for confrontation.

Rhys spoke in a rush: incomplete sentences piled on top of one another uneven and jagged as broken glass. She was a victim—a junkie (although she did not mention that part of her life in the group), a habitual fuckup who could not hold down a job or keep an apartment, always on the verge of not surviving because she managed to alienate even the friends who offered her temporary places to stay, fed her, loaned her money that she never repaid. Rhys had a lot of friends for a girl who never put out. But it was no surprise to Adulfa that givers outnumbered takers in this world, and she did not think ill of Rhys for her unthinking consumption of other people's love, money, peanut butter, and smack.

Rhys had been raped by virtually every male relative she had, and by some of their friends. Pictures had been taken. Movies had been made. Some of the violation had been scripted as Satanic ritual. She did not need hypnotherapy or truth serum to remember this. She remembered it all. In fact, what she really wanted from the group was a way to forget.

When Rhys was done speaking, Adulfa—who knew what such a thing would look like—visualized everyone trying to sit quietly with her abdomen slit open and her intestines steaming in her lap. She got a little too preoccupied with embellishing this vision, until she realized the silence in the group had gone on too long for even a therapist's patience.

"Adulfa," Amy said pleasantly, "do you have anything you'd like to share with us?"

Adulfa gave her back a smile, an exact copy of that I-feel-so-much-compassion-for-you-because-I-know-something-you-don't-know look. "Once," she said, deliberately spacing out her words to get their attention, "a long time ago, my brother did something to me that I did not wish him to do. And I have never forgiven him for it. One day, he will do penance."

Everyone kept looking at her, hanging on her words. When it became clear that there would be no more to the story, they shook themselves as if they were waking up or flicking water off their faces. Even Amy Ross had to shudder to cast off the spell of Adulfa's honeyed, foreign-sounding tenor.

The meeting went on for another hour. Amy managed to persuade the woman who had not been abused to pretend she was talking to her father, to confront him with accusations that Adulfa could hardly refrain from laughing at. Eventually she beat up a pillow that represented him. Then Amy dismissed them all with a short, upbeat speech about liberating themselves from the tyranny of the past, which would happen only if they kept coming back!

The therapist asked Rhys to stay behind. She wanted to tell her that there were more resources available for healing herself—in other words, she wanted Rhys to start seeing her for individual therapy, in addition to the group. Adulfa heard all of this from her place on the landing, where she was waiting so she could watch Rhys walk down the stairs. She heard Rhys complain that she could not afford so much therapy, and Amy offered to run a tab. Adulfa bit her own tongue to keep herself from laughing out loud. Rhys was going to go into debt to satisfy Amy

Ross' appetite for suffering. That was like asking people to pay for the privilege of being bled. Although, come to think of it, there was that mad transvestite Daytona Bitch, who kept a dungeon on the east side of Detroit and did exactly that.

Rhys said she would think about it, and left. It took only the lightest touch against her mind to stop her from wondering why Adulfa was lurking on the landing. The vampire descended two steps behind her quarry, aching to cup her hands around the cheeks of her ass. Rhys smelled like water lilies and snow. The aura she gave off was violet-tinged, and its texture reminded Adulfa of a Victorian quilt she had once seen, made out of one-inch squares of jewel-toned velvet. Inside her chest was the claw of an eagle, which tore and tore at Rhys' heart. She was in so much psychic pain, all the time, it was as if her own blood were scalding her to death.

It would be so sweet to take her now. Adulfa knew it could be done with ease. All she had to do was prevent Rhys' Shadow 350cc motorcycle from starting, say she knew something about bikes, pretend to fix it, invite her out for a beer to celebrate. Of course, even these preliminaries were not necessary. Adulfa could simply take Rhys in her arms, rip her head off, and empty her right here on the street. People would part around them and keep on walking, as if they had seen nothing at all. Adulfa had the power to make even a grandiloquent kill invisible to innocent bystanders. But she loved the dance of seduction. She would never do what her foolish brother Ulric had done and take a mortal consort. Though she would, someday, be sure to punish the fellow immortals who had sent her gleeful email or called her cellphone to tell her the gossip about his embarrassing sentimentality. Still, there were pleasures other than blood lust.

And she did not intend to kill Rhys. At least, not yet, not now. So Adulfa satisfied herself with breathing into Rhys' body, a warm and subversive gust of air that started around her ankles, ran up her legs into her cunt, and from there spread into her chest and face, opening her up to a lightning-flash of pure pleasure. Rhys made a small sound and stumbled. Adulfa caught her by the elbow, steadied her, and gave her a conspiratorial wink. It came to Rhys, despite everything she did to shield herself from the information, that this was the first time she had felt a delicious sensation of her own in any of her orifices, rather than being held hostage as a witness to other people taking their own pleasure there.

Adulfa shrugged. Human beings were cruel to each other. It was one of the things that justified her hunting among them. This was the latest episode in the predatory game of her life, and that was all. The musician's soul had been mangled, but countless others had been treated with even more brutality. She felt no pang of separation as she walked away from her latest human hobby.

The darkness would last for another six hours. Adulfa squeezed herself as small as a fist — *wrinkled face with a monkey-snout, soft brown fur, thin-skinned wings stretched taut between cartilage struts, and agile, grasping paws.* In this guise, she flew to a much more interesting part of town, where the clubs were located. After spending so much time in the company of women, she had a fancy for boy meat, some brash young thing who would be appalled to find himself alone with a woman he could not force or intimidate. Frat boys were especially yummy, full of testosterone, their faces prickly with nubile beards. The scrape of male fur against her lips and tongue gave Adulfa goosebumps. She loved the flavor of brandy mingled with a human being's blood. It was her little way to sit next to her intended and manipulate the bartender into pouring — and her beloved into drinking — whatever flavor she thought would make her feeding most piquant.

It took three more weekly sessions for Amy to persuade Rhys to make an appointment for individual therapy. In that short amount of time, the lives of the women in the group deteriorated quickly. Two of them lost their jobs. The graduate student severed all ties with her family, who were paying for school, which solved the problem of the unwritten dissertation. Some of them had broken up with their lovers. All of them were depressed. It amazed Adulfa to see them draw closer together, caught in the net of their despair. Why was it that adversity made human beings so stupid and stubborn? Any other animal would try to escape from a situation that was causing them such unhappiness, but these women simply dug their heels in and became even more loyal to their therapist and the process that was drowning them.

It was Amy Ross, with her turquoise jewelry and cloisonné bracelets and silver earrings from Thailand, her cashmere cardigans and her batik skirts and linen jackets, and her promises of nurturance and healing, who had them spellbound. She loved to dabble her clean white fingers in someone else's emotional wounds. If she saw any signs of healing, she did not flinch from yanking hard on the sides of it and ripping it open again. Women in her groups who were not sure they had been molested became convinced that it was so. Those who had been able to name one perpetrator were now able to name two, or half a dozen. Those who had remembered only fondling, which had been obnoxious but not painful, were now sobbing through hysterical narratives about being torn by penetration. They saw signs of abuse in every relationship that they had with employers, friends, lovers, family members. They stopped making love, stopped masturbating, and saw every sexual fantasy as just one more symptom of damage.

Adulfa had to admit it was a perfect scam. Find a group of people whose early life experience has convinced them that they are unworthy, that bad things will always happen to them, a group of people who expect to be hurt by their caretakers, who have never experienced nurturing or unselfish love. And then put yourself in the position of their caretaker, and promise to help them. After most of the group therapy sessions, Adulfa was convinced that if Amy Ross had tried to do real therapy with them and promote resolution or healing, she would have lost every client she had. They were that embedded in old patterns, the repetition of injury and insult and violation.

Rhys never spoke to her or even looked at her. But she always sat next to Adulfa, on her left, like a dog that automatically assumes its place at the feet of its master. Adulfa could not, of course, wait a whole week to see Rhys again. She had taken to feeding herself quickly and then hovering outside Rhys' bedroom window, every night, in the witching hours before dawn. There were so many games she could play with Rhys once sleep had dismantled some of her defenses. One of Adulfa's favorite ploys was to make Rhys' tattoos come alive. First she would warm them, until Rhys threw off her covers and lay naked before Adulfa's hungry eyes. Then she would make them move slightly, quickly. It was like being caressed with the barest tips of butterfly wings. She would make the rings in Rhys' nipples and clitoral hood vibrate subtly, until the parts they pierced were swollen and erect. Slowly, gradually, Adulfa would pour sensuality into the ink, suffusing Rhys' body with delight until she groaned and came in her sleep.

The best moment of all was when Rhys would wake up, heart pounding and cunt wet, unable to remember exactly what had happened, rubbing herself all over, trying to figure out how the flat ink on her skin had become raised and inflamed. Adulfa wanted her so much then, wanted to flick her tongue against Rhys' clit and sink her hand into Rhys' cunt. But she knew that Rhys took no pleasure in sex and would barely feel the most savage rapine. So she continued to devise new ways to make Rhys tremble in her sleep.

Of course, she could have simply walked into Rhys' mind and taken away the horrors that had made sex a ruined palace for her, but she did not. That would spoil the game, and Adulfa was relishing this hunt.

She was there the first evening that Amy Ross met with Rhys one-on-one to begin a new phase of treatment. Ironically enough, it was the weird evenings of onanistic pleasure that had made Rhys think the therapy was effective, and more of it would probably be a good idea.

Adulfa slipped in the door behind her, accidentally catching the fact that Rhys had no idea where she was going to sleep tonight; probably the bus station. There was no time to find out who had given her those knee-length leather overalls.

Amy, wearing a tan linen jumper over a white cotton blouse with white embroidery, indicated the couch and told Rhys to lay down on it. She obeyed the order, as she had obeyed many like it. Adulfa could barely contain herself when Amy began to hypnotize Rhys. She had to dig her fingernails (cut at sundown, now a half-inch long and sharp as razors) into the palms of her hands to make herself stay silent and hidden. It was a surprise to feel so much jealousy. The clumsy trance state that Amy Ross induced could not be compared to the deep glamour that Adulfa could cast, but it was enough to peel back Rhys' inhibitions and make her suggestible.

Amy Ross began with the usual reassurances that Rhys was safe. They were going to watch a movie together, and maybe there would be some upsetting things in the movie, but it wasn't really happening, and Rhys could stop the tape at any time. The movie was about Rhys when she was little, and some bad people had done bad things to her. Did Rhys remember when that had begun? Who was there? What did he say? What had been done to her?

Adulfa hissed as she listened to the narrative. So far it was standard desensitization, giving Rhys power over the narrative of her life, allowing her to stop and thus control the replay of her memories. But Adulfa did not think it was standard practice for Amy Ross to keep demanding additional details (which Rhys gave her in the voice of a frightened child), nor was it ethical for her to put her right hand inside her own panties and rub her bikini-waxed pussy. Adulfa was not surprised to find herself becoming aroused by the pathos of Rhys' tale of rape and voyeurism, but she didn't approve of mortals who had gourmet appetites.

Then Amy suggested that it was hot in the room, very hot, and it was hard to breathe, so Rhys should pull up her T-shirt and unbutton her jeans. Adulfa's eyebrows shot up at the sheer temerity of it. When Amy succeeded in directing Rhys to stroke her own nipples and finger her clit, Adulfa cracked. She would not tolerate someone else coming this close to the gift she had picked out for her own enjoyment.

The look on Amy Ross' face as Adulfa came out of the shadows was priceless, a mixture of fury and abject guilt. Still, she managed to cling to the mantle of her profession. "Adulfa, I am afraid I will have to ask you to leave. You are jeopardizing the confidentiality of one of my clients!"

Adulfa advanced on the brazen huckster, plucked her wanton hand from between her thighs, and thrust the fingers of that hand into Amy

Ross' painted-pink mouth. "Is this what you mean by in-depth work?" she sneered.

The vampire took the therapist's hand out of her mouth, so she could hear what she had to say. But she kept a tight grip on her wrist. Amy Ross did not try to escape. She seemed to believe that if she did not acknowledge her captivity, it would have no meaning. She gave the intruder that pitying trademark smile. "I'm afraid you don't have the background to understand the intricacies of psychotherapy, dear. Sometimes it takes unorthodox methods to clean up the garbage that's left behind by incest. But I stand by my results. "

"Oh, really?" Adulfa asked, with one eyebrow raised. "What about Evelyn Harkness? Do you stand by the results you got with her? Because you might as well have been standing by her side when she blew her brains out with a .45."

"I must acknowledge that it's a great tragedy when a long-term client commits suicide," Amy Ross whispered. "But I can't take responsibility for her decision to end her own life. Each one of us is the only person who can really shoulder that existential burden."

"I don't know about that, you seem to have more burdens than most shrinks. Do you recall the name of Ellen Bauer? What about Linda Treat? Jocelyn Dewars? Or little Eddy Silverstein? Come on, Amy, I know you can't reveal the identities of your clients, but these people all happen to be very very dead. And I think it's your fault."

Amy Ross finally realized that she was in deep trouble, and began to struggle. But Adulfa was not ready to take her yet. "Wake Rhys up," she ordered, turning Amy to face the reclining young musician. Rhys still lay there with her clothing askew, and her mouth was slightly open. She looked as if she was in REM sleep. One of her hands twitched a little as she dreamed.

"Tell her the movie is over, she doesn't need to watch it any more, and wake her up!" Adulfa said, getting impatient. She shook Amy to let her know she meant business. The out-of-breath counselor repeated Adulfa's words, and snapped her fingers. Rhys sat up slowly, realized her breasts were exposed, and yanked her shirt down. Then she realized her fly was open, and she glared up at both of them, humiliated and furious. "What the hell is going on here?" she yelled.

"Why, it's time for Amy Ross to realize that she's not the only vampire in this town," Adulfa said, feeling quite cheerful now. Amy Ross' eyes went wide as Adulfa took her by the shoulders. She was facing Rhys as Adulfa sank three-inch ivory fangs into her neck and sucked out her life as fast as it could come. She beat on Adulfa's back and tried to free herself, but it was no use. Adulfa was too strong, and too quick. Rhys made a muffled sound and tried to back away, but the couch was too heavy to move, and she was too frightened to think of a way out of its sticky pastel embrace.

Adulfa dropped Amy Ross' body. It fell akimbo, with as much dignity as she had allowed her patients. Rhys threw her hands out, an ineffectual gesture of warding, as Adulfa came toward her with her fangs fully extended, a snake woman, a wolf spirit. Her face was bloody, and her eyes were full of glee.

"Don't hurt me," Rhys pleaded. "Please, leave me alone, don't hurt me!"

Adulfa shook her head, spraying Rhys with a little of Amy Ross' jugular vintage. "Don't hurt me," she mocked in a little girl's high-pitched whine. "Please, leave me alone! What a wimp you are, Rhys, a weak member of a pathetic species. You have no idea how short your life is, do you? In fact, you imagine that your life has already gone on for far too long. You whimper and bitch and live like a fool, and hope that fate will take a hand and deal you out of the game. I have lived for many long centuries. My victims number in the millions. Sometimes I take the best, the strongest, the most beautiful, the most talented. And sometimes I am in a mood to take the evil, the wicked, or the sick whose time is almost up. But I tell you this, every person I have ever embraced has fought to live. And now, it is your turn to discover the naked brute instinct to survive."

Rhys' sleeveless white T-shirt was speckled red, and a few fine drops of blood had been sprayed across her forehead. Her blue pigtail hung over one shoulder, and her guitar-callused hands dug into the leather upholstery, ripping it. She smelled like absolute terror. There was no hot, coppery smell of anger in her. She was a little brown rabbit who knew it had been spotted moving through the autumn leaves. The sight of her small breasts, rising and falling with her frail mortal breath, enraged Adulfa, and she hurled herself at her, lifting her until they were chest to chest, eye to eye. There was still no resistance. Rhys stared straight at her, but her eyes were blind. And so Adulfa gathered her up like a lover, nuzzled the crook of her neck, and went deep into the muscle.

The pain must have been intense. But Rhys didn't even scream. Adulfa thought she might be crying. So she worried the wounds that she had made, and at that, Rhys responded by pulling away slightly. "I can't do this," she cried, and Adulfa knew she was weeping. "I can't do this, I can't fight you. Take me, let me die, I don't want to live. I don't want to live. I'm a fucked up mess, I'm a junkie and a loser. You're strong and beautiful, and it's right for me to feed you. So take what you want, just do it quick, and if you don't have to hurt me, please don't, I can't stand the pain."

Adulfa shrugged and resumed feeding. It took her no more than a few minutes to take a life, but she prolonged this kill. Amy Ross had sated most of her hunger and rage, and now she felt almost playful. She refused to take quite enough blood to make Rhys lose consciousness. Instead, she bit deeper and deeper, making multiple wounds, deliberately inflicting the pain that Rhys was begging to avoid.

Finally she lifted Rhys up and sank her fangs into the musician's left breast. Rhys was dangling from her arms, and she screamed when the sharp incisors penetrated her delicate tissues. Still she did not really resist. This was maddening. When her own brother had come for her, Adulfa had not shrieked or tried to escape. She was too proud. But this was not pride, it was weakness, and Rhys had no right to stir the ancient pool of her memories!

Physical pain was not having the effect she wanted. Forever flexible, Adulfa changed tactics, and unleashed a series of fierce orgasms in her victim, pressing on the pleasure centers of her brain. She kept it up until Rhys' thighs were as wet as her neck. Rhys had never come in someone else's arms before. "You're going to get at least one good fuck before you die," Adulfa vowed. She threw Rhys back onto the sofa and herself on top of her. She ripped off her jeans. Now the musician was struggling, calling Adulfa filthy names, trying to fend her off and protect her cunt. But Adulfa brushed aside her hands and went in deep, then said, "You are under my power, Rhys, and you will come every time I say your name."

She proved that it was so. The only break that Rhys got were the few seconds Adulfa needed to lick her nipples in between the soft, caressing repetitions of her name. Adulfa put her hands everywhere that Rhys' abusers had: in her cunt, her mouth, her ass. And everywhere she touched, she left behind a legacy of inhuman pleasure, the total response that can be wrung from human flesh only when it is on the brink of death, or under supernatural sway.

"So there you are," Adulfa said, withdrawing from her victim. Her belly was full of blood, and she felt warm and replete. Ready for sleep.

"You're not going to kill me, are you?" Rhys asked gloomily, legs splayed against a stained couch. The murderous hue of blood looked terribly out of place against the soothing, neutral pastel leather. Her arms and legs trembled with fatigue from their combat.

"I don't think so," the vampire said.

"Where are you going? What will I do now?" Rhys sobbed with dry eyes, looking wildly about, smeared with blood, furious at the building fear that would keep her stuck in the hateful meat of her own body.

"If I were you, I'd call an attorney," Adulfa said, stepping down. "Then I'd call the police. You might want to ask them to take a look at Amy Ross' private video collection, over there on the bookshelf, between Malamuth and Goldsmith. She taped all of the private sessions." Adulfa took the Georgia O'Keefe off the wall. A tiny hole had been cut in it, and it concealed a niche in the wall that held a small video camera. "Just like she was videotaping you, sweet thing."

"But I didn't kill her. You—"

"Please be my guest, Rhys. Tell the district attorney that you were raped by a vampire who had just murdered your therapist. They'll still put you away, and I suppose mental hospitals *are* a lot more fun than prison. Or I guess you could tell the cops that the cult that was abusing you took revenge upon the kindly shrink who was trying to give you psychic first aid. In which case, you should probably destroy Amy Ross' library of dual-relationship pornography before you call anybody. Or you could steal her Day Runner, pull your file, and hope none of the other group members tell the cops to interview you along with all of her other clients. I guess you could pilfer their files as well. I don't care what you do, my little steak-and-kidney pie."

"I can't believe you're just going to walk away and leave me to deal with all this!"

Adulfa gave her a withering look. "Believe it or not, as you like. I'm out of here. You'll clean up this mess just fine, Rhys. You'll do it because you have to if you want to live. I wonder why you're not grateful to me for putting you in touch with that. Like Amy Ross said, we're all survivors. You're not well, but you're better."

Adulfa opened a window and thought, *fist-size, warm night sky, bouncing ping of radar, insect scooping crunchy-squishy midnight snack, soothing moonlight bath,* and vanished, eager to feel the narrow sides of some secure hiding place pressing against her well-fed flesh.

Several nights later, Rhys was kicked awake. She had shrouded herself in a sleeping bag in the corner of a room that had been occupied by punk dykes, young fags, and a few hip straight people. The building was abandoned, but the squatters had been quite ingenious; they had electric lights and enough power to run CD players and guitars. Rhys had been huddled in that sleeping bag ever since she had escaped from the bloody chaos of Amy Ross' office. She hadn't even bathed. (Then again, there was no hot water.) Used to the catastrophes that accompanied life on the street, her fellow squatters had avoided bugging her about what had happened. They had enough injuries of their own to lick. If she had asked for help, they would have been as generous as their own scarce resources and precarious states of mind allowed. But if somebody just wanted to be left alone, it wasn't cool to barge in. So Rhys shook in her down cocoon and hoped she would never have to hatch and leave it.

The foot that nudged her in the ribs, too painfully to be ignored, was clad in a pointy-toed shoe that Rhys knew quite well was also spike-heeled and made of patent leather. She unzipped her bag before the kick could land again and said reproachfully, "That hurts." She had been wrong. Adulfa was wearing knee-high platform boots with wedge heels.

"Pardon me. Next time I'll whip you out of there. Get up."

It was the voice of the terrible creature who had killed Amy Ross, then turned on Rhys—she was too traumatized by everything that had happened to think of Adulfa as her rescuer. Nevertheless, she sat up. It wasn't the first time a gorgeous, hard-assed babe had told her what to do. But Adulfa was scarier than any femme Rhys had run into in a mosh pit.

A file folder and a Palm Pilot landed beside her nest of thrift-store pillows and rugs salvaged from dumpsters. "You forgot some of the evidence," Adulfa said dryly. "Don't be stupid and pawn the PDA, chickie. Smash it to smithereens and burn the paper. Now take off your clothes."

Rhys stripped, shivering. The resources of the squat did not include space heaters. At least four other people had crashed in the same room, largely because it had no broken windows, so it was nominally warmer. Why weren't any of them waking up? The air seemed colder than it had been when she went to sleep, and there was a vibration or a smell coming from Adulfa that was like a forest after it rains. But it wasn't a happy, fresh, friendly smell. This was an old forest, one that contained dark gods and no paths made by the feet of mankind.

Adulfa took her by the chin, jerked her head to one side, examined the wounds on her neck. "Lovely," she pronounced. "You look like you're headed for a deli counter. I'd like a pound of prosciutto, please, sliced extra-thin."

"They're your marks," Rhys dared to sullenly reply.

Adulfa slapped her. The blow made Rhys smile. Chicks didn't hit you if they didn't want something from you. Adulfa took the smile off her face by lifting her off the ground by her neck. In the few seconds between her feet leaving the floor and then mercifully returning to earth, Rhys decided that she was going to kiss Adulfa's ass, thoroughly. Because if she had her face buried in that sumptuous Aryan ass, there would be no way for the vampire to tell if she was pulling faces at her.

"You're wrong," Adulfa said, slapping the sides of Rhys' face with both of her hands, left, right, left, right, but these were lighter taps, not strong enough to snap her head to the side. "I know everything about you, Rhys. And you know nothing about me. No matter what you think you've gleaned from books and television and movies. Unfortunately for you, I believe you are so self-absorbed that you will know little more about me at the end of our association than you do right here and now." She punctuated the end of her sentence with a punch in the stomach.

Rhys doubled up and retched, but Adulfa hauled her upright by her T-shirt, not allowing her to huddle over her innards.

"What association?" Rhys coughed, wishing Adulfa would leave her alone so she could crawl into the corner and vomit.

"This," Adulfa said, and sent a mental scalpel into the musician's mind. There were so many submissive tendencies there already that it wasn't very difficult to forge a strong bond between them. Rhys' mouth was open and she was drooling, a loony expression of ecstasy on her face. "I don't want you to do anything different than what you do already, Rhys. Just go about your business. Go to the clubs. Go to bars. Score drugs, because if you don't, everybody will think there's something wrong with you. But you won't be doing them. At least, not in lethal quantities. Screw whoever you want to screw. But when you come, Rhys, you will see my face above you. And when you see this face," (Adulfa flashed several pictures of her brother Ulric) "I will know because you will tell me, like this." Then Adulfa gave up a smidgen of her power to Rhys, just enough to make her capable of using the emotional cable that she had spun between the two of them. Now she would know what Rhys observed, and she would also be able to send the grubby and eccentric little creature on various errands.

When she had finished scrambling Rhys' mind, Adulfa told her to kneel. She pulled up the hem of her skirt and exposed her Brazilian wax job. "From now on, this is what sex is to you, Rhys. My body. My scent. The feel of my cunt in your mouth. Lick me slowly. Oh, yes, you queer little butch slut. What a good pussy slave you are. Now touch yourself. I want you to stroke your clit and think about how much you'd like to come. How much you wish someone was licking you. But nobody is, Rhys, because you are just a sex slave, something I use and then cast aside. So any pleasure you might have is at my behest, and I choose to leave you wanting. No, you may not come. But you can make me come. And if you can do it more than once, maybe I will take pity upon you and consider your needs. Yes, finger that wet hole. I know you've got a dildo under your pillow, Rhys. Go get it and stick that suction cup to the floor. No, you don't need any lube. Climb on top of it, Rhys, and hump it for me while you suck on my clit. Yes, I'm getting your face all wet, aren't I? How does it feel to eat my pussy while you have to fuck yourself, without being able to come? I actually think you like it. Yes, do that. Just like that. Don't stop."

Adulfa did not leave Rhys alone until dawn was dangerously near. The brutal bout of sex, interspersed with two heavy spankings, had reinforced their telepathic connection. (The dildo had snapped in two, but it lost its life in a glorious cause.) Rhys had even begged Adulfa to take more blood from her. Adulfa had refused, knowing that the frustration of wanting something she could not have would draw Rhys more powerfully than granting her request.

Now she had eyes and ears in her brother's favorite city. Rhys was her decoy and her beacon. Adulfa had already scouted out his overdecorated Victorian house, and the cats had warned her away. So she knew he was not at home, but she assumed he would return sooner or later, because he was stupid enough to take pets and pretend that he was the sort of creature who deserved them. The cats might think they could protect Ulric's house, but they were not powerful enough to keep her from staying in San Francisco as long as she liked. But she didn't want to risk being here when Ulric arrived. Let him think she had come and gone like the fog on the bay.

She had waited long enough to have her revenge upon him.

CHAPTER 5
You Will Never Be Free

They had taken only a few steps over the threshold when Lilith knew this was the wrong place for them to be. She no longer felt that this place was her sanctuary from the world. Just being there made her feel stifled. The walls seem to come together at odd angles. The lights were too bright, yet she could not focus, and it felt as if a shimmering film had laid itself on top of all she saw. Ulric sensed that something was wrong. He put her down, stepped in front of her so she was sheltered behind him, and scanned the room with dangerously alert eyes. Lilith stared at his back and contemplated her ambivalence about having such a powerful creature as her bodyguard. She didn't want to be hurt by a prowler, but how would she feel about what Ulric would do to anyone who threatened her? "There is no one else here," he told her, offering her a hand out of the blind spot he had tucked her into.

"I know—I believe you. But I can't stay here. Not tonight. I can't lay down on that bed and pretend we're just two normal people who are going to watch the evening news, kiss for five minutes, have sex in the missionary position, and go to sleep."

He was a little offended by that image of the evening he had planned for her, then realized she was not being literal. "A hotel?" he suggested, then remembered there was none in this small town. "The motel?"

She laughed. "I might as well fire myself right now. Everybody knows me here, Ulric, but nobody knows you. Single women don't have one-night stands and then read Dr. Seuss to six-year-olds on Saturday afternoon."

"Ah." Now that he was attuned to her discomfort, Ulric felt uneasy too. His growing desire to leave this place distracted him from searching for a solution. Lilith had disappeared into the kitchen. She returned with a sandwich in a Ziploc baggie and then grabbed the down comforter from the top shelf of her closet. It had been packed into a square, zippered plastic container until fall would make it a welcome presence on her bed, the soft roof that guarded the nest of her sleeping body. He wanted his arms to be a part of that nest as well.

"We'll go to your place," she said briskly, stowing a few other items along with the sandwich in a shoulder bag.

"My place?" He had no idea what she was talking about.

"The crypt," she said, in a businesslike tone of voice. "Come on. I'll drive us."

"You will not!" Ulric said, and tried to catch her elbow.

She evaded him. Her hair fell over her face and she allowed it to conceal her expression from him. "Don't tell me you're too macho to take the passenger seat."

"No! But I'm not—we're not—"

"Going where they keep the dead people? Oh, yes, we are."

"But there are bones there—raccoons. Drunk teenagers. Litter. It's a cemetery, Lilith!"

"And it's where you sleep all day, correct?"

She had him there. "Yes, my beloved librarian."

Lilith did not respond to his small attempt at humor. "Then I will go there and see how the other half—the undead half—lives. Look, you can't expect me to pretend that we haven't crossed the line into a reality that nobody knows about. A horrifying reality, Ulric, and if I am going to be your lover, I have to know what I'm getting into. Not just the past but the present too."

"You won't like it."

"Then I'll leave," she said, jingling her keys. "Carry the blanket, will you?"

"You're a stubborn woman, Lilith."

"And you're not?"

"I'm not...a woman."

She laughed and hung the shoulder bag upon him. Then she walked quickly away, and he sighed and followed her, shaking his head. What kind of woman voluntarily enters a room full of coffins—used ones? His kind, apparently. Should that really be a surprise? He had himself smiling by the time they arrived at her vehicle.

The car resided in a long carport behind the apartment building. It was a beige Toyota, four doors, eight years old but not banged up, clean but not fussily immaculate. It was an invisible, completely ordinary car. Still, it surprised him. He had imagined her walking everywhere. But then he recalled that if you did not have a car in America, you were unusual. Lilith had constructed Mary Beth's image in this town with great attention to detail.

"No air freshener hanging from the rearview mirror," he murmured. "Thank you." Those odious paper pine trees and vanilla-drenched smiley faces hurt his sensitive nasal passages and made him sneeze like an old dog.

"But of course." She put the car into reverse and rapidly got them onto the main road. "Are you afraid to have me see you when the sun comes up?"

The hits just kept on coming. "Hmm. I don't think anyone's ever asked me that before. Should I be?" He searched under the seat for the lever that would let him move it back, and suddenly lurched away from her. She didn't acknowledge the abrupt change in his position, and he tried to adjust his seat belt with aplomb.

"No," she replied. "Even if I decide I can't deal with being with you, Ulric, I would never hurt you. Well," she amended, "I guess I mean I wouldn't want to destroy you."

"What if you decide I'm a thing of evil?" he asked, quite seriously. "There's a ruthless streak in you, dear one. Something I take seriously despite the fact that so far it's been bloodless. And you were raised Catholic."

"Lapsed."

He gave her a sideways view of his lifted eyebrows. "Just like that? Do you really think you can undo a childhood of indoctrination? Could you put another sword through Mary's bleeding heart, or add even one thorn to the crown of her crucified son?"

"I stopped believing what the nuns told me when my best friend was molested by our catechism teacher. Doesn't the past color your feelings about me? Can you dispense with six hundred years of hating Christians when you deal with me? Besides my time in Catholic school only felt like it went on for centuries."

"I don't think of you as one of them," he admitted. "Turn here." Should he tell her that in his own spirituality she represented a pagan goddess? Should he risk adding the label "witch" to the corrupt modern notion of "vampire"? He didn't want to recall the odor of those public burnings, horrific spectacles in which the pious prayers and celebratory laughter of the spectators were as disorienting as the poor women ablaze and choking in the smoke.

"Thank you. I guess. Don't you think there's more to this spending an entire day together than whether or not I let in the daylight, or put a stake through your heart?" She was trying to make this a joke, but her voice trembled minutely and her hands were gripping the steering wheel hard enough to crack it in two. But what could he say to reassure her? "Well?" she prompted after the silence had become uncomfortably long. He shrugged, then realized she could not see that gesture with her eyes on the road.

"I wonder how you will feel about seeing me when I'm a prisoner of the sun," he admitted, resenting her directness. He had hoped American society had become secular enough to allow a human being to see him as something other than a demon that had to be executed. If he was wrong, centuries spent successfully evading extermination by priests and policemen had gone for naught.

"And how do you look?" Oh, what the question cost her. And how her heart ached, to think the two of them would never be able to enjoy the simple pleasure of sharing a bed, asleep in one another's arms.

Lilith coasted into the gravel lot that passed for graveyard parking, and they got out of the car. She refused to let him pick her up, using a flashlight to direct her around the marble and granite monuments and flower vases sunk into the dirt. But she did let him hold her hand.

"I don't know what I look like," he replied, picking up the thread of their interrupted conversation. "I can't see myself. But I don't feel like I'm asleep. I don't believe I dream or move. I never feel too cold or hot, or thirsty or itchy. I just—blank out. When I wake up, I know time must have passed, but it's not like waking up from a nap. I am suddenly alert and wary. The difference between the two states is more extreme for me, and the transitions are much more rapid."

He opened the heavy iron door of the mausoleum he had chosen for his own and let her pass in front of him. Then he sealed it shut. She was looking around and had already spied the concrete slab where he habitually posed himself for immobilization. The crypt held a few other pedestals, all of which had already been used to deposit a casket. He hurried to brush the dirt from his "bed," using his bare hands, and arranged the comforter. Rather than burn out the flashlight's battery, Lilith set candles around the tomb and lit them one at a time with matches. She accepted no help, even though the wind or her own nerves made the matches difficult to keep going. He couldn't tell if she had just lost track of the conversation and so didn't respond to his description of the daytime dead zone, or if she was unwilling to tell him how she felt about it.

As she settled herself on the comforter, he said defensively, "I'm not like Adulfa, you know. She lives like a wild animal, or like something more feral than any animal could be. I try to preserve as much of my humanity as possible. She'd be quite happy sleeping here, but I have a house in San Francisco. A very nice house too. I collect stained glass windows, and I have cats who miss me. I just took this place because I wanted to be near you and didn't have time to find a vacant house to rent." (*Or make room for myself in a home that was already occupied*, he thought but did not say.)

"Who is Adulfa?" Lilith wanted to know. *Now!* she thought.

In this age, jealousy was a sign of love, so Ulric was at least a little happy to see her unconsciously bracing to defend her lover against another woman's prior claim. But he also cursed himself for letting this bit of information slip out. Back in the woods by the stream, he had been prepared to tell Lilith everything, but she had stopped him, and he did not want to go back there again.

But she had a right to know. And what else were they going to do? Ulric tried to see this tiny room the way she must see it. But he had been a hunted creature for so long that he could only see its normalcy. The crypt resembled thousands of other secret places he had inhabited, the necropolis that was usually his only safe haven.

"She was my sister," he conceded. "Don't you remember? I looked for her among the dead. And I was glad she was on one of her larcenous forays, and had escaped."

Lilith went back to the horrific images he had shown her. She had been so overwhelmed by all the blood and displaced limbs that she had not quite taken in his guilty memory of rejoicing in Adulfa's survival.

"But you talked about her in the present tense," she recalled, back on the scent. "Adulfa is still alive."

He mentally cursed her thorough mind. "Do you want to see?" he asked.

Lilith knew she could say no. And her rational self told her to do just that. But her rational self also told her to pick up her flashlight and take her car keys in her hand and run away from this place and its sad inhabitant. How many people had died so that Ulric could continue to live? What was to save her from being one of them?

Ulric was standing in front of her. She found her arms around his slender waist, drawing him close for a kiss. He waited shyly for her to place her lips next to his, followed her lead each step of the way as the kiss became more intimate. Lost in the taste of his mouth, she took one of his hands and placed it between her legs. He cupped the heel of his hand against her mound and agitated it gently. She came, an orgasm that built slowly, seemed to last forever, and then lingered, generating a half dozen smaller aftershocks. She put her hand over his, and smiled to think how much she loved the way he touched her. Just thinking of his long-fingered, strong hands was arousing.

"I should do my thinking with my big head," she said in his ear. "Because my little head is even smaller than yours. Fuck me."

Whenever someone topped Ulric, he rebounded from it with an energetic desire to return the favor. By the creek, where she had thrown him onto his back, that experience had been deferred. So he was happy to oblige and would have been even if he hadn't wanted to delay explaining why there was such bitter enmity between him and Adulfa.

Lilith was at just the right height, and her panties were quickly extricated and sent to the dusty red granite floor at his feet. Solicitous of her broken hymen, he inched forward slowly, but she was wet enough to reassure him that his cock was welcome. Lilith kept him close to her, allowing him to move only a little. He was near the point where even the blood of another vampire and what he had taken from her would fail him. So he was glad when she clasped him snugly with her pelvic muscles. The sex they had was less a matter of him thrusting into her than it was of him rocking slightly as she gripped and released him. It was as if her cunt had a mind of her own, and like a mouth with no tongue took her time exploring and hefting every inch of him. He wasn't sure if he came or not, though there were certainly peaks and valleys in his pleasure. "Look at me," Ulric begged the woman in his arms. "Don't look around, don't see where we are, just see me. See how I adore you."

Ulric thought that she was as caught up in this strange experience as he was—coupling, utterly connected, in the realm of Eros but on some track other than the one that led to orgasm. Higher and higher she took him, and they were suspended together in long minutes of bliss that were experienced on a physical as well as a mental and emotional plane, but this led only to climbing to yet another level of closeness and peace, not the hard contractions of physical release. They both knew when they had flown as high as they could for that one attempt, and yet remained bound together by their bodies, and slowly descended. The process of returning to the here and now was almost as amazing as their ascent.

The slab was narrow, so they reclined on their sides, pressed front-to-back so that neither one could fall off the edge. Lilith took Ulric's right hand and covered her eyes with it. He was behind her, spooning her, and she had flipped half of the large comforter over the two of them. "Roll it, mister," she commanded.

"What do you wish to see?" he asked, just to make sure.

"The second portion of our premiere feature," she gibed.

Ulric's sex was aching. His erection had slowly receded, and would not revive until another complete feeding. Did she want him to enter her again? He could not, but wanted her still. What was love but the maddening impossibility of ever having enough of your She? Did Lilith feel unfulfilled? Had their union been good for her as well? At the time, he had been sure of it, but now he was insecure. He could find out by entering her mind, but so many things were unsettled between them. He dared not risk a quarrel over the boundary between her inner self and his powers of intuition. Let that fester for another day!

Then he realized that she was asking for the rest of his story. His physical exhaustion made it easier for the barriers to come down. He took her into his past.

Ulric was feverish, nauseated, and yet exalted. The sand-colored cat had become his constant companion, licking his wounds and sleeping in the crook of his arm. Her purring was a counterpoint to the songs that he sang over and over again, whenever Hilbert was not in the room to smash him in the face. He had only seen one elder made, and he knew that part of that ritual was secret. Perhaps it meant nothing to give voice to the prayers that he remembered. But singing helped him to get through the radical revision of his body. He would not scream in front of his enemies, and the pain was too much to bear in complete silence. But his ability to step aside from his own body and relax into the pain was stretched to its limit. He was starving, and his only food was the blood he sometimes managed to draw from Hilbert when the knight raped him.

He tried desperately not to think of himself as being contaminated by his enemy. It was Rowan's lineage he had inherited, his beloved granny. He remembered the elder who had carved him toy horses and taught him to recite his ancestors. Rowan had shown him useful tricks when he fletched his first arrows, and he had learned how to imitate the call of a pheasant from her. She had brewed teas for his sore throats and given him salve when his dog had a cut foot.

Every night Hilbert raged about his changed condition. He would demand that Ulric explain what was happening to him—that he could feed only on blood, could not walk in the light of the sun, and would live as long as he avoided being decapitated or set on fire. Then the crusader would punish Ulric for these answers. At least the change was making Ulric's body stronger and more resilient. Eventually Hilbert seemed to really believe what Ulric told him, and began feeding upon other prisoners. Sometimes he insisted that Ulric join him at these feasts or participate in the sexual degradation of Hilbert's newest target. Ulric tried, when he was in physical proximity to these victims, to use his nascent powers to ease their pain. But he also knew he was the tool of an evil man, and did evil to others to save himself even more pain. Thus did a portion of Hilbert's guilt become his prisoner's to bear. For Hilbert kept him chained, especially during the day, allowing him no opportunity for escape.

One evening, Hilbert kicked Ulric awake and also aimed a kick at the cat, who had awakened more rapidly and escaped with a contemptuous flick of her tail. The knight took Ulric down into the dungeons and told him that it was his responsibility to select someone to take back to his room and torture, then drain. When Ulric refused, Hilbert had him hooded, bound hand and foot, and tossed into an empty cell. "I'll kill them all eventually," Hilbert said, giving him hard kicks in his kidneys and ribs and head. "I'll redeem myself by purging the earth of unrepentant heathens. God will welcome me in heaven and make me the general of a host of angels. As for you, you'll always be nothing but a slave to that whore you think is a goddess, an idol-worshiper dancing naked around obscene statues and committing all manner of filth in the open air, where the sun wishes he could avert his face from your shame. And my victim."

Ulric felt his kneecap shatter as the toe of Hilbert's boot collided with the bone. So the leader of the Germanic Knights thought that the sun was male? How strange. And what colorful pictures he had of their festivals and rituals. Why dance naked around a statue when you could dance with a fair maiden with tattooed breasts or a willing freckled lad with flowers in his hair? Ulric ground his teeth together to hold back a scream until he heard the cell door crash shut and lock. By the time Hilbert had gone beyond earshot, he no longer wanted to scream, only groan. His body could repair itself, but without blood, the healing would be very slow.

"I am your slave," he said, and his moving lips wet the inside of the hood. "Goddess, there is no shame in it. I am your willing slave. Despite all they do. If they kill me for loving you, help me to die bravely. There were many things I wanted to do before I died, and I confess this was not one of them. So I must put myself in your hands."

Painkilling love filled his blinded and contorted body. He accepted the gift of trance and gave himself up to it, knowing he could not remain conscious in the present if there was an alternative. The kindness of the Lady of the Mountain endured for a long, long time, and when he came to himself, he was still tied and hooded, but it seemed that the worst of his bruises had faded, and even his broken bones had been replaced by new and strong ones. But thirst overcame him when he tried to make a plan to use his strength to escape. It was all he could feel or visualize: the need to receive the coppery red elixir that would soothe his arid throat.

Who knows how many nights passed? Ulric was a fledgling; his need for blood was a rage in his soul. And he was a young man, vigorous, without the lifetime of training in self-discipline that made elders able to control their hunger. His newly sharpened senses rebelled against the hood and silence of his cell. He knew he could go mad; his mind would eventually begin to supply its own creations to replace his disabled senses.

So Ulric talked to himself. He rubbed his wrists and ankles together so that he had some external stimulation. He reminded himself that this agony could not kill him. He kept hope for as long as possible, and when that failed, he became obsessed with revenge. But the darkness crept ever closer, and eventually he was reduced to nothing more than hunger. His teeth grew until he shredded the hood and tore at his own shoulder. He thrashed in the darkness, taunted by the taste of his own blood. The ropes they had bound him with fell away, and he groped along the floor, knowing there was nothing over his eyes, but he could still see nothing. A froth of crystal lace revolved in front of his eyes; random patterns and colors broke apart and reformed, dissolving just as they were about the make sense. His sense of smell was expanded, but insanely so; he could not really smell the presence of other living beings through the rock, he told himself.

Amid this raving need—a hunger so great that it threatened to reduce him to chewing on his own bones—Ulric suddenly heard the cell door open and shut. He scented something warm and soft. He closed on its heartbeat with hands that had become iron claws, and tore open a vein. He drank and drank, oblivious to any resistance. It was not until he had sated himself that his vision cleared and sanity returned.

His sister Adulfa lay crumpled at his feet, gravely injured but no longer able to bleed. She had cut her hair short, like a page, and wore one of the Germanic Knights' tunics, complete with their heraldic device. Her hose was ripped and shabby, and someone had stolen her boots. She had only a few more moments to live. How had she fallen into Hilbert's grasp? There was no time to ask any questions, no time for the remorse and recrimination he knew would come. He used one of his long, sharp fingernails to open his own chest, picked her up like a scarecrow, and forced her mouth to his flesh. He brought her across the same way Hilbert had brought him.

He discovered too late that this melding carried its own madness. The feeding triggered an intense and involuntary erotic response. Somehow, as Adulfa struggled to free herself and resist the gift of long life, he came to believe that she was enticing him. So he took possession of her body—he was too strong for even her to defeat. The taboo that forbade sex between children of the same mother had evaporated. He barely even recognized her. It was not until he had accomplished penetration and orgasm that he recognized her again. But was it her? And who was he? It was like being two people who did not know each other and could not share memories. Adulfa had never taken a male lover. What was happening to him? Was this what Ulric had saved her life for, to become his victim, to be treated the way he had been treated by Hilbert?

He heard familiar laughter outside the cell. It was Hilbert. His yellow teeth were bared in a self-righteous grimace. "I knew you were just like me," the Germanic knight said with disgust. He had washed and combed out his long hair, and he no longer stank like meat that had turned to charcoal. But there was blood on his clothing and hands that betrayed his murderous status. "The only difference between us is that you're in there and I'm out here." He showed Ulric the key to the cell, dangling it on a red ribbon, then left, dragging a prisoner with him. "When all these are gone, I'm coming back for you," Hilbert howled triumphantly. "You can watch me take her before I kill the both of you."

Ulric wept, and sank to his knees. He drew Adulfa into his arms and begged her forgiveness. She shoved him away, but he could not leave her alone. For as long as it took for her condition to stabilize, he monitored her and gave her the only medicine he had—his own blood. His guilt was quadrupled when she raged at him that she had been apprehended trying to rescue him and the other young men held by the knights. He had attacked his benefactor, and assaulted her doubly. She would forgive the rape before she would forgive being made a parody of the elders who had once protected and guided their people. The elders were sacred and esteemed, yes, but they were also feared. That was the nature of holy things and people. Mothers did not usually hope that their children would be chosen to follow that path; it removed them from the normal cycle of human life. Both he and his sister had no priestly calling or unusual gifts of the spirit. They had embraced a short life with all of its joy, trouble, and freedom, and were content to be reborn again after they had used up their days.

Eventually Adulfa became Ulric's equal in strength, and he knew she no longer needed nursing. Though what life would hold for either of them, he could not say. He begged Adulfa to do what she must to survive even if it meant taking his own life. Perhaps if she tore at him and threw him at Hilbert, the general of the knights would be distracted enough to let her escape. "Oh, don't worry. I will," she replied bitterly. "But not at *his* behest. I have other plans for Hilbert and his eunuchs."

A third party interrupted their conference. It was Luna, the cat. During the fever and pain of his transformation, Ulric had learned that she was descended from Egyptian animals that had been traded throughout the Middle East to guard granaries and keep ships rodent-free. In Egypt, there were temples to a goddess who had the head of a cat, and Luna expected to be treated like her holy emissary on earth. The cat was different, somehow — more lithe and magical now. So she, too, had been changed. Then Ulric heard her in his head.

"Been looking for you," she said, trying to sound indifferent. She licked one of her paws clean.

"I missed you," he said.

"Of course."

"Are you hungry, Luna?"

"No."

Ulric cut one of his fingers open on a fang and extended the bead of scarlet toward her. When he looked away, she wandered over to him and licked his finger clean. Eventually she was satisfied and came winding through the bars of the cell to sit upon his lap. "Dirty floor," she complained.

"Luna," he said, "there's something I want you to do for me."

She stared at him indignantly. "First you think I'm a deformed rabbit, and now you think I'm a dog?"

The word "dog" carried the same contempt as "excrement" or "running water."

"No — I thought you were a great hunter."

"I am quick and lethal."

"The key is very clever. Its keeper is stronger than you," he conceded. "Perhaps you do not wish to embarrass yourself by leaping when you know you will miss. I understand."

"Lies!" He had her full attention now. Her yellow eyes blazed into his. "Who is this keeper of the key?"

He painted a mental portrait of Hilbert.

"The kicker," she cursed. "The thrower. No reverence is in him for my sacred person. He is a slow and stupid man."

Ulric shrugged. "Until I see the key between your jaws..."

Luna was gone in a flurry of wounded pride. Ulric waited in an agony of anticipation, afraid he had sent his only friend into harm's way. But she came back, mere hours later, dragging the key by its ribbon.

"You may abase yourself and serve me," she told him haughtily, posing with the ribbon pinned beneath her spread claws.

"All my days," he pledged, and knocked his forehead on the floor. "I will gladly serve you till my dying breath."

"Then all is as it should be," the cat replied, settling once more into his lap. Ulric scratched her under the chin till she fell asleep, then scooped her up and stuck his other arm through the bars. He didn't think he would be able to bend his hand back far enough to use the key but found that his joints were unusually supple. He pushed on the door, and it gave.

"We're free," he told Adulfa, trying to take her hand to lead her out.

She warned him off with a hissing growl that woke Luna up and made her fur puff out. The little cat hissed back, and her claws dug deep into Ulric's shoulder. He mentally soothed her, and she settled back into his arms. "Queens have more daggers than they do dead birds to give away," she told him, picturing herself lying on her side, all four feet poised to gut an unwanted suitor.

"You will never be free," Adulfa told Ulric. The intensity of her anger hit him like a killing wave of poison. The natural barriers between their kind asserted themselves suddenly, bolstered by her declaration of a lethal feud between them. With Hilbert no longer there to compel them to remain in such close quarters, Ulric staggered away from her as fast as he could run, carrying Luna with him. He vaguely remembered dropping the key so he could cradle the cat more securely.

The vision ended.

Lilith was out of control. She was punching Ulric in the face and chest as hard as she could. The injuries she inflicted would heal by morning, but Ulric was afraid she would break her fingers or fall onto the hard granite floor. He slid away from her, standing at one side of the pedestal, and reached for her hands. But as soon as he captured them, she began to kick him, and even though she was not wearing boots, her legs were strong, and an ordinary man would have been incapacitated by some of the blows she landed. An ordinary man would also have kicked her back.

"Bastard!" she said as he let go of her hands and stepped away from her. She slid to the ground and stood facing him, as angry as Adulfa had been. "How could you?"

Suddenly his own anger erupted. After centuries of self-blame and hatred, he rose to his own defense. "How could I stand being kept in chains? Raped? Starved? Abused and beaten? Is that what you are asking me?"

"Noooooo," she wailed, beating her arms on the comforter that she had laid over the concrete block. Tears were running down her face, and she scratched at her own cheeks, her upper arms.

"Stop!" he begged, reaching for her. But his arms fell short.

"I know—I was there. The pain. Oh, my God, the fear and the pain. You were so helpless and he treated you like...nothing. Like something that wasn't even human. But then you gave in to that same lust for power and control. You violated the one person left free and alive from Red Springs village. She loved you enough to risk her own life, to come to the castle, that huge fortified heap of stone. She'd never seen a fortress that big or men so well-armed, but she tried to get you out. Her courage and her humiliation! Oh—no, no, I can't bear the sorrow and the hurt. Both of you. No hope. No escape. And I can't bear the need. I feel it in me—your addiction to blood, your ravaged mind reaching out for her heartbeat, the way you crumpled her in your arms and tore her open with your teeth. I feel your cock get hard and the mindless joy you took in fucking her. You've made me into a rapist. I was there in your body. I did it too, I couldn't stop myself—or you. Oh—God—!" She screamed, and Ulric was surprised to look around and see the roof and walls of the crypt were still intact.

"Then you also felt my panic when I knew what I had done! My regret—the knowledge I can never erase my crime. And she will never give me absolution. But I was not myself. I had no one to help me transition, to control me until I learned to control myself. I am a young man. I was never supposed to receive such lethal powers. By the time Adulfa was thrown into my cell, I had been reduced to a brute, and everything primal in me took over. If I could pay this debt I would. I have ensured that Adulfa will never want for anything. But I know that money can never wash out that assault. I have no excuse—and every excuse. Have you never heard of people who were tortured enough to become torturers themselves?"

Lilith had her hands over her ears, but she heard him anyway. Was he still inside her mind? Did he think he could just *live* there? "Stop thinking for me," she said. "Get out! Get out of my mind!"

"Lilith, I'm not trying to be inside your mind. I'm not sharing with you anymore, not my opinions, not my memories."

"Then why do I still feel you there?"

"I don't know." He wanted to say, Because I am your beloved. Your horned consort who comes to you, snake in hand. I am the lord of the green wood, and you are the high, royal purple places that surround me and keep my wild children safe. When you look down from your snowy throne, armed with lightning and thunder, dressed in silver mist, everything I do is readily apparent to you.

"Well, stop it," Lilith said irrationally. Ulric could only spread his hands and shrug helplessly. This made her even more angry. "Do you know what you've done to me? I can still taste her blood in my mouth. Still feel myself shuddering with pleasure when I came inside her, knowing I was going to live at her expense, rejoicing in my triumph over her. I've become the one thing I hate the most." She threw the last sentence at him in a steadily rising shriek that had him backing away from her. He was tempted to leave, but he was afraid to abandon her when this madness was upon her. And daylight was near.

"What's to stop you from doing the same thing to me that you did to her?"

"Six hundred years of penance."

"Oh, yes? Don't you mean six hundred years of indulging your parasitical bloodsucking perversion? If you're ever in a crisis, you will take me by force. Do you plan to turn me into what you are? Is that what this whole seduction has been for? Have you been laughing at me inside while you toyed with me, made me want you, persuaded me to trust you and submit to you, knowing all the while that when I was completely vulnerable to you, you would smash my dignity to pieces and use me, for what? A model in a snuff movie? A necrophiliac's sex doll? Was that what you had planned?"

He had never thought of changing Lilith into a vampire, much less violating her sexually. He had been too immersed in the present to think about her fragility. So he was silent, his mind working hard to conjure up the future. Lilith in a car wreck or simply growing old—how could he ever let her die?"

"Don't lie to me, Ulric. I saw it all, remember? I know the whole truth about why she hates you. You all hate each other. The day you convert me is the last day we will ever spend together. My body and soul will cry out for you, and you will be denied to me. Forever!"

"If you fear and hate me so much, why do you care?" Ulric asked.

"I hate you because you've made me love something ugly. But I promised I would never destroy you. I gave you your life and now you have to give me mine. I will never drink your blood, Ulric. Never become what you are. Swear it!"

"I will never give you my blood against your will."

"You're hedging. You can go into my mind and make me want whatever you find amusing. Can't you?"

"Lilith, please. I love you. How can I stand by and let you die? Please let me spare you. Any lover would want to save his beloved if he could. The pain of aging and death is so cruel. Even if we were parted, at least I would know I had saved you instead of destroying you. I don't want to live knowing you have gone on to the blessed isles."

"No! Never. I have obeyed you, Ulric. Submitted to you. Because I trusted you. But I will not bend upon this point."

"It will be as you wish," he said dully.

"Damn right it will be," Lilith said, scuttling after her things. "Keep the comforter," she said, and went to the door. Of course, she could not open it. Ulric was there in a split second, making an exit for her. "Don't touch me," she said.

"What you saw was the very worst of me. Since then I never—"

She faced him for one blazing moment. "I'll tell you what's never. You are *never* seeing me again."

He could not go after her. False dawn was seeping in all around her body. So he shut his love and the new day out of his grim gatehouse and hurried to the now-grimy comforter. He didn't even have time to draw it over his face for a trace of her scent before somnolence laid him out. He would have twelve hours or so of rest before he had to figure out how to go on living without her.

He did not like this new experience with loss. Weren't masters supposed to be in control, calm, free of the need that their slaves groveled to express? No. She was not replaceable, and he was more than a witness to her desire. He shared it. He had made a place for her in his psyche, and she had torn herself away, leaving a huge injury behind, the way the moon had ripped itself away from the earth. The oceans were the tears the earth shed in mourning for its escape. He wished he could cry an ocean's worth of waterless tears.

Training Lilith to become his sex slave had altered him as well. Losing her was worse than having an arm cut off. An arm could regenerate. But once love had turned to hate, there was no going back. Adulfa was proof of that maxim.

CHAPTER 6
Your Name Is My Only Prayer

Ah, but it's never as simple as that, is it?

Lilith...no, Mary Beth. Mary Beth!

She thought she had really thrown Ulric out of her life forever. But as soon as she got home, dumped her things on the floor, and went to undress, she encountered a reminder of his tenderness and cunt-twinging dominance. She skimmed the dress up over her arms. She had left her panties on the floor of the crypt. Let Ulric go on the Internet and sell them to get his plane fare home. But before she could step into the shower, to try to make water wash away things it could not touch, she had to unfasten the hooks of her corset and take it off. The plum-colored brocade with its rows of stays was like a feminine piece of armor. Ulric had gotten it made for her, brought it to her, and laced her into it while she stood tied naked in the doorway. The feeling of having her waist constricted, brought in so that her breasts and hips were made more prominent, made her slippery inside. He had told her to wear it every day, that he was having a smaller one made for her and expected her to be able to fit into it in six months.

After that, every time he put the corset on her and tightened the laces, she wanted to swoon from the heat that came up from her needy little pussy. Her whole body seemed to blush. He could make her gasp just by putting one of his fingers through the laces and tugging on them. During the day, at work, she was afraid her co-workers or the library patrons would notice that she was wearing the Victorian undergarment, but nobody ever seemed to pick up on the change. The corset made her feel as if he was embracing her, controlling her, even when he slept. It reminded her that he was real, that he would really be with her that night, to collar and lash her. To make her finger herself while he watched. And her erotic response to the tight-lacing reminded her that she had consented to allow her fantasies to come to life.

Mary Beth threw the corset into the wastebasket in her bedroom, and ran for the shower. She stayed under its spray until the hot water ran out. Then she left voicemail at the library, calling in sick, something she had never done before. She got into bed, which seemed awfully big, and closed her eyes, fully expecting to have them snap open. How could she not have insomnia after all that had happened? But she was wrong; her body shut down immediately.

She woke up masturbating. She had been dreaming about Ulric, dreaming about kneeling to suck his cock. Her waist had been cruelly nipped in by the corset, and her ass was still smarting from a spanking.

There was no resistance in her when she saw his cock, only eagerness. And it went down her throat like a perfect fit. She was begging to masturbate, to make herself come while she sucked his cock. He had taken his hard dick out of her mouth just long enough to hear the whispered pleas, then he shoved it back in, hard enough to startle her, and put his hand on the back of her head.

"Stroke yourself," he said, "but don't you dare come before I do. Slave girls have to wait to come until they are given permission to let themselves go. So go ahead and torment yourself, but don't forget for one second that your real purpose is to worship the big club in your throat. I'm going to fuck your face so long that you'll never be able to get the taste of me out of your mouth. Suck, girl. Suck me like the cock-hungry slut we both know you are. You love me as much as you love pain, baby. And that's because you know I will give you as much pain as you can handle and more."

She was so close to coming that she kept on manipulating her clit. The dream had faded, but she could supply the rest of the fantasy from her memories and aching cunt. Ulric would pull her hair a little, come out of her mouth all the way, then slowly insist on complete occupation of her body. He would say, "Take it down, all the way, that's it, that's it. Aren't you a sight? Do you know how pretty you are with your mouth stretched wide around my cock? I can see the tears starting to run down your face. I love it when you cry. If you suck me really good, maybe I won't come in your mouth. Maybe I'll pull out and fuck you up the ass. You'd like that, wouldn't you baby? You'd like some stud to come along behind you and lift your ass up just enough so he could slide his prick into you. Plug you. You need to be plugged, don't you?"

"Yes!" she heard herself say as she came.

Ulric woke up to find a large moth perched on his sternum, opening and closing its wings of brown and gold. On each wing was a huge eye, outlined in black, with a white cornea and black pupils edged in bold. How had it gotten in to the crypt? It must have been attracted to his sweat, and been feeding off of his sticky skin. Could moths become vampires? The slow flutter of its wings was hypnotic. And then the eyes became Lilith's eyes, and he could see her face, nestled against his chest, full of love.

He stood up slowly, giving the moth time to fly away, and physically waved his hands to and fro, clearing away the vision. She was not here and never would be again. And he must feed.

The easiest thing to do would be to go to the cluster of trailers parked just outside the town's limits and avail himself of the services of a prostitute. He could take one of them into her room, take some of what he needed, and leave her with the memory of a torrid encounter. If he was still hungry, another girl would be there for the taking. This was too small a town for him to kill, so he would have to swallow his queasiness about slipping into the mind of a stranger and inserting a false version of events.

But he could not do it. Sex was a convenient excuse for getting close enough to a mortal to take hold of them and suck them dry. But he wanted to preserve his memory of Lilith for as long as possible. He did not want someone else's face or body imprinted upon his view, like a greasy film on a windshield. Instead, he wandered over to an old folks' home and spent the evening playing checkers with a man who was physically healthy but not in his right mind. Ulric didn't care if the man simply laid out checkers on the board and rearranged them over and over again. The futility of the activity suited his mood. When attendants came to take his checker player up to his room, Ulric followed, protected by a see-me-not, and took what he needed while he gave the old man a dream about a happy day spent fishing with his son. He wanted to stop himself before he took too much, but the hours spent in daylight had taken more out of him than he had realized. And so the old man slipped into final darkness with a smile on his face.

Standing over the bed, sucking the last drops of blood from his fangs, Ulric knew that his victim would rather have died at the peak of his physical and mental vigor than suffer from years of the indignity and confusion of Alzheimer's. But killing someone when he had not intended to made him feel like a whipped dog. He was, after all, as bad a man as Lilith had told him he was.

The body did not appear grossly abnormal. He had had the presence of mind to heal the puncture marks as he withdrew from the old man's neck. Ulric had also stopped feeding before taking every ounce of moisture from his flesh, so there was no dehydration. On his way out, Ulric stopped by one of the attendants and planted the suggestion of a sudden cerebral hemorrhage in his mind. The doctor who the home had hired to sign death certificates and such for their residents was easygoing and near retirement himself. Ulric doubted he would make a fuss. Old people should die, and that probably included people who were more than a few hundred years old.

The befuddled man's life was in him in more than one way now; Ulric had imbibed his story along with his blood. It was like having to watch a bad movie, a movie in which you relived everything along with the characters you saw. Perhaps because he was already full-up with his own romantic tragedy, Ulric found himself doing something he had never been able to do before. It was as if a pair of hands had plunged wrist-deep into his mind, bundled up the old man's memories, tucked them into a trash bag, and thrown them away.

So Ulric left the facility, intending to wander aimlessly until impending daylight became an emergency, and he would either have to hurry to his crypt or let himself burn. It would probably be wise to find a new place to hole up. Despite her cruel parting words, he trusted Lilith, but he was angry with her. Why make it easy for her to find him again?

Oddly enough, he found himself exactly where he had told himself he had no desire to go. He was standing in the middle of a patch of withered crabgrass and weeds, looking at three trailers that had been parked around a large patio. There were three tables and several chairs, but only one man sat there, apparently thinking of nothing but the next drag on his cigarette. The walls of the trailers were so thin that Ulric could hear music, laughter, and more guttural sounds. The smoker was oblivious to it all. Ulric had a feeling that he would react in an instant if anything out of the ordinary happened, but for now, it was just another night of babysitting a posse of women who were in between their stints in Nevada brothels or strip clubs in Canada. It was a weeknight, so business was slow, but a few furtive, middle-aged regulars and a couple of boisterous farm boys just out of high school were horny enough to show up and fork over some cash.

Ulric walked closer, making sure he was not seen. There was only a thin curtain over the window that he came to first, and he peered through a bit of clear glass. There was a blonde woman inside, a pretty one. She was getting undressed and talking to her customer. "I sure am glad to see you again," she said, sounding genuinely excited. "Looks like you're glad to see me too. Oh, Lord, look at that thing. You sure do have what it takes. You want a little half-and-half, baby? Which half first?" Then her head disappeared, but Ulric's sensitive hearing could detect the sounds of a cock being sucked, and he could see the grimacing face of her client, a young tall man with a tractor tan and callused hands that looked big even for his height.

"Get up on the bed," the man said, letting go of her head. The prostitute scrambled up onto the mattress, her head down at the head of the bed, giggling and motioning for him to join her. He was taking off his pants and underwear, but left on his T-shirt. He got behind her and clamped his hands upon her hips, placing her at just the right angle. He had to stroke his cock a time or two to get a full erection back, and then he was leaning forward, whispering something to her that made her giggle again. In he went. He had a cock to match his size, and it would feel so good to suck it. Ulric suddenly wanted to climb in the window and take the woman's place on that bed. Like a Peeping Tom, he slipped his hand into his pants and took out his own cock so he could fondle it.

What business did he have being a top, and seducing a woman?

Men were so much easier to understand. (And much more available.) Ulric reveled in the fantasy of being fucked by the young farmer, kept in a stall to serve his whim, being forced to service his friends. The depth of Lilith's submission was terrifying at times, tempting him to take her with more force than her mortal body could sustain. And when she was not unconsciously offering up her jugular vein, she was resisting him, fighting him so hard that he sometimes felt guilty about the pleasure he took in grabbing her thrashing arms, bending her over, spanking her until she cried, and then fucking her, not letting her come until she had groveled for provoking him. He wasn't ready for the responsibility of training, owning, protecting, anticipating, understanding, and cherishing her.

It certainly was not what he had anticipated when he had envisioned meeting the love of his life. Alain had been all that.

Oh, how expertly the young farmer in the trailer worked his cock; surely the woman he was fucking wasn't moaning just because she wanted a tip. How long had it been since Ulric had felt a man's hands on his butt, holding it open? Perhaps this upwelling of a need to be taken was a natural reaction to preying on the old man. No, it was a genuine part of him, and it was only the insanity of this age that insisted you had to love either men or women, not both. Lilith had seen that in him. She had understood, and for a girl who had never fucked a boy before, she was damned good at it.

At the thought of Lilith stroking his prostate while she choked him, Ulric came. Ah, well, at least there was no mess to clean up. Being a vampire had its perks, after all. No trick towels to launder—if you didn't count the occasional gout of blood that had to be mopped up.

It occurred to him to scout out the rest of the trailer park and see if there were any unoccupied units. When that turned out to be a false lead, he stole a can of paint from a toolshed and headed to the junkyard and got lucky there. He picked out a big, old American car with a back seat big enough to stretch out on, and piled enough crap around it to keep out any midnight visitors. Just for good measure, he coated the windows with spray paint (on the outside, thank you, because the stuff stank worse than a tanning vat).

But when he climbed into his lair and had no further distractions, he had to give up and admit that he was still inside Lilith's head. He knew where she was. He knew that she was sleeping. If he pushed, just a little, on that connection, he would find out more about her. "There's your leash and collar upon me, my lady," he said in a snit just before he lost consciousness.

The next day was going to be better, Mary Beth decided. She got up, had a good breakfast, and was ready for work in plenty of time to walk to the library. She was looking forward to getting back to her books and videos, the computers and newspapers. There would be a pile of phone messages on her desk, no doubt. And people would be worried because she had told them she was sick.

When she got to the library, however, nobody asked her how she was. She had the strange feeling that her co-workers were ignoring her. Halfway through the morning, she went into the employees' bathroom to wash some ink off her hands, and realized that she had not put her hair up before coming to work. It curled slightly all around her face, making her look five years younger. She had put on the makeup that Ulric had bought for her, not the drab stuff that she usually wore to work, which made her look like she had bags under her eyes and a thin mouth. Upset by these slips, she put her hands on her hips to scold herself mentally, and realized she was wearing the corset.

She had no memory of putting it on.

She had come to work wearing no bra, and no panties.

She went into one of the stalls and masturbated.

She couldn't help it. The knowledge that she was wearing his corset was like an aphrodisiac. His cock would get hard when he put it on her; he would make sure she felt it against her naked flank. Why hadn't she done everything you could do with a cock, while she still had access to his body? He had already made her feel so many unexpected pleasures. What could they have done together that she would never know, never experience, never even guess existed? Oh, the silky weight of his balls in her hand; the way he pulled her off her feet to kiss her.

She tried desperately to keep quiet, to hurry, so no one else would come into the ladies' room. But she found herself sobbing as she came, pinching one of her own nipples while her other hand was frantic between her legs, unable to do enough to quiet the uproar of her loss. When she composed herself enough to return to her desk, she caught the looks the other women threw at her. *Traitor,* those looks said. *You've gone over to the other side. You've got a man in your life, and everybody knows it. How could you show your face here? You're not decent, Mary Beth Wolcott.*

She went home early, and didn't even bother to make the excuse that perhaps she wasn't quite well yet.

Ulric found out where the farm boy lived. He went there. He had sex with him. And with his brother. And then with his father. He showed them no mercy. If he encountered any resistance in their minds to servicing him, he relentlessly eliminated it. They took him into the barn and hung him from the rafters by his hands. They strapped him and spit on him. He sucked all of their cocks. They fucked him over hay bales, up against a barbed wire fence. They pissed on him. And in payment for these acts of savage kindness, he left them anemic and forgetful, with a farm full of neglected crops and animals.

She needed him. She missed him. But she had told him he would never see her again. What was he supposed to do? Why couldn't he scream at her to get out of *his* head?

The longer she stayed away from him, the worse it got. She lost weight. Someone at the library made a catty comment about her roots showing. She began getting obscene phone calls from someone she suspected was the sheriff. People who had placidly sold her groceries or put gas in her car became either less helpful or far too friendly. The former were women; the latter were men. She got online and ordered a dildo. When she used it, she called Ulric's name again and again. One night, she picked up the green branch he had used to whip her thighs, and gave herself a set of marks from her hips to her knees. She woke up with the dildo in her mouth, sucking on it like a pacifier. She kept seeing men who looked like him, and repressing an impulse to run to him and kneel at his feet.

He had done terrible things. But terrible things had been done to him. He was a killer. He had committed rape. But every living thing had a right to try to feed itself and survive.

Life without him was a dull cacophony of anticlimaxes.

Ulric went to her window once and saw her sleeping. She looked peaceful and happy. So he went away. He told himself he would get on the train that night and leave. Pickings were beyond slim. She would get over him easier if he left.

He didn't leave.

Lilith (for she was determined to be Mary Beth no more) resigned her position at the library and cashed out all of her retirement benefits. She bought a fast little car that only had room for two people and one suitcase. She paid cash. The car was red. The salesman didn't suggest, not even once, that it was too much car for a woman to drive. He didn't dare. She drove her Scarlet Streak to a big department store and bought one little black dress, and didn't even blink when the price tag was more than her monthly salary. The shoes she chose to go with it were almost as expensive, so she made sure the thigh-high stockings she bought were silk. She changed in the store's dressing room and left her old clothes behind on the floor.

It was surprisingly easy to drive the car really fast; the high heels gave her more leverage on the gas pedal. When she drove past a beautician's shop that was all-pink and spied a pretty, middle-aged woman inside whose hair nearly reached the light fixtures, she parked, went in, and told the beautician that she wanted her drab brown hair dyed to match her blonde roots. She had been letting them grow out ever since Ulric had said goodbye, to the consternation of her staff and the library patrons.

As the proprietress of Queenie's Beauty Salon was throwing a plastic cloak over Lilith's shoulders, she noticed the silver scar on her customer's neck and brushed it with her maroon enameled fingertips. "You're doing this to get your man back," she said wisely, using her comb to gather up a strand of Lilith's hair, then twisting and pinning up the rest. The beauty parlor's track lighting refracted off the small diamond on her wedding ring, temporarily making it look as large and bright as the North Star. "Don't worry, honey, I'll get rid of all this ugly and make you as pretty as a bride. It ain't popular to say so, but a man who really loves you always hurts you. Even if he's not mean. He just forgets his own strength if he's really caught up in you. That's all. I been married thirteen years now, and my husband and I have left our marks on one another many a time. For better or for worse, you heard that. We fight hard but that's okay with me because we love hard, too. You know just what I mean, don't you, sugar?"

When Lilith allowed as how she might, the beautician laughed as if she'd made a delightful and original gibe. She wasn't nearly as amused after Lilith paid for the renewal of her blonde birthright and bluntly asked where local bikers went to party. Lilith got the name of an intersection in a bad part of town, but no more empathy on the joys and travails of standing by your man. Why is it, exactly, that the good girls always know where to find the bad men?

Darkness was falling as she pulled in front of a small building with a plain brick front. Small windows set high up were either frosted or blacked out by grime. The bar's neon sign was in the shape of a Confederate flag and bore the name Alabama. When Lilith looked to the left and the right of her car, all she saw were two rows of hulking, big-shouldered stallion machines trimmed with leather and chrome. Red, green, black, purple, and gold—but Harleys every one. She took off the glasses with the plain lenses that had been her ridiculous shield for so long, and dropped them onto the pavement as she opened the door and swung her legs out. The useless glass and ugly frames made a satisfying crunch under her lethal heels.

She studied the moon, and it was so beautiful that she felt reinforced in her decision to make it the new sun in her sky. To choose this darkness for her daylight, and the dangers of love over the punishment of duty. "Ulric!" she cried aloud to the moon. No more than that.

The dress could have come off in seconds. She slowed herself down, took the same time that she would have taken if he was watching, because she had to believe that he was. All she really had to do was untie the dress at her left shoulder, and it slipped from her like ebony water. The cool air made her nipples tighten painfully, and she reveled in the startling pleasure of being naked beneath an open sky. She had been blessed by an ardent lover's touch, and wherever his hands had caressed her, she had no self-doubt, only a happy knowledge of her own beauty. She stepped out of the dress and dropped it onto the driver's seat, the only sign she was willing to make that she might have a future.

Lilith took six steps across gravel and two concrete steps up to the door of the bar. When she put her hand on the wood, it was vibrating from the loud music that was being played inside. The worst had already happened; she had lost him. So there was no more fear in her, except for the fear of surviving his loss. Young, naked, and beautiful, she opened the door and walked into a room full of men she did not know, but had every reason to assume were thugs, criminals, and outlaws. So much the better.

It being a weeknight, the bar was only about half-full, so there was no crowd to block her entrance. Weekends would usually bring a few couples to Alabama, but on this particular evening, there was only one woman in the place. Her naked self. The nonplussed silence of the men nearest the door spread rapidly in this group of people with the finely honed survival skill of paranoia. Everyone at the bar swiveled away from his drink to see what had come in, and more than a few of them put his hand on a weapon as he turned. The long-haired, fifty-two-year-old bartender in an Army Ranger T-shirt shook his head and let go of the sawed-off shotgun he kept out of sight under the counter that held a sink and ranks of glasses. He muttered a prayer under his breath that this crazy chick was over eighteen, because the boys were going to have their fun whether she was or wasn't, and poured himself a shot of the Grand Marnier he kept in a Jack Daniel's bottle.

Fuck it and fuck them, he had it on the rocks.

There was money down on a corner of the pool table, but the game stopped anyway, and cigarettes everywhere ran down into ashes, untouched on the lips of souvenir ashtrays the patrons had pilfered from various motels and donated as joke gifts to their favorite bar. Only the jukebox went on and on, droning the extended version of "Freebird." A displaced Southerner had his eyes closed, tears running down his cheeks while he mouthed the words, until his buddy smacked him on the shoulder and gestured at the blonde who was gathering all eyes to her, the way Penelope had gathered the threads of her loom when she unraveled each day's mournful weaving.

Nobody said anything, and nobody made a move. Time had slowed down for Lilith. It felt to her as if she had time to study each one of the faces that was turned toward her, and drink in her intuition about these men's temperaments and lives. As soon as this scan was complete, she walked over to the man who stood at the nearest edge of the pool table, cue in hand. His dirty-blond hair had been combed back from his face, and he had a ponytail that was held in place with a brown leather lace. He was taller than Ulric, maybe the tallest man in the room, and his T-shirt was tight enough to show off his well-built, working man's chest. Black grease was embedded in his cuticles and under his nails. He wore chaps over his jeans, chaps with the zippers on the outside of his legs so they wouldn't scratch his bike. There was intelligence in his eyes, and hell to pay for the harsh lessons life had taught him. He was aggressive, maybe even a bit sadistic; slightly less predictable than a .45.

Perfect.

"Want to play?" she said clearly.

He took his dark glasses off and gave her a smile that said he understood the game and would play his part well. "This?" he asked, pointing his stick at the green felt.

"I'm not very interested in *those* balls," she replied coolly, and ran her hand down his zipper, then cupped the weight she found within the crotch of his jeans.

"I didn't think so," he said, trying to match her nonchalance. But his voice shook just a bit, and he took a sharp breath in when she gently squeezed the part of him that she'd come to see and use. "Can I offer you a seat?" he said next, his voice full of good humor, trying to match her cool-for-cool.

"Please," she said. Their eyes were locked on one another, and she liked what she saw in his face, admiration and unapologetic desire.

He swept the balls on his half of the table away from them, without looking, and doffed his leather jacket. Looking down at her, still smiling, but looking a little more sinister, he rolled up the squeaky, heavy garment and wedged it against the rail of the table. Then he slid his big but gentle hands under her ass and lifted her straight up into the air. It was always a little shocking to be reminded how strong men could be, and Lilith gasped, to the biker's satisfaction. She parted her legs to wrap around him, and he pivoted and deposited her on his makeshift bed. He was used to handling women's bodies; he put her down in such a way that her hair was not trapped underneath her, where it would pull. As Lilith relaxed back, reclining on her tawdry throne, the glare from the light above the pool table blinded her. "Turn that off," she ordered.

"Gettin' shy?" the man she had chosen drawled.

"No. I can't see you. And I want to see you."

Somebody hit a switch somewhere, and she could open her eyes without wincing.

"And here I thought you just wanted to feel me," he teased, undoing his fly.

"That too," she shot back.

"Well, here I am," he said, and shot his cock up her. "Feel all you want."

Thrilled to be full, she reached for him and their hands met, fingers twined together. "Oh, I'm doing everything I want to do right now," she said, eyes locked upon his amber brown gaze. "Do it to me, big daddy. Give me everything you've got."

Six strokes later, he had let go of her hands so he could pick her up by her waist and slam her into his body. She was unable to talk, amazed once more by the fact that contact between her cunt and a cock made her entire body awash in sensation. Her legs, belly, breasts, lungs, and throat were as involved in the experience of sex as her well-pounded pussy. Other men, made bolder by the noises she was making, came closer, and she was glad then that she had her hands free, because she could fill them with hard cocks. Most of the men she touched were just waiting for a turn to fuck her, but not all of them could wait; she laughed in triumph when she made one of them ejaculate all over her breasts. But she refused to take any of them into her mouth, and oddly enough, none of them forced the issue. That act she had reserved for someone else.

That "someone else" was already present. Only Lilith had heard the door open and shut, or felt the midnight-cold wind of his passing by. The man who rode her was close to coming, and she turned her attention on him, bearing down, milking him as he shot, wringing every drop of cream from his softening prick. "Oh, what a ride!" he gasped, leaning forward to give her a kiss. As he got close to her ear, he whispered, "You sure you want to stick around?" Lilith was startled by his chivalry. He would have to fight to get her out of this bar with only one man's leavings in her. Jostling over the next place in line had already begun, and could easily get ugly.

She shook her head minutely, then pushed herself away from him to lay full-out in the middle of the interrupted game pieces. "Party's just getting started," she said loudly, lifting her hair and letting it filter through her fingers till it fanned out around her head. "Does a girl have to buy you all a drink to get a fuck around here?"

There was a chorus of "Sure!"s and "Why not?"s, but an older and wiser man who knew that pussy was harder to come by than a beer was edging between her legs, his fat dick in hand, giving her the lewd grin of a satyr. Lilith's first stud relinquished his place reluctantly, shaking his head at her determination to be gang-banged. He took a place nearby, however, pasting his tired body to the wall with a half-empty beer bottle on his thigh. His replacement said to Lilith, "So you wanna get me a drink?"

She laughed, then propped herself up on her elbows and drew a bead on the bartender. He had given up any pretense of serving his customers and was watching her like a hungry wild animal. "Can I run a tab?" she yelled at him. That made everybody dissolve into ribald merriment.

"Come on!" a redheaded man who was bare-chested beneath his leather vest shouted. "Give our new mama a line of credit, you cheap bastard." A barrage of similar sentiments goaded the bartender into throwing both of his hands (clad in fingerless leather gloves) up into the air. "Round of drinks on Sweetie over there," he growled. "But you gotta pay up before you leave, sugar tits."

"Wonder how she's going to do that?" some anonymous wag yelled. "Harharhar," Lilith heard the other bikers roar. But the man between her legs was rubbing the fat head of his cock up and down her slit, teasing her clitoris, and she really had eyes and ears only for him.

"I don't want a drink of nothin' ole Five Ears has got behind that greezy-grimy bar of his," the gray-haired biker told her, as if he was revealing a secret. He took off his gold-framed, round spectacles and stowed them in his shirt pocket. Then he bent over, separated her legs and held them straight up in the air, and ran his tongue along the track that his cock had traveled. The bar broke up into raucous shouts of encouragement and a few cries of feigned disgust. "She's sweeter than manna and cleaner than the armpit of the Holy Ghost," he stood up briefly to declare. When the heckling continued unabated, he shouted, "You wish the seat of your bike smelled this good!" and went back to eating her out.

Lilith grabbed the top of his head and said, clearly and firmly, "Slow down!" To her surprise, he did. His technique was completely different than Ulric's; her lover had always been slow and gentle, spending a long time sucking and licking on her inner lips before he tickled her clit, barely touching it with his tongue. This guy seemed determined to lick it right off; but after she rebuked him, he changed what he was doing just enough to make it feel good. He moved his tongue to the top of her clit and gave her a good, steady lapping, firm and confident of his results. Her body, already at fever pitch with an excellent fuck and the knowledge that Ulric was watching, quickly gave him what he wanted. She yanked on his long hair as he made her come, and felt him laughing in between her fuzzy outer lips. He was clean-shaven, but his five-o'clock shadow burned that tender place.

"Oh, my, cherry pie!" he proclaimed, and hunched his hips, working his cock in a half-inch at a time while he wiped his face on the sleeve of his flannel shirt. When Lilith got impatient about taking him in, he held her down on the table and took control. "What's your hurry?" he asked, giving her another segment of his cock. "You gonna turn into a pumpkin at midnight?"

"No, but I'm not a goddamned glass slipper either, so stop acting like you're going to break me!" Hilarity and high-fives ensued around them; she had won the crowd over to her side in a hurry.

"Don't flatter yourself, bitch, you ain't been broken in yet." The biker's voice was more reassuring than hostile. In fact, Lilith was surprised to realize that the atmosphere in the room was more energized and cheerfully lustful than threatening or ugly. The men seemed to take it for granted that she wanted sex and was asking for it plainly; and they didn't seem to have any doubts about their ability to satisfy her, or the propriety of doing so.

Her second shooter adjusted his gut so that his cock, which was wide but not too long, could crawl forward once more. When Lilith knew she finally had the whole thing, she howled in triumph. "See?" he said, triumphant as well. "I know how to drive that thing. Got you good, don't I?"

"Oh, yes! Oh, yes, you do. I'm a believer."

"Praise god and all his works," he said between gritted teeth, and flashed her an utterly pagan grin, then ground his hips in circles. It was like being reamed out by a relentless power tool. She was used to an in-and-out pressure, not this masculine force that went after her response in all directions, and she couldn't help but say so. Once the vulgarly worded flattery was out of her mouth, she had a brief moment of guilt, hoping that Ulric would not be wounded by her enjoyment of another man. That was when he unveiled himself to her, and leaned over the table to give her the shadow of a kiss. "You're beautiful," he said simply, and then withdrew, leaving her with the reassurance of his appreciation.

The preacher's debauched and merry son sensed the moment when his thick tool had opened her up, and said, "Giddyup!" The new tempo made her come almost at once. When she calmed down, and found that he was still at it, and likely to make her come again, Lilith dug her high heels into his chest as he pummeled her sex. Even with the careful preliminaries, the way his cock was shaped made taking his thrusts a challenge. So it seemed only fair. "Think you can hurt me?" he dared her.

"Yes," she replied, a stiletto aside each of his nipples.

"Might just encourage me," he said, sounding out of breath. He was fucking her faster now, and his eyes were wild.

"Maybe that's the idea," she said bitchily, and pushed her heels into him hard enough to pierce the skin.

"Oh! God!" he shouted, and threw his head back and came. "My redeemer lives. Wildcat bitch," he said fondly as his flaccid prick slipped out of her. He touched the blood that ran down one side of his chest, looked at it, looked at her, and said, "Bravo, girl, you drew first blood." Then he licked his fingers, put his cock away, and bowed low to the next man in line.

Lilith wasn't sure that she wanted yet another full-out fuck. She was getting a little sore, and her legs were tired. Luckily, the next two men who did her simply propped her feet on their shoulders and thrust into her for mere moments before they came. The first man of this pair was as stiff as a board. He looked at the wall behind her as he screwed her. The only part of him that seemed alive was his cock. Lilith believed that he was doing her simply because that was what the other men in the bar were doing; he wanted to be able to tell the story, but his orgasm was stunted and brief. Well, if he could use her, she could use him. Lilith speeded up her breathing and willed herself to climax as well, and shuddered with the delicious shamelessness she felt. The second man was simply a quick draw. He fucked like a rabbit, excited beyond endurance by the fact that his cock was sliding in other men's sperm. He added his load to the rest like a good soldier, which in fact he had been. *Where's all this weird information coming from?* she wondered. It was as if she could see into them, as long as they were within her.

But when the next guy, a bald-headed bruiser with Plexiglas grommets in his ears and an Iron Cross around his neck, shouldered his way through the crowd to claim her, Ulric emerged from the multitude and got in his way. "No," he said. And Lilith thought, *Ah-hah! He has been feeding me the things that he sees.* For the first time, she understood his complaint about the way it made him feel to go deeply enough into a stranger's mind to change his memory or alter his behavior. It must be overwhelming.

"Hey, dude, I don't recognize you, and in this bar, we don't let outsiders come in and take our tail away," the man said belligerently. Lilith realized that he had a tattoo of a riled-up cobra running down the back of his head and onto his neck. The serpent's tail disappeared within his clothing. It was disturbingly realistic work.

Ulric was unruffled. "Remember how bad it burned the last time you had to take a piss? Well, you need to go home now, and you don't want to have sex with anybody until you get that clap taken care of."

As Lilith watched tensely, all of the rooster seeped out of the man, and his facial expression went lax. Looking rather vacant, he turned away from Ulric and went toward the door. "Wait a minute," Ulric said, and the man whose mind he had changed stopped in mid-stride. "There is a service you can provide for my lady after all," Ulric continued, and motioned him close. The biker stood before him, and Ulric tenderly pulled the other man's leather jacket off his left shoulder and tilted his head to the right.

Lilith caught her breath. The sight of them embracing was like an ember in her cunt, a sudden heat that surprised her. Ulric was wearing leather pants with fringes down his legs, and a jacket to match. His belt had a large silver and turquoise buckle that made her think of rodeos and Indian reservations. She wanted to bury her face and hands in the soft weight of his hair. But he was doing something important now; she must watch and learn. This was such a significant part of who her lover was — his sexual response to other men. Where was her jealousy? Where was her revulsion? All she could see was male beauty, perfectly matched, flesh against flesh, no harm, no sin, only sensuality that did not injure anyone's soul. If seeing Ulric with another man made her want to masturbate, made her wish they would go further and show her more, could it be that loving her master with an open hand would bring the two of them even closer together? And why shouldn't two become three, if only for an evening?

It took most of the power that Ulric possessed to keep everyone in the bar from reacting as he bit into the big vein in their friend's neck and stole his blood. He could feel his own Adam's apple move up and down as he swallowed. The man was relaxed and happy within Ulric's arms, giving with pleasure. The erection he had thought to use on Lilith, although he did not know her name, returned, and when Ulric took his last swallow, his victim quietly but emphatically came in his pants. The vampire stifled the impulse to say, "Now, who is daddy's good little boy?"

Drunk now with his own desire and the wherewithal to fulfill it, Ulric shoved his suborned donor away and reminded him, almost as an afterthought, "Home!" Like a well-trained dog, the biker promptly left the bar, thinking nothing of the wound in his neck or the strange way the gangbang had been interrupted. All he could think of was tomorrow's visit to the city clinic. Eagerly anticipating getting a Q-tip stuffed down his urethra and a huge shot of antibiotics in the heinie, he rode home, obeying every traffic light.

But Lilith and Ulric had no thought for anything but each other. He claimed his place between her legs and crooked one eyebrow. "I'd ask you if you come here often," he quipped, "but I've seen you come so many times it's a pointless question."

She wrapped her legs around him and drew him close to her body, then sat up. He wrapped his arms around her until their chests were pressed together. Her naked breasts stuck to the leather jacket that he wore, and the fringes on his sleeves tickled her bare thighs. "I'm a slut," she told him, and caught her lower lip in her teeth.

"Yes," he said. "Congratulations. You've had almost as much fun with these boys as I would have had if I were in your place."

"Have you ever been where I am now?"

"Maybe..." he said coquettishly.

"That's a story I'd like to hear."

"It's a story I'd be happy to tell you."

They kissed. His fangs were still prominent, and she was careful to move her tongue between them, but Ulric was even more careful to ensure that he did not bite himself and allow his blood to flow into her body. He had to respect her wishes. She would not allow him to preserve her from death. He must treasure every moment that he had with her, for she was mortal, and he was not. His hands traced her back, then slid between the two of them and smoothed her breasts, wandered to her nipples. She moved enough to allow him to reach her chest, and whimpered when he pinched those nubs and twisted them just enough to make them ache.

"Can I be your girl?" she whispered.

"Only if I can be your Sir," he said, and circled her throat with his hands, then squeezed. Lilith threw her head back and allowed him to support her weight, and gradually shut off her air. He stopped when her vision began to dim, then throttled her again, marveling at the grace with which she relaxed into his control. She was beautiful, and she was his. He let go of her throat and kissed her again, feeling his whole body focus on her, preparing itself to give her pleasure and take it from her.

"I have a surprise for you," she said, and wiggled to be let down from the table. He made her slide down the length of him, and she wound up on the floor, kneeling between his boots. The entire bar seemed to gasp when she opened his pants and exposed his cock, displayed it to them in her small, white hand. She leaned forward and licked the head of his cock, both hands wrapped around the base so she could feed it to herself. Ulric was almost afraid to move or feel what she was doing, he was so surprised. But the reality of her wet, warm mouth sliding down his cock finally sank in, and he rested his hands on her beautiful golden hair, urging her on. "You look so pretty with your mouth stretched wide around my cock. Just looking at you makes me want to come," he said. Just like in her dream.

She could not swallow all of him, though, and looked up at him with cocksucker's tears running down her face, on the brink of despair. She thought, *I want my mouth back*. By that, she did not mean that she wanted to relinquish his cock; instead, she wanted the freedom to suck him better than any other whore or faggot whose face he had fucked. She wanted to own her lips, tongue, and throat the same way she owned her clitoris, labia, vagina, and cervix. And that meant being liberated from the tyranny of trauma, the superstition of shame. She had chosen this man, and the past must not come between his beloved cock and any part that she might use to lavish attention upon it.

"Shall I help you?" Ulric asked, and she nodded, not willing to let his cock slide out of her mouth so that she could talk to him. Ulric sent the most delicate probe he could fashion into the place in her psyche where sexuality was housed. He found some tinges of fear and washed them away. He eased her physical discomfort and soothed her agitation. He played with the oxygen content in her bloodstream, boosting it and slowed her gag reflex down. And he found a fantasy that he could bring forward to help her, the fantasy of belonging to a cruel master who deprived his slave girls of any sexual stimulation other than sucking his cock while they rubbed their cunts upon his boot. At just the right moment, Ulric slid his own boot between her thighs and pressed against her sex.

United with her, he was able to enjoy both the enormous pleasure of being sucked all the way down her throat and the pleasure she felt at being taken this way. Her tongue played all over the sensitive underside of his cock, and he lost track of her limitations or enjoyment then. He came, experiencing all of the sensations of ejaculation with none of the liquid release, and just as he opened his eyes and regained some of his composure, Lilith ground down upon his boot and came as well, making a pretty show of submissive sexual release. She was sobbing so hard that her shoulders were shaking. He had done it, the magic had worked. The taste of his cock and its fulfillment had exorcised her mouth and made her whole.

At that moment, most of the men in the bar would have killed Ulric to possess his slave, and a few of them would have died to be as owned and abandoned as Lilith was.

"Get back on the table," he ordered, and when she looked confused, he picked her up and put her there. He had taken enough blood to will himself into a second erection, and he slid into her cunt, fucked her just enough to get her excited again and lubricate his prick.

"I've got another surprise for you," he said, and linked them together once more as he positioned his cockhead at her asshole. "I'm going to show you how to love this," he promised, and slowly speared that virgin hole. With Ulric forcing her body to relax and feeding her sensory images of how good it felt to be fucked in the ass, Lilith screamed at the intensity of accepting this new form of mastery. "I won't accept any resistance," Ulric told her. "This is mine, just as your mouth and your cunt are mine. Your hands. Your mouth. Your lovely breasts and sweet, sweet ass. You can't stop me and I won't stop myself. I'm going to fuck you until you cry."

"No!" Lilith said. "If you take everything, I'll have no place left to hide. You'll know everything about me. And then you won't want me anymore."

But his cock was relentless, as was the merging of their hearts and minds, and she could not help but give herself over and feel what he wanted her to feel, as if she had a prostate that hungered for the stroke of an invading cockhead. He made her like it, and tears of frustration as well as joy were not far away.

Ulric kissed her again, his black hair mingling with her blonde tresses. His tongue was as tender as his cock was outrageous, and he told her that he would always want her. "As if I could ever know everything there is to know about you," he chided her. "And even if I could, I would simply want to start all over at the beginning and discover it all again."

That was when she began to cry again. She fought him with every bit of strength that she had, wrecked herself against the breakwater of his determination. He was strong enough to catch her and keep her. She knew that and the knowledge made her come under him, come even though he was fucking her the way he would fuck another man. Then he bit her, and that sent her over the edge. How could she have been stupid enough to send him away, to give up this communion? She screamed again, begging for his mercy and his cruelty. He told her to come hard, to give her master the orgasm of a slave girl who knows who holds her leash. "I belong to you," she replied, and her body obeyed him, because he was her harbor and her home. It was a strange orgasm with an alien flavor, but she suspected its very strangeness might be addicting.

When he had finished using her, Ulric withdrew slowly and gently, and let her clasp her exhausted legs together. Then he took her in his arms. The bar broke into mad applause. "This is my bitch, and I'm taking her out of here," he announced to no one in particular, and backed out of the door. She had her arms around his neck and he could smell the sex on her, and her tears and her happiness. They were both soaking wet and tired. He took her to her car, put her on her feet, and dropped the dress over her head, then retied the ornamental knot at its shoulder.

"Beautiful dress," he commented. "Not that the car and the shoes aren't excellent as well. By the way, don't you think this was a dangerous thing to do?"

"No," Lilith replied. "I knew that you would come. Your name is my only prayer now, Ulric. You are my lord and I live to serve you. If you will let me, I will be your mortal companion."

He picked her up again (she thinking, *I could get used to this*) and deposited her in the passenger seat. She had left the keys in the ignition.

He shook his head, amused beyond telling by her fine sense of drama. He got in the car and decided to leave the top down so the moonlight could bathe them and the wind could clear his head.

"Where are we going?" she asked as he pulled away from Alabama and its barricade of evil-looking and expensive motorcycles.

"To a motel," he said. "It's almost dawn. And then I will drive you to my home in San Francisco, where you will be my slave and my queen. Only if my cats approve of you, you understand. But they will love you because you will give them many little white mice to eat. And maybe a few drops of your blood. Then you will ride behind me on *my* motorcycle, scantily clad, of course, since you seem to fancy being a biker's hot mama."

"I don't know about that," she teased him. "Is your motorcycle as nice as the ones I just saw?"

"Nobody has a nicer motorcycle than me," he said, dead serious, and she took his free hand and put it on her lap.

"You will not kill when you feed, unless you have chosen someone who deserves to die," she told him.

"In this, you are my master," he acquiesced.

They did not speak again until he found a place where he could hide from the dawn and she could guard his rest and share it. As his heart stopped beating, there was only one wish in it, that he would never be parted from her.

Lilith slept almost as soundly as her lover, her arms and legs wrapped around his insensible flesh, and just before she dreamed, she vowed, "I will never leave you. Never again. No matter what. We belong together." But the lips she kissed were cold, unresponsive as a graven image.

CHAPTER 7
The Wolf Is My Shepherd, I Shall Not Want

On their way west and south, across the heartland of America and back to Ulric's home in San Francisco, Lilith had her first taste of what it might mean to relinquish the daylight and cleave to her lover and the shadows that preserved his life. The daylight world was ruled by the seasons of the sun: summer solstice, fall equinox, winter solstice, spring equinox. But the seasons of the night changed every evening, a twenty-eight-day cycle ruled by the moon. She knew it was summer because the temperatures, even at night, were warm enough for them to leave the top down and let the wind surf around their bodies as they soared down the highway. But the details of summer were blurred by the darkness; with this absence of color, how would she know when fall approached? The temperature would drop; the farmland they drove through and the forests would smell slightly different. But the darkness would claim even the winter, turning the snow dark blue, even snowflakes in the headlights would look dark gray. She hoped her eyesight would sharpen. Perhaps the memory of the daylight was enough to help her color what she saw as Ulric's traveling companion. He never demanded that she keep to his schedule; she knew he would not object if she arranged her life to include some time in the daylight. But while they were driving it would delay them, and so for now, she awoke when he did and put head to pillow at the same instant her lover laid himself out for the sleep of the dead.

Although Ulric often spoke of the pleasure of riding his motorcycle and described imaginary trips he would take her on, Lilith's lover preferred to have her drive the little red sports car. He had brought her a black leather miniskirt one night after he returned from his foray through the town that surrounded their motel. It was still warm. She put it on for him, and wore it after that to drive. He said he liked the way the skirt pulled up onto her thighs when she drove, and the interplay of her high heeled shoes with the gas pedal and brake. Certainly he loved to show passing truck drivers what she wore underneath it, usually nothing more than his fingers.

Driving at night, she knew she was more bold with this exhibitionism than she would have been during the daylight. There was something anonymous about the car, surrounded by darkness and the moving headlights of other vehicles. Sometimes he would convey the truckers' excitement to her, and it would heat her so much that she would have to pull off the road so he could finish her off.

Huddled in her car, making love with their clothes half-on, Lilith tasted a little bit of her lost adolescence. The next car she bought, however, was going to be an old American automobile with a large back seat. "Are you jealous of these other men?" she asked him once, her legs astride him, resting in the middle of an impulsive midnight fuck.

He laughed. "I think they are jealous of me."

"No, really."

"No. Really." He knew she was talking about the barroom scene, probing for his complete reactions, wanting to make sure no scorpion lurked in the garden of her happiness. He reached up to finger her nipples, tasted her mouth, nudged his cock into her, wanting her to ride him again. She resisted, so he put his arms around her and whispered in her ear, "Among my people, you know, we had certain occasions in which it was expected that women would take their pleasure with as many men as they could find to service them. And any time a woman wanted sex, all she needed to do was go to the door of the house where the young men lived. If she waited by the door, one of them who found her comely would go out to her. If she stepped across the threshold, their cocks were hers to command."

"I can't imagine living in a world like that," Lilith said. "Being a woman in a world like that. It almost sounds like too much freedom. But how can I say that after what I've just done?" She laughed softly at herself. "I'm afraid of being punished if I become too free, and I'm not talking about getting a paddling from you."

Ulric nodded. "It's broken my heart again and again to see women lose all power and respect, and become the brutalized objects of a world run by the worst of men. But I will be your ally in winning your autonomy. I don't want to see you get hurt. I want you to have what you want. And if you fell in love with someone else perhaps I'd be insecure or anxious. But I'm not jealous. I love that outrageous streak in you that flashes cops. Did you think I didn't see you show your breast to the motorcycle patrolman today? Well, I did. Did it make you hot to do that? I thought so. Show me. Show me."

"My thighs—I can't—too tired."

"Then I'll help you," he said, and lifted her up, then dragged her back down onto his shaft. She gave her body over to him and worked her clit in time with his thrusts, until they both fell back against the seat, gasping. "It'll take us a year to get to San Francisco at this rate," he joked.

"Well, I could put you in the trunk and drive all day, then you could drive all night."

"My dear, there are a lot of things you own that I'd like to get inside, but you are forgetting that this natty little streak of a car doesn't even have a trunk."

"Oh. Oh! Oh! Oooooooooh."

116

Each night just as the light might impinge upon their journey, Ulric would signal her to start looking for a motel. They had learned to ask for a room with two double beds because she was uncomfortable sleeping next to his impeccably quiet body. Once evening fell, he would make sure she had something to eat, then slip out the door to get his own sustenance. "Kill only the wicked," she would remind him with a kiss.

"Such a bother," he teased her. "There aren't as many wicked people about as you might assume."

"Then you will have to settle for quantity instead of quality. Take a little from several good people instead of hitting the jackpot with one villain."

"Easy for you to say. It's not that easy to stop some things once they get started. Who is good enough to live? Who is bad enough to die? And why do I have to be the judge, jury, and executioner? Does lightning feel guilty when it strikes a person instead of a dead tree? Before I met you I was like a crocodile lurking in the water. Smug and lethal and—"

"Crying crocodile tears. Just like now," she said, turning him toward the door.

When Ulric came back with a book of poetry, a string of pearls, a riding crop, or a box of chocolates, she would have their things packed up, and they would leave, and drive as long as the darkness would permit.

What Ulric treasured about this time was the plenitude of her touch. He had gone for decades knowing only the brief embrace of his prey, and such caresses were rarely reciprocal. He reached out for what he wanted, grasped, imprisoned, and fed from it. If he wanted to, he could have created a simulation of mutual lovemaking. He had in fact done it, and he knew that Adulfa gloried in the power she felt in such humiliating dumb shows. But since he had to initiate every movement of his partner by the machinations of his own mind, Ulrich usually found the whole thing completely frustrating and even faintly ridiculous. It was masturbation with a living sex toy, and his dominance was not appeased by such fakery. He wanted genuine submission, the adoring abundance of one who willingly gave over body and soul.

And that was Lilith. She hated to be further away from him than the length of her arms. It seemed that her hands were always upon him— massaging his shoulders or stroking his thigh, teasing the back of his neck, or pressing the length of her body against him. She didn't touch him simply to solicit his sexual attention, either. She loved the texture of his skin, and she wanted the smell of him close to her face. She was as hungry for the experience of touching another human being as he was for the delight of being noticed, accepted, and welcomed. No one could have mistaken them for friends, brother and sister, or anything other than lovers. They walked in step, finished one another's sentences, fell into embraces both casual and passionate with the ready ease of a perfectly compatible and infatuated couple. Each time she took his hand and merely held it, Ulrich held his breath, waiting for the miracle to end. But it did not end; it merely changed into another reassuring and tantalizing meeting of their skin.

It was about ten o'clock one night, by the glowing green letters of the dashboard clock, when Lilith said, "You seem to have highly developed standards for which truck drivers or highway patrolmen you want to see our little sex shows."

He stiffened in the seat beside her, and stifled an impulse to turn on the radio and drown out this conversation. "Does that bother you?" he asked, trying for a neutral tone of voice and almost managing it.

She laughed, a low and sexy sound, then poked him in the ribs. "My boyfriend is a big fag," she said, mimicking the vapid speech of a Valley Girl. "For sure. He is!"

"Well, duh!"

"So tell me about it."

He knew that she wanted the truth. "My last attempt to form a relationship with a mortal was very short-lived," he said slowly, and each word tasted of a deep and abiding sorrow. "He was not fated to live a full span of years, and he did not want to become as I am. Much like my present perverse companion."

"We won't have that argument again just now. I want to know about him."

"It's a tragic tale," he warned her. "Won't you see me differently if I show you how it was between us?"

"Honey, after all we've done together, do you really think I'm some kind of stupid fundamentalist homophobe? The only thing that would have turned me on more than taking on all those bikers would have been to see you with them. Top or bottom. Yes, I'm your sex slave, and a fledgling masochist, but I love you enough to see all of who you are. It won't tarnish your mastery. Are you afraid to let me see him fuck you? I swear all I want is to know as much as I can about you, about how you've survived. But I also respect your privacy. So if you're not ready to relive that relationship, I won't insist. But maybe you could let me have it bit by bit, as a bedtime story?"

"It wouldn't be a good idea to try to share my memories with you while either of us is driving," he conceded. "When we stop then, let's take an hour or so, and we'll see how far into the story we get."

It took several nights for them to complete the narrative, nights in which she comforted him and gave him the courage to conjure up the ghost of his lover Alain, and bid him a less bitter farewell.

Ulric awoke. A fever was upon him. He burned with a hunger that made his toes and fingers ache, and shriveled his balls. The darkness that beckoned beyond the glossy windowpanes was not enough to hide the heat and light of the glowing embers in his belly. Surely if he walked the streets in this state, people would run for the nearest door and bolt themselves behind it, frightened by his intensity. But this was San Francisco, and a winter fog had wrapped the city as stylishly and flirtatiously as a drag queen's feather boa. He could walk these damp streets as safely as a phantom, and the fire that drove him would keep off the drizzly cold that ate into other men's bones.

His guardians ringed his sleeping place, and came to brush their elegant bodies against his ankles and calves as he sat up and stretched, trying to work the stiffness of eight unmoving hours from his limbs. "Hungry," they each said, and the word was as substantial in his mind as a goblet of AB-negative in his hand. There had been no intruders, or they would have been plaintive in their demands that he get up and rid the house of what remained of the prowler.

There was Luna, the mystical Abyssinian he'd rescued from Sir Hilbert's keep; Anastasia, the regal Russian blue; and Charley, the enormous alley cat with long black fur and a white ruff. He particularly loved Luna because of all the cats, she was the only one who bothered to still speak aloud to him, even though it was much more difficult for him to decipher her yowls and rumbles than it was to understand the compelling mental pictures the others gave him of their immediate needs.

It was Luna's turn tonight to watch the house while he hunted. The rest of them Ulric released through the back door, having no fear that these cats would be crumpled by a speeding car or crushed in the jaws of a pit bull. Luna waited gravely until he brought her the puzzle-ball containing her dinner, a half-dozen clever white mice. He reset the combination and placed it on the floor, and as he walked away, he could hear her already calculating her strategy for breaking into the little cage and releasing its tasty bits of animated fur. In the meantime, though, it was important to punch the spherical cage with her right paw and send it rolling. There were some bells in the box along with the mice, to make her sport more merry.

His hunger was cocked within his body like a snake coiled to strike, but he kept it at bay for a little while, puttering about the house, touching this book and that painting, reassuring himself that his treasures were still there. Unlike Adulfa, who scorned the comfort of mortal trappings and preferred to sleep in crawl spaces and rafters, Ulric always made himself a lavish home. He found that the camouflage of wealth was at least as effective as the camouflage Adulfa shared with wild bats, owls, and raccoons.

He went into the bath that adjoined his bedroom and prepared himself for the evening's festivities. He had always been meticulous about his grooming, unlike many men of his era. He bathed and washed his hair, and paid especial attention to cleaning his teeth. In the bathroom mirror, he saw another difference between himself and his sister, and sighed. Adulfa had hair the color of corn silk, and she religiously shaved it every evening, so that by dawn it had grown out only a few inches. Ulric's hair was black as a raven's wing, and he wore it long about his shoulders. It curled a little, as did the edges of his blue-black mustache and beard. Was Adulfa still shaving her head? Was she still living in nooks and crannies, sneering at his masquerade of antique furniture and Persian rugs? Better, perhaps, to do without an update. Ulric shuddered, and went to dress.

The leathers he pulled on were skintight and soft from frequent contact with his body. It's easy to get good tailoring when your weight never alters by so much as half a pound. He still found trousers a little awkward, but one must change with the times, or be left behind. Snaps, however, were a great improvement over troublesome lacing or buttons, and practically everything he wore could be doffed or donned with the bright clicks of these handy little metal appliances. What would they think of next? Ulric shook out the fringes along the edges of his shirt sleeves and the outer seams of his leather pants. A man liked to have a little dash, a little panache, a little something that cried *Peacock!* rather than peahen.

His hair seemed to repel water, like the fur of an elk. It was already half-dry. There were a few annoying little cramps in his stomach, threats of what was to come if he did not go courting soon. He opened a window and let the breeze in to complete his toilette. He could feel his hair breaking into additional curls. By the time he hit the street, he would look like a pirate. Then he saw the full moon, shining through fog like a lamp swathed in gauze, and knew why his hunger tonight was especially keen. Was it his imagination, or did he hear a wolf howling somewhere over in the green hills of this beautiful city? For the second time that night, Ulric shuddered, and put the thought of Adulfa firmly from his mind.

He tugged on his boots, hooked keys to the right side of his belt, and left, stopping only to give Luna an encouraging caress. The tawny little cat flipped onto her stomach, took his hand between her teeth, and gave him an arrogant look that invited him to move. "You are the queen of my home and my heart," Ulric acknowledged, and she graciously released him without breaking the skin.

His motorcycle was waiting in the garage. Ulric started it up and rode toward the door. At the last possible moment, it swung open. He rode away chuckling, hearing the door fall shut behind him. It was not quite the same thing as jumping a high fence on a hot-blooded Arabian, but it was important to avoid boredom even in the little things. Adulfa was such a sourpuss. The world had never been so full of amusing toys, and he had enough money to buy all the amusement he could enjoy. It was good to be alive in 1975.

There was a fisters' bar on Market Street, and a brand-new leather bar down on Capp in the Mission. But Ulric was not interested in either of these places. He wanted to surround himself with other stallions, and become just another stud in a herd of wild horses. And so he went South of Market, to Folsom Street, where half a dozen bars and three times that many sex clubs and bathhouses had men in denim and leather queuing up in lines three deep for blocks and blocks. The thick smell of sex and the acrid scent of poppers almost managed to defeat the faint whiff of sewage from bad drains. Music from the bars and clubs spilled into the streets until it seemed that the entire neighborhood was partying. He supposed other people must live here, people who were not leathermen, but he never saw them. Small wonder that so many of the men did not wait to get indoors before they began to take pleasure from one another.

It all reminded Ulric of his youth and the sexual frenzy of warriors after a battle. His feral good looks and hard muscles made him an easy sell in this part of the city. Few of the men he cruised had bodies as impressive. But then, they had never trained for eight hours a day in a full set of armor. And that had been Ulric's upbringing, under the harsh eyes of the Germanic Knights who had slaughtered most of his people. Thinking of those days still made Ulric's fists clench, and he went down Folsom Street at freeway speed, angry at his own helplessness. He could not save his folk or, for that matter, himself. One day, he vowed, the banners of the Christian armies would be trampled in the mud, and Ulric would be there to make sure that no man lifted a hand to preserve them. It was one of the hopes that kept him alive, after so many years.

Along with the hope that tonight would provide an unusual feast, something savory and out of the ordinary. His ears were ringing with hunger, and he was sweating, despite the chilly wind that bathed his upper body. He brought his bike to a halt in front of the Eagle's Lair and backed it into a parking space as if he was in a dream. His consciousness seemed to be floating slightly outside of the boundaries of his skin, as if he were watching himself perform in a trance.

There was bar called the Eagle in every city. Ulric should know. It was one of the first things he looked for when he scouted a new territory. Even in this age of the machine, men still remembered their true heritage. The warrior's totem of the eagle lived on, and would probably survive after the last living eagle had fallen from the poisoned sky.

It had been a long time since Ulric had been drawn to a woman. If he thought about it, he would have to confess that he kept himself from looking. Well, he would not be the first or the last man who hid a broken heart behind a hard-on. And what he needed now was the direct simplicity of contact with another man's flesh, to slip in among his brothers as a black sheep is slipped into the herd to keep its silly white flockmates from straying.

The sweating, oiled bodies that packed the Eagle were indeed as slippery as raw wool, rich with lanolin. Ulric picked up a beer because it was such a useful social prop. He had to admit that he was also glad to see his favorite bartender, Alain. Alain had six inches of height on Ulric, and twenty pounds of muscle. He had shaved his balding head and his beard, but his hair was so thick and black that the outline of it could be clearly seen against his white scalp and ruddy cheeks. His earrings were solid gold, thick hoops of wealth and disdain for heterosexual convention. His oversized earlobes jutted out rudely, as if to say, *Fuck you*. He wore what he always wore, a leather vest and a dirty pair of 501s. Rings as big as the earrings were shoved through his raspberry-sized nipples. The bottom button of the jeans was undone, not because Alain wanted to create the illusion that he had a big dick. He *did* have a big dick, and there was no way his cock and balls were going to fit into those jeans with the fly buttoned all the way down. On the left he wore a hefty bunch of keys and a coiled-up whip. Ulric scented old blood streaking its tip.

Alain was a sadist. His reputation was such that even in this bottom-heavy city, he often went without a weekend tryst. He always looked at Ulric as if he knew secret things about him. Ulric, on the other hand, was never sure he would actually get the order he placed with Alain, and felt sheepish about having such a chieftain wait on him. In another age, Alain would have been the leader of a war band or a great king. Ulric supposed he had done the best he could to find his own domain. The part of him that was still a stripling longed to please Alain, dedicate some service to him, obey and perform great deeds for his approving eyes. But the very great danger of walking into Alain's iron chains kept Ulric's troubled eyes down and a civil tongue in his head.

Alain handed him the beer with a little shake of his head, as if he were saying, *Too bad*, and Ulric almost snatched it out of his hand. He turned his back on the impossible man and rolled the sweating brown glass over his forehead, trying to cool his drenched face. The cramps in his stomach were spreading to other parts of his body, so that his hands were making small, involuntary gripping motions, and his lip was threatening to curl up and permanently expose his teeth. Ulric handed the beer to someone who had been waiting in line for twenty minutes to get one, gave and accepted the obligatory pat on the crotch, and followed his nose and his memory toward the back room.

The further you went into the Eagle's Lair, the darker it became. Too dark for video games or pool, too dark to make sure you were hitting what (or who) you were pissing at. Out of the darkness came groans and sighs, bellows and shrieking, as if a horde of men were being slowly roasted. It was this braiding of pleasure and pain that made human beings such ideal victims. And tonight, Ulric wanted to approach that state himself, to kneel as close as he could actually come to the flames of true submission. He supposed that anyone who knew about his physical strength and his other powers would have expected him to dominate other men, and sometimes he did. But more often, Ulric was compelled to sink into a state of passivity and response. He wanted to be swept up, carried along, to feel as if he had no choice. The hunger had taught him that. It was a hard master, this pain in his heart and throat, and now he would find the wherewithal to drown his longing.

He went a little way into the room, which was twice as big as the rest of the bar, and dropped to his knees. Now he was in a forest of boots—laced-up lumberjack and combat boots, cowboy boots, engineer boots, and tall riding boots and Dehners. Levi's, leather chaps, jodhpurs, police uniform trousers, and fireman's rubber waders towered above him like the trunks of trees. He ran his hand up the nearest leg and cupped the balls that rested at the bottom of an undone fly. He never saw the man's face. He knew him by the funk of his crotch and the size of his quadriceps and the fur of his scrotum and shaft. His touch was permitted, and so Ulric brought his face closer and tongued, then swallowed, both balls. This got him the gift of two hands, clasped behind his head, and a belly-deep groan of surprise.

He managed to bring his tongue back into play, and turned his head to one side, applying pressure that compressed the testicles and made the skin over them more thin, taut, and sensitive. Stretching and licking, he resisted as long as he could the cues he was receiving to spit out this man's nuts and pay attention to his cock. He got a brief reprieve by reaching up and milking the rampant organ with his hand. The shaft was fat, long, and already half-hard. Ulric didn't mean to pry, but he understood (as precum slicked his palm) that this was a man who liked to play for hours before he came. It would be a real triumph for Ulric to get him to shoot. He had been letting cocksuckers try to make him come ever since the bar opened. The slightly raw foreskin that slid back from his cockhead was one of the things that had probably drawn Ulric to him in the darkness.

Other men, sensing passion, were gathering around them. Ulric could hear other cocks being beaten off nearby, could smell the crowd's voyeurism and approval. So he carefully expelled his victim's balls and swallowed—more slowly than any sane man would have permitted—the steadily leaking length of his sex. The hands locked behind his neck could do nothing to speed him up; Ulric was so close to getting what he wanted now that no mortal's strength would avail against him.

He took a perverse pride in being good at what he did on his knees, in the dark, and he never liked to think he had to cheat to attract his prey. So he had not tampered with the other man's mind. But now it was necessary to shift his chosen one's perceptions just a bit, and provide a few distractions as well. So Ulric called the men around them, and they began to unbutton the stud's shirt and suck his armpits and nipples. Someone else was kissing him. Ulric could tell, from the little discreet nibbling he had done upon the man's balls, that he was not entirely averse to a little pain. Getting your dick deep-throated for hours was, after all, as much about abrasion as it was about suction.

So Ulric drew his teeth up the length of the cock, and delicately dragged them along the cockhead too. He fiddled with the way this felt just enough to make it seem more exquisite than damaging. He also encouraged the men who were holding up his victim to begin to explore his furry ass. First tongues, then fingers, and eventually a cock were sent between those square, heavy cheeks. Ulric thought it was a bonus that this man did not normally enjoy getting fucked. All the more reason to give him an excellent suck job, and take his mind off his troubles.

When he slid his mouth back down the length of the scored erect cock, he was at last rewarded with the delicious taste of something hotter, saltier, and sweeter than cum: the red red blood that had enslaved Ulric so long ago, when the Grand Master gave him the unwelcome gift of perpetual darkness. After all these years, each time was as glorious as the first. Ulric had been reborn to do this: to feed and adore this virile, handsome animal who made it possible for him to live.

The cock in his mouth suddenly became even more rigid, and Ulric's eyes flew open with surprise. One, two, three, it pulsed, and filled his throat with bitter jism. There was enough blood mingled with the cum to make it palatable, but Ulric could not stifle a cry of disappointment. It would be virtually impossible to feed until he was satisfied now. His victim's arousal dissipated rapidly, no longer providing a concealing intoxication to cover the pain of Ulric's fangs.

He got up and took himself to another corner of the room, licking his teeth with frustration and hissing like a wet cat. About the man who had been on the brink of giving him everything, he did not spare a second thought. Somewhere in the back of his mind, he could hear the man's confusion and self-hatred, as he was forced to all fours on the floor of the bar, and a second man began to piston his ass, and a third took possession of his head. This was not how the evening was supposed to go, this was not what he wanted or liked, this was not who he was—why wouldn't anyone help him?

Screw you, Ulric thought. *How does it feel to be lost in a crowd?*

He calmed himself enough to look around for a second victim. This time, there must be no mistake. In the past, this bar had always been so good to him. In fact, Ulric realized, he could not remember exactly how often he had fed here. Was it seven, or was it more? Tomorrow, he would find another place to quell his hunger. But it was too late to start all over again. There had to be somebody here, somebody who was a sure bet, an easy score.

The atmosphere in the back room was suddenly stifling. Panicked by claustrophobia, Ulric scooted for the door. To reach the main bar, he had to pass the urinals. A blond boy with a bad haircut that marked him as a recent arrival from the Midwest was staggering to his feet. His hair and chest were rank with piss. But Ulric found those human secretions which were akin to blood to be rather attractive, if a bit of a tease. The kid had been on his knees drinking piss. He was fucked up from the shame and excitement of performing this forbidden act, and he was also flying very high on the acid, cocaine, MDA, and alcohol he had ingested along with the hot jets of piss and clots of cum.

Ulric did not even bother to move his keys to the left. He just beckoned to the woozy young man, and took him by the arm. He was not about to go back into the darkness and risk losing this quarry to other hunters with lesser appetites. No, it was into the alley with this one, a quick kill, and then he could spend the rest of the night dawdling on his bike or head for home and listen to music.

The alley was, for a miracle, empty. Of course, until closing time, with a back room available, few of the patrons would be likely to take their tricks out here. Even for a raunch pig, it was an intimidatingly filthy scene. But what did that matter to the boy who had been used as a human toilet?

Ulric had received just enough blood to make his cock swell in a painful imitation of a human erection. Arousal made him rough. He knocked the kid down, and the boy sprawled on the pavement, immune to the garbage, as loose-jointed as an abandoned puppet. Sighing, Ulric hoisted him up to his knees. He nuzzled Ulric's fly, and got backhanded away from it. *Easier and safer to take it out myself*, Ulric thought, and fumbled his equipment out into the breeze. His cock didn't have time to get cold, though; the wanton farmboy swallowed it whole, showing an enthusiasm that made up for his lack of experience. Ulric was always ambivalent about these situations. Was it worth it to give the kid some coaching? It was hardly likely to benefit him in future encounters.

Ah, well, but that slobbering and gnawing had to stop. Ulric stepped into his mind, not being nice about it, and snapped out some quick orders. The pressure on his cock became more even, the tongue more insistent, the teeth less bothersome. Yes, that was much better. Ulric let his frustration out now, and gave the kid a skull-fucking that expressed some of his displeasure at losing his first choice. The young man was sobbing, beating on his own dick, and Ulric snarled, "If you get one drop of that scum on my boots, I'll kill you." Caught between the need to laugh at his own joke and the sudden surprising need to come, he came instead. Ulric did not let the boy register the lack of ejaculate before he picked him up off the ground and raped his carotid artery.

Vampires take body fluids from human beings; they do not reciprocate.

Ulric's teeth went into the boy's throat more quickly than the piss had run down it. Now, this was satisfaction. The blood was thick and rich, a vintage like no other, unfermented but utterly intoxicating. The mad fire that had threatened to capsize him in agony all evening subsided. He could almost feel every cell of his body drinking its fill. Life was grand, when you were the one who was going to go on living.

The back door of the bar opened, and out came Alain with a double-barreled shotgun. "Put that son of a bitch down," Alain said. Ulric did as he was ordered with hatred in his heart, and hatred of the bittersweet longing he had to fling himself at the trash that had been quelled under the thick soles of Alain's work boots. He wanted to feel the weight of those boots on his neck, his back, and felt an irrational pang of jealousy for the cigarette butts and used condoms the big man ground into the muddy surface of the alley.

Ulric looked into the perfectly round nostrils of the sawed-off firearm and wondered if this was the last face he would ever see. He had survived some terrible wounds in his time, but he knew a stake through the heart would kill him, and thought perhaps a couple of shotgun shells in the chest would do the same thing. There was no way to be sure, and he would much rather not undertake the experiment.

Then the gun roared, and he was sure the last page of his life story had been written. It took him long seconds to figure out that his own body was intact. Alain had defaced Ulric's victim. Now he took a razor blade from his vest pocket, unwrapped it, and handed it to Ulric. "Wipe off our fingerprints, and put it in his hand," he said curtly.

Ulric performed the task requested of him, protecting the steel from fingertips with a corner of the victim's T-shirt. He even thought to wipe his prints from the dead boy's chipped and bitten fingernails.

"Business has been pretty good since you started coming around here," Alain said. Ulric jerked around to stare at him. The gigantic bartender lit a match on the sole of his boot and twirled the tip of a cigar in the blue flame. "Once word got out somebody was murdering guys in the back rooms, practically biting their cocks off, we started getting so many new customers there were nights when I thought we might run out of beer before midnight." He pointed the cigar at Ulric, who was hard again after feasting in earnest and weak in the knees from shock and relief.

"You did that, didn't you? You're the bastard who's been turnin' all this prime beef into dead meat."

"What do you want?" Ulric whispered.

"I just want to hear you admit it."

Ulric put his hands up, showing open palms that held no tricks. "I am the one," he acknowledged.

Alain pursed his brutal lips, and blue cigar smoke shot at Ulric, curling lazily about him. The bartender was waiting for something. Finally Ulric could not bear the silence anymore and said, "What are you going to do with me?"

A long parade of conflicting emotions flew across Alain's face. He wanted this dandified longhaired rebel biker with his piratical good looks. He had wanted to chain him up, whip him raw, and ride his narrow ass since the first moment he'd set eyes on him. Now that he knew Ulric was more than he seemed, this desire took on another twist, like the loops of a hangman's noose. The presence of genuine danger was such a challenge. And then there was the other side of Alain, which he had locked screaming into a cell many years ago.

The two men stared at each other, not even aware they were leaning toward each other. Their cocks also strained toward each other, tenting their trousers, as if to say, let us out and we'll figure out a solution to this standoff.

Ulric could not endure the suspense. He took a gamble. "What is your pleasure, my lord?" he asked softly, resurrecting the courtly speech of the pageboy and squire he had once been.

Alain's face closed up like a Bible being slammed shut by a pastor done with his sermon. "Once word gets out about this," he said, nudging the body with his shotgun, "things will go back to normal. If I were you, I'd stay away from the Eagle's Lair for a while. Give Folsom Street a rest, if you want to keep your pretty face intact."

Ulric shrugged and turned to go. It was ever this way between him and humankind. They were natural enemies, after all. His quest for a soulmate among them was pathetic, as mad as a cougar singing love songs to a white-tailed deer. Loneliness was his ordained and proper lot, and if he were half as sane as Adulfa, he would accept it. He was nearly to his bike when something else Alain said made him stop and turn.

"You might come back in a couple of years," Alain allowed. "Business might need to get jump-started again. I don't mind selling more booze." He blew more smoke at Ulric, who took it in his face like a kiss. His whole body was erect and trembling with desire. The single word *please* resonated again and again within him; but he could not say it out loud. He bit his own lips until they bled to keep himself from saying it.

Alain had no idea that he had just been shown a rare sort of tribute. He gave a little bark of laughter, and waved Ulric away. "Be off with you now," he half-shouted, hand on the blessed door that would let him back into the music and frenzied coupling that heated the bar. How hard it is to break the habit of never having what you really want, the habit of refusing to see what is marvelous in the world.

Shaking his head, Ulric mounted his bike and drifted home. Without turning to look back at Alain, he lifted a hand in a graceful gesture of farewell and surrender. The vibrations from the motorcycle's V-8 engine made his balls ache like a bad tooth. He longed to find a suitable niche for his aching cock before dawn made him impotent, and knew it for a futile desire.

CHAPTER 8
Parting Is Such Sweet Sorrow

"But that can't be the end of the story," Lilith said, stroking Ulric's back as he lay upon her shoulder. He was breathing shallowly, still wrapped up in his pain. "You fell in love with him when you saw him with that shotgun in his hands, didn't you? Or maybe you were a little in love with him before you smelled gunpowder and the possibility of your own death. How terrible to have to leave him standing there. But you did what he told you. You obeyed him even though it hurt you more than any whipping could have done. But I know you, and you are nothing if not persistent. You went back, didn't you?"

He nodded, eyes closed tight, unwilling to leave the safety of self-imposed darkness and the shroud of her perfume. She bathed him in the soft strokes of her hands, soothing him. "Don't fuss about it now," she said. "Compose yourself. I'll sing to you, and then you'll be ready to hunt. We can continue tomorrow, or whenever you are ready. We are going to be together forever, so we can take our time."

He grimaced at her innocence. No, they would not be together forever. There was an expiration date, an execution date, stamped upon their affair. He might be able to keep her safe from car accidents, men with guns, and a thousand other mishaps, but time would wither her before his appalled eyes. He could love her when her hair turned gray, but he dreaded cancer, osteoporosis, cardiac arrest. Some mortal ailments were beyond his power to heal without sharing his own blood. Still, he knew that his ability to take her back into his past was used up for the night. She was right. He should listen to her sweet voice, the love song she made up for him, and calm himself. Tonight, like every other night, he must take his ration of blood, and perhaps it would cleanse him of the poison of grieving for Alain.

Bit by bit, night after night, as their trip came to a close she coaxed the rest of Alain's story out of him, like a medieval doctor applying leeches to a festering wound. And he found that as he walked through the story with her at his side, it became both more real and also more bearable. He no longer had to keep a thick iron door shut between himself and Alain. Thoughts of his lover could come and go, and sometimes they even brought him pleasure instead of pain. Lilith remembered what he told her as one consecutive story, a true tale that broke her heart.

Ulric stood in the living room of his Victorian mansion, using a small crowbar to pry the top and sides off a crate that contained his harpsichord. His long black hair was getting in the way, so he stopped to scrape it back and bind it in a ponytail. If he had been able to sweat, his beard and mustache would have been damp with perspiration. And if water would have done him any good, he probably would have chugged a quart of it by now. Other crates, bearing stickers from Europe, stood nearby, waiting to be unpacked. It was good to be home, back in San Francisco.

Not that Amsterdam hadn't been fun. The weather was cool and damp and social attitudes were so liberal that sometimes, if he kept his eyes and mind out of focus, he could almost believe that he was still in the city of gaudily painted Victorians and buff young men. It seemed as if the whole gay world had fallen in love with San Francisco and was trying to imitate its sensual openness, its lascivious pride. Very little distinguished the adult bookstores with their glory-hole-riddled booths, the backroom bars, and the bathhouses in Amsterdam, Paris, Berlin, London, and Madrid from the militantly masculine and hopelessly homosexual haunts of Baghdad by the Bay.

But there were always these annoying differences that plucked at Ulric, distracting him even in the middle of a hunt, and making him homesick for the city where a very butch bartender had helped him to conceal a kill, then warned him not to return until things had cooled off. He would be flirting with a longhaired beauty in a coffee shop, for example, and the man would say something in Dutch. Although cafés in San Francisco reeked of pot smoke too, they didn't have thirteen different brands of hash on a menu posted above the espresso machines. And San Francisco had more than its share of erotic entertainment, but nothing like the boy brothels that floated down the canals, barges full of choice meat.

The flight over had been stressful. Ulric's muscles still made cranky comments about being confined inside a trunk. He needed a safe container to protect himself from harm while he slept the sleep of the dead. But during the dark hours of the night, he was as awake as any other man, and it was tedious beyond belief to have nothing to do but count the studs that held the trunk together. The vampire cats who were his guardians and companions had been irate, and refused to entertain him. He could have booked a passenger seat and flown with everyone else, but he was afraid a perky and conscientious stewardess would notice his total lethargy and decide that he was dead. The thought of some self-appointed hero cutting him open with grubby airline cutlery to give him open-heart massage was disgusting.

He had tried flying as a passenger once, but the big dark cloak he had wrapped himself in to sleep had drawn unwanted attention from the other passengers, and they were also startled when he applied duct tape to the window to keep it shut. The controlling powers that normally kept him safe from mortal malice or curiosity didn't function while he was asleep, so he couldn't count on that to make everybody draw their shades and leave them alone. He could endure daylight, but he didn't like it much, and if his sleep was interrupted by the sun, he would awaken in such hunger that no one would deplane alive.

In a similar predicament, Adulfa would no doubt have taken one of the many animal forms that were her forte, and simply flown or swam across the ocean under her own steam. Or she would have boarded an ocean liner, stayed on it until she had fed on all the passengers and crew, then sunk the damn thing and taken bird or bat form to wing a few miles to the harbor. With her great power to make people forget what they had seen, Adulfa could afford to be fond of slaughter on a grand scale. But Ulric had only one animal form, and wolves did not take to the sea like pinnipeds. He could, however, compel people to do things they normally would not do, and make them forget what they had seen, but he shrank from intimate contact with their minds. Perhaps Adulfa was able to alter mortals in a more surgical fashion. Afterward, Ulric always found his own mind cluttered by unwelcome bits and pieces of their lives and personalities.

But Adulfa was not in San Francisco now. Ulric knew it because he felt happy and comfortable. There had been one vampire in residence, a young and confused prostitute who had probably been created accidentally. At any rate, she had been abandoned by her maker, and it was no problem for Ulric to dispatch her. He liked killing other vampires, when he didn't know them personally. That sort of blood lasted longer than a day. He might have as much as a week in which he would wake up without feeling the pulsing in his temples and his gut that told him he must feed right away.

There were other vampires across the bay, in Oakland, in Berkeley. The natural aversion of their kind for one another made vampires space themselves out, as other sorts of predators do, so that each had an adequate territory to meet his or her needs. In cities, where population density was higher, vampires tended to cluster more closely together than they did in smaller towns or rural areas. But Ulric was famous for forcing other vampires to give him a wide berth. He would tolerate no challenges to his dominance in a city as small and lovely as San Francisco. She belonged to him, her streets were his to caress and her hills were his to embrace. And all her people were under his patronage. The only vampire he could share a city with was his sister, Adulfa, and that was only because when it pleased her to crowd him, there was nothing he could do to stop her.

One nice thing about cities was that people moved around. Ulric had already checked out his neighbors, and there was only one old man still living there who had seen him during his previous tenancy. It was easy to make him forget someone he had only glimpsed a time or two. So Ulric kept the same house, rejoicing in the shipments of antique furniture, Persian rugs, and first editions that arrived from Europe. Each time a crate arrived and he opened and unpacked it, he felt as if he were coming home again. Soon everything would look just as it had the night when he had been told to leave San Francisco.

Well, plus a harpsichord, a set of originals by Aubrey Beardsley, a Tiffany lamp, and several stained glass windows that would have to be installed somewhere. You couldn't expect him to be gone for six years and stop shopping. That would be inhumane. He wrestled the musical instrument into a corner and dusted off his hands. The rest of the boxes could be dealt with tomorrow. Night had fallen an hour ago, and he wanted to go out.

The cats were also glad to be back. They loved the backyard of Ulric's Victorian, and now that it was overgrown, wild creatures had made their home there. They might catch anything, perhaps even a raccoon. Ulric hoped that no one in his neighborhood let their dog run free. The cats would pack together to hunt an obnoxious canine. "Just leave the skunks alone," he warned them as he let Anastasia, Luna, and Charley out to forage. Russian blue, Abyssinian, and black-and-white tomcat sent him identical images, cats licking their buttholes with great absorption, to tell him what they thought of his fussing.

Charley was going to be left behind to guard the house while Ulric went out on reconnaissance. Before he left, the vampire opened a vein in his wrist to let the longhaired tomcat feed. He had blood to spare, thanks to the little streetwalker, and all the cats could use a tonic after being cooped up for so long at high altitudes. He shook his head to rid himself of the memory of her welcoming smile. She had been so glad to see one of her own kind at last, someone who could explain the painful metamorphosis that had changed her body and given her needs she did not understand. She had thought that Ulric was going to take care of her. The nasty feel of her fake leather jacket still clung to the palms of his hands.

The purring cat at his wrist brought him back to himself. Life was not fair, was it? Even if he had wanted to become her master, Ulric knew she would have been hopeless as a student. She was not independent enough to endure immortality. And Ulric was not about to burden himself with responsibility for an inferior. A relationship of that sort was slavery for the ostensibly dominant partner.

He had purchased a new motorcycle yesterday. But before he went to straddle it and conquer the night, Ulric picked up Charley and held him. He loved the big white ruff that outlined the male cat's chest. His fluffy fur made his big feet look even larger, and between the ebony toes sprouted tufts of more white fur. The cat had a long spray of thick white whiskers that pricked Ulric's face. Charley went limp in his arms, a sure sign of deep contentment. Ulric sometimes carried him around the house for hours, over his shoulder, while Charley purred and drooled. Ulric hoarded the feeling of Charley's vibrating body against his chest, storing up the animal's deep love for him in his own undying heart. In a mental picture that included smells as well as visuals, Charley told Ulric that he loved him as much as a bowl full of goldfish, though he would love him even more once the fish tank was set up. The amorality and pitiless nature of the cats was a great comfort to Ulric. They took the sort of joy in life eternal that sometimes eluded their formerly human caretaker.

Ulric put Charley down and dusted cat hair off his leathers. The last time he had been here, he had gone in for a lot of fringe, if memory served. Now he was into a sleeker look, and wore an expensive, body-hugging racer's jumpsuit. It was amazing how persistent cat fur was. How often had he interrupted a killing bite so he could brush a cat hair from his victim's neck? Almost reluctantly, he went to the garage to start his brand-new bike. It was strange to travel out into the world without being driven by the great hunger. He almost wanted to stay home and putter with his things, alphabetize his tapes and albums, reshelf the books according to topic, author, and age.

But he knew what he had really come to San Francisco to do. He had come to see Alain. He still got goosebumps when he remembered the cool tones of his voice, informing him in Cajun-flavored English that the kills he had scored in the Eagle's Lair had been good for business. It wasn't like a mortal to see him in a positive light, or have such callous feelings toward his own kind. Alain's sadomasochism was linked to power and vulnerability in the real world, not posturing in an expensive costume.

Unlike a hundred other mortals who panicked or denied his true nature, Alain had seen him. And he had not flinched, not turned away, not denied the truth or tried to run from it. Surely six years was enough time to let the titillating scandal about a South of Market murderer subside. Alain had said he could come back. And Ulric wanted to see him, but he was also afraid. Mortals changed so much in such a short time. Besides, Ulric knew nothing about him except that he was a bartender at the Eagle's Lair. He didn't even know his last name.

Lacking any other place to start, he went back to his old haunts South of Market. The new Harley handled easily, and Ulric realized the BMW he had been driving in Amsterdam had needed its front fork aligned. *Oh, well.* The student he had tossed the keys and papers to would have to worry about that. Ulric was at the Eagle's Lair before he was aware of much time passing. Unfortunately, the place was now boarded up, the sign faded, the backroom no doubt full of ghosts who still hadn't found a trick for the night. *Shit.* This quest wasn't going to be as smoothly plotted as a Falcon video, was it?

Ulric turned the bike and went down Folsom Street, looking for other places he remembered. Most of them had closed their doors. A few of the bars had simply changed their names. The Combat Zone was The OK Corral now, and Ulric shuddered as he listened to the country music that poured out of its doors as faux cowboys came and went. Appalling stuff, that, the aural equivalent of possum cooked in molasses. The boots were nice, though. Colorful. Ulric had always liked a bit more of a heel on his boots than this century found appropriate for men.

Finally he spotted another man on the street who was wearing leather. Two men, actually, a well-groomed couple in their forties. The top was in leather pants, a leather uniform shirt, and a cap with a thin chain about its brim. The bottom was in chaps and a leather vest, and had an attack dog's choke chain draped loosely around his neck. Under the chaps he wore a jockstrap, nothing else. Ulric made a little face. What use was a collar that did not lock? Still, these men were the closest he had seen to brothers in an hour and a half of searching, so he let his bike drift to a crawl beside them and said, "Good evening."

"Evening," the top said, turning to face him. Ulric adored his gray handlebar mustache and big sideburns. The pocket of the uniform shirt bulged with hefty brown cigars, which smelled wonderful but did not compensate for the lack of a big bulge further down. The bottom turned as well and waited a little behind his master, although he leaned over to make sure he got a good look at Ulric's body. *Smack that boy*, Ulric thought impatiently, then focused his attention once more on the older of the two.

"I just got into town," he explained. "Where's the party? Seems like it's been hidden pretty good."

The top chuckled. "Eager for action, huh?"

Ulric gave him a look that would have made him step back if he were any smarter. "Oh, yes," he said finally. "Action."

"Well, you can't do any better than the Bear Cave," the man with the bodacious mustache said. "But it's not on the main drag." He gave Ulric directions to a side street. "We're headed that way ourselves," he said, and put a hand out to drag his boy forward. "Wait for us, and we'll buy you a drink. Welcome you to San Francisco in style."

Ulric did not say yes or no. He just nodded, raised his hand, and sped away. Could it be that in this thriving queer metropolis there was only one leather bar? What had happened to this town? Back in 1975, he'd been aware that many of the butch men who stood around in hundreds of dollars worth of cowhide couldn't wait to take all that hot, cumbersome clothing off the minute they got home with a trick. The number of sadomasochists, as opposed to the number of men who simply liked the masculine look of leather, had been small. Could it be that leather was no longer a fashionable fad? Was he going to have to go hunting in preppy sweater bars?

Shuddering at that humiliating thought, Ulric raced to the location the couple on Folsom Street had given him. He parked his bike between a little Suzuki and a good-sized Yamaha that had seen better days and went in, eager to inhale the scent of beer, cigar smoke, piss and sweat that colored and thickened the air of such places.

There it was in abundance, and Ulric's nostrils happily drank it in. He took off his gloves, tucked them under the epaulet of his jacket, and went to the bar. There were two men behind it, but neither of them were Alain. He ordered a single-malt scotch that he could not drink, just to enjoy the incense of its fiery aroma. The young man who brought it was pretty in a common way, and clearly thought himself a great beauty. The silver bar pinned to his leather vest said "Billy." Ulric scanned the patrons of the bar, and was bitterly disappointed to see that Alain was not among them. He got the bartender's attention again by holding out a fifty-dollar bill, and leaned toward his ear.

"I'm looking for somebody," he said, and the upstart laughed.

"You came to the right place," the bartender said, and made a grand gesture that included everyone in the place.

"No," Ulric said emphatically, slamming one hand on the bar. Billy jumped away. Ulric summoned him closer with a crooked finger. "I am looking for a particular man," Ulric hissed. "An old friend. Someone I lost touch with a few years ago. I need to find him now." He gave Billy the limited information he had, and was delighted to see comprehension dawn in those weakly handsome features.

"Why, that's one of the owners," Billy said. "He doesn't come around much anymore. Sometimes he's here on weekends."

"Where does he live?" Ulric demanded.

"Well, I can't just give you his address," Billy protested. "I mean, I'm not even sure I know it. It would be worth my job to give you his telephone number."

"Then give him mine," Ulric said through clenched teeth, and wrote it down on one of the cards the bar provided its customers. It said, "Here I am falling in love with you and I don't even know your name _____ or telephone number _____." Billy took the card with the tips of his fingers, and Ulric suddenly knew that he was in love with Alain and not about to pass another man's telephone number on to him. As if this puppy could endure what Alain's lust demanded! Furious, Ulric went into the young man's mind, and took the information he wanted.

But first, he found out that the bartender had about six more months to live. His death would have something to do with the red marks upon his chest, marks that looked almost like bruises, except that they were raised. Coming back to himself, Ulric had an ugly moment in which the vapid face behind the bar had turned into a grinning skull. He turned away to escape this macabre vision, and his opened consciousness was invaded by information about everyone in the bar.

All of these men were sick. Well, not all of them. Perhaps half a dozen were whole. But the rest would die sometime over the next year, mostly of pneumonia. Ulric turned and almost ran for the door. He collided with the couple who had directed him to the Bear Cave, and knew for a fact that the master would barely have time to bury his boy before he himself was in the hospital, dying of an infection that was not supposed to be fatal, something he caught from the tropical birds he loved to keep.

It normally took a lot to turn Ulric's stomach, but this onslaught of death in a place where he had hoped to renew his own life was just too much. He muttered an incoherent apology to the master, handed his boy back to him, and darted out the door.

"Daddy, what's wrong with that man?" the boy asked.

"I don't know, son," said the master. "I'd rather know he's crazy now, though, than find out after we took him home. Go get your old man a beer, now, and try to do it without shaking your ass at every big dick in this place."

It took Ulric two tries to start his Harley. Too bad the people who made these things could never get certain details right, like making them start up when you turned the key. Finally he kicked it alive, and the violent gesture calmed him down. Some of the shaking went away as the big bike's vibrations went through his hands, up his arms, and into the rest of his body. He went back to Folsom, got his bearings, and took Howard Street back toward the Eagle's Lair. Alain had bought a building close to the bar. There were three apartments in the building. He lived on the top floor.

Ulric parked outside the somewhat dilapidated facade of the building and went to the front door. There were buzzers for each apartment, but the front door was unlocked, so he simply went in. The stairs were a nuisance, but he bolted up them, more and more angry with himself for staying away so long. Why let Alain send him away in the first place, hmm? Vampire reflexes were so much quicker than mortal ones, it wouldn't have been that risky to take the gun away from him. If only he had dragged Alain out of the alley and taken him home! When you lived forever, it was too easy to lose touch with mortal frailty, the brevity of their life spans. Ulric cursed himself in the Old Prussian dialect of his boyhood, a language he used only when he was very upset or surprised.

Then he was at Alain's front door, and he did not know what to do. He wanted to break it down, but that would be crass, and might attract unwanted attention. He gently rattled the knob. This door was locked. Ulric shrugged and rapped it hard with his knuckles.

There was no response. But he could feel warmth inside the apartment, the heat of a human body. So he knocked again, more sharply this time, leaning into it. Someone on the other side opened the door abruptly, and Ulric stumbled in.

"What's your goddamned hurry?" Alain snapped, then he saw who had troubled his day off. "Well, speak of the devil," he said in an awed tone of voice, and grinned. Ulric found himself being picked up and vigorously hugged, an embrace that would have cracked a normal man's ribs. Then Alain was kissing him, the black stubble on his cheeks scraping Ulric's face. His tongue was big, his mouth tasted like sex and cigar smoke. Ulric petted his shaved head (more coarse black stubble there) and massaged the big muscles in Alain's broad shoulders. He had not been wearing a shirt, just a pair of dirty 501s, so Ulric could run his hands across the planes of muscle that outlined his back. There were more tattoos than there had been when they last met, and the rings in Alain's nipples were a bigger gauge.

When Alain was done smooching him, he put him down, and Ulric gasped. He had not been able to expand his chest to draw a full breath for several minutes. Alain was talking a mile a minute, and Ulric was having trouble following it all. The phrase "you bastard" appeared frequently. "How the hell did you ever find me?" Alain demanded.

"The Bear Cave—Billy—" he gasped, and Alain nodded.

When Alain spoke, Ulric could hear the faint remnants of an accent leftover from his bayou childhood. He didn't use a lot of Cajun slang, but Ulric loved the French tang of his Louisiana-paced sentences. Alain could read the phone book in that voice and make it sound like the dirtiest dressing-down a cowering slave ever got from a belligerent master. Ulric was so lost in a potent desire to fall to his knees that he jumped when he realized Alain was talking about something other than raw, mean, no-holds-barred sex.

"I should can his weasly little ass for handing out personal information," Alain said. "But I'm so goddamned glad to see you, it can wait until tomorrow. What can I get you? I know it's early, but let's have a drink. Or would you rather smoke a little bud?"

Ulric gave him a look that said, *Be real*.

"Oh, no, I guess you wouldn't." Alain stood three feet away, chewing his full lower lip, trying to think of some other form of hospitality he could offer his strange visitor. Ulric had a few moments to examine the furnishings of the room, which were simple but expensive, all the furniture made of oak and upholstered in brown leather. While he was distracted, Alain advanced upon him, embraced him a little more gently this time, and began to unzip his leathers. "Get your clothes off, man," he said impatiently. "I'm not going to let you get away this time."

If Ulric had been able to weep, he would have been in tears. His sexual encounters with mortals had been brief, controlled affairs. It was hard to let go when you had to keep your true nature a secret. (Thank the Horned God for the vampire blood he had ingested less than two days ago. It made it possible for him to be erect between Alain's hands without feeding on him first.)

The experience of being undressed and fondled was terrifying. Ulric found himself hyperventilating, straining to get away and straining to get closer to the big man who had gone straight to the heart of a hunger that was much more difficult to satisfy than a mere need for blood.

Then Alain picked him up again and was taking him into another room. Ulric once again felt the panicky sensation of wanting to escape and wanting to have this moment last forever. He was being held, comforted, practically abducted by a handsome, brutal man who knew he was a vampire and wanted him anyway. He stared wildly around the room, trying to distract himself. It was a cross between a bedroom and a dungeon. There was equipment hanging on all of the walls, workmanlike stuff that was obviously used frequently. There were a couple of posters, framed, from bars that Ulric remembered, places where he had found sweet young men who tasted of springtime and workouts in the gym. On his way into the room, Alain had punched a button on his tape player, and the big reel had started to turn, surrounding them with the spacey sound effects and insistent beat of queer disco, the kind of raunchy, high-tech music straight people were afraid to dance to.

Alain dumped him on the bed, wound his hands in Ulric's long, black hair, and stretched out on top of him. By the way their bodies sank into the mattress, Ulric guessed it was a waterbed. Heated, fortunately. Then Alain was kissing him again, taking the time to do it right, and Ulric almost came from the wonderful feeling of having his mouth explored with so much ruthless tenderness. He dared to put his hand on the buttons of Alain's fly and ease them out of their holes. When he palmed Alain's erection, the bartender groaned and dug his tongue so deeply into Ulric's mouth, he was about to hit his tonsils.

Ulric had seen Alain's cock a time or two years before, when he took a piss at the Eagle's Lair. The Prince Albert was still there, the thick ring that went through his piss-hole and came out just below the rim of his cockhead. But he also had a series of smaller rings that went down the underside of his cock, and a couple in his ball sack. Figuring anybody who liked to get pierced this much wouldn't be able to do without a certain classic ornament, Ulric reached a little farther back and found the guiche that pierced Alain's perineum. When he tugged on it, Alain's cock jumped, and his precum stained Ulric's thighs.

His own cock was painfully rigid. Alain was stroking it with one hand, and running his thumb across the head. Ulric made himself meet Alain's gaze, saw the question that made one of his eyebrows go up. "I don't do that," he explained. "I mean, I come, and I come really hard, but it's dry. No jizz."

Alain shrugged and began to play with Ulric's nipples. His broad thumbs were capable of small, delicate motions, and Ulric felt his pelvis lurching forward, toward Alain, driven by the arousal that was heating up his chest. Alain, sadist that he was, quit toying with Ulric's nipples and stuck his fingers in his mouth. He felt his pointed fangs, then stuck another finger in, and moved them in and out. "Did you ever think of getting your tongue pierced?" Alain asked. "It's already a wild trip, kissing you with those big, sharp canines. But a ball in your tongue would be too much. I'd come just from swapping spit with you."

"I don't know if my body would hold a piercing," Ulric said, trying to sound thoughtful and objective. The truth was that the idea of it frightened him to death (well, not quite that much). "Does it hurt a lot?" he asked, trying not to sound as timid as he was.

Alain wasn't fooled, and laughed so hard that Ulric thought he might suffer internal damage. "Oh, what a big old chicken you are," Alain guffawed. "Mister Nightmare, creeping around in shadows, has to catch and kill his own dinner every goddamned day, and he's afraid to get a little old needle stuck through his tongue. What would you do if I made a big fucking hole in the head of your dick, Ulric? Pass out on me?"

Ulric hid his head against Alain's chest and swore he was blushing. "I hate you," he said.

"Well, of course you do," Alain said comfortably. "Everybody I bring into this room comes to hate me sooner or later. Why else do you think I do it? Nothing makes my cock get harder than that cold stare of pure hostility, when I know if a guy could get loose he'd break my neck. Except he can't get away, all he can do is rage against me, and he's so frustrated he's ready to cry. Pure gold, that is pure gold. Better than a case of champagne or a pile of cocaine. So, scaredy-cat, get your nose down there and lick around those big old rings of mine. If you can't stand the thought of getting a few of your own, you better admire the ones that I've got."

Ulric was happy to oblige. He slid the head of Alain's cock into his mouth and down his throat, carefully guiding the shaft so that it ran between his fangs. It wasn't easy to keep from puncturing or scratching it. None of Ulric's teeth were dull. But he wrapped his lips around them, trying to cushion their edges. He didn't care if he cut his own mouth up a little in the process. His tongue was equally problematic. It was thin and raspy, more of a file than a human tongue. But Alain seemed to enjoy the way it felt, moving back and forth on the underside of his dick.

If he thought about it, Ulric would have had to admit that he was not protecting Alain from the sensation of having his cock scored. Anybody with this much gold in his equipment would probably love to be nibbled by vampire teeth. He was protecting himself from Alain's blood, and from the unwelcome knowledge it might contain.

Alain rapped him on top of his head. "Quit daydreamin' and tend to business," he snapped.

Ulric obeyed. Soon he was rewarded by a dose of hot cum that nearly choked him. Alain hauled him up so they were face-to-face and licked off the spit and white stuff that had spattered Ulric's mustache and beard. "I always like to come before I play," Alain murmured in his ear. "It makes me so much meaner if I'm not distracted by a hard dick. Know what I mean?"

Ulric did not know, but he was certainly trying to figure it out now. Alain interrupted this anxious reverie. "So, tell me about yourself," he said, tugging on Ulric's hair to force his head back and focus his eyes on Alain's face.

"What do you want to know?" Ulric replied.

"Don't be a smartass." Alain tightened his grip on Ulric's hair and slapped him lightly on one cheek.

"I'm honestly not being flippant," Ulric said patiently, relishing the smart along one side of his face. "I don't know what you are planning. I don't know what you need to know. Ask me questions, and I will answer them honestly."

"Stand up," Alain said, and roughly dragged him off the bed and onto his feet. Ulric played along, allowing himself to be manhandled. It was delicious to be able to pretend he was out of control. Alain handed him a piece of chain. "Can you break that?" he demanded.

"Of course not," Ulric said, relishing the way each cool link slid through his hands, like the scales on snakeskin. But he could not look Alain in the eye and say it, and the master sensed his lie. For that, he was kicked to the floor.

"Don't jerk me around, grab that chain and show me just how strong you are," Alain said impatiently.

Ulric shrugged, yanked the chain taut, and snapped it like a piece of string. "I'm sorry," he said, when he saw Alain's look of disbelief.

"Bend over the horse," Alain said, not acknowledging his apology.

Ulric went on his knees to the piece of equipment Alain indicated, stood, and bent over it. The padded surface was comfortable and sturdy enough to make him feel quite secure. "I'm going to hit you with something," Alain said. "You tell me how it feels." A braided cat-o'-nine-tails landed hard across his shoulders. Ulric sighed happily. "Well?" Alain said impatiently, poised for another blow.

"It's hard to know what to say," Ulric said sadly. "It's been a long time since I was changed, and there are so many things I've forgotten. And other things I don't know how to describe, since you have never experienced them." He took a deep breath and did his best to explain private facts about his body that he had rarely shared with another person. "I'm not very sensitive to pain. I don't need to be, my body can repair almost any injury. That insensitivity helps me to ignore the risk to myself when I go out to feed. When you hit me, I know it should hurt, but it doesn't exactly. It's more as if it makes me remember what pain used to feel like."

"Well, goddammit, that sucks," Alain said. Ulric knew without looking that he would be chewing his lower lip.

"I want you," Ulric said. "I've wanted you for years. Think of it this way, Alain. You can do your worst with me."

"You've got my attention now," Alain said. "Go on."

"Haven't you ever wanted to go as far as you could? You're a sadist, Alain. But you're smart about it. You don't go around kidnapping and torturing strangers. You ask for permission. You prefer men who don't have a lot of limits, but you stay within those boundaries. But surely you've wondered about it. What are *your* limits, Alain? I'm willing to bet that no bottom has ever been able to give you carte blanche. And I'm hungry for this. Think about how horny you get if you've got to do without sex for two weeks. Then imagine what it would be like to be me. I'm a creature of physical, sensual appetites, Alain. That's all that I am. I live to satisfy the cravings of my body. I manage to get a few other things done from time to time, but mostly I exist to feed, to feel the pleasure that comes from satisfying that hunger. But I have other appetites, just like you do, and this has never happened to me before. I've never had this opportunity. It's been centuries, Alain. If you tell me to stand inside your chains and leave them unbroken, I will do that. I will. You are the only person here who needs to set any limits. Not me."

His long-lost master knelt on his heels where Ulric could see his face, and slapped him to make sure he saw the sharp look he gave him. "That sounds too good to be true. So there's nothing that can permanently damage you or threaten your life? You're just immortal, you live forever, nothing can kill you?"

Ulric had thought he was completely open to this man, and would hold nothing back from him. But he balked at answering this question.

"I thought so. Well, that's okay. We've all got our little secrets. I like secrets. Just promise me you won't hate yourself when I make you give them up. I'm going to take you up on your offer, Ulric. I haven't been this horny for months. Don't know what's been wrong with me. Ever since this winter I haven't been myself." Alain shook himself like a wet dog. "Well, nothing's more boring than having to listen to somebody whine about their health like a senile old lady."

He took Ulric by the shoulders and guided him to a wall where chains dangled from heavy eyebolts that were sunk deep into the building's supporting timbers. After turning Ulric to face that wall, Alain wrapped the chains around Ulric's wrists and secured them with large padlocks. "No need to protect your nerves and tendons with a pair of wrist cuffs, is there?" he jeered. "So, just to make this official, I'm telling you: Leave those chains alone. If one of them breaks, I'll find a way to make you sorry. It's a tough order to find a way to punish somebody like you, but I've got a few tricks up my sleeve that might surprise you."

Ulric bowed his head and waited while Alain sorted through the whips that hung from a circular cast-iron frame that was probably manufactured for gourmet chefs to hang up their anodized aluminum pans. His sharp hearing caught Alain murmuring under his breath. "Forget that, too light. Too candy-assed. Ha, ha, don't need to bother with that bugger. Well, fuck all. I don't need to warm him up at all, do I? Goddamn. Let's see. What have I got that's really effective? Yes, you, and you, and you. You too. Come to the party, babies, daddy's about to have himself a *good* time."

Alain began with a wire brush that he'd bought at an auto supply store. Ulric supposed it was used to clean machine parts. The brass bristles were sharp and stiff. Alain pulverized the skin over his shoulders, back, butt, and thighs. It felt to Ulric like lying out naked under a hailstorm. There was more of a feeling of pressure than anything else, although occasionally a bright thin spatter of pain would penetrate his consciousness.

"Yesss," Alain hissed. "Gonna have myself a *good* time."

A rubber cat was next. The heavy latex cords had been tipped with metal nuts, knotted to hold them in place. This made Ulric grunt a bit. It was a nice, deep massage. Then he felt Alain's hands all over his back and butt, smearing thick liquid across his skin. "Baby," Alain said gently, "you're a mess. Let me make it all better," and turned his head to kiss him. The kiss created far more sensation than the beating. Ulric drank it in, giddy with pleasure. Alain was full of fierce joy, and it made Ulric happy to be able to put him in that altered state.

Other implements followed. It made Alain cheerful to show him each one before using it, and tell him a little story about where it had come from and how it had been used in the past (if ever). The truck antenna had been set into a steel handle by a tool and die worker in Seattle who promised Alain he would make him a new one if it ever broke. Alain had managed to bend it on its maker, but it remained intact. And the little flail tipped with hooks was something Alain made himself to frighten away a persistent would-be slave who was not his type. The beautifully shaped wooden club was acquired on a fishing trip. (It was made to knock out big salmon.) Until now, it had mostly been used to fuck boys who wanted something bigger than a dick up their asses.

Ulric's feet slipped. He was apparently standing in a puddle of his own fluids. Alain was growing progressively more and more excited. Finally he left Ulric's side and came back with a blacksnake, six feet long. "If this won't make you dance for me, nothing will," Alain declared, and let it snap.

This was not a massage. This was a slicing caress, with just enough of an edge to it to make Ulric wonder if it was pleasure or pain. The novel sensation made him crazy. He panted, whined for it, and almost forgot his vow to leave the chains unbroken, just because he was so excited. Again and again Alain let him taste the snakebite edge of the long braided whip, until Ulric was chewing his own lips and crying, "More, more, more!"

But before he had enough, Alain was at his side, unlocking the padlocks and catching his limp body, turning him around, locking him up again so he faced out from the wall. He drew a bowie knife from a scabbard that ran down his right thigh. *That's a monster knife*, Ulric thought. Not quite big enough to be a bayonet or a sword, but definitely longer than the four-inch limit on a legal pocketknife.

"Remember," Alain said evenly, "I told you not to break those chains. And you told me you would obey me. Do you have honor?" The point of the knife came to rest between Ulric's nipples, slightly to the left of his breastbone. Ulric keened in terror at the sight of it, but Alain was still talking. "And if you have honor, how far does it go?" he asked thoughtfully. The point of the knife went into Ulric's body a full half-inch. "Far enough to trust me with your precious overextended life?" Alain wondered.

Ulric was shrieking, rattling the chains that he had given his word to leave intact. Alain's face was set in a snarl, the lips drawn back in exactly the same expression as Ulric's when he was ready to drink. To the excited vampire's senses, Alain's hand seemed to draw back in slow motion. This was it, the killing stroke, the knife to the heart that could end his life. Ulric found himself howling in his wolf-voice, driven by desperation back to the animal part of his nature, and then the knife arced forward—

And lodged in his chest only a quarter of an inch away from his heart. Alain pulled it out, and a spout of blood hit him in the chest. The two men stood facing one another, panting, marked by a nearly identical gout of blood. Then Alain sheathed his knife, laughed a little at both of them, and released the padlocks. Ulric allowed himself to fall into his arms. By the spear of the Sky Father, he had never been so scared.

Alain half-carried, half-threw Ulric facedown onto the bed and shoved a big piece of Crisco up his ass. Ulric's ability to feel pleasure was the opposite of his numbness to pain. His predator's body was more sensitive to arousal than mortal flesh. It seemed as if he could feel every vein on Alain's swollen cock, and he could certainly feel the outline of every single ring that pierced his dick. By the time Alain had gone in and out of him a half-dozen times, Ulric swore he could have told you the gauge of each piece of jewelry. Never had he been fucked like this, with so much dedication and determination. Alain reached around in front of him, hauled him to his knees, and wrapped his fingers around Ulric's cock. With the big tool lodged firmly in his guts, Ulric shouted from the intensity of the pleasure he felt as Alain jacked him off again and again.

"Tell me you want it," Alain said, slightly out of breath, the words jerky because of the pounding he was giving Ulric's ass. "Tell me you want my cum, cocksucker. Tell me how bad you want it. Beg for it or I'll pull out, I swear I will."

Ulric was surprised by the little speech he made. Who would have guessed he could be that abject, or that poetic? Apparently it was effective, because Alain came hard, and Ulric's thirsty flesh drank up each drop of the white blood.

And now he knew. He had known since Alain came in his mouth, but he had been too impatient, distracted by his own hard cock, to let the information sink in. Alain had it, this new disease, whatever it was. He was doomed.

They snuggled together on the bed, Ulric sticking to the leather bedspread. "We made quite a mess," he said fondly.

"I feel wonderful," Alain exclaimed. "I haven't been so happy since Kip died. He was a hell of a masochist, but nothing like you, baby. My arms are burning like I bench-pressed 300 pounds."

"Kip was your boy?" Ulric asked.

"No, he hated all that role-playing shit. He just liked to turn up at my house once a week, down half a bottle of Jack Daniel's, and get the shit kicked out of him. No games. He was a good man and a good friend."

Ulric didn't want to ask, but found himself voicing a question anyway. "How did he go?"

"Some weird-assed kind of pneumonia that the doctors couldn't cure. Or at least that's what they said. I think they just didn't give a damn. He was just some fag to them. What did they care if he died?"

"So he had it too," Ulric said, then wanted to cut his own throat.

"Huh?" Alain knew he had heard something important, and he would not let Ulric take it back. Eventually he got the whole story out of him: Billy, the skull face, the premature mortality looming over the patrons of the bar. Then, of course, he wanted to know, "What about me?"

Ulric could not answer him directly. "I could make you like me," he said.

Alain studied him coldly. "So you can tell I'm sick, even though I feel fine?"

Ulric nodded.

Alain thought it over. "So what would that mean? You have to feed every day, right?"

"Usually," Ulric said. "Unless I've fed on another vampire. Then I can go for a few days without mortal blood."

"So you guys don't hang together? There's no fraternal bond?"

"No, there's not." Ulric's body was still singing from the pleasure this man had given to him, and he could not withhold the information he needed to make a decision. "We can't tolerate each other, in fact. Vampires don't like to be around other hunters. We need to keep a certain zone of space between us."

"So you and I would not be spending eternity playing perverted leather games with one another?"

Ulric shook his head.

"And you say it's bad? Everybody's got it?"

Ulric nodded. "These things happen periodically, Alain. I've seen lots of plagues sweep through the human population and decimate it, about once every hundred years or so. This one is too new to have a name yet, but it's every bit as nasty as bubonic plague, typhoid, or cholera. Millions of people will die."

"Including all of my friends. My God. In a few more years, San Francisco will be a ghost town. Do you have any idea what we've built here, Ulric? How many men have sacrificed careers and their families and come here to make this a gay Mecca? This is the only place on earth where we can be ourselves and live without fear. We have this city by the balls." He took his arm out from under Ulric's body but stayed close to him, stroking his chest. Ulric waited patiently for him to speak again.

"I killed somebody once," Alain said finally. The confession came out in awkward bits and pieces. "A basher. I was cruising this rest area down on the interstate, and I blew this big trucker. Got up in his cab to do him, just like some kind of Jack Fritscher fantasy. Motherfucker came at me with a tire iron when I was done. If he hadn't gotten himself a really great blow job before he tried to kill me, I probably wouldn't have been so pissed off. I might have just run away. But the nerve of him, to get his dick sucked and then turn all self-righteous and call *me* a queer? Forget that shit. I took that tire iron away from him and beat his head in. Took it home, washed it off, kept it in the trunk of my car. I've still got it. That's weird, huh?"

"How did you feel about it?" Ulric wanted to know.

"Well, that's an interesting question. I guess I had fantasized about it often enough, what it would be like to kill someone. Because of course you know that's what I'm supposed to be all about. If I like to hurt people I must secretly be a killer. But it made me sick. I threw up for about an hour. And then I went to sleep for two days. I don't think I liked it much. Certainly didn't give me a boner. I was just glad to be alive myself. And pissed at him for getting me in a corner."

"It's different when you feel the hunger," Ulric said, yawning. How far away was dawn?

Alain put out his hand and grabbed one of the big canines. Ulric let him, loving the feeling of having this man put his hands in his mouth. "I'll just bet it is," he whispered. "But I don't think I want to find out." Ulric stared at him, stricken. "I know you mean it kindly," Alain said gently, withdrawing his hand. "But my whole life is about fucking other men. I gave up everything in order to have a life where I do whatever gets me hard. My family is the men who come to me to get tied up and spit on and beaten and fucked. I don't want to live long enough to see the end of what we've made here. I can't stand the thought of watching them die and leave me behind. It makes me too sad. And I couldn't do what you've done, Ulric. I couldn't wait a year to get my rocks off, much less a century."

"Feeding is very pleasurable," Ulric argued. "I wish I could show you how it feels, Alain. It's—"

"It's lonely," Alain said flatly, and Ulric knew the verdict was final. For the first time in his immortal life, he felt what might have been tears in the corners of his eyes. Alain reached out and wiped them away, and Ulric saw the bloody traces on his fingers. "I could make you," he said fiercely. "I could force you to drink my blood. And I should do it, I should, I should!"

Alain pinned the clenched fists that were beating on his chest. "No, you shouldn't, baby." Alain gathered him up and patted him on the back, treating him like a mourning child. "I know you love me, and you want to keep me with you, Ulric, but that's just not in the cards." He kissed him on the nose, and the fond gesture made Ulric weep again, painful thin strands of diluted blood.

"There's one thing you can do for me. Two, actually," Alain said.

"What—is it?" Ulric hiccupped.

Alain got a firm grip on his bearded chin. "Let me put a big fuckin' stud in your tongue, honey. Then I want you to fuck me. It's been a long time since I met a man whose dick I wanted up my ass. Then bite me, and let me go when I'm in your arms, doing the stuff I love the best."

"Are you sure?" Ulric demanded.

"Yes, I'm sure. Now let me get up and deal with a couple of things. No, you stay in bed." Ulric watched from the leather-covered waterbed, which was gently rocking from the sudden absence of Alain's bulk. He was moving decisively through his apartment, pulling a few things together: a manila envelope ("my last will and testament"), some keys ("this here's the truck, this here is to the bar, and that's the summer cabin on the Russian River"), a locked strongbox ("somebody oughta get rid of all this primo dope before the cops arrive"), and some jewelry ("won't ever have to pawn my diamonds to get out of the country now"). He sat on the edge of the bed and wrote a note on the manila envelope. "Harvey," it said, "you probably won't believe this, but it was the best time I ever had. Everything in here belongs to you. I love you, man, take care. Throw me a hell of a going-away party. p.s. Fire Billy." Alain signed his name, then went away, presumably to leave everything on the kitchen table.

He stuck his head in the door and gestured for Ulric to come out. "The light's better out here," he said. The kitchen was well-lit, furnished with a yellow Formica table and some buttercup yellow chairs that matched. "Pretty queeny, huh?" Alain said, and got him to sit down in one of the chairs. There was a surgical drape on the table, a needle, and a few different studs. "Stick out your tongue," Alain said, and grabbed it with a pair of forceps. The stick wasn't too bad. Ulric crossed his eyes so he couldn't see it coming. But it made his eyes tingle. The thick post in his tongue was a trip, the stud pressing against the roof of his mouth. He supposed he would get used to it in time.

"Now you belong to me," Alain said, clapping him on the shoulder. "You don't know how many times I've had men beg to wear my rings and be my property, Ulric. You are the only one who's gotten me to do it. Now a little bit of me will be with you every time you punch open some poor fucker's neck and drink him dry. Feed for my sake, buddy."

Alain just stood there looking at him, and Ulric felt unaccountably shy. "Thanks," he muttered, looking at the toes of his bare feet. Then he looked up at Alain again, and marveled at the man's sheer ballsiness. Anybody else who had heard Ulric's bad news would have shrugged it off. They would have preferred denial to a cold confrontation with the certainty of their own death. But Alain faced it the same way he had faced the revelation of Ulric, standing over a bled-white body, fangs out, hunger not quite sated. He saw things as they were, and if they were weird, that simply excited him. His first question about any novel fact seemed to be, What unique sexual opportunities lie in this bizarre event for me?

Ulric decided that he did not care if dawn was pending. He put away his own sorrow and sealed it in a deep, dark, faraway place. He could mourn later, when it would not taint Alain's last hours. It was the face he had seen bending over the boy's body in the alley that Alain wanted to see now. From somewhere, Ulric found the strength to become his most amoral, ferocious self. He was up off the chair and had Alain by the throat before the big man even saw him coming. "So you like to pick people up, " Ulric sneered, and lifted him with one hand. "You like to make other men think they are helpless." He shook Alain like a woman shakes out a tablecloth. "Let me show you what it's like to be helpless. Let me show you, oh, all kinds of interesting things."

They were back in the bedroom, and Ulric bound him facedown to the bed the way he had been bound to the wall, with chains wrapped around wrists and ankles and padlocked in place. The coroner wouldn't have to think much to figure out where those marks came from. He went to the cast-iron carousel full of whips and picked out a handful. Alain had good taste. There was no junk in his collection. Everything was well-made, the braids tight, the leather well cared for. Ulric had hidden out during the French Revolution in a brothel where he dressed as an aristocrat and flogged Citizen Liberté, Égalité, and Fraternité, who felt a little guilty about chopping off the king's head. It was pleasant to have such responsive whips in his hands again.

"I don't believe I asked for all this," Alain said menacingly from his spread-eagle position on the bed.

"Like I care," Ulric retorted, and lashed out. "You have wanted this from me since you first laid eyes on me. And you are not leaving this world until you have taken everything that I feel like handing out."

The beating he administered was thorough, but tempered with mercy. Alain did not have the experience or the tolerance of a devoted bottom. Still, he took more than Ulric would have gambled on. One of the things he loved about gay men in this city, and in this era, was their shamelessness. Top or bottom, when they saw or felt something they liked, they went for it wholeheartedly, without apology. Alain liked what he was feeling. Ulric worked him up to a frenzy, then tossed the whips aside, unchained him, and turned him onto his back.

"Are you ready?" Ulric asked, but Alain was already greasing up his cock, which responded as if it had not been milked dozens of times already this evening. Ulric settled on his knees between Alain's spread thighs, and rested the other man's feet on his own shoulders. "Just hang on me," he said. "Don't worry about holding yourself up. I'll hold you up."

Then he picked up Alain's torso, and slid him onto his cock. It was hot in there and tight, which pleased Ulric a great deal. Apparently

Alain had not been lying about the fact that this was a rare experience. "Does it feel good, baby?" he asked the other man, who had spread his arms out like Jesus on the cross.

"Yeah, oh, yeah," Alain moaned, eyes rolled back in his head.

"Think about this," Ulric warned. "Think about what you're giving up. This beautiful body that feels so good when I touch it here and pinch it here. The feel of my fat dick taking you on a good hard ride. My lips." He kissed the other man, broke off the kiss, fucked him a little harder, a little faster. "Can you say goodbye to all this? Because you don't have to, honestly. You can change your mind. Even now."

"Shut up and fuck me," Alain whispered. "Oh, my God, this feels so good I think I'm going to—"

"Die?" Ulric said.

"Come," Alain corrected. "Yes, baby, just like that, do me just like that. Oh, you are so good, such a stud. Now come on and kiss my neck. Right there, baby. Put your lips right there."

Alain suddenly shoved Ulric's head into his throat with all his might, and Ulric's reflexes took over. He bit deep, and gasped at the wealth that filled his mouth. Then a smack on his ass reminded him to keep his butt moving.

"Harder," Alain said, and Ulric didn't know if he meant the bite or the fuck, so he doubled the force of both, and Alain's cum spilled between their bellies as his life ran free and ran out into Ulric's grieving mouth.

He called the bar before he left Alain's apartment, and left an urgent message for Harvey. Then he carefully rifled the mind of everybody in the building and made sure they had seen and heard nothing, not even fucking. He got on his bike, and he rode away slowly, deliberately lagging until the sun came up and scorched his worthless hide. By the time he got home, he was burned all over, but he had no more tears. He thought he would never cry again.

He fell asleep clicking the ball in his tongue against the left fang, the right fang, the left fang again, a lonely little ditty that could only be played by someone whose mouth was not being glutted by Alain's voracious tongue.

After he relived Alain's last moments, Ulric came back into the present in a hotel bed with Lilith's unmistakably female body pressed up against his. He thrashed in her arms, disoriented and frightened. The taste and memory of Alain's muscles, furry chest, and thick cock were still palpable, temporarily making his lover into a stranger. The nearness of dawn was adding to his alarm. He had spent too much time with his mind linked to hers, burning through his vital energy as well as the past, and Ulric felt as if he needed to feed, even though there was no time to hunt and return to her.

She didn't even stop to think that with his greater strength, he might hurt her without intending to lash out so vehemently. Lilith's instinct was to protect him, to contain him and keep him from hurting himself. She wrapped him tighter in her arms and said, "Shussh, shussh," as if he were a child. But she did not offer him any platitudes or sympathy. He could not have borne such presumption. No one knew how he felt; the so-called cycle of grief had no end. No acceptance and no resolution. Alain's death had broken something inside of him, and it would never be whole again.

It was awful to cry when no tears would come to wash the grief from his heart. But he sobbed anyway, holding on to the tender nude skin of her breasts, his face pressed between them as if she could shelter him from the terrible truth of his own loss. There was a primeval comfort in kneading the resilient flesh of her bosom, and the dumb beaten animal within him was relieved to not be alone. Was it because she was a woman that she realized he needed physical nourishment as well as the shelter of her body?

"Don't let sleep find you starving," she said, and put her breast to his lips. "Take what you need from me, don't wander out-of-doors when you are in such a state."

The long-forgotten taste of Alain's slaughter was still fresh in his mouth. How could Ulric feed again on someone he loved? But she would not leave him be, and the third time she offered him her breasts, his instincts took over, and he punctured the lovely living cushion beneath his cheek. He blurred her pain and gave her pleasure instead, perhaps too much pleasure, because he needed to feel united with her in a fierce ecstasy, so that his own mind would be clouded enough to forget that she too would someday leave him. Goddess grant she would not contract a lingering, painful illness and need him to send her to the Land Behind the Moon. It would be a blasphemous reversal of the natural order of things for a man to sacrifice his feminine link to the divine.

Just before dawn captured his consciousness, a blood-drunk Ulric recalled that he did not have to go on living if he did not wish to. He could refuse to walk the earth alone, a solitary prisoner of the moonlight, when she was gone. Fortunately, the sun-struck stillness made him blank and cold before he could wonder if he should have left his own body in Alain's bloody bed, mute as the strong but sick man he had loved enough to kill.

Back in San Francisco, Rhys discovered that being in a twenty-four-hours-a-day, seven-days-a-week D/S relationship with a vampire dominatrix was hard labor. For all the footwork she did, she might as well have gotten a job chasing her own tail at Bad Boy Boots. At least in retail you got occasional breaks, days off, and an opportunity to appropriate the cash from fake returns or discover clothes that were determined to run away so they could live with you.

Adulfa had her patrolling the city like a damn Canadian Mountie trying to get his man. At least she didn't have to wear a stupid double-breasted red coat and a pair of jodhpurs. People got killed for dressing that way. Or if they didn't, they should.

Clad in her ragamuffin splendor, Rhys' long sapphire braid was seen at every leather bar, sex club, and S/M play party in town. She even sneaked into men-only places like Brothers Suck and the Libertine Lounge, but she suspected that was more for Adulfa's amusement than for genuine sleuthing. What would a guy with a hot chick like that blonde babe be doing haunting glory holes or slings? He'd find it as much of a turnoff as Rhys did. Well, there had been that cute chicken, that fat boy with a sparkly purple barrette in his hair. She'd lay odds he was still in high school. None of the older men would give Freckled Farmboy the time of day, but Rhys thought he looked like a good time. For somebody else, of course.

Adulfa said she had to get off the streets for winter and found her a room in a crazy cat-lady's house. Rhys scrubbed the room from floor to ceiling before she started dragging in furniture that other people had left on the street. Every time she left she padlocked the door shut so the cats wouldn't get in and ruin her bed. Adulfa made her dress warm, got her a leather jacket big enough to fit over a hoodie, put her in thermal socks and knee-high boots. Adulfa also made her eat. Three meals a day. It was enough to make you gag. Meat. Eggs. Cheese. Bread. Things Rhys the vegan had shunned for years. There was no way to cook in the cat lady's apartment, and Adulfa wouldn't give Rhys money. But there were three or four restaurants around town where she seemed to have an open account or something, because Rhys could walk in and order anything she wanted (or rather, what Adulfa wanted her to eat), and nobody ever brought Rhys a check.

The biggest drag was that it was all for nothing. She wasn't supposed to get herself noticed or lose her focus and actually party. It ran completely against Rhys' nature to enter a social situation without scoping out the foxes and blowin' shade at the other dudes. How could Adulfa expect her to ignore the short-skirted deliciousness that flaunted itself on dance floors or on stages with Saint Andrew's crosses? "It's not like I have a girlfriend," she had once sassed, and the punishment for that had involved way too many twenty-gauge needles and a staple gun.

Maybe she did have a girlfriend, Rhys mused. Adulfa was jealous enough of her time to be her sweetie. But who could use the word "sweet" in the same sentence with Adulfa's name? That was so not happening. Still for a butch who had fallen in love with straight razors and switchblades in junior high school, maybe that *was* sweetness. With a sour note of pain. If Adulfa was a drink, she'd make you choke and get you drunk on the first sip. And she wouldn't let you have more than one taste. Count on it.

But whoever Adulfa was looking for, he wasn't here. Day after day, he wasn't here and neither was his "hussy," as Adulfa termed her. Rhys thought displaying so much interest in your brother's love life was a sign of poor boundaries, but she wasn't about to tell somebody who could turn herself into a snake that there were places she shouldn't slither. Rhys happened to be afraid of snakes. And being tied up while a fourteen-foot-long boa constrictor as thick as her waist climbed her body like a tropical tree and French-kissed her while its muscular and inventive tail reamed out her ass had not been a sunny walk in the rainforest. Ecology be damned.

As Mordecai had once told her, "Check it out, bro. She is right and you are wrong. That's it. No appeal, no argument. Want love? Then prepare to be the stooge. Give her props while you take hold of the burning paper bag full of doggy doo. Because it's your job to be wrong, my man. Just remember, while she has you on the floor, you get to look up her dress."

That outrageous statement had proven itself to be true on many occasions. But there was a hell of a lot of difference between a girl who hung up the phone every time you called until you coughed up the cash to get her some roses and a girl who would take those roses and beat the skin off your back, then lick the blood off with a tongue that felt like a steel file. Not to mention what came next. *I am not tall enough to take this ride*, Rhys thought, *but here I go anyway. Wheeeeee! And I never even looked up her damn dress.*

Then came the night when Adulfa had said, "I'm leaving you." Tears of pain had turned to tears of fear and confusion. "Stop it," Adulfa had said irritably. "There's not enough moisture left in your veins for you to be able to spare water for tears. I won't be far away. But don't slack on your route, Rhys, because I will be watching you."

"Why?" Rhys asked, trying not to sob. She didn't want to ask if Adulfa was leaving because she'd done something wrong; she just assumed she had committed some misdeed.

"Because he's on his way. Him and that brown-eyed, blonde hussy. But her sweet tits and plump, pale behind will be mine to savor. And he will twist in the wind like a dope on a rope." She grabbed Rhys and dragged her near, close enough to smell her own blood in Adulfa's mouth. "And you will get him for me? Won't you?"

"Yes," Rhys said, and meant it. *But not his fluffy little sidekick,* she thought. *I'm not enough of a chump to hand you another girl, even if she is his bitch.* She meant that too.

Then Adulfa touched her mind. Cold twigs from a snow-covered tree grew arrow-fast into her brain, which made way for the intruders. *FIND HIM FOR ME. AND HER,* Adulfa said. *GO HERE AND HERE AND HERE AND HERE.* She repeated her instructions over and over again—or was that Rhys, chanting them mentally to herself?

Then the long-legged blonde terror was gone, and Rhys was in a cab that was taking her to yet another leather bar, sex club, or play party. She was about to see a level of sexual excess and deviance that would give Keith Richards a heart attack. Handsome men in full leather. Women in latex dresses. Engineer boots and high-heeled ballet slippers that kept the wearer on permanent point. Japanese bondage, corsets, clothespins, hot wax, ultraviolet wands crackling, caged slaves protesting, straps landing on cherry red butts, gags so big that they made their wearers cry, music so loud it shook your fillings into your boots, and hot cigar ashes falling into boys' mouths.

Life sucked bowling balls through a garden hose.

CHAPTER 9
Let Her Thighs Revive You

They got into San Francisco at midnight, entering the city via the Bay Bridge. Lilith was expecting to feel intimidated by this big city, but all she could see were the bright lights and skyscrapers of downtown. These old and new buildings were like a history of high-rise architecture. She admired the Transamerica Pyramid and the comparatively tiny but more explicitly phallic pillar of Coit Tower. They whipped across the wide span of the bridge, surrounded by only a little traffic, while Ulric talked about how much he loved this city. From time to time, he fell silent, and Lilith knew he was trying to contact his cats and let them know how close he was to home. For the last few nights he had been busy making phone calls and sending email, hiring people to clean the house and prepare it for their arrival, and making other, secret arrangements that seemed to make him both happy and nervous.

Lilith was sick of traveling. She wanted a place to unpack, even if she didn't have much to set out in a room to claim it as her own. She wanted to take a bath in a place where she had her own toiletries and a towel that wasn't coarse motel-issue white terry cloth, and sleep in a bed that didn't sag from contact with thousands of other people's weary butts. She wanted to cook a meal in her own kitchen, walk over to a familiar shelf of books and select something new to read, go out into a garden and pick some basil or rosemary or cut flowers for the table. Her shoulders ached from maneuvering the wheel of the swift little car. It had been tempting to let Ulric drive just this once, but he seemed too agitated, so she let him be the navigator. "After this, bucko, we're taking the train," she said, and he was so distracted by homecoming that he took her seriously and said reassuringly, "Of course, dear, of course."

He directed her off the main street and up a steep hill. His house was located on Woodhull Court, a relatively level cul-de-sac that branched off a street lined with bottlebrush trees. The long, bristly blossoms had left the streets coated with coarse, scarlet pollen. When she coasted to a halt in the driveway, he jumped out and found a hidden remote control for the garage in a fake rock along the base of the wrought iron fence. The spears of the fence had been painted a midnight blue, and the points were highlighted with gold. They parked the car inside the garage, next to his motorcycle, then closed the door so he could show her the front yard and facade of the three-story Victorian he'd been renovating for decades.

A series of steps with one switchback went up to the front door. The garden was terraced. As they passed various points on the stairs, floodlights automatically came on to highlight different parts of the garden. She saw a cluster of bright orange birds of paradise; a swathe of white, night-blooming lilies that emitted a sweet scent; tall Asian grasses, moss, and ferns grouped around river rocks and boulders; a small Japanese maple tree with purple leaves; and a veritable herd of elephant-ear plants with white stripes around the edges of their dark green, huge, glossy leaves.

When the house itself became more visible, Lilith felt as if she had already been there. She chalked this eerie moment of déjà vu up to the potency of Ulric's shared memories. The ornately carved wooden pillars of the entryway were wreathed by thick, hanging purple bougainvillea. He put a protective arm around her to keep the thorns at a safe distance. And while the house may have begun life as a Victorian, there was nothing staid about its color scheme. It was a cream and gold confection with green and purple accents that matched the bougainvillea, as if a carousel horse had been turned into a residence.

To her weary feet, the four steps up to the front porch of the house felt as tiring as the hill she had just climbed. "There's an elevator from the garage up to the other floors," Ulric said apologetically, sensing her body's protest. She nodded and said something to him about her fantasy about the house's bright colors. He giggled and took her up onto the front porch, then pointed to the secluded nook to the left of the front door.

A porch swing hung there, with two carousel animals for its supports. To her left was a pony, caparisoned for a gypsy. To the right was an ostrich escapee from the Dream Time. The black horse's saddle was made of braided, gaudy scarves, the ends of which seemed to blow free in the wind of its passage. Its sparkling, jeweled bridle was rich enough for a king's ransom, and a curved dagger hung to one side of the pommel. There was a leather bag full of stolen golden coins, or perhaps cards that would foretell the future, on its other shoulder. The dancing hooves were painted with flames, and the horse had a devilish look in his eye. This was a flesh-eater, a wild mustang, a horse as roguish as any fairy-tale Romany could be. The ostrich was white and silver. The saddle was made of bits of broken mirror. The stirrups that hung below its glittering saddle were shaped like human feet, and a didgeridoo was tucked on one side of its tackle. The bridle was made of plaited tropical flowers that were probably not native to Australia but looked very pretty. The enormous bird had a far-seeing look in its eye, too much intelligence for this bird to bury its head in the sand. The ostrich's feet looked lethal, and the legs were easily stronger than any man's. No human would be able to run fast enough to catch up with this striding bird.

They looked like museum pieces, but Lilith could not resist

touching them. Her hands were so tired of gripping a steering wheel. The irritated palms and aching fingers were soothed by the cool, thick enamel paint and smoothly carved wood. Ulric seemed delighted by the interest that she took in them. "I have a buyer on the lookout for a tiger," he told her. "When you've rested, maybe we can brainstorm about what to do with it. There's some space in the backyard. I thought of building a gazebo with carousel animals all around the sides."

"That would be something to see," she said. "How about a rotating gazebo or how about just setting up a merry-go-round? I'll sit on it."

Ulric laughed at the raunchy implication of her wiggling eyebrows and took her hand to draw her toward the front door. "If I don't introduce you soon, I'll make myself truly unpopular," he said. The door's gently aged brown wood framed an art nouveau stained glass window of dragonflies and narcissus. The dragonflies had subtly iridescent wings. The doorknob was ornate, cast metal but turned smoothly to admit them once he inserted and rotated the old-fashioned key. "There's a modern security system," he said under his breath, "but I had to install it without informing my roommates. They would have taken it as a personal affront. So I'll show it to you later."

"How could you have a better security system than this?" she asked as a posse of cats sauntered into view and struck various poses of indifference or outright disapproval. The first to break ranks was an adult but medium-sized Abyssinian who had a small diamond earring and eyes only for Ulric. After thoroughly cleaning both sides of her butt, she walked up to him and then sat, front paws in the air, clearly assuming he would pick her up. Lilith was approached by the other cats, but she gave them only cursory attention, not wanting to break protocol with the alpha feline. Besides, rushing to slather cats with petting and baby talk only insulted them. She knew enough to wait patiently while they smelled her and decided whether or not to arch their backs, indicating permission (if not an order) to be touched.

Luna kissed Ulric on one side of his face and then the other. Her purr was loud enough to be heard where Lilith stood, at a discreet distance away from her lover. This was the other woman in his life, and she wanted to be on friendly terms with her.

She startled when a regal female voice began reciting in her head something in a foreign language. From the images that accompanied the litany, she guessed that she was hearing ancient Egyptian. Luna was greeting Ulric with a poem or a prayer.

Lord, while you have lain in your coffin,
Slept in the tree that was hollowed out for you by your enemy,
The mother of waters has not risen to greet the shore.
No greenery spreads upon the parched land.

Your people perish.
Sand covers your monuments.

But now she comes:
Your sister, your bride,
Dressed in transparent linen,
Draped with necklaces of turquoise and gold.
She has hunted the earth to retrieve
The fragments of your being.
Let her set the missing piece into place,
Rise up for the sake of her love.

As the hawk above screams his triumph,
Let her thighs revive you.
Open your eyes so that you can see
The perfect breasts of the one who adores you.
Return to her, so the river will return to us.
Be as a very child at her breasts,
For those who drink the milk of Isis
Will live rejoicing, his souls united.

My beloved brother,
My virile husband,
My pharaoh of the abundant mane,
Let the lion's roar of your awakening pleasure
Shake the two kingdoms.
Take up your crook and flail,
Assume your crown,
Fill the lonely throne and let us see your countenance once more.
Your beauty is terrible as justice.

Live forever, my beloved.
She will defend you as the lioness defends her cubs.
She has power over the poison of the serpents that lurk in the
  swamps.
She utters the word that closes the malicious mouths of
Crocodiles, and sends away the lurking hippopotamus.
Assassins cannot outwit her;
The perfume of her lotus will render them insensible.

Enter the gate of your palace.
Here is your cup.
Here is my hand.
Here are your musicians and your ministers.

Be seated. Allow this perfume to cool your brow.
All this is your birthright.
Enter; let the order of nature be restored.

Lilith closed her eyes and allowed herself to enjoy the succession of images of the mourning of Isis and her resurrection of her murdered lover, Osiris, and his re-establishment upon the throne. When a suitable interval had passed, Lilith smiled at the loving pair, man and cat, and said, "You are indeed his savior. I am grateful to you for preserving his life." She came just an inch or two closer. The golden brindle cat stopped rubbing her face on Ulric's chest long enough to sniff at Lilith's offered fingers.

"Gratitude?" the cat scoffed. "This is a human feeling, I think."

"It means I intend to serve you as Ulric does," she replied quietly. "Though I am of course unworthy."

"I understand *unworthy*." The cat returned to giving Ulric her undivided attention. Lilith understood their audience was at an end, and she was at liberty to introduce herself to the others, a tiny tortoiseshell, a Russian blue who was almost as regal as Luna, and a longhaired black tomcat with a white ruff and paws.

She settled into an overstuffed burgundy armchair, noticing the Persian carpet on the floor, the fireplace well-stocked with tinder and three different kinds of hardwood, Ulric's harpsichord, and a sofa that matched the chair. The room was done to match the colors in the rug— tan, dark blue, maroon. The walls had been painted matte cream, but there was also a pattern embossed beneath it, white acanthus leaves with a glossy finish. You could not see them unless you looked at just the right angle. The ceiling was an upside-down sheet of wedding cake done in white plaster with a crystal chandelier in the middle. But at the moment, all the light came from floor lamps with art nouveau shades that complemented the front door. The moldings and wallboards were of maple.

The kitten jumped into her lap, but was offended by her slick leather miniskirt and bare thighs, and left the room, tail twitching. The Russian blue trailed the little cat, looking as concerned as a cat can. Not so easily deterred was Charley, who was broadcasting Roy Orbison's "Oh, Pretty Woman" as loud as a radio station. Lilith wondered if Ulric would have to give her lessons about how to modulate the cats' contributions to her stream of consciousness. Charley plunked himself down in her lap, providing welcome warmth. His weight seemed out of proportion to his bulk. He must be mostly hair. He spread his claws, letting her see the long tufts of fur on his toes, as he purred and drooled. Lilith got nothing from him like the cool complexity of Luna's priestess mind. "Love give love give," he chanted as he made biscuits in the air and his chest went *rrrrr Rrrrr RRRRRRR*.

When she actually touched him, Lilith was surprised to find that his fur was silky soft. His ecstasy when she scratched him gently behind the ear and under his chin overflowed the boundaries of his skull and made her feel as if the purr had been displaced behind her own breastbone. She was feeling as goofy as a college girl who'd killed a six-pack. Charley suddenly flipped himself over, assuming she would catch him, and Lilith found herself cupping his head and neck in one hand, kneading his shoulder muscles. His joy brought the beginnings of tears to her eyes. He regarded her with big baleful green eyes that defied her to stop touching him. His vampire teeth made him look quite sinister, but it was hard to remember how dangerous he was with pearls of drool regularly forming at the corners of his mouth.

Luna had arranged herself like a collar around the back of Ulric's neck. He was fussing around with a rag. "Dusty," he complained, dabbing at this and that.

"Stop," Lilith said. "You must have had a cleaning service come in, because it's immaculate."

"We'll see if they remembered to change the sheets," Ulric said darkly. "It wasn't easy to find help who would put up with this lot, you know. Don't let those cute little pointy ears and whiskers fool you. Lethal con artists in teeny fur coats, that's my kids. If they do in the staff one more time, I'll have to blackmail some brownies, and the Fair Folk don't like that, I'll tell you. Though you can't beat help who'll work for beer."

Wondering if he was kidding, Lilith went with him on a tour of her new home. He suddenly turned to her and said, "You don't *have* to live with me, you know. If you want another place, I can rent one for you." She squeezed his arm for the lovely thought, but being apart did not appeal to either of them. In between pointing out the stereo and other features of the living room, Ulric was apparently having a spat with Luna. Lilith could hear only one side of it. "About the kitten. Fine, Hecate. You promised me there wouldn't be any more," he said crossly. "You can't save every stray in town, dear. Yes, I know Anastasia is broody. But I really have to draw the line here, Luna. Oh, stop it, there aren't that many pit bulls out mauling children. How did you get access to the sex offender database? You know, some of those people haven't done anything wrong, they were just unlucky enough to stand next to a vice cop in a park. Well, who do you think you are, the Mod Squad?" He snorted, all the while continuing to pet the sand-colored cat he was wearing as a collar. "Cleopatra, Queen of Denial."

The fight ended when Lilith heard the cat say, this time in English, "A queen must have her court." Ulric had paused at the door to the kitchen. Its window depicted a woman like Botticelli's Venus solemnly offering an Easter lily to a regal stag. Lilith put Charley, who had been lying in her arms like a baby, carefully on the floor, where he began to turn figure eights around her ankles. She took Ulric's face in both of her hands and brought him down for a kiss. Luna slipped off his neck and onto a kitchen counter. "I already love this house almost as much as I love you," she whispered. "I think we're going to be very happy here."

"Do you really think so? I've told myself a million times I should sell this place, that it's too big and empty for one person. So it's become a bit of a museum, I think."

As Lilith inspected the kitchen, she was aware of Anastasia and the kitten regarding her from a safe distance. If Ulric had asked her point-blank, she would have had to agree that the room had a stage set quality. The appliances were beautiful—two huge modern stoves with six burners apiece, a refrigerator and a freezer, a convection oven, a dishwasher, and a butcher-block island. Copper, steel, and cast-iron pots and pans hung from ceiling racks. Knives were arrayed on a magnetic strip at one side of the island. It was a gourmet chef's dream workplace. But the chrome and pebbled gray surfaces looked as if they had never been touched. The utensils were department store bright, and there was no lingering aroma of garlic, cooked meat, vegetables, or other food.

Feeling uneasy, she went to the refrigerator and opened it. It had been stocked with butter, milk, eggs, and an array of other staples. Not a single carton had been opened, and all the groceries were lined up like toy soldiers in a shop window. She jumped when Ulric came up behind her and spoke in his melodramatic "I'm-Vincent-Price" voice. "What did you expect? An icebox full of red plastic bags from the blood bank?"

Lilith had become so accustomed to what he was that this made her laugh. "The thought did cross my mind," she confessed.

"Packaged blood is no good," he said. "You can survive on it, but not comfortably and not indefinitely. Even animal blood is better than human blood that has been processed."

"Why?" The librarian in her had taken control. Lilith really wanted to know. A part of her had assumed (or hoped) that once they had a stable location, he could quit hunting every night and rely on donated blood. Though she had no idea how you obtained such a thing without a trip to the emergency room in an ambulance. Stealing it or buying it on the black market would have its own perils.

"It has no *önd*," he explained. "Living things have a quality, a vitality that fades if they die or are separated from their source. Water fresh from a spring or lake has *önd*; bottled water, even Perrier, does not. Sap has it; maple syrup does not."

"Like a tree being different from a board in a lumber mill," she guessed.

He nodded and began walking toward the dining room. "Exactly. There's a bathroom there, by the way."

Sliding double doors separated the kitchen and dining room. Lilith looked up and saw a rose window, albeit not the size of the cathedral version, lit from behind. It threw deep hues of crimson, green, royal blue, and violet onto the pale table, large enough to seat twelve.

"It's made of pear wood," Ulric said. "And the sideboard is cherry."

"Lovely," she breathed, caressing the fine grain of the wood. A breakfront full of china stood on the wall opposite the sideboard. Both of these pieces were the dark purplish-red of cherry wood, with mother-of-pearl inlays. The floor was inlaid parquet wood, also of cherry and pear. "Could we have a really elegant dinner party?" she begged. "This is such a wonderful setting for it. Do we dare?"

"I dare anything for you, sweetheart," he replied. "But I'm afraid I don't have much experience with such things."

"Me either. But I bet I could learn." Lilith circled the room, savoring the four windows that depicted a dragon, a unicorn, a griffon, and a mermaid. The dragon looked like it was trying to get the last delicious bite of roasted knight out of an iron gauntlet. On the unicorn's wall, the virgin had taken out a sword to protect her odd consort, who had a goat's beard. The griffon was coming to life, as if it were emerging, stone turning to flesh and blood, from the gate of a Babylonian city. With one hand, the mermaid poured tea for a drowned sailor she had dressed in a dozen necklaces, while her other hand held up a mirror so she could regard her own impish countenance.

"You won't make me write out two hundred invitations by hand, will you?" Ulric pleaded. He had his fill of the social whirl during the Regency period in England. Had there really been a time when his day was ruined if he did not have a brand new pair of kid gloves each morning? And what was he thinking, wearing yellow pants and a vest with a maroon-and-white-striped lining? But that was then—he had to come back to the present.

Lilith silently counted the seats at the table and shook her head. "Less than a dozen," she said, "because you and I will sit at the head and the foot of the table. The flowers and candles will be arranged so that I can still see your face, and we will quietly flirt with each other while our guests rave about the food and make elegant small talk with each other. Everyone will be beautifully dressed. There will be place cards and handwritten menus. Napkin rings. Napkins! Linen napkins! No—damask. I have no idea what the difference is but I want them anyway. They sound more luxurious."

He nodded as if he were making note of each detail of her fantasy. Knowing Ulric, he probably was doing exactly that. She could imagine him looking up all the rules in Emily Post about how to do such things properly.

"Yes, I actually have a copy in here," Ulric said, and went through a discreet door into a large room behind the dining room. This one really took Lilith's breath away. It was a library, an old-fashioned study with a mahogany desk and two big, comfortable brown leather chairs. The lamps had beaded shades. There was a rug on the floor that laid out the pattern of a labyrinth. The back wall of the library had sliding-glass doors that opened to a patio, which was screened from the neighbors' view by potted bamboo plants that had grown as tall as Ulric. "I thought we could put your desk here," he said, coughing politely first to get her attention. "Or if you like we could turn one of the upstairs bedrooms into an office for you. There's room in this house for all of the books you might want for yourself."

She stood at the doorway, gaping. When she gave Ulric her heart and her hymen and left her job, she had believed that she was giving up her beloved sanctuary of learning. Now it had been returned to her. It made her want to cry. Ulric steadied her elbow. They were both very tired, he reminded her as he led her back to the staircase. "Let me show you what's above," he said. They took the carpeted stairs slowly, arm in arm, trailed by a pack of cats. "I could use a shower," Lilith confided. "Or even a nice, hot bath."

The cats registered their disapproval of that notion but also a voyeuristic fascination with the funny pink skin that naked humans wore and their fondness for being immersed in water. "Sounds like they'll help me to give you a bath," Ulric said. "Won't you, kids?"

The cats disappeared. Later, Lilith realized they had gone into one of the front bedrooms, which was fitted out as a cat entertainment center, with a complicated jungle gym, a tropical fish tank, a television that played nothing but DVDs of birds in flight, and a computer that was logged on to a mouse warren's webcam. When the cats became bored, they could tap the keyboard and change the program to cartoons in which dogs met horrible ends.

At the head of the stairs, all she could see for now was an open area containing gym equipment. Did vampires need to exercise? She couldn't imagine being lonely or bored enough to pump iron. But she wouldn't mind seeing Ulric doing it, especially if he had a handsome friend to spot for him. The doors to the two front bedrooms were on the far side of this indoor version of Venice Beach. "Sauna," Ulric said, pointing to a redwood closet. "Shall we go left to the master bedroom, or straight into the elevator so I can show you the dungeon that's behind the garage?"

"The master bedroom," Lilith said, suddenly shy. She took his hand, and he gently squeezed her fingers. "Will you introduce me to the dungeon properly, in a day or two, when I'm not so limp and woozy?"

"Count on it," Ulric said. "Do you think you can get some rest in here?" He opened the door of a huge bedroom. Its walls were covered in raw yellow silk. Lilith had to touch the slubs in the fabric, irregular bits of texture in the weave. The carpet was a cream-colored Berber, soft and thick enough to give palpably beneath her feet. She took off her shoes so she could walk on it barefoot. The walls were decorated with nineteenth-century Japanese prints of famous actresses, and drawings of cats in repose, hunting, or bathing their young. A carved four-panel screen depicting the seasons set aside a private space for a vanity table. There was a walk-in closet for Ulric's clothes. The other was stuffed with a wardrobe for her that would take a week just to try on. "I gave your sizes to my personal shoppers at Nordstrom's. North Beach Leather too, I think. There's a wonderful Italian shoe shop on Hayes Street where they picked out some boots and high heels. Dark Gardens made corsets to match your dresses. I called up Mister S for something fun and butch. I'd love to see you in that pair of chaps. If anything doesn't fit or you don't like it, we can return it."

So this was the surprise that had him so jumpy and yet pleased with himself. "Hmm," Lilith said thoughtfully, thinking that the closet looked as big as the living room in her old apartment. "My favorite boutique is Target." She pronounced it *Tar-jay*.

Ulric laughed. "Yes, I've got things from that couturier, and from the Mart brothers, Kay and Wal, as well. But I want the best for you. I want to spoil you with expensive things." He went into the bathroom and turned on the taps of a large marble tub. "Let's get you into the water jets," he said, returning, and began undressing her. Lilith suddenly felt rancid from travel, and almost wanted to push him away, afraid she smelled sour. But he was persistent, and she reminded herself that he hadn't been forced to take off her clothes. "I'm so tired my manners are disappearing," she said, scolding herself. "Ulric, I love all those beautiful clothes. Thank you for being so considerate. But you're scaring me. How rich can you be?!"

He laughed again, shaking his head at her class consciousness. While they waited for the sunken tub to fill, he led her to the bed and helped her up into it.

The bed frame was made of carved black Chinese lacquer. It looked like an elaborate flower cradling the oval mattress. The sheets were the color of parchment, and the bedding was topped with a black satin, embroidered duvet cover that depicted at least a dozen groups of people enjoying various carnal pleasures. A woman in a swing was preparing herself to enjoy the erect cock of her suitor in a scene near Lilith's elbow. The two lady's maids who were pushing her toward the rampant man had discreetly covered their eyes with fans.

Black nylon rope was threaded through openings in the carving at the four corners of the bed. Ulric showed her the toys hidden in drawers along the sides of the bed, and the lights in the headboard. He stretched her out with her back upon the satin and pressed his body against hers, loved her with his hands and mouth. As absorbed as she was in the pleasure he gave her, Lilith still had a glance or two around the room, and noticed that in one corner there was a heavy wooden beam three-quarters of the way up to the ceiling, perfectly positioned for Japanese bondage. She had seen intriguing pictures of girls suspended from beams like that with artful twists and coils of rope. Hanks of the same kind of rope, a mellow gray brown color, were looped around the plain, heavy beam.

Every sigh he heard from her, the way she closed her eyes and turned her head away when she began to get aroused, the contours of her upper arms, collarbones, waist and hips, seemed to imprint itself deeply on Ulric's soul. He tried to memorize every variation in her face and body, but there was no way to keep pace with the detail and variety of her. It was as if she were a hundred different women, and he fell in love more deeply with each one he saw and caressed.

Charley insinuated himself between the two of them, breaking the mood. Luna said crossly, "Drown yourselves if you like, but please don't flood the house." Anastasia was at the foot of the bed. She had one paw on the tortoiseshell kitten Hecate, and was washing her face. Ulric slid off the bed, careful not to dislodge them, and hurried to turn off the taps. Lilith followed, and he eased her into the white marble tub. The bathroom was tiled in cobalt blue and white, and the faucets looked like silver swans.

"Come in with me," she said sleepily, and he shed his boots, leather pants, and T-shirt then tested the temperature with one toe. "Don't be such a big chicken," she teased.

He folded his arms at the elbow, flapped his "wings," and cawed. "How did chickens get a reputation for cowardice when men will bet on two roosters fighting to the death?" he asked indignantly.

"It was a rhetorical question, and I'm too wet to look that up for you," she said, gathering a cloud of bubbles on the palm of one hand. She blew them at him, and a cluster of frothy soap wound up on his beard. He laughed and turned to get a nylon net pouf and a bottle of peppermint soap, then drifted through the water and began to gently wash her.

"Don't go out tonight," she said suddenly, opening her eyes. Ulric jumped and dropped the blue pouf. It floated away, buoyantly entertained by the four whirling jets of water that circulated through the tub.

"What are you saying?" he asked, feeling addled and a little embarrassed.

"You haven't taken anything from me for a long time," she replied, studying his face. She swam toward him and embraced him, took his cock and balls in one hand and squeezed him just enough to get his attention. "I don't think it would harm me if you—if we—" He turned his back to her so he could switch the jets to high. They were surrounded by vigorously bubbling water. He kept his back to her. "Ulric!" she warned, pursuing him. "Don't you want me?"

"Want you?" He shifted to kiss her, his tongue conveying the subtle madness of his desire. Releasing her, he repeated, "Want you?"

She had retrieved the bathing accessories and scrubbed his chest, gesturing for him to raise his arms so she could rub the minty soap into his armpits. With fingertips on his shoulders, she pressed him under the water to rinse himself off.

"You should have everything you want," she said softly, embracing him from behind, her hands tracing the shape of his pecs, his nipples. She switched off the jets, climbed out of the tub, and wrapped herself in a plush gray bath sheet. He came after her, so mesmerized by her naked body that he would have forgotten to dry himself off if she hadn't wrapped him in his own oversized towel.

He lifted her off her feet and carried her to the high, elaborately carved bed. Their towels cast aside, he tossed her onto the memory foam mattress, and she drew the coverlet to her, trying to conceal herself again. "No," he said, and hid her body with his own. He had his arms around her torso, and his legs pinned the rest of her to the bed. She struggled against him, exciting both of them, and watched his face become more and more intent upon possessing her. With one hand, he positioned her head, licked her exposed neck. Lilith moaned, suddenly afraid to stand by her offer. "Shall I get you a black velvet choker to cover the marks of my fangs?" he asked.

She was shivering. "I don't care if everyone sees them. I'm proud to belong to you."

"But we must keep ourselves safe," he reminded her.

"To hell with safety!" Her eyes were full of scorn and need.

"I—want—you—so," he panted. Ulric licked her again, his tongue scraping up her salty scent and taste. The skin was powdery soft between her earlobe and shoulder. The tendons below the surface would be so satisfying to take between his teeth for a judicious grinding bite. "Do you shiver because you're frightened?"

"Yes, of the pain," she admitted.

"I can take all of your pain away," Ulric offered her. Lilith. His slave. She was doing something for him that had not been done for hundreds of years, voluntarily giving up her blood to nourish his immortality. Because she trusted him to care for her, to provide for her, because she was loyal to him and loved him. Had taken him for her own just as surely as he had claimed her.

"Take *all* of the pain away? What fun is that?" she retorted bravely.

"You want it to be real?" he asked, sounding mean. His teeth worried her earlobe. She screamed, and that triggered an almost involuntary attack. Ulric slapped her head to the side with one hand and pulled her shoulder down with the other. His long canines went into her thin, downy skin, fangs not quite as sharp as razors, so the wound felt like flesh tearing as well as the sensation of being sliced open. Face-first in the fountain of her life, Ulric reminded himself he must regain control. This was not a victim who wanted or deserved to die. Then Lilith said, "Be sure you take enough," and he almost lost it again. It was the quaver of fear combined with resolute masochistic tenderness in her voice that brought his predatory need to the fore once more.

But another intensely pleasurable sensation burgeoned, pulling him away from a terminal feast of her hot, tangy blood. She had, despite his greater weight and size, managed to separate her legs. The wet fur of her cunt teased his wolfish hard-on. While he continued to drink, Lilith brought their sexes together, united their bodies. It was excruciating to have her love, her blood, and the rut all together in one bed. Ulric lifted his head and moved to kiss her. Lilith hesitated for a moment, then accepted contact with his bloody muzzle. When he caught himself thinking of his own face this way, Ulric wondered how close the real wolf in him was to emerging. Feeling a little scared of himself and cruel, he did not heal her wound. As he penetrated her with his cock, he paused from time to time to worry it open again. "Don't fight me," he warned her. "I am barely able to contain myself and remember that I love you."

She held still, breathing hard, but his hips threw her back into the bed, again and again. The resilient mattress mimicked the responsiveness that she would have demonstrated if he had given her liberty to move. Crazed by the soft domes of her breasts moving against his thickly furred chest, Ulric turned his attention to them and left her neck alone. Lilith stifled a terrified impulse to press one of her hands to the gouges there. If she behaved as if he was bound to eventually heal her and keep her alive, it would increase the odds of Ulric remaining in touch with his pledge to cherish her. She licked her dry mouth, feeling feverish and frightened. It was humiliating to be aroused by a man who could treat her with such disregard, as if she were nothing more than a thing to be consumed. But when the awareness of that feeling of humiliation intensified her need for him and her enjoyment of him, how could she ever escape it? And wasn't there something special about being able to stand up to him this way, to pit her mortal frailty against his centuries of slaughter? Did she feel shame or triumph over it? Was she supposed to be able to feel her own cunt getting wetter, and then wetter still? Was that physically possible?

"Come and get what *you* want," he told her. They came together, clawing at each other. Ulric urged Lilith to bite him, twisted one of her nipples and told her he would keep increasing the pressure until she sank her teeth into him, but she refused, and distracted him by clamping her vaginal muscles around his cock, again and again, hard enough to make him cry out. Once more, Ulric was angry and frustrated by her refusal to save herself from death.

Lilith had other things on her mind. "Hurt me with your cock," she hissed, writhing, and he changed the angle of his thrusts to accommodate her whim for pain. How did men ever make love to women, he wondered, if they could not read their minds? His body was giving back to her, returning the gift of blood with his gift of sensation. "You'll never be happy with a mortal lover," he told her, wanting it to be true. "Not after this. Not after you've experienced everything that I can do to you."

"No," she agreed. "No one else can do what you can do to my mind. And my body. And my heart. I hate you! Oh—I—I hate you so much I could die."

"No, you don't," he chastised her, fucking harder. "Tell me you love me. You know you're not going to be able to come until you admit it. You can't resist me. *Say it.*"

She threw her own arm across her face, bit deep into her flesh to keep the words from crossing her lips. He was twisting her other nipple, and to her, both of them felt as big as the balls of his thumbs. Lilith could smell her own drying blood; knew that when they stopped having sex, the pain would be hard to ignore. Oh, God, the things he could do with his cock! "Hate," she managed to get out.

Ulric dragged her arm away from her face and held her hands down. "Beg me for the privilege of telling me you love me," he said, coldly pleased with himself for escalating the game.

"No!"

"Do you know what it feels like to be right on the edge of coming, to have that first contraction happen, and then the sex stops, and all of a sudden there's nothing, and the biggest orgasm in the world has been put on hold, while your whole body is screaming for relief? Do you?"

"Yes, damn you!"

"Uh huh. Because I've showed you what that feels like, haven't I? Yes, I have. So do it. Because the next time I slide into you, you are going to turn, that wave is going to build and try to crest."

"No, please, I beg—I do, I beg."

"The whole thing, girl. Chapter and verse."

"I beg you, please, let me tell you how much I love you."

"Show me. Don't tell me. Show me."

After that climax had come and gone, Ulric held himself back, attending to her until she was sated. He allowed himself to ride a wave of sensation to its completion just as she pushed at him, no longer playing the erotic game of frightened victim, and said, "Enough. Please. Enough." Ulric gave himself up to enjoying his own release, then thought what a shame it was that vampirism dried up a man's spunk. He wondered if giving her his cum would have the same effect as feeding her his blood. But was he ready to have this be the last time he ever caressed or fucked her?

He rolled away from her, sat, and propped her up on pillows and cushions. But he left the two puncture marks on her neck intact. "Stay here," he said, and went down to the pristine kitchen. She didn't even have the energy to wonder what he did there. But when the cats lined up, eager to make her intimate acquaintance, she gingerly touched her fingertips to her bloody neck and allowed each of the cats to lick up the scarlet traces of Ulric's only sustenance. Even the feral kitten approached to accept her homage, and then they arranged themselves in various positions close to her legs, cuddling up to her and protesting if she moved a hair. When Ulric returned, she had gathered enough energy to pet Charley and Luna, who were the closest to her hands.

He had brought her a chilled mound of freshly ground, raw beef, toast points, and a cup of tea. The peak of the steak tartare had a raw egg yolk in its center, and a moat of capers was heaped at its feet. Ulric settled a breakfast tray on her lap, dislodging the cats, and curled up next to her to feed her one delicious spoonful after another.

"I know what you're doing," she said when the tea had cooled enough to take a sip. Black Earl Grey with one spoonful of sugar.

"Expose my skullduggery, then," he invited, jauntily waving the spoon.

"You're just building up my blood so I can feed you again."

"Yes," he said, glancing at her neck. "Should I apologize? Did I frighten you?"

"Never explain and never apologize," she quoted. "Whoever said that had a perfect strategy for modern life. You did scare me and hurt me. But I liked it. I love the fact that you're so quick and strong, you could take me against my will."

"I think you want a bad man who will just be nice to you," he teased.

"Well—not too nice." She looked at his face, touched his bare, hairy chest. "I never thought I would like a man this much. I wasn't about to let myself feel desire. But if and when I did, I couldn't imagine being so attracted to maleness. Your furry chest, your big shoulders, your beard—they all turn me on so much I think I'll go crazy just watching you walk across the room. I get wet just watching you climb the stairs, do you know that? The way you strut and stalk, the pride in your stance, the danger that surrounds you." She leaned forward and kissed him, wincing as her neck creased. "No, leave it alone," she said, responding to an unspoken question. "I want to know what it feels like."

"So...did you ever think you would love women instead of men?" he asked, chasing the last caper around with the spoon and a judicious fingertip.

"Mmm. Good question. I don't know. I fantasized about it sometimes. But sex between two girls was supposed to be so gentle and equal, I guess I never constructed an erotic image of a woman who was dominant. If I was bisexual, don't you think I would have created an imaginary woman I could think about when I masturbated? But I don't think I can say no to any possibility, Ulric. Do you want to see me with another woman?"

Ulric disapproved of the Western male's preoccupation with "lesbian" pornography. He'd been taught to keep his nose out of women's affairs. "I think you should do whatever pleases you," he replied. "I don't know how I'd feel about it. I know what another man can do for you, so in some ways I feel less competitive about that. I can beat another man at the Casanova game, but I couldn't be a woman for you. But if you wanted another girl, it would make me happy to get her for you or let you go and get her yourself. As long as I wasn't going to be replaced as your first and best sweetheart."

"No. Not ever." She drank some more tea and declined the last bite of food. "Ulric, there are clubs here in San Francisco, aren't there?"

"All kinds of clubs, my lovely. Golf clubs, club feet, police truncheons, a club for gay fathers who collect stamps."

She cuffed at him. "You know what I mean. Clubs where people go who are like us. Who make love the way that we do."

"Yes."

"I want to go to them."

"Very well. Once we get some clothes for you and I put your name on my bank accounts, we can scout out the local scene."

Lilith pawed at the covers, made an opening, and slid in between the sheets. "Luscious bed. I'll sleep for a week." Ulric settled beside her, wanting to watch over her sleep. There was enough time for him to retire to one of the secret, fireproof crypts he had built into the house. But before she slept, Lilith unsettled him again, reminding him why he had fallen in love with her. "Do you ever think that maybe you're supposed to be an elder, even if you don't think you can do it?" she asked, half asleep. He loved the slightly lower voice she spoke in when she was drowsy.

"Lilith, the Boar People are gone. I would be an elder without a tribe."

"Okay, but that *is* what you are now. The elder of an extinct nation.

I can't believe you've survived this long without learning anything useful. Tribes can be founded as well as extinguished."

"I suppose they can," he said, truthfully agog, and fussed with the sheets around her shoulders.

"Just let me take a little nap and I'll go find a damn tribe for you," Lilith said, woozily belligerent. "The Old Religion isn't dead quite yet."

"Sleep first," Ulric said. And for once in their relationship, she did as he bid her, without putting up a fight.

He took a long flannel nightshirt out of his closet and donned some tube socks. After bumming around for so long, and then road-tripping with his new lover, it felt a little silly to pick up his old domestic routines. But he hated waking up with cold feet. Only someone with the aplomb of Bela Lugosi could go to sleep in a tuxedo without looking like an ass. He was tempted to remain with Lilith, but she didn't like seeing him in daytime catatonia, even though she was too sweet to say so out loud. He thought he would take up the false bottom of the elevator and sleep in the niche there. Might as well take a comforter from the closet too.

Before he left the bedroom, he went to Lilith's side and put his hand on her forehead. He skated upon the surface of her mind, not hard to do when the two of them had been joined physically just a short while ago and her blood was sizzling in his veins. She accepted him as her partner for a dance across the ice, nothing to hold them up but the knives on their feet as they twirled and jumped in graceful defiance of winter. He had to go only a bit deeper to instruct her to sleep a little past the time when evening would awaken him, so that he could come back to her. That way she would not wake up alone with the injuries from the night before.

It was hard to resist the temptation to tell her neck to begin to heal as well. But she had said she wanted to know what it felt like, so he abstained. Hopefully she would feel differently about it in the morning. However, if she wanted scars, that was her affair. He had been born in a time when women were proud of their scars and men did not shudder at the proofs of female bravery.

As he arranged his quilt on the floor of the elevator compartment, then stretched himself out and fit the panels back over his head, Ulric thought how bright the house seemed with Lilith in it. She had brought color and excitement into rooms that had merely been pretty or expensive before. Perhaps he had been designing this house for her all along, without knowing it. His mind was full of endless lists of things to get for her or changes to make to the house to accommodate what he knew of her taste. This house was Art Nouveau Central. What would she make of the ultramodern New York City penthouse with all the post-Impressionist artwork? Or the villa on Crete? Could he manage an ocean cruise with her? Feeding arrangements would be tricky. How many passengers would the ship need to carry for, say, a two-week jaunt?

Just before the sun came up, he heard a small body scratching its way through the ventilation duct. To his surprise, a tortoiseshell kitten settled on his head, made a nest for herself out of his long hair, and fell asleep with her claws in his scalp, just as he himself lost track of the story of time.

CHAPTER 10
Transubstantiation

In the days (or rather, the nights) that followed, Lilith found herself in a life that she could not have imagined. She was constantly in the company of a man she loved who was, if it was possible, even more in love with her. She barely had time to form a clear picture of a fantasy or a need before he had intuited it and arranged it for her. The library was rearranged to accommodate her literary tastes, and a desk and computer for her use were set up there, across from his own. She had vaguely imagined that some business matters would be difficult for him to arrange with his nocturnal lifestyle. There were a few daylight matters he delegated to her. But for the most part it seemed that the rules that applied to working people did not apply to the rich.

Ulric had made money as a lark (albeit one that had lasted several centuries). For when the moon's rise forced his eyes open each night, the hunger was so strong that it could override virtually any other thought. And the pleasure that came from feeding was strong enough to tempt an immortal to continue to hunt even if enough blood had been taken to live another day. But Ulric had bent his will toward mastering the instinct to feed. The elders of his people had not been wanton killers, and they had participated in every aspect of the tribe's life. He, too, would have something besides a belly full of blood to occupy his hours—even though he had often felt empty and depressed once he had accomplished whatever task he set for himself. Lilith empathized with his drive to hang on to some portion of his humanity and make productive use of the attenuated span of his life.

There were phases when he sought out the most chaotic part of the world, and used the ugliness of battle or famine to hide his activities. He lived sparely then, trying to give himself up to the cycle of sleep and rapacious consumption of blood, willing his vampiric instincts to quiet his conscience and his loneliness. He realized at some point that wealth created even more freedom of movement and camouflage than a nation given over to genocidal fury or civil war. He did not forbid himself the option of bumming around, mimicking a thoughtless killer. But he had also entertained himself by creating sanctuaries for himself wherever he could, so that when he could not bear the stench of human misery, he could retreat into a place where there was more beauty, if not just as much unhappiness.

Ulric didn't really need anything other than a dark nook in which to hide during the day. Lilith gathered that this was how his fearful sister Adulfa preferred to live. Professing to hate everything human, she usually kept no home of her own, but lodged in hollow trees or attics. Nevertheless, she did venture into cities from time to time and so Ulric had arranged accounts for her. Each time he changed his legal identity, he made another available for her as well. The majority of his gifts she disdained, but there were occasional withdrawals from ATM machines or safe-deposit boxes that indicated Adulfa had found it more convenient—or amusing—to pay for something rather than to compel some human to give it to her.

Ulric put Lilith's name on all of his accounts and set aside some independent sources of income that she could rely on regardless of what happened to their relationship. She now had access to funds in every major city in the world. Furthermore, she learned, he was obtaining a selection of false identities for her. She wanted to ask him why this was necessary, but he seemed to believe it was a sensible and important security precaution to take, so she did not object.

It was disquieting but liberating to know that Mary Beth Wolcott was about to drop off the grid and a multitude of aliases were waiting like cloned bodies to take her place. When she described this image to Ulric, he said, "Actually, that might attract too much attention. You are living in Portland, Oregon right now and working for the post office. There will be just enough activity in your bank records, credit cards, mail, and other traceable factors to make it look like you just moved to another city where you resumed a quiet life. A conscientious investigator would be able to see through that deceit, but I would be alerted in time for us to evade confrontation."

"Why is it so important to keep anyone from finding me?" she asked. The look he gave her, kind but grave, told her she was being naïve. "If they find you, they can find me," he replied. "And an injury to you is an injury to me. So I must protect you the same way I protect my own life."

They visited expensive department stores after hours, where personal shoppers had set aside a selection of clothing, shoes, and accessories for her to try on. He made appointments with fetish shops, a tailor, and a dressmaker, to ensure she would have a wickedly varied wardrobe of leather, latex, and Victorian fashion. Since corsetry was so important to their romance, Ulric had period clothing made for himself as well, and this was what they wore at home and eventually at the clubs as well.

If she wanted to, Lilith could do nothing at all but entertain herself and her master. After a young adulthood spent in secular monasticism, Lilith waded eagerly into a life of luxury, rest, and sensual gratification. She feared that this easy dedication to loveliness and passion would only be a brief respite, but she honestly hoped it would never end. What was wrong with spending a day rearranging the cats' gymnasium, ordering dinner, or cooking, sewing a little, reading, watching movies, or working in the garden? It wasn't as if Ulric didn't work her hard when he arose and made his will clear to her.

There were times when she felt as if she were all erogenous zones. Practical use did not define any part of her body. Her feet were not for walking, they were for being massaged or fitted into high heels or rolled steel fetters. Her legs were not there to support her body; they were for being spread apart so that her inner thighs could be caressed and her sex forced open. Her belly, lower back, and upper arms were covered with skin that yearned for his touch. Her mouth was for kissing him, sucking him — not for speech, unless it was the talk that excited him, the false and genuine pleas for mercy, the shameless begging to kiss his boots or lick his balls, the profane chant to urge him deeper into her ass. Her nipples had become as much a sense organ as her eyes and ears. They seemed to sense his presence and felt as if they began to glow whenever he was near.

Books were no longer her most important source of knowledge. His body was her field of study. His body and her own. One day she would perfect the choreography of throwing one leg over his body, kneeling astride him, and rising slightly to take his cock and ride him while he watched her moan and sweat. There were a dozen ways to walk toward him when he summoned her, thirty ways to kneel, a hundred ways to look up at him from the floor. She had never felt graceful or deft before, but his response to her movements — a catch in his breath, widened eyes, an admiring shake of the head — made her for the first time in her life into an unself-conscious animal, happy in her body. She didn't lose touch with her intelligence. Instead a whole other joyous set of abilities was added to her power of rational thought. The knowledge contained in her body shocked her. How had she ever lived without this sensory richness? Her constrained life had been impoverishing indeed. The self she had known all too well before had quadrupled in scope, and given her a wisdom that made her almost as powerful as Ulric.

That tall, dark-haired man would awaken at dusk, go out to feed, and then return to rouse her. Sometimes he left her to sleep in a cage in the dungeon, and she would have to scheme to win his mercy and release. (She came to relish the feel of cold steel bars on either side of her ass, holding her open, while what felt like a molten rod of steel moved inside of her.) Sometimes Ulric concealed his presence in the room, sliding into bed behind her as she slumbered on her side. She would wake up with his cock churning inside her, wake up on the brink of an orgasm in a strange between-time when she was not sure who or where she was. Once he held her naked in standing bondage and made her come without touching her. Over and over again, until her cunt was as numb as her hands. That was one of the most frightening things he had ever done—shown her that he held enormous power over her that he usually chose not to wield. He could make her feel excruciating pleasure by merely looking at her and willing it to be so.

What terror, then, might his displeasure hold? She knew even when he fed from her, at carefully spaced intervals, that she had no idea how it felt to be hunted by him when he was in earnest. And this was one game he would not play; she had been punished soundly for making suggestive comments about whether she should dress in pitiful grubby rags or whorish elegance so he could feign being Jack the Ripper on the prowl, coming at her through the fog. It was his Victorian dress coat and top hot that put her in mind of that scenario. He had stayed away one entire night, and would not, when he returned, discuss the matter again.

Lilith felt she had to become the perfect submissive because Ulric was the perfect master. He never forgot a rule or a promise, and he was alert to every nuance of her acquiescence or resistance. The microscopic accuracy of his empathy made him a devious and devastating sadist. Lilith gave herself up to his imagination. He usually restricted himself to whips and clips and the other standard S/M paraphernalia. But he could also do things beyond the power of a mortal master. There was a night when he took her to the ocean and made her walk into and under the water. He allowed her to imagine she had drowned, then resuscitated her from that terror and took her for a walk along the bottom of the sea. With Ulric at her side, she could be an eagle or a mermaid, both slave and princess, one night hung from flesh hooks and another night healed, depilated, dipped in chocolate, and given to the tongues of every tourist in Ghirardelli Square.

But most importantly of all, he loved her. He was the perfect immortal companion, knowing when to leave her alone, when to chase her and tickle her, when to spank her and when to make gentle love to her. Lilith would have died for him. Had he not already died for her, and lived for long, lonely centuries without knowing her love was waiting for him?

It was the strength of the bond between them that made Lilith feel safe about venturing into gay men's leather bars with him. She was never in any danger, and Ulric was entertained by her fantasies about being exposed in public or used by more than one person at the same time. She also wanted to test her dream of finding a group of people who could be trusted with the truth about Ulric's nature. A pool of willing volunteers would be less demanding for him than a nightly search for the appropriate target. He was so skeptical about her dream of creating a tribe that she hesitated to explore it with him. In the Falcon's Roost and the Galley, they did find men who were willing to let Ulric feed from them, but they thought it was simply very heavy "edge play." They didn't know their blood provided the longhaired, green-eyed man in well-aged and oiled leather with more than a dangerous cock-throb. Ulric allowed them that illusion.

Lilith could admit only to herself, not Ulric, that she was searching for her own replacement. If anything should happen to her, she didn't want him to be alone again. Since a man had preceded her in his affections, it seemed to her that a man should be her understudy for his love. She was young still, but accidents happened. By the time she was in her fifties, she must have some ingénue in her stable, learning her master's ways. Perhaps she should find him a pair of lovers, a master and slave who would gratify both aspects of his erotic abilities and needs.

There was only so much that could be learned from reading about S/M (or BDSM or D/S, as it was more commonly called) in books or on the Internet. It seemed silly to cultivate acquaintances via email when she lived in one of the largest kinky communities in the world. She attended a few men's parties under Ulric's veil of invisibility, but it was not the ideal situation for finding men who would accept her as part of their intimate network. So she compiled a list of groups that met to discuss bondage and other kinds of kinky sex and asked Ulric if they could attend. If people were willing to join a group, maybe they had put more time into thinking about the politics of sex than most of the men and women they encountered at play parties. Someone who was willing to be out of the closet about being kinky might be radical enough to wrap their head around the concept of blood-drinking immortals.

Ulric was baffled by the rationale for an S/M support group. "Why talk about fist-fucking or cock-and-ball torture when you can go out and do it?" he asked. She had to admit that she wasn't sure how to answer that, but then, she had a very good teacher with centuries of experience. It looked like some of these groups held educational events as well as parties. "Until I met you, I don't think I knew it was possible to do these things. I was too afraid to try them on myself, let alone look for another person to bind me. There's an attempt here, I think, to pass on a craft from one person to another, to keep a sort of oral tradition alive. Isn't that the way your people passed on their skills? Can't we just try a meeting or two? If they bore you, or me, we don't have to stay. I'm still too intimidated to go to a mixed S/M club with you."

Actually joining such a group proved to be more difficult than she had thought. She tried email, letters, and phone calls. None of her communications were returned. "Is there something wrong with my spelling?" she worried aloud to Ulric. "I know my mother isn't dressing me funny."

"Dear, I don't think they care how you spell," he replied, laughing. "They're just disorganized volunteers. Let's go out, and I'll lower my standards and do some snooping. If we can find somebody who's already a member, I can find out where their next meeting is, and we'll just go. I should be able to turn any questions about our status into a warm welcome."

What he did snag at a beer bust raising money for the AIDS Emergency Fund was the woman who led orientation meetings for new members, and Lilith told him to be content with the time and location of that gathering. "You look like you're getting a migraine," she worried, and he confessed that he was nauseous from contact with other people's grocery lists of anxieties, guilt, and resentment. Why was the top layer of human consciousness such a mess? All the good stuff was buried underneath a thick layer of sludgy angst and barely controlled anger, with a heavy seasoning of denial.

A few weeks later, sitting in a cold classroom in the LGBT Community Center (What did all those letters stand for?), Lilith wished she had Ulric's power of telepathy so she could amuse herself by seeing if these people's memories were more interesting than their droning on about their group's policies and S/M safety and consensuality. The safety demonstrations were a little more attention-getting, but she and Ulric had already gone far beyond that point with each other. She spent most of the three hours kneeling at his side, and his light touches upon her hair were all that kept her alert in her place.

After the meeting, there was time for coffee and desserts. Any place other than San Francisco, it would also have been the signal for all of the smokers to light up, but here there were only two smokers, who slunk apologetically out the door to enjoy their vice in the chilly evening air. Ulric told her to get up and help herself to any beverage or snack she desired, then stood behind her, embracing her while she sipped a cup of mint tea and nibbled on a chocolate chip cookie. "Do you like any of these people?" he asked discreetly, close to her ear.

She pointed out Janice, a plump and cheerful bisexual woman with short gray hair who had introduced herself as a switch (whatever that was) and made a few biting comments about how long it had taken the organization to require party participants to follow safer-sex guidelines, a young couple of articulate leathermen, Fox and Lynyrd, who seemed as out of their element as Lilith and Ulric, and a shy girl who barely got out her first name. She had asked no questions as members of the group delivered their prepared remarks. After the meeting, Ulric mingled with the crowd just enough to make brief skin-to-skin contact with each of them. "When we go out, if you want them to be there, I can call them," he explained. With the handful of people he had tagged during their outings, that brought the total of their gang to about twenty souls.

It wasn't exactly like making friends by asking them to go out for coffee, but Lilith accepted it as a shortcut. If it turned out that any of these people didn't like them or were not appropriate for her purpose, they could be released, she supposed. Ulric agreed. "It's not as impossible as trying to get your name off a bulk mailing list," he joked.

Lilith could stomach only a few of the meetings that the onerous membership process allowed them to attend. It wasn't that she thought they wouldn't be helpful to someone who was new, alone, and looking for technical information or scene-wise friendship. But many of these people had been coming to these programs for years. How often did you need to sit through Bondage 101 or Introductory Flogging? Did the demonstrations really teach people how to play, or were they a soft-core sex show, a substitute for an encounter with a real person? Yes, these displays were often scary and beautiful, carefully planned and well-enacted, and she respected most of the people who taught the classes. But it had nothing to do with how she and Ulric related to one another. Did she need to know about which kind of candles to melt on someone's body or how to quickly extinguish a blaze of rubbing alcohol that had been dabbed on someone's back when her master could have asked her to walk through a burning building and kept her safe from harm even as she entered the heart of the flame, in perfect love, trust, wonder, and obedience?

When she saw a similar yearning for intensity between some of the couples and triads who taught classes, Ulric tagged them for her. When they were ready to make their debut at a mixed S/M club, they could have a small crowd of familiar faces around them.

Rumors about the new "lifestyle 24/7 couple" had begun to circulate. Who was this full-breasted blonde woman in a tiny corset who attended to her lord in flawless silence? And how had that dark-haired brigand captured her heart and trained her to take pain that would have made a Marine faint dead away? The single-tail marks she had gotten in private and wore in public raised knowing eyebrows, cocks, and clits. Jonathan Steel, a master who had founded a club for Gorean role-playing, Pipe, a butch dyke who ran with the Biker Bitches from Hell, and a transgendered dominatrix named Fortunata Noir circled Lilith cautiously, hoping she would fall out with Ulric and become vulnerable to their advances, or be given to them for an hour or two. Boys who dreamed of being ravished by an evil biker and girls who had a strident taste for the lash competed with Lilith for Ulric's attention. But they searched in vain for a way to upstage her or drive a wedge between the blood-drinking pirate and his busty, laughing tavern wench.

They visited every club and play party in the Bay Area, but did nothing their fans could carry home to fuel a session of strung-out, I-stayed-up-all-night masturbation. For their debut scene in public, they selected their favorite club, Tight. It was above a large dance club that catered to Goths, punks, queer leatherpeople, and kinky straight couples who preferred a pansexual ambience and DJs who would stay away from heavy metal. The building sat between a three-story sex club for men only and a warehouse with For Rent signs all over it. The owner of Tight was well-connected; he drew no attention from the vice squad. The mayor's mistress was rumored to be a part-owner, and it was not unusual to see slumming celebrities there or fetish devotees visiting from Buenos Aires, Tokyo, London, and Germany. Professional dominatrices seeking to build a clientele frequently showed off their wares and regulars at Tight, and masters with fantasies of owning a harem of slave girls would come looking for fresh faces and flanks.

Club security was impartial about the sexual orientation or role-playing dynamic of the attendees. Leathermen and S/M dykes were as welcome as the dommes with their collared dogboys or English schoolmasters with their plaid-skirted and pigtailed charges. Tight etiquette said you could ask anyone for anything once (provided they were not in session). But a single "no" had to suffice. Voyeurs were permitted no closer than a top's backswing. This is not to say that men were never bound there on all fours and left to suffer the lust and cruel whims of excited spectators. Most of the play at Tight was prearranged, but single men got lucky (or at least got an email address) often enough to keep a good stock of willing volunteers on hand if a top was in the mood for something spontaneous and anonymous.

Before Ulric and Lilith got into the car to go to Tight, they stood on the porch, facing each other, palm to palm. "I'm calling those who feel a bond with us," Ulric said. His breath on her face was as intimate as a kiss. "But I do not compel them. If they are supposed to be there, they will come." She nodded, privately believing there was not one person she had selected who would be able to stay away from this premiere.

As they got into her car and Ulric backed it down the driveway, Lilith looked regretfully at the motorcycle. It had quickly become her favorite mode of transportation. The Hein Gericke leathers Ulric had bought for her were perfect for San Francisco's cold nights. But tonight she was going to surprise Ulric. She wore a cloak that covered her from her chin to her toes. Not appropriate garb for a bike. The temptation to pick a fight with him and stay home was tricky to spot and difficult to resist. And she shook with a bad case of nerves. So she had let him drive her car for the first time.

Lilith felt Ulric extend a calming tendril toward her, questing for her consent to lower the level of adrenaline in her blood. "No," she said. "I'm psyching myself up to do something completely out of character." But as her heartbeat spiraled out of control and her palms bled cold sweat, she drew his kindness back to her. "Maybe just a little," she said, and he was scrupulous with his control, so she was on edge but not quite ready to vomit.

They weren't early, but they got lucky with parking anyway—a space just across from the club's entrance. Ulric opened her door and helped her out, retrieved his bag from the back seat, and locked the car. He walked her across the street with fatherly courtesy and took care of the business of signing them in, paying their fee, getting their hands stamped. Just before they left the anteroom counter and entered the first proper play room, Ulric kissed the back of her hand. Betty Page's shocked face was neon purple under the room's black lights. "I don't like seeing anyone else's mark on you," he said softly, next to her ear, then bit it just hard enough to bring her out of her stage fright and back into the present. He smelled like the meaning of life to her, and she stopped anguishing about what any stranger would think of her.

Their friends had prepared a surprise for them. Alice and her girlfriend Moe had stretched a velvet banker's rope between the rest of the room and the stage at the far end that contained a spiderweb of chain. They had taken up all the nearby play stations, claiming them with their coats, toy bags, and whips hung wherever hooks were provided. As newcomers entered the club, they flowed past this marked territory, looking for more open space. A few of them paused, and Lilith knew that more of them would stay once they saw that something was happening. A certain proportion of Tight's customers behaved like minnows, clustering wherever there was something novel or dramatic to watch, then drifting off en masse in pursuit of another opportunity to feed their senses.

Lilith's Canadian co-conspirator, Curtis, wrestled a heavy wooden chair from its normal position against a wall and settled it near the stage. She led Ulric to it, and he settled there, looking almost as nervous as she was. The bodies of their friends were arranged behind him, permitting the spectators to catch tantalizing glimpses, but not allowing strangers to intrude on her physically or psychically.

She took the stage in her long cloak and rather conservative high heels, only three inches high. They teetered on the border between sexy eveningwear and flashy business shoes. She stood, gathering herself, eyes closed, seeking a calm center where nothing mattered but her own body, heart, and mind and her love for the dark-haired immortal man in the chair ten feet away. The club's industrial dance music became her music, a soundtrack for her hips. It was an internal silent strengthening that seemed to last for several long minutes, but she knew only a few seconds had passed.

She opened her eyes, put her arms out, and whirled half a turn so her back was to him. *I don't know how to dance*, a panicky part of her mind said. *But you do know how to take your cloak off*, the calm center replied. Moving with deliberate slowness, exaggerating each motion just a little, she undid the clasp of the cloak and let it fall bit by bit. When the full weight of the fabric hung from her fingertips, she gave it a swirl and dropped it. It became a black puddle on the floor. Lilith turned and forced herself to meet Ulric's eyes. A little smile played upon his lips.

She was wearing the same outfit she had on when they first met on the steps of her Midwestern library. A black skirt, a white blouse, and a frumpy purse. His smile became an innocent grin as she reached up to open the top button of the thin, loose blouse. The grin became overtly lewd when she put her hands in her hair and began to undo her bun. The rest of her body moved just a little, then a little more. It was a combination of dancing and strutting. When her hair had slithered free, she shook it loose, twirled, and began to take off the blouse. Again, she reminded herself, *Take it slow.*

Ulric was leaning forward, an admiring and encouraging look on his face. The tiny, white plastic buttons felt oily slick against the tips of her fingers. She gently tugged the shirt out of the waistband of the skirt and shrugged it off in dramatic, teasing steps. *Bare left shoulder, put back to the audience, right shoulder exposed, let the blouse slip down a bit to show half my back, turn, almost reveal one breast, laugh, and then shed it like a winter coat in an overheated room.*

She was wearing a bra made out of silver chain. Bells hung from its lower edge. A pair of silver embroidery clamps dangled from the links of its straps. Every eye was on her as she caressed her own breasts, but his hungry look was the only one that mattered. Dancing to the persistent throb of blood between her legs, Lilith drew her left nipple out between the thumb and forefinger of one hand and used the other to open and attach the gleaming metal clamp. Everyone gasped. Ulric's hand dropped to his crotch, applying slight pressure to his aching dick. She was like a flirtatious nymph out of Richard Burton's uncensored translation of *The Arabian Nights.* Who knew his girl had so much talent as a performer?

When she cupped and squeezed her other breast, preparing it to receive the same treatment, Ulric was surprised to feel his own nipples grow hard. One of them burned as if a small, determined animal had bitten it. He gasped when she completed her movement and clamped the second nipple. But he refocused on Lilith's motions on the low stage. She had placed both hands at the waistband of her black wool skirt.

Striding like a model to the back of the stage and then toward him again, she abruptly snapped the skirt open. It had been held shut with Velcro along one side. Around her waist was a strap of leather and a short skirt of more small-gauge chain and bells. Under that disguise was a leather thong with a zipper in it.

The shoes were the next to go, thrown off into the audience. She raised her hair and let it run through her hands, threw her head back and around so it circled her head like golden flames, and sent him a burning look of accusation and promise. She seized the chain that connected the clamps, and then she really danced for him. The music was quicker and harder than it had been when they first entered the club. Now it was peak party time, and the music was selected to impel people who were not playing to consummate their cruising, and to prolong the scenes of people who had already hooked up.

Lilith felt as if she danced in a setting far removed from a warehouse club in the twenty-first century. She was by a campfire, and the camels were bedded down for the night, to one side of a row of tents. Or maybe the fire was in a cave. The steps she chose with her bare feet seemed that ancient. Her longing for his touch was easy to express with her body if she allowed it to guide her. The sweet ferocity of his response reached her in a rush, and she cried out and almost stumbled to feel his intention to collar and leash her. Something very like an orgasm made her shudder, and she could not trust her legs to carry her through one more swaying set of urgent movements. She dropped to her knees, unclipped one of the chains at the side of her skirt, and attached it to the chain between her nipple clamps. The flesh in their grip had nearly become numb. She mutely offered him the leash and all that it would draw toward his sovereignty.

"The offering is sufficient," he said dryly, "and I accept it." He came to his feet, took the leash from her hands, and drew her to his boots. There were some quiet cheers.

Ulric vaulted onto the stage and took her by her hair. The pressure of his hand on the chain awakened the compressed tips of her breasts, and she sobbed aloud. When he applied a sharp yank that freed their jaws from her flesh, she screamed. The cheers and lewd congratulations grew louder, and their escort began to break apart. Toy bags were unzipped, rope went onto the eyebolts in crosses and horses, and leather cuffs were applied to wrists and ankles. The swish of floggers became a hissing counterpoint to the broadcast music.

What Ulric and Lilith did after that was less important than where they were and the fact that their play was witnessed by a community of intimate acquaintances. At the end of their play, he chose to do something that brought everyone running again. He took out a single-tail whip and gave her six stripes across her back. This was a whipping in a different league than sensuous play with heavy, unbraided leather whips and short suede cats. Lilith could not hold back her screams, but even to herself they did not sound like the wretched involuntary noise emitted by a chain gang convict or a galley slave. They were in almost musical harmony with the snakebite crack of the black whip, screams to make Ulric's dick hard, not screams to summon rescue.

The genuine and extreme sound of both whip and woman had everyone in the club holding their breath. Masochists who had gone too long without a drubbing had tears of jealousy in their eyes, and those who thought dressing up and a bit of bondage were going far enough felt indignant and assaulted.

When he took her down from the cross, he picked her up and cradled her. Lilith hung limp in the strong sling of his arms, her hair brushing the floor. "Blood of my blood," he said, kissing her closed eyelids. "Dearer to me than the spoor of a hundred lightly injured victims who imagine they can escape. I give myself over to you, Lilith. You are the love of my wicked life."

"You are not wicked," she said, kissing him back hard. "Except to me. For which blessing I am eternally grateful."

"Shall I take you here, or would you prefer the privacy of your own bed? I intend to fuck you so hard you won't be able to walk tomorrow."

"There is something you need from me that moves me more than sex. Take that, here and now. Let them see it."

He was rigid with fear and doubt. Lilith beckoned to the special members of their club who played with knives, needles, and blood. Most of them had felt the sharp edge of Ulric's teeth and prized this forbidden experience. But Ulric had fed on them discreetly, and he had taken the memory of witnesses away and erased the marks upon his victims. Not only was he afraid to give his secret into the profane hands of mortals, the rules of Tight about blood play were draconian. Being seen drinking Lilith's blood might make them a legend, but it would also be enough to get them thrown out for life. He would have to wade in mental sewage up to his knees to expunge such a juicy scandal. For a prime piece of gossip was hard to send into oblivion, making him wonder if swapping secrets was not an underrated drive, right up there with reproduction and locating clean drinking water.

"Hide us," Lilith said succinctly to the people she was not sure how she had called to the forefront. A screen of human bodies went up around them, clambering onto the stage. Ulric took a deep breath and decided he must trust her, even though he suspected she might regret this in the morning. She was giddy with the endorphins engendered by a severe whipping, and light-headed from the breakdown of adrenaline in her bloodstream. Her world had shrunk to the size of the floor that she knelt upon or the cross that refused to budge when she flung herself away from agony. The glamour they had both cast upon this dingy place would not hold back bullets or newspaper headlines.

"These are your people, Ulric. If you show yourself to them, it will only consolidate your position as our leader. Let us all be woven together in truth. I am not the only person capable of loyalty to you, or love."

Ulric chided himself for his dick-wilting paranoia. He had survived the Inquisition and World War II. What did he have to fear from a small group of mortals who were themselves outcasts? She had crossed her hands behind her back. He stood behind her and lifted her hair, shifted its glossy weight to her other shoulder. Despite the dim light of the club, her skin looked as if she were in sunlight, not cheap industrial fluorescents. Golden. But the treasure he sought was another color.

"You have given me your pain, and because you were willing I was able to take your pain into me and transform it into a rare delight, for you and for me. Now you offer me your blood, and I will imbibe it and transform it into life everlasting. Because of the fealty you offer me, I will uphold and nourish you as well. You will want for nothing that is in my power to grant you. Open your senses to me as I open your veins, Lilith."

His teeth seemed to become longer, thinner, sharper. A warm sensation of arousal and approval warring with fear went up his back. She tasted so good, her blood full of adoration instead of abhorrence. The people around them were reliving their own interludes in his arms, and the sites where he had broken them open tingled and burned. The significance of his words to her was slowly sinking in. Ulric silently questioned each of them in turn. Their conscious minds said this was only a fantasy, but their unconscious minds were lighting up like police cars. In the part of them where dreams and myths made sense, and fairy tales were real (the largest part), the map of reality was being changed to accommodate him, a genuine nightwalker, an undying nightmare. Could Lilith's ability to bring brightness into his life also shift their deep-seated conviction that a vampire was nothing more than a supernatural sociopath? If these people did begin to see him as some sort of guide or leader, what would he offer them in return for that allegiance? Who would have to change more to make this dynamic a reality, him or the people envying the beautiful slave he wanted to drink dry?

"Can we have some?" Isabeau, an ebony-skinned émigré from New Orleans with the facial features of a white Southern belle, asked shyly. She knelt fearlessly at the feet of Ulric and his love. Not understanding why he did so, Ulric took a bead of Lilith's blood on the tips of his fingers and touched them to her lips.

"Me next, eh?" Curtis decided, stroking his thick straight bristle of a mustache. He too kissed Ulric's bloody fingertips and went back to his place, making the blood last as long as possible by holding it in his cupped tongue.

One by one they each received tribute from her. They had become both givers and takers of blood, bound to Ulric and Lilith alike.

By the time that circle had dissolved, and Ulric had tidied Lilith up enough to walk her out of the club, their sexual heat had been banked. But the original fire had burned so high and hot that it left a glowing wealth of embers behind. They sailed out to the car like carnal hot-air balloons, with their feet barely touching the ground. Neither of them remembered any of the scenes they walked past or remembered the drive home. They climbed into bed together, and found themselves naked under the sheets with no sense of having undressed. There, they pressed their bodies together and savored a connection that resonated with tenderness and gratitude. Sex could not have brought them any closer. And that night, Ulric remained where he was, trusting Lilith to guard his unconscious body with the same love that she felt for him during the dark hours of the night.

He had gone to the club prepared to claim her publicly, to enhance their relationship by putting her perfection on display. So much more than that had happened. How weird was it to be coming out at his advanced age? Weirder still to imagine that someone besides Lilith would come into his world knowing the truth about him. It had been centuries since he had thought of himself as the member of a family, let alone a tribe or a larger community. What would he do with them all?

"Love us," Lilith said, reading his mind as well as he read hers. "Just love us, sweetheart. Like I love you. Feel the sun coming up? We've been awake all night long. I'm so tired. Sleep with me. I'll be with you even when you sleep, Ulric. And you will be with me."

He didn't believe it, but when the involuntary quiescence came upon him, he was startled by a dream. Such a thing was extremely rare. But there it was. And in the middle of it was Lilith, slumbering alongside him, stroking his chest in her sleep. What could he do but accept this miracle, and settle into the daylight sojourn with a new sense of restfulness and ease?

Someone other than Janice, Fox and Lynyrd, Curtis, Alice and Moe, Isabeau, Fortescu, Jonathan, Madison, Chloe, Evan, Horace, Pipe, and Fortunata Noir was watching as Ulric publicly took scarlet tribute from Lilith's swanlike neck. Rhys had slithered between bodies until she was able to catch a glimpse of them between the anonymous elbows of other spectators—one clad in a leather jacket, the other sheathed in black and brown Maori tattoos. She was chewing on the end of her off-center sapphire braid. She had seen Ulric and Lilith before, but when they walked into Tight tonight, the sexual energy between them was a gold crackle in the atmosphere. She knew Ulric from the pictures Adulfa had imprinted upon her memory. Now she sweated to photograph Lilith with equal clarity so that Adulfa could take this spectacle from her mind.

When Ulric bared his lover's neck, Rhys dug her fingernails into the palm of her hand. She was jealous of the pretty lady who had danced so provocatively and was now about to be taken as Rhys longed to be taken by Adulfa. No—jealousy was a pale thing compared to the blind yearning that possessed her when he spoke so gently and bit—bit and drank—oh, God, there could be no God because any merciful deity would turn that man into Adulfa and place Rhys within her grasp. The musician's neck and groin felt as if teeth were rending them. She could smell her own blood, and realized she had broken the skin on the inside of her hand.

"Hey!" someone said, and jostled her loose. She had been gripping the sleeve of his leather jacket, holding herself up so she would not swoon. The fact that this was a man loving a woman made her own response to Ulric and Lilith almost offensive. How dare he touch her that way, and how stupid did she have to be to allow it? And why were they trespassing on Rhys' libido?

She left the club, mastering all her willpower to glide through the crowd, drawing no attention, until she was close enough to an exit to bolt out into the chilly night air.

COME TO ME.

"Okay, okay," Rhys said. "Let me walk home and get the bike. I need some warmer clothes and my helmet." Home was still one room in a flat leased by a woman who seemed determined to own one cat for every orgasm she had missed in her wasted youth. Couldn't someone with supernatural powers do better for her faithful servant than a perch at the edge of that squalor?

TOO DANGEROUS.

"I suppose you want me to take BART?" Rhys said sarcastically. Cool people walked, rode skateboards or bicycles, rollerbladed, or owned a motorcycle or a truck. Being seen on public transportation was humiliating.

Ten minutes later, she found herself at the Powell Street BART station.

"I don't have any money."

LOOK AROUND.

A woman with an FAO Schwarz shopping bag was walking toward the stairs. She had the clipped body language of a middle-class person in what they perceive to be a dangerous environment—eyes down, elbows clamped to her sides, going so fast she was almost breaking into a trot.

TOUCH HER.

"Hey, lady," Rhys said, and put her hand on the wrist that was braceleted by the shopping bag's handle.

Without acknowledging her, the woman went to the ticket machine, put in a twenty-dollar bill, and gave the ticket to Rhys. Then she calmly went her own way.

WALNUT CREEK.

"Nagging bitch," Rhys swore under her breath, and got on the escalator down to the trains. "I would get there just as fast on the Shadow."

TOO DANGEROUS.

"If I'm not supposed to do anything dangerous, does that mean I don't have to see you?" Rhys realized she was talking so loudly that other passengers were avoiding her. Adulfa sent her an image of being cradled in the vampire's shockingly sharp kiss, with one of Adulfa's narrow hands buried in Rhys up to the wrist. Teeth and fist moved with equal deliberate slowness, drawing out the sensations of penetration, bleeding, and punch-fuck fullness. Rhys cried out, "Mother *fucker!*" and fell to her knees. She caught herself palms down on the dirty concrete floor of the BART platform.

A train pulled up. Rhys couldn't see the blinking destination sign. A man brushed past her. Then he came back, picked her up by the elbows, walked her to a vacant seat, and then took himself to the back of that coach. Rhys heard the pneumatic doors open and shut as he made his way to a different car on the train. "Mother of all bitches," she muttered to herself, and scouted around her padded bench seat. There weren't very many passengers, just a few yuppies headed home with Christmas shopping and some people who worked the late shift at San Francisco restaurants and hotels. Rhys spied a piece of paper on the floor across the aisle and snatched it. Most of the front was blank and all of the back. Someone had crossed off items on a grocery list and then lost it. Rhys got a pen out of the pocket in her denim overlay and thought carefully. There wasn't enough room to doodle or start with a rough draft.

"I run to the wolf," she wrote carefully in small capital letters. "Ice howls. She calls me and I run to the wolf. Wild to feed the wild hunger in her. There is no love, only ice and appetite. Voracious appetite. My blood and her teeth. I run to the wolf and she teaches me to howl."

Grunting satisfaction, Rhys turned the paper over and drew straight lines for bars of music. The opening chords were the most important. The chorus of this song would be a shriek. Somehow she would force herself to reproduce what she heard in her skull when Adulfa wounded her and fed. Punk chicks would love this song. She felt a bleak regret for the days when she would have had some use for fans like that. She had always thought her life was fucked up because chicks were mean, and all she needed was a girl to be nice to her and take care of her. Before Adulfa. Before she knew herself better, understood that garbage has to stay in the alleys and gutters. Knew what she had wanted was a girl who would never let her go because it was too damn much fun to kick the crap out of her.

Her last song about Adulfa had been called "Kickboxing in High-Heeled Shoes." Femmes all over San Francisco had made it their anthem. Butches hated it. "Not all of us are masochists," Mordecai the bass player had said, scowling at the lyrics.

"If you want to sing about little girls comin' to you to do it for daddy, write it yourself," Rhys had snarled.

"Chill, bro, I ain't tryin' to pierce your clit with a dull needle. We'll sing this shit, but we also gotta represent for the dyke dudes who're all stone. Feinberg it once in a while, poet."

"Naw," Rhys said to the almost-empty BART car. "I'm stone no more. A pussy and a whore just like they always said. Only this time I really do like it. And she ain't nobody's daddy."

Rhys heard a snatch of music and wrote it down. There was another bit, so she scribbled notes to record it. The struggle to follow her erratic music generator took up the rest of the ride. Problem was, the lyrics to a song popped out whole usually, like a baby. But the music was more coy. She could tell already that the phrases on her scavenged notepaper weren't sequential. It would take some tinkering around on Mordecai's keyboard to put it in order. For some reason, she couldn't compose music on her own guitar. And even though Mordecai was a bass player, and she never used the keyboard, she refused to give it to Rhys. "You sit right where I can watch you, and you can get your fingerprints all over it for a coupla hours. But if I want it to wind up in a pawn shop I can walk it over there myself."

"I wouldn't pawn your Kawasaki," Rhys had protested.

"Not if you could get more for it at Sixteenth and Mission," Mordecai agreed, and straightened her yarmulke. Rhys always wanted to twist Mordecai's *payess* around her index finger. The golden brown hair looked so soft. But Mordecai hated having her hair touched. "Don't go disrespecting my cultural and religious heritage!" she would yell. "You just fetishize Jewish girls. I'm not going to collaborate in your anti-Semitic wet dreams."

If Rhys replied, "How many of your girlfriends are Jewish, 'daddy'?" Mordecai would erupt, and they'd spend the afternoon arguing about the validity of Mordecai's attempt to bring Orthodox Judaism into a dyke context. No music would be finalized.

GET UP HERE NOW.

Rhys came back to the present. Adulfa would be waiting for her outside the station. She climbed a long flight of stairs, but didn't see her at first. Then she sensed rather than saw her in the back seat of an orange cab. It was a stupid retro car made to look like something from the fifties.

GET IN.

"I'm within earshot, you can talk to me out loud now," Rhys said irritably. Adulfa yanked her into the cab and pressed her facedown into her lap. Rhys scrambled to slide off the seat and onto her knees, even though there really wasn't room between the edge of the back seat and the back of the front seat for someone to be on the floor. Adulfa didn't help, just kept up the same relentless pressure so that Rhys was unable to breathe in anything save her chilled champagne sweetness. How could a girl smell fizzy? Rhys wondered. Shouldn't a vampire smell rotten? But Adulfa never did. It was as if she was hyper-alive rather than undead.

The driver let them off in a parking garage underground, below a complex of several two- and three-story office buildings that looked like corporate cottages. Walnut Creek was a precious little enclave of white people who made too much money, Rhys thought, reflecting on all the dead trees sacrificed to this bad taste. The small block of buildings was set at the edge of a large tract of woods and bordered on two sides by a stream large enough to need a bridge.

A van was parked next to a maintenance shed, and Rhys expected Adulfa to push her into the back of that dented vehicle, which had a certain "I-live-on-the-street" cachet. Instead, Adulfa dragged her into the woods, and nothing would have freaked Rhys out more. One word: *bugs*. When the vampire tried to push her onto the ground, Rhys actually resisted. Adulfa just swept her feet out from under her with a roundhouse kick. It was more of a *Road House* maneuver than *Pulp Fiction*, but Rhys landed in a pile of dead leaves and grass all the same. She could smell eucalyptus leaves and hear running water. Thankfully, it wasn't as cold as it was in San Francisco this time of year.

"Hey! I'm in the dirt!" she protested.

"You don't mind dirt when it's ground into concrete or asphalt," Adulfa said, lying beside her, pinning her to the ground by her throat.

"That's civilization." Was that a eucalyptus pod digging into her left buttcheek, or a rock? Rhys tried to squirm away from it or drive it deeper into the ground where it would not bother her, which Adulfa interpreted as more hapless resistance. The stars of looming unconsciousness overlaid the brighter stars of the night sky as Adulfa cut off her air.

SHOW ME.

Rhys was really annoyed by the way her body thrashed around when she couldn't breathe. Was it too stupid to understand that there was nothing so great about living? Adulfa's hand must have eased up because she settled back into the mat of vegetation and dirt (the pebble or pod gone, hopefully kicked over to Adulfa's side of the bower). The movie of Ulric's breaching and enjoyment of Lilith unfolded in slow motion, each detail sharper than Rhys remembered seeing it the first time around.

"How dare he?" Adulfa hissed. Rhys flinched away from the horror-movie mouth open above her own, ringed with white razors. So much for her romantic fantasies about being vampire bait. Might as well fantasize about being savaged by a police dog. "How dare he love *that*! A human. A mere mortal. How dare he love at all!"

"Don't dis us for having a short shelf life," Rhys said testily, then wondered why she was championing the cause of the authors of nuclear weapons and female circumcision. But since when had she ever been able to know when to shut up? "Talk to the friggin' manufacturer, for Christ's sake."

Adulfa slapped her on the cunt. Hard. Rhys said "ooof" and wanted to throw up. "Don't utter that weakling's name in my presence," she warned. "You are less amusing than you believe." She straddled Rhys and took both of her hands. Terrible pain (*As if there was any other kind*, Rhys thought) lanced down her fingers and back up to her palms and wrists. It felt like every bone was being crushed.

"Stop it! Please!" Rhys cried. "My hands—I won't be able to play my guitar."

"Or diddle yourself," Adulfa sneered, but released her hands. Rhys tucked them into her armpits and silently sobbed. Crying out loud always made things worse. "You and I have nothing in common," Adulfa expounded. "I am at the top of the food chain. You are meat. And you have all the vices mortals display. Principally, cowardice." She crinkled her nose to indicate the depth of her distaste, which Rhys thought made her look like Samantha from *Bewitched*. Adulfa continued her lecture, unaware of Rhys' disrespect or choosing to ignore it. "We are meant to be hunters, and Ulric should dedicate himself to taking revenge on those who made us and ruined our world. He has no business dabbling in this masque of mortality. The fox does not wed the pheasant. It is disgusting. And he does not deserve to have even one moment of happiness. Not if he lives *five thousand years*!"

Rhys had shoved herself back into the dirt as hard as she could, but there was no escaping Adulfa's tirade or the mad look in her eyes. The eighth of an inch of space she created didn't count for much. Adulfa's rant ran down sooner rather than later, and she gradually took notice once more of the woman beneath her thighs.

"Still here?" she crooned, playing with Rhys' braid.

Damn it, Adulfa was beautiful. Like a Fury. A kind of beauty that predated patriarchy. Literally. Those cheekbones, that bone white hair, her mouth as firm as an Amazon general's... "Yes," Rhys could barely admit. Her throat was dry. "I am still here."

"What do you want?"

"To be your sacrament," Rhys replied, and wondered, *Where the hell did that come from?*

"More religious cant," Adulfa said dismissively.

"There are unholy sacraments," Rhys retorted, and thought, *That's a great opening line for another song. If I live that long.*

Adulfa touched her. Cold fingers, colder looks. Ice howls. "You can choose between the kisses of my teeth," Adulfa decided, "or a ride home."

Rhys knew if she protested the injustice of this, Adulfa might refuse her both boons. She had no idea where she was, and being lost in the middle of all of these white-bread homophobes scared the piss out of her.

"I pick the lady who's the tiger," she said, and knew by the blank look on Adulfa's face that she didn't get the joke or care about it. Then Rhys' T-shirt tore, and she couldn't think, only scream. There was nothing human about the strength of Adulfa's embrace, it was like being crushed in an iron maiden. Someone was holding a chainsaw to her neck. No, a wolverine. It hurt wicked bad. Why didn't she remember how bad it hurt? How come the only thing that lived in her memory was Adulfa's gluttonous and dreamy smile of satisfaction?

Toward dawn, the Walnut Creek police found a queer wandering around downtown. They did what fascist suburban pigs always do with gender-ambiguous hate crime victims, and arrested "it" for vagrancy. But when they saw the bloody shirt and extensive injuries, they took her to the hospital rather than jail. Rhys was handcuffed to the bed, sutured, and given a blood transfusion. Because the prisoner had tattoos, the doctor on duty didn't order any pain medication; no drug addict was going to get opiates on his watch.

When Rhys came to, revived by agony, she retrieved the key she had taped to the inside of her belt and let herself go. It may not have been prudent to take the time to unlock the handcuffs from the bedrail and pocket them before sneaking past a skeleton crew of nurse's aides. A cabdriver outside the hospital took Rhys to BART in return for a wet joint, and she retrieved the ticket from her jacket and barely made it home.

What was she going to call the CD?

CHAPTER 11
The Angel at the Top of My Tree

Caught up in the Christmas spirit, Adulfa decided to go shopping.

She had awakened in the tiny attic of a mortuary, where she had used the office shredder after-hours to make herself a comfortable bed out of the important financial records that had been stored there. She discovered the room downstairs where corpses were embalmed was full of amenities. After shaving her cornsilk blonde hair down to the scalp, she stretched out on one of the steel tabletops and rinsed herself off with the flexible sprayer that was used to wash off the bodies. Still naked, which was how she preferred to sleep, she strolled outside to the car she had stolen from a recent victim, expressly chosen because she wore clothes that Adulfa liked, and shared her dress size.

Tonight she would be wearing a very brief leather miniskirt and a matching black leather jacket, lined with scarlet silk, of course. The tailoring was Italian, very chic, very naughty. The cold was all the artifice she needed to put a cruel blush of color on her Teutonic cheekbones, and her mouth had always been blood-red. She thought the clothes would have been expensive if she'd had to buy them, but Adulfa never carried cash or American Express. Her mesmerizing, big ice-blue eyes were her line of credit. Underneath her leathers she wore nothing at all, being immune to the chill. Her black stockings were held up by lacy elastic tops, and she maneuvered on seven-inch stilettos as if the brick sidewalk were just another Paris runway.

Since she intended to visit Ulric's territory to acquire and distribute holiday cheer, she first had to acquire enough power to conceal herself from him and, if necessary, walk in the daylight. So she had paid a visit to a monastery in Marin County, a cloistered order that made its living raising llamas and selling yarn made from their hair. Or so they told any curious outsiders. They were actually a satanic cult run by a vampire master who forced his fledgling immortal novitiates to remain with him, despite the suffering that it caused them. It had taken her quite a while to literally sniff them out. They had planted a high hedge of look-not around the farm. But the crushed flowers of that bramble had a distinctive smell, if you knew what you were looking for, and so Adulfa had followed the grazing llamas to the hedges.

The underling that Adulfa released from painful servitude was wearing a reddish brown habit to soak up the fine mist of blood that perpetually seeped from his naked scalp and back. Beneath the habit, however, was a well-nourished body that yielded quite enough blood for her to be freed of hunger for a few days at least. She was discovered at her feast by the monk who had been placed over her victim, and he too wore a long cordovan frock with a hood. Adulfa was quite happy to speak to someone with seniority, someone in charge, someone with the power to make decisions. He decided he would rather die in her arms than continue another day in bondage to this order's master. It almost took all the fun out of killing him.

Filled with a sense of infinite strength and energy, she was tempted to destroy the entire place, but it might prove useful in the future. The order was a squalid thing; they had business dealings that she loathed. Eventually, she would return and clean out their nest. But for now, she had more important things to do. Humming "Moon River," she walked out of the monastery and down to the parking lot, where a Lexus was waiting to ferry her across the Golden Gate Bridge.

How nice it was of all the merchants to remain open well after dark. In downtown San Francisco, the antique steel-blue lights along Market Street were decorated with enormous candy canes and reindeer. Shop windows were lushly lit, golden boxes full of expensive and precious things. Well-dressed and well-fed men and women hurried along the street, loaded down with shopping bags and parcels, eager to pick up one last present or head for home with the bundles they had already amassed. Between them lurked figures who had not partaken of the season's bounty, dirty, thin people who begged change from their betters or begged their invisible tormentors to leave them alone.

Before allowing the warm air, silver tinsel, and discreetly secular carols of Nordstrom's to suck her in through its thick glass doors, Adulfa paused and took a deep whiff of the street. Really, she could not see that cities had changed much since 1887. Victorian London had its clouds of coal smoke; more than a hundred years later, San Francisco had carbon monoxide. The gutters still smelled of sewage and rotten food. Horse-drawn carriages and electric trolleys seemed equally indifferent to the welfare of pedestrians, and the street people were, if anything, even more desperate, despite the absence of snow. She took in the crowds with the delighted smile of a vegetarian gourmand contemplating the glossy rows of organic produce at the Berkeley Bowl, and swept into Nordstrom's, eager to enjoy her portion of greed, the joy that comes from avid consumption.

Riding the escalator was a treat, although she had to resist the temptation to rise an inch or so above the steps and alarm the shoppers thronged behind her. She had artfully positioned herself in line so she would be ahead of a matronly woman who was taking a young boy shopping for a suit. It was delightful to hear their twin reactions to the view, like an operatic dialogue in her head, the older woman's fear and dismay paired with the adolescent's disbelief and delight. It was sweet to be adored, and equally savory to scare someone. She resisted the temptation to introduce them to a whole new set of family values. There was time, still, and she was fresh from her kills at the far edge of the monastery's grounds and wanted to look around a bit.

Of course, she headed straight for the shoe department. The buyers at Nordstrom's had to be perverts. Just look at all the thigh-high boots, platform heels, leopard prints, Lucite pumps, sharp metal spikes, little-girl shoes with padlocks on the straps. These shoes were positively pornographic, erotic verses in latex, patent leather, kid, and steel. She found a row of seats, made everyone who was seated there leave, and positioned herself in the middle of the row. The chairs were not upholstered with leather, and she frowned at the sensation of plastic against her half-bare bottom. It was annoying to be reminded of the store's faux elegance, its pretentiousness. Americans craved only the illusion of exclusivity.

Now, that salesgirl over there, perhaps *she* was the one to drag under the mistletoe for a nice, long kiss. Adulfa stared at the back of her head until she abandoned her customer, turned, and came to inquire submissively if there was anything that Madam would like to see. She was a cute little thing, with her dark brown hair cut in a Dutch boy's bob. Adulfa liked girls who wore ties with boy's shirts. She was a little thin in her dark slacks and fashionable loafers, but there was no time to fatten her up. Her name was Jamie, this was not what she had in mind when she graduated from high school, she was from Santa Monica, San Francisco was sooo cliquey and drinks were too expensive, she was thinking about moving back to Southern California and staying with her parents for a while, and Adulfa did not care to pay attention to the rest of it.

"I think you should measure my foot first," Adulfa purred, and crossed her long, long legs. Jamie sank to her knees and removed one of Adulfa's viciously high heels. The foot arched in her hand like a cat imperiously ordering to be petted right there. So Jamie stroked it, and for some reason the rasp of the black silk stocking against the palm of her hand made her feel hot and sweaty inside the button-down Oxford shirt that concealed her small breasts. She wanted to loosen her tie.

Instead, she ran her hands up Adulfa's legs, confirming with her fingertips that the stockings were perfectly taut and the seams aligned as if they'd been painted on with a laser. The muscles in the calves bunched beneath her hands, and she kneaded them, and continued kneading up, shifting her hands to palm the inside of a pair of perfect slender thighs. The silk stockings were like sandpaper on the sensitive inner surfaces of her hands, and she wanted so much to soothe them against this woman's skin.

Somehow she had forgotten to put the foot-measurer beneath her customer's feet, and was kneeling instead between her legs. She could see Adulfa's sex, the pink lips clearly visible because the pale pubic hair had been severely clipped. Jamie's breath caught in her chest. She ran her hands off the tops of the silk stockings, toward skin. But she barely got to experience the downy texture of Adulfa's thighs before her head was rudely shoved down, into the gray industrial-but-chic carpet.

"Measure me with your mouth," Adulfa said, and the words were like a sonorous hymn in Jamie's head, a Gregorian chant that heralded and sanctioned the forbidden. She was afraid, afraid! But then there was a warm feeling like a touch behind her eyes, and she knew only desire. She took Adulfa's stockinged toes into her mouth, and adored them with her tongue. She was vaguely aware that customers were standing around in shock, watching a tall blonde woman with a crewcut spread her legs and feed a salesgirl her feet. The manager of the department was heading toward them, and Jamie did not understand why he had not already shouted at her to stop, stop! But then it seemed to her that everyone was frozen in place, because Jesus told us to love one another, and here she was loving someone perfectly. *It's like a Nativity Scene*, she thought as she licked up toward Adulfa's kneecaps. People would stand in front of them with their hats in their hands and admire them and think deep and beautiful thoughts, they would be inspired and awestruck because it was holy, holy to press her mouth against the elastic roses and hunger for Adulfa's asymmetrical art deco labia and the pink topaz of her clitoris.

Then her mouth was on rose petals, skin at last, and Adulfa's long fingers were in her hair, guiding her. Jamie had vague memories of a drunken party long ago, falling backward onto a friend's bed, an awkward pleasure provided by pearl-tipped cheerleader fingers and lips that tasted of peach, passing out more because she was not sure she wanted to reciprocate than because of her blood alcohol level...but this was not like that. There was no intoxication except the sweet smell of Adulfa's body, no awkwardness at all because she was firmly held, directed, and there was no possibility of failure. She would give anything, anything to do this perfectly, to hear just one small sigh of delight from the woman who had gathered her up and given her a purpose.

So she used her puppy tongue and dizzy lips to give Adulfa pleasure for as long as she would graciously suffer it. And Adulfa was happy to take from her, to muss her hair and smear her face, and brand her soul with a deep hunger for cunt. It was delicious to allow a human being to feed on her, Adulfa found. It felt so wicked, and it was also endearing, to see them parody the act that sustained her own life. Caught up in fantasies about Jamie's fragile neck and strong young heart, Adulfa came, and quickly came again, mercifully blinding Jamie to light and sound by enclosing her in the grip of her strong pale legs.

Jamie thought she would weep; she was so delirious and glad.

Then she was tossed back on the floor, out of breath, confused and bereft. The carpet burned her hands, and she had a bump on her head — she had landed that hard. Adulfa had spotted her prey. As she got to her feet, ready for the hunt, she did Jamie the favor of making everyone forget what they had just seen. Everyone except Jamie, that is. *Let her sort it out*, Adulfa thought, amused by the many possibilities that presented themselves. There was room for one more sweet young submissive in this wicked world. Let her find her proper place. Adulfa grinned, and mentally whistled for her quarry as she slipped back into her high heels.

This was Monica Bradshaw, who had honey brown hair with artificially enhanced blonde highlights, freckles on her shoulders, and a mouth that was too tight to be beautiful. Monica Bradshaw was terrified of turning thirty. She had an MBA from Harvard, and she was working as a manager for a company that was not a bank and not a stockbrokerage, but it did something with money; Adulfa was too impatient to figure out exactly what. Monica Bradshaw was pissed off because she kept hitting the glass ceiling. She wanted out of her current job, which was supervising secretarial services, so she could get her smart-yet-sensible pumps on the fast track to real money and prestige.

Just one week ago, the higher echelons of her company had okayed her proposal to downsize her department. Monica had promised them the same level of service with a much smaller investment in employees' salaries and benefits. One-fourth of her staff was going to get their layoff notices tomorrow, a week before Christmas. If this didn't catch the eye of the old boys' network and put her in line for a promotion, she had a backup plan, which was to fire everybody and outsource "administrative support" from independent contractors.

Adulfa was more than happy to give Monica Bradshaw the recognition that her talents deserved. Almost lovingly, she petted her way through the obsessions, phobias, traumas, irritations, and fetishes hidden in the cortices of Monica Bradshaw's maniacal little mind. Adulfa did this as she stalked behind her intended, who was whisking through the lingerie department. Her first act of possession was to take hold of Monica's frantic wolverine personality, tear up her list of rush-rush-rush things to do, and send it away on a tropical puff of indolent air. Slowing down, looking a little confused and concerned, Monica began to actually look at all the lovely silky things around her. And she dutifully picked up the items that Adulfa selected for her. Looking a little distracted, she shed, one by one, her navy blue blazer, her blouse, a white satin Bali bra, a gold chain, a skirt that matched the blazer, white flats, pantyhose, and a scrungy pair of old Jockeys for Her, which had been the only clean underwear in Monica's drawer when she got dressed for work that morning.

"What, no ankle chain?" Adulfa laughed, and pivoted the puppet to make it face her for the first time.

Monica Bradshaw was not happy with what she saw. Adulfa reminded her of the white trash punk girls who occasionally intruded on her much more middle-class circle in high school, girls with wild colors in their hair and switchblades in their Hello Kitty pocketbooks. No one could have mistaken Adulfa for anything other than a woman, but her affect was far from womanly. The ultrashort hair combined with the micromini, deep cleavage, and nasty shoes sent strong conflicting signals. "Come here, if you want to be killed," was the slogan that came to Monica Bradshaw's mind.

"Aren't you the clever one?" Adulfa said aloud, and erased the insight. She made her chosen one pirouette in the aisle, and as she turned, she donned, one by one, the pieces of the costume that Adulfa had made her glean from the pastel rows of slinky merchandise.

First she rolled stockings up her shapely, aerobicized legs. They were a dark brown color, and had no seams, but they were silk, thirty dollars the pair if anyone was counting anything other than Monica Bradshaw's perky, ruddy nipples. Adulfa abhorred nylons. Then the AWOL middle manager stepped into a pale pink G-string, and a matching push-up bra. Over that went a champagne-colored, mid-thigh–length slip in moiré silk. It was slit up the back far enough to provide a glimpse of the top of Monica's stockings, and cut so exquisitely that lace would have been superfluous.

"You don't really need shoes, because you're not going to be walking much," Adulfa said. She allowed Monica to come to a halt. She was a bit out of breath. But she had performed the difficult maneuvers with an unusual amount of grace. Could it be that there was another side to this petty bully, something in her soul besides a pocket calculator and the day's NASDAQ quotes? She looked lovely, dressed this way. The colors Adulfa had picked made her skin look translucent. Adulfa bit her lower lip and made Monica perform a series of ballet exercises, using a rack of garter belts as a barre. Not half bad. "Perhaps you do need shoes. Dancing shoes," Adulfa said, and with that thought a star was born.

On their way out of Nordstrom's, Adulfa snagged a pair of pink satin slingbacks and personally slipped them onto Monica's somewhat oversized feet. "Let's find a more appreciative audience," she told the shivering woman, and took her down the escalator toward the street. "The women in this place look as if they've never had an orgasm, and the men look as if they dribble out their spunk."

They headed for the Tenderloin, protected from unwanted attention by Adulfa's fierce powers. It was dark and cold. The wind had picked up, and sped between the tall buildings with a vengeance.

Adulfa disliked the taste that exhaustion lends to the blood, so she picked Monica up and carried her along. She did not bother to dispense forgetfulness as they traveled. What were these weaklings going to do, stop her and take Monica away from her? That would be amusing.

Besides, she was busy working on Monica, fondling her breasts and her consciousness. The tits were nice, but the rest of it was such a mess. It would have taken hours for Adulfa to change the root directory of Monica's mind. The fundamental assumptions ("I will never have enough," "No one cares for me," "I am not safe," "I must ignore other people's needs to get what *I* want," etc.) were as hard as bedrock. Adulfa tried dislodging Monica's obsession with money, and met with surprisingly stiff resistance. So she planted a little seed in the granite of Monica's heart, a little spark of erotic hunger. The red vine of sex-need grew quickly, twining itself about the green vine of cash-hunger, and Adulfa laughed to think where she was taking this rare orchid to flower.

Finding the red-light district is the same in every city, she thought. *As drunks and shit get thicker on the street, so do hookers and drug dealers.* Soon she was in the middle of a neighborhood that offered wares every bit as expensive as the big department stores on the main thoroughfare. But this sort of business could not put its merchandise in bright windows. The darker and dingier an establishment was, the more piquant its commodities. Adulfa stopped outside a place she knew quite well, a dance emporium called Sugar and Spice. Its signs declared: "And everything naughty, that's what our girls are made of!"

Adulfa sent Monica through the door ahead of her. She wanted to see the reactions of the patrons to her new acquisition. Feeling cruel, she did not soften Monica's perceptions of the place. She just kept her walking forward, making her stalk like a panther in heat toward the stage. But inside her, it was the soul of a prim, bright young woman who looked down on sluts and strumpets, an ambitious professional who would never dream of sleeping with her boss to get ahead, who heard men hoot their lust at her and smelled the freshly spilt semen in the private video booths.

The main attraction at Sugar and Spice was a large, glass-enclosed stage surrounded by booths, where patrons kept a blind from coming down and closing off their view of the dancers by constantly feeding quarters into a slot. This created a distance between the strippers and their admirers that Adulfa found completely appropriate. Let men hang their dripping tongues and dicks out, panting like the dogs they were for a favor they would never receive. She sent Monica among them like a clipper ship, majestically overturning dinghies with its wake. And like the noble wolf she was named for, Adulfa followed her, declaring the boundaries of her territory. A lucky few of the customers managed to touch the tips of their fingers to Monica's silk slip, creamy breast, or dusky thigh, but when they saw Adulfa's snarling mouth and prominent, pointed teeth, they suddenly felt rather the opposite of being blessed by fortune.

Adulfa had been here before. It was one of her favorite places to hunt. In a small city like San Francisco, it was necessary to become familiar with the few places where prey could be snatched that would not be missed. One of her favorite dancers was performing, a tough little Asian punk who wore combat boots with a ballerina's tutu. Since she had already removed her top, there was no telling what blasphemy she had done to fashion and femininity to cover her breasts long enough to get up on stage. She had a platinum-blonde stripe in her long, thick black hair, and she wore kabuki makeup. Her name was Poison, and her dance was full of martial arts moves that made the more traditional shimmying she did seem ironic to any observer who was not a half-wit. Adulfa thought Poison was delightful, as touchy about her independence as a Shinto priestess, as thoughtless about displaying her sexuality as if the world had already been made a safe place where women ruled, as inviolable as Amaterasu.

Adulfa ejected one of the spectators from his tiny enclosure and sent him away with a strong suggestion that he find a video viewing booth with a glory hole and suck cock until his throat was pummeled raw. She directed Monica to take his place, and stood behind her to prevent her from being violated by anything other than the spectacle of female flesh, pride, and hostility. She also sorted out some of the male reactions that were going on all around them and funneled a few of them into Monica's mind, so she could feel her own body charged with the adoration and raw need the audience had brought into the dark plywood stalls along with their heavy rolls of quarters.

"I am going to make you do that," she told Monica Bradshaw, who was breathlessly observing Poison's hands, cupping tits and crotch, and tits again. "Then *you* will be the one who makes them feel that way." The stripper made an elaborate show of licking her fingers, circling her nipples, wetting her fingertips again, and slowly running them down her body to her clit.

There was enough left of Monica's original consciousness for her to feel a great deal of panic and denial at this threat.

"But I thought you were a heterosexual," Adulfa said, teeth gleaming. "This is what it means to have traffic with men, my oh-so-ornamental one. Now go like the little lamb you are, and do me proud."

She took Monica out of the booth and sent her backstage, past a sleepy-looking, dirty-blonde butch whose neck was ringed with hickeys. Adulfa's mouth tingled at the smell of blood so close to the surface, but she made herself wait. This was Bo. As the houseboy of Poison and two other bitch goddess strippers, her life was almost as hard as Adulfa would have made it. *Best not to tamper with another she-wolf's province*, Adulfa thought, chuckling at Bo's memory of her weekend, which seemed to have been spent in front of the fireplace, fisting two of her mistresses while the third whipped her shoulders. Having been in Bo's mind before, it was child's play for Adulfa to suppress the bodyguard's complaint about Monica's trespassing, and whisk the new toy up on stage.

Poison was not pleased to have another woman join her. She was collecting a decent amount of tips, and she did not want to share. For some reason, Adulfa disliked the idea of toying with Poison's perceptions. Perhaps it was the kinship of their sadism that made her feel as if this would be poaching. So she put Monica on her knees and stretched out her lovely hands in the universal gesture of submission. "You're so beautiful," Monica said. "Please let me serve you."

She began with adoring Poison's combat boots, petting them with her hands and then with her mouth. Adulfa enjoyed applying just enough pressure to Monica to force her to commit these strange and humiliating acts. It took a high level of skill and concentration to get the behavior she desired out of her quarry without actually changing her personality enough to make her enjoy it and begin to submit voluntarily.

Of course, there was a natural feedback process that Adulfa could not control, that was bound to change Monica into another woman altogether, even without the vampire's mental manipulation. She knew that men were watching her and becoming terribly aroused. She also knew she was safe from their intrusive touch, and so their arousal became contagious. The fact that money was being shoved through peepholes toward her satin-encased pussy was also a powerful aphrodisiac. As Poison rubbed Monica's clit with the tip of her boot, she got wet, and the wetness was a most effective reinforcer, miles ahead of M&Ms. Adulfa found herself becoming a little annoyed when Monica unlaced Poison's boots and removed them without prompting, so she could lick her feet and ankles. The sudden absence of resistance made Adulfa feel as if she was going to tip over.

"If you try to go higher than that, I'm going to slap you," Poison warned Monica, who was taking off Poison's tutu and revealing her trademark gold lamé G-string.

Adulfa bet herself it would take a dozen slaps for Monica to persuade Poison to let her put her tongue on the metallic strip of fabric. She relished, vicariously, the oiled and polished sensation of Poison's thighs beneath Monica's hands. The dancer's old-ivory skin was incredibly smooth and soft, and the muscles underneath it were like liquid steel. Bullets would bounce off her hard little ass. She smelled, Adulfa thought, like the most wonderful incense in the world, and wasn't it exciting to participate like this in someone else's first experience of approaching a woman's cunt? Shouldn't every woman have a lesbian experience at least once before she dies? *Yes*, Adulfa thought, *oh yes*. However, she declined to stay in Monica's place while the promised slaps were administered. Those she was content to watch from the outside, dipping briefly into Poison's riled-up mood as one dips nigiri into soy sauce that has been made explosive with wasabi.

Things were getting very hot on stage. Poison was about to break management's strange regulations that prohibited certain sex acts on stage. In her opinion, the owners' hope that this would prevent the theater from being busted was all in vain. Come election time, the cops would appear. Adulfa was not sure that she wanted to share all of Monica's cherries, and so she strolled on stage, pleased to hear the gasp of surprise and recognition that burst from Poison, who just now remembered having seen her before in all kinds of strange situations. "Go," Adulfa advised her, not unkindly. "Take all this money and go home, and forget."

The assembled crowd could not believe their good fortune. Adulfa strolled the perimeter of her Plexiglas arena, letting them get a good look at her light-year-long legs and melon-round asscheeks. She unbuttoned her jacket enough to give them all a peek at her cleavage, but as the dominant member of this duo, she was not about to shuck everything and shake it for them. Oh, no. That was someone else's job.

"Now that you have begun your instruction, you may proceed to a more advanced level of service," she said gravely to Monica Bradshaw, who was groveling on the floor, all purpose evaporated from her scrambled and cornered mind. "Put your succulent mouth to my shoe, little girl, and make it pretty. That's it. Yes, you are right to be cautious. I am hard to please. Ass higher in the air, my dear, let everyone see you in this state of need. Now peel them down, my babeling, softly, slowly, panties off an eighth of an inch at a time. Oh, yes, let us all see how wet the shiny curls of your little parts have become. What is it that the sweet one needs? Come follow me, now, my darling little slut, and we will make sure all the gentlemen are equally educated about your base and bottomless need."

Adulfa pivoted, forcing Monica to come after her, shambling awkwardly on hands and knees, legs spread in a hapless invitation, heart aching for something, but no image to answer her mind's question about what it was she wanted with such fervor.

"Why, this, of course," Adulfa answered, overflowing with charity. She bent and touched Monica there, in the place that was sore and chafed from being wet for so long, and as Monica came so did many other people. Adulfa's slender finger was like a claw upon her clit, and the impromptu stripper gave herself up to pleasure as the fallen deer gives itself up to the arrow in its heart. There was so much money on the stage that Adulfa kicked up a bit of a breeze to blow it toward the exit, where Bo could collect it. The houseboy butch was still standing guard for Poison, who was changing into street clothes backstage and getting one hell of a headache.

"'Tis the season to be jolly," Adulfa announced. She waited a bit, then added, "It is better to give than to receive." She bent to Monica, kissed her tear-stained cheeks (much saltier than blood, those tears), and stage-whispered, "What have you gotten me for Christmas, my angel?"

Monica stared about herself in shock and disarray. The spaghetti straps of her slip had slunk down her arms, and her body was half-bare, looking hauntingly lovely even in the nasty greenish fluorescent light. Her voice was rusty from lack of use, but a pressure between her ears told her she must answer this unfair and ridiculous question. "I—I'm afraid I haven't got anything for you," she quavered.

"Oh, but you're wrong. So very wrong," Adulfa said, shaking her head. "You have so much to give me. All that you are, all that you could have been, that is the fruit that I am about to pluck."

Adulfa picked her up with one hand. Monica gasped to feel her feet leave the floor. "Put your soles on my shoulders," Adulfa advised, and so she did, not having any choice. "Pretend I am a tree that you are going to climb," Adulfa said, twisting her other hand between Monica's thighs. "A Christmas tree, I think, ablaze with glorious tapers, decked with every bonbon and gimcrack a child's greedy fancy could hope to see. And you are about to become the angel at the top of my tree."

Monica screamed as Adulfa's hand took possession of her channel. It was a cry of outrage, not a cry of pain. She was angry to discover that she could be made to receive so much; afraid of what it implied about her character. She cried out again in fear and triumph when Adulfa, glaring from the mental effort it took, levitated her until she stood without support upon the air. It looked as if the only thing that held her up was Adulfa's upraised arm and fist.

It was a pretty sight, but it apparently had blown the audience's fuses, because the tips had faltered and a deadly silence had fallen over them all. Even those who had run out of quarters half an hour ago were compelled to remain and witness what was about to occur. For once in their lives, they wished an obscuring curtain would fall to protect what was left of their innocence, but they were not about to be granted the mercy of blindness.

Adulfa began to turn Monica's body, still holding her up in the air. Slowly, slowly, she made her rotate, gradually picking up speed until she was swimming in a circle upon the impaling fist of her captor. Despite the sobs of orgasm and terror that came from her victim, Adulfa insisted that she hold a graceful pose straight out of *Swan Lake*. This was supposed to be a dance club, after all.

And then the ballerina came to earth, soaked with sweat and other juices, wrung out and exhausted by passion fulfilled, fucked beyond her wildest dreams of sexual excess. (Which, in Monica Bradshaw's case, had actually been domesticated dreams of passion defeated. She wanted a man with a regular paycheck and unreliable erections—lesbian bed-death without the stigma of homosexuality.)

Adulfa slowly and deliberately tore the clothing from her body, discarding each tiny rag as if it were putrid. She bared her fangs and approached the cringing woman. Once, twice, three times she slowly chased her widdershins about the stage, and now some of the men in their booths were screaming and pissing themselves with fear, beating on the walls to try to smash their way out.

Really, it is a pity, Adulfa thought, *by all rights it should be the men whose lives I take.* They were the ones she hated. And she didn't mind killing them on general principle, especially if she happened upon one in the act of assaulting or abusing a woman. But she didn't like the way they smelled. Their blood had an offensive taste, as if it was slightly spoiled. And then there were those prickly necks, ugh, it was like trying to eat a salad of stinging nettles.

Adulfa loved other women. Their bodies stirred her the same way that works of fine art or great vistas stirred other people. Women were her passion, firmly at the center of her life. She had always felt that way, even before the world had a word for gay girls or bulldaggers or lesbians or dykes. This exclusive obsession had made her peculiar even in a culture that had no strictures against same-sex intimacy. And now, because this was where her lust had taken her, she would not even need to harden her heart before she took the gift that could never be returned.

And so she took Monica in her arms, caressed her back and shoulders, and granted her the favor of one last climax, one that was so intense it brought tears to both of their eyes. The shaken girl was too far gone to even notice that she was coming without anyone touching her vulva. Monica hardly noticed the fangs in her neck or the fading of her own vital signs as her blood passed obediently into Adulfa's painfully hungry mouth. As Adulfa's arms tightened about her, Monica's loosened until they fell back limply. There was barely enough blood left in her body to leave a faint trail down Monica's shoulder and breast. Adulfa dropped the body before she could see the pitiful red drops kiss the chilly, lifeless nipple. She felt no gratitude, just repletion.

She was warm now, heated to boiling, full of light and life, happy and sleepy and not a little high. She licked her teeth and contemplated the little crowd that was motionless and mute, still in thrall to her terrible will. She was tempted to simply leave the body and go, and let them all deal with the consequences, as expiation for their crimes against women. While she thought about it, she made all of them wail for Monica's death and scratch their own cheeks and chests. She tweaked each one of them, pinching out the bits of them that were mean or thoughtless toward women. By the time they left this place, they would not remember what they had seen, and none of these men would ever again fondle his secretary's bottom, slap his wife, pay a housekeeper minimum wage, or slight his daughter's ambition. For the rest of their lives, all of them would sleep with their hands clasped tightly around their own necks, curled up in the fetal position, as if they dreaded the sharp teeth of some night-flying succubus.

Adulfa forced herself to pick up Monica's remains. Her skin cringed instinctively from contact with the corpse. Humans were so distasteful when they were empty, as unsightly as used-up tins of soup. Her brother Ulric was fond of mortals, wasn't he? Then he ought to pay his last respects to this one! His insufferable mortal companion could help Ulric to fill in her grave. Lilith, that was the name he had given her. He *would* choose a blonde, as if there could ever be another fair-haired woman in his life who would mean as much as his half-sister.

There was just time enough to leave them both this little token of her affection, before dawn crowded night from the sky. She sought the wild dark wind, thinking how very glad she was that she had not left all of her Christmas shopping till the very last minute this year.

CHAPTER 12
She's Coming for You

The music at Tight was, as usual, almost too loud; the lights so low that play with a whip became a perilous proposal. Still, people appeared to be talking, arranging encounters, and carrying them out. Lilith sat on a crudely made chair upholstered in black leather and brass tacks. It was butch dungeon chic, a modern recasting of Inquisition aesthetics, and she could still smell the stain and varnish that colored the bare lumber of its limbs. *She would* not *get a headache*, she vowed, though she knew that Ulric could put his hands on her head and remove the pain. He was jumpy tonight. They both were. Although there was no reason for discord between them, they were in a funk. Lilith had thought she was coming down with the flu until Ulric confessed he felt the same malaise. "If you are feeling unhappy," he said, "the best thing to do is to leave the house and make someone else feel even more unhappy." But Lilith thought that coming to the club had not really helped improve her mood.

Ulric sat at her feet, massaging them, and she did not want him to stop. The two of them were wearing modern fetish apparel tonight. The Victorian dresses that she usually loved seemed like too much trouble tonight. That kind of outfit would take up too much space in a crowded club. Instead Lilith was wearing a strapless black leather sheath that ended at mid-thigh. Her stockings were held up with lace elastic tops, so there were no garters to disturb the smooth column of the dress. The little patch of the leather G-string felt cool against her sex. She was also wearing an elaborate necklace that Ulric had given her, a wide fan of diamonds and rubies that almost took attention away from her cleavage. She had a matching ring on her wedding finger, and a few scarlet and crystal ornaments to hold up the loose chignon of her blonde hair. She had been wearing English pumps with six-inch heels, but Ulric had taken those off. They sat on the arms of the chair on either side of her, like strange guardian birds.

It was only because of the speed and strength of the inhuman creature who lovingly worked the joints of her toes that she dared sit in such a place, wearing a sheik's ransom in precious jewels, with her hair its natural honey gold, and her breasts thrust out as a warning and a lure, her slender bare legs crossed at the knee, so that anyone could look at them. Ulric had the capacity to deflect most forms of unwanted attention, and the power to put a stop to anything else. He also had the siren's capacity to draw whatever adventure she might crave into their sphere of influence. Tonight she wanted very badly to flog someone, and he was sorting through the crowd, looking for just the right sort of masochist. She had figured out what the word "switch" meant now, though she thought of herself as a bottom who occasionally got feisty.

There were plenty of warm bodies for Ulric to squeeze like sponges for the information they contained. The large room was crowded with metal cages, wooden stocks, Saint Andrew's crosses, bondage tables, a dentist's chair, slings, and other thrones like the one that Lilith had commandeered (which could also be used for bondage). The music drowned out the sound of cat-o'-nine-tails and unbraided floggers hitting bare backs and buttocks, and erased the sizzle of an ultraviolet wand being used to torment a giggling girl in a cage, so that the scenes involving these implements looked like old silent movies with a frantic soundtrack. But occasionally you could hear the rifle-shot of a blacksnake or bullwhip breaking the sound barrier, even over the pounding bass of disco gone bad. Yelping protests and heartfelt "Yes Sir!"s also soared above the music's infernal syncopation.

But something else was going on in the club that was at least as interesting as contemplating the tangled mess that Lilith's bad mood was making of her past, present, and future. Now, there was something that you didn't see very often in this club—a scene between two men. Why had this couple chosen to perform for this particular audience? There were plenty of S/M play spaces and private parties for men only. Nevertheless, an older man in a Los Angeles Police Department uniform, with silver hair cut military style, had draped the young and nicely muscled body of his slave upon one of the X-shaped crosses. Each hand was restrained with a separate set of handcuffs that ran around the wrist and back to an eyebolt on the cross. Lilith raised one eyebrow at this potentially dangerous arrangement. A bottom who thrashed around a lot could hurt their joints or cause nerve damage by banging their hands against those steel bands. They were American handcuffs with sharp edges; none of the rounded thick steel that you saw in its English cousin.

Without so much as a by-your-leave, the cop took his belt off and doubled it up. He showed it to the boy, then beat him, zero to sixty, no warm-up, no breaks. The kid took it like a trooper, kept both feet planted on the ground, did not protest or dance about. When his entire backside was the color of a livid sunset, the cop stood aside and looked out at the crowd, a challenge on his face.

Somehow, by the psychic currents that circulate through such places, a bevy of beautiful young submissives were sent over to the pinioned boy. They all had long hair, albeit of various colors, and wore collars and had initials tattooed or branded on their hips. Most of them had pierced nipples, a few also had pierced labia or clits, and some wore little chain mail tops that did not quite cover their nipples, or beaded

Cleopatra headdresses, or a bit of bright silk tied about the waist. They took over the boy, running their hands down his helpless body, handling his cock and balls. One girl took him by the hair and bent his head back and kissed him deeply. Other girls were busy with his nipples or pressed their sassy young breasts against his sore back.

The cop looked very amused. From the way his young slave's huge, dripping hard-on went soft as soon as the women touched him, Lilith guessed he was a Kinsey 6. When the master had enough of watching his property being taunted, the cop sent the slave girls away by snapping the doubled-up belt in his hands. The sound was almost as loud as a bullwhip, and it scattered the slave girls back to their own handlers. Another belting followed, and this one turned the streaks of red to blue blossoms, which must have been quite deep, Lilith thought, if she could see them from across the room.

Then the cop took out his cock, broke a bubble of lubricant over it, spread the boy's asscheeks, and entered him a little too quickly to allow him time to open for the assault. Lilith's jaw dropped. She realized that Ulric was as alert as she was, trembling with excitement as he watched. The young slave was sodomized at length, and still he kept his peace, his big dick jerking as it held back the cum he had not been ordered to spill. The cop's thumbs and forefingers used his nipples like reins, yanking him to and fro. This was a selfish master who seemed a little careless with his property, as if he did not care whether or not he broke it. Still, Lilith noticed, he had not broken the boy; he kept him on the proverbial short leash.

Finally the master wrapped his hand around the boy's cock and made him shoot after half a dozen short strokes. When the big cock hung soft and wrinkled against the slave's emptied balls, he picked up the pace of the fucking and hammered into his property, finally reaching his own climax. Lilith patted Ulric's shoulder in sympathy. She knew (because he knew) how hard it was to keep on taking a big cock up the ass after you'd come. This cop was so mean to his pretty possession. And that looked like such a tender ass.

The handcuffs fell open, and the cop turned the boy around and kissed him, then forced him to his knees to clean his cock and put it away. Lilith realized a condom had never been in evidence—another transgression against house rules. She didn't think she'd ever even seen one of the straight masters' cocks. They got their girls all hot and bothered here, then took them home to fuck, or had a leatherdyke give them a good pounding with a strap-on. Lilith assumed that the straight masters at the club didn't trust one another to copulate publicly; it would make them too physically vulnerable. This man didn't seem to have any fear of being attacked or interfered with in mid-swing. He didn't doubt his own ability to complete what he set out to do, regardless of any spectator's opinion. She wasn't sure who this scene had been staged to shock—the gay boy who had to endure being handled by women, or the straight men who had to watch another man's ass being plundered. The cop was good; he had basically gotten to top every single person in the room. It made her laugh with glee.

"Good boy, Davy," the cop said, and snapped a lead to the boy's chrome collar.

"Thank you, sir," the young man replied, and followed the cop, a prince who had just performed a difficult service for his liege. He was not haughty, but he knew his own worth. Lilith approved. It looked like they were on their way home—or to another club.

"Excuse me," Ulric said, and got to his feet. "I'll just have a word with them, if you don't mind," he said, looking distracted and disheveled. She could always tell when Ulric got turned on because his hair seemed to spring out in half a dozen cowlicks. He pressed her hand and then hurried after the master and his beloved. Lilith grinned at his back indulgently. She wasn't surprised. Ulric was her one true love, but he was also a big slut, bless him. "Hos of a feather flock together," she whispered, and put her shoes back on. Her feet felt lovely after Ulric's ministrations, light as clouds.

When Lilith first realized that Ulric had taken at least as many male lovers as female, she was surprised to find that it didn't bother her. It simply made other things she'd noticed about him make more sense. He didn't use the word "gay" or call himself bisexual. He simply noticed attractive people of both sexes and commented on them with equal enthusiasm, as if he expected her to also be looking appreciatively at bodies both like and unlike her own. Ulric also seemed to have radar for people who had begun life in one gender and then transitioned into the other. Lilith had had no idea before how many of the pretty girls she saw in a typical day in a big city had been born male. And after a week of window-shopping in New York with Ulric pointing out every female-to-male transsexual who went by, she began to suspect any man who had a beard and was under five foot six to be an FTM.

Ulric caused a little stir in Tight when he reentered with the two men in tow, the one still in an LAPD police uniform, the other in a baggy pair of jeans held up with a red sparkly belt. Lilith saw at once that he'd taken blood from the master, who made no attempt to hide the wounds on his neck. The cop's eyes, in fact, glittered with a dark amusement. He wore the two puncture marks as a soldier would wear a Purple Heart.

"Lilith," Ulric said, indicating the crop-haired master, "this is Patrick Kelly."

The cop murmured something that may have been "charmed," and bent over her hand without actually kissing it. Straightening, he put his hand on the young man who attended him. "Davy," he said without looking at him. Then he gave the slave a gentle push in Ulric's direction. "Stay with Ulric, Davy," he ordered. "Do what he says. And do not interfere."

Davy gulped, and Ulric gathered him up. The vampire opened his leather jacket and tucked the young man's face into its shelter, where he would discover that Ulric's body was barely warm, and held almost no odor of its own.

"So," Patrick Kelly said, looking her up and down with clinical courtesy, "I understand you need a back to beat."

Lilith expected him to hand over Davy, and was about to ask whether the slave had not had enough corporal punishment for one evening. She did not particularly enjoy getting the second shot at a penitent. But the cop unclipped his breakaway necktie (it was at that point Lilith realized he was a real police officer) and began unbuttoning his shirt. She stood so she could take these items from him and lay them over the arm of the chair. He was wearing an old-fashioned, sleeveless undershirt, and that came off too. The hair on his chest had not yet turned as completely silver as the hair on his head. She could not help but inhale some of his pheromones as she handled his clothing. Behind the smell of a clean male who has just had some heavy exercise, there were hints of more sinister things — steel and rubber, gunpowder and tear gas.

His body had the visible muscles of someone who has sculpted his torso by hoisting iron. The shirt must have been custom-made to fit those shoulders and biceps. His left nipple was pierced, and a bullet decorated the gold ring that hung below his pectoral muscle. His left arm was tattooed with an image of the Egyptian god Set, the Adversary, while on his right arm Prometheus endured the eagle's punishment for trying to bring light to mankind. On his left forearm was a long scar, a defensive wound. Whoever had taken a slice at him had barely missed the artery. If they hadn't, he would have bled so heavily that no call to 911 could have saved his life.

Lilith's knees felt a little weak, her legs wobbly. Who was she to corral this much violence and cynicism? She knew without having any proof that he was a bad cop, as much of a criminal as the people he arrested. What gall (or stupidity) it took to wear that uniform to this quasi-legal club, thumbing his nose at any authority that might imagine it could stop or punish him.

Kelly apparently felt he had endured enough of her scrutiny. He walked to the same cross where Davy had been pinioned and took hold of a pair of greasy old ropes that hung from eyebolts at the top of each arm. He never knew when the uncharacteristic desire to get the shit kicked out of him would manifest itself. He thought it had something to do with his fear of being trapped and forced, through some physical weakness, to do or say things that he found repellent. The ability to travel through pain with enthusiasm and welcome it was part of his notion of freedom. And he didn't mind that it was a shocking thing to do. "Do your worst," he said cheerfully, "since I believe that it will also be your best."

Lilith laughed, and he briefly joined her. She heard a small noise behind her and turned to see Ulric fondling Davy. Her lover had his hand inside the boy's fly and was extracting his thick rod, bringing it out where it could be teased and controlled. His other hand was wrapped around Davy's neck, and Lilith knew he was intending to blood him here in this crowd, even if he must touch a dozen grubby minds to censor their witnessing of the act. She could see the white points of his fangs descending, and shivered to recall the pain of them sinking into her own flesh, a hot pang that became a pulse, a drumbeat, and then, through Ulric's intercession, the first contractions of an orgasm.

She was this creature's paramour, the chosen one of an ancient undead warrior who did not give his love away lightly. The cop was scary, but the terror he inflicted on the street was of an entirely different order than the nightmare that was Ulric when the full moon drove him mad with hunger, and he became oblivious to right or wrong. Lilith did not make the mistake of imagining that Ulric's power was her own, but by living alongside him, she had acquired enough mojo of her own to handle this cocky sadist who had decided, God knows why, to take a walk on the other side of the dungeon. Associating with Ulric had made her a predator as well.

She went into her bag and picked three whips, nothing nice, though each had its own sensuality. Kelly waited for her first blow, not smiling. He had obviously sized her up and decided that she had whatever quality he looked for in a confessor. Though, she thought, she would not care to hear his confession aloud. She was also fairly certain she could skip the pathos of that and move straight to the penance, and get no complaint from him.

The normal course of a whipping is to lay down a foundation of soft, firm strokes, and escalate slowly. Lilith had a number of beautifully made unbraided whips with suede lashes in a variety of lengths and weights. She had not bothered with those. Kelly was not looking for a top who would ease open the doorway of pain and prop it ajar without ever letting the sharp-clawed beast come all the way out. He lived, son of a bitch that he was, on the edge, exactly where it suited him— in jeopardy, and relishing it. He was also not looking for a stronger will to subsume his own. He knew no one's will could exceed the scope of his own arrogance. He wanted to be hurt, not dominated, and the fact that this would upset Davy (who was weeping while Ulric tongued his nipples and forced his balls to the bottom of his scrotum) was a tasty bonus.

She knew these things just as she knew it would be a mistake to hit the cop on the ass with a cane. Lilith knew also that he was mighty entertained by having met and fed a vampire. Ulric's existence simply confirmed his misanthropic view of reality. His evil was a rational response, he believed, to an utterly corrupt world where anything could happen, as long as it was worse than the last thing that had happened.

The first thing she wrapped her fingers around was a tawse. This was a yard-long tongue of leather a half-inch thick, split into three fingers at one end. It was difficult to find an authentic one, cut out of a single thick hide rather than being made of layers of leather stacked up and stitched together. There was one small family firm in Scotland that still made them, despite the fact that corporal punishment of schoolchildren was no longer legal in Great Britain.

The tawse was not easy to use. It had a tendency to double back and bite the hand that snapped it. For hours, Lilith had practiced the exact flip of the wrist that would send it home. Now she marched over to Patrick Kelly with a cat-o'-nine-tails draped over her left shoulder and a six-foot signal whip made of kangaroo hide wrapped around her waist, and she lambasted him.

"Yes!" he shouted. Pedal to the metal. He liked her style. He did not recognize the implement, and Lilith could have sworn his ears twitched and turned backward, like a wolf's, to better catch its sound. Unable to identify the source of his stripes, he relaxed his shoulders and let his curiosity go. The blow had settled him down, made him determined to go on. She hit him again, so there were two matching stripes running diagonally across each of his shoulders. He was so ready, so eager for the next bolt of pain.

Instead, she walked over to the cross and touched him, putting her cool fingertips to the hot edges of the marks, getting a sense of the quality of his skin and muscles, the depth of the bones' placement within his flesh. He turned his head a little and audibly inhaled. The gesture was as intimate as a lover's kiss upon her parted inner lips. What he drew in made his sharp nostrils quiver. His smile knew a nasty secret.

"You like doing this," he said, his voice low and conspiratorial.

"Indeed I do," Lilith replied, and took up her stance to repeat the attack. She overlapped blows until the officer wore a scarlet peacock's tail on his broad back. Then she spared Ulric and his catamite another glance. The vampire held Davy's face in both his hands, ignoring the bobbing, jutting cock that seemed to be weeping as copiously as its silent owner. Ulric was licking the tears from Davy's immobile face. His fangs were fully extended. She turned back to her subject.

Davy cried out, his pain-sound truly pitiful, as he was tapped. Kelly's back flexed, and Lilith knew he had heard it too, and knew what it meant. Nothing that happened to Davy escaped his notice, even if he couldn't see the boy.

Ulric tightened his grip upon Davy's chest, lifting the lithe body until the cop's slave stood on his toes. He opened his mind and Davy's as well, and shared the bliss that he felt as the hot iron-flavored blood brought wave after wave of life and heat into his mouth. He marveled at the obedience that kept Davy quiet in his arms, offering up his life. The fact that his own blood was flowing rapidly into another man's body troubled him less than the spectacle of his master, marked by Lilith's sport.

Davy had moved through a dozen emotions while watching his owner being flogged, emotions that were heightened by dreading the inevitable violation of Ulric's bestial and destructive kiss. At first he had felt numb incomprehension—why was his master doing this?—and shame because he, Davy, was not suffering in his place. Then he had moved into rage at Ulric and Lilith for taking advantage of Patrick Kelly's odd personality, his tendency to enjoy things that made most people queasy. But the rage had not lasted long, because he had never known anyone to successfully manipulate the boss. Kelly's rule was, "We either have to be making money, or having fun," and Davy had never seen him break it. And he thought he understood now that something important was happening, that his master was receiving something that he needed to go on, a purging or a refueling. So Davy's only task was to try to hold back and wait, just wait for this to be done so he could take his master home, back to the routine he superstitiously relied on to keep the sadistic cop who owned him from being killed by one of the many powerful and unkind people that Kelly loved to fuck with.

A little annoyed at being upstaged, by someone who had his back turned, no less, Ulric wrapped his hand around the last third of Davy's cock and used his thumb to smear the clear viscous precum back onto the sensitive red mushroom head. He manipulated the foreskin, loving the way it moved over the shaft of the young man's cock, like a velvet skin over sponge over bone. With this oddly pure mind, he felt no need to restrict himself, and so he felt free to drive Davy wild with enhanced sensations. The feeling of being jacked off so slowly would be an excruciating sweaty memory for a long, long time.

Davy didn't fight him much. He saw no reason to deny himself this enjoyment since he was under orders to obey the creature who stroked and tantalized his overeager, wine-red meat. Ulric made Davy come just as he finished drinking and took his teeth out of the boy's neck. There was a puddle of white blood on the floor at their feet, its surface spattered with a fine net of red droplets.

A slight shift in Davy's muscles warned Ulric that he was about to lunge forward, and he easily prevented the hustler boy's escape. "My lady is not finished with your lord and master," he whispered in Davy's ear. "Do you think he's had enough, your master? I think not. Stay with me and watch. Watch and learn, little one. The cop who has taken you over has a very interesting inner life."

"Fuck you," Davy said, nevertheless being careful to keep his voice down so Patrick Kelly would not hear him. "You don't care about him or me. We're just food to you. Just...just the evening sideshow. Let me go. Let him go. Please. Let him go. I'll come back to you later, I'll let you drink again. Just let me take him home."

"But he doesn't want to go home just yet, Davy," Ulric reminded him. "You were told to stay with me, and you were ordered not to interfere. Are you going to embarrass him by disobeying such simple, clear instructions?"

Davy stood stock-still in Ulric's embrace, impervious to his caresses, eyes locked on Patrick Kelly's back, the very picture of a dog not allowed to drag his drowning owner from the river.

Abandoning the tawse, Lilith took the cat in hand and made a few experimental figure eights in the air. The tails were thin and so tightly braided they could have cut the facets of a gemstone in her accurate hand. This was a sound that the cop recognized. He put his feet apart a bit to brace himself, and she quickly made him glad he had this foresight.

Lilith used a forehand stroke, switching to her backhand when she felt the muscles in her forearm burn. It was not quite the powerhouse of a belting that the cop had laid on Davy. She did not have the same amount of meat to put behind the blows. What she had instead was precision, an implement that sliced instead of crushed, and a cruelty that matched her subject's. Whether it was guilt, despair, or a warped sense of humor, she could face the bleakest of his moods with one of her own. Whether he was here to be punished, to punish Davy by forcing him to witness an act that overturned the order of his world, or simply because he wanted to fly weightless before the whip, Lilith had her own equally mad agenda.

She was here to forget the fact that the love of her life was a killer who wore the guise of a man as the ultimate sort of camouflage. He pleasured her with an organ that was like a leech, bloated with the blood of another creature. Yet she loved him. He was wise and kind, he took care of her, he knew her better than anyone ever had. He was in his own way innocent, and yet he had chosen to embrace evil. And what was she, to take this thing into her bed, a being who could never be warmed by her unless he stole the essence of the heart that adored him? Despite the comfort, security, and sensuality of her life, did she not have much to atone for? The painful labor of lashing the back of this despicable man was her punishment, as it was Ulric's, to watch his love-slave torture another. Could she not forget herself in the cloud of sweat, the curses that came up off him? Was there not a way out of the dilemma of loving Ulric by losing herself, if only for a little while, in the psyche and wounds of another?

She took the single-tail in her two hands when she sensed that she might soon lose the ability to make it go where she intended. This sound Kelly also knew, and he began to bellow his satisfaction before the leather actually cracked against his skin. He did not speak actual words. Such dialogue always runs the risk of being kitschy, like the stilted soundtrack of a bad porn movie. These were primal sounds, the guttural cries that even deaf-mutes and unfortunates who have had their tongues cut out are able to utter. He was mad with relief—joy, even—and howled as if Satan had dipped his balls into brimstone.

Lilith's hair was soaking wet. Her arms felt as heavy as the concrete limbs of a garden statue. She stumbled over to Kelly and touched him for the second time, felt electricity come from his body into hers. She turned his head, and he thought for a moment that she meant to kiss him. Instead they hung face-to-face, looking upon each other's secrets with open eyes, holding nothing back. She was the first to look down.

"I absolve you," he whispered to her. "You are not what you fear you are, Lilith. I know because I can feel your light shining on me. Love is always a virtue, Lady, even if its object is most wretched."

With tears in her eyes, Lilith said, "I wish I had absolution to offer you."

"He is my absolution," Patrick Kelly said. "Where is Davy? Bring me my boy."

Lilith went to her lover and gently pried the weeping young man from his side. For the first time, she noticed that Davy was barefoot. On his narrow, beautiful feet, he went to the cross and opened the fists that seemed welded to the ropes that had supported Kelly during his ordeal. Davy put one of the cop's arms around his shoulder and took him away. The master's free hand beat a tempo in the air, and blood ran freely down his back from the long cuts left by Lilith's signal whip. He did not bother to put his shirt back on, and the crowd parted to let him through, afraid of his blood and his macabre joy.

A girl with a blue braid sprouting out of the side of her otherwise shaved head crashed into Lilith, knocking her back into Ulric's arms. Both of them had been too absorbed in the sight and smell of the master's blood to notice her staggering toward them. She was wearing paint-spattered overalls cut off at the knee and red Converse high-top sneakers. Under the overalls was an incongruous turtleneck sweater. She did not look old enough to be in a place like this.

"She is coming," the girl babbled, plucking at Lilith's arm. Ulric, trapped behind her, was going slightly mad because he could not reach this interloper and throw her across the room. How dare she put hands on his lover?

"Don't imagine you can hide," the stranger said, drawing back as if she had been offended. She glared at both of them, as if to say, *I know who you are. Don't think you can fool me.* "She can get you whenever she wants you!" she shouted suddenly, pointing at Lilith's face, making her jump.

Ulric had finally gotten around Lilith, but when he tried to put hands on the waif, she evaded him. Since she appeared to be leaving, he let her go; but he was obviously disturbed. "Lunatic," he snapped, and Lilith thought he was about to be angry with *her*.

"Take me home," she said, suddenly exhausted and depressed. Ulric swept up her scattered equipment and stowed her belongings in the black leather toy bag. He escorted her across the floor between couples and small groups hard at play, and a faceless crowd of lonely straight men who came only to watch. Before she knew it, they were on the bike, then home. It was later than she had thought. The midnight blue of pure darkness was being watered down by impending dawn. They took the elevator from the garage straight up to her bedroom.

"Did I not bring you a proper sort of lamb?" Ulric asked anxiously, hoping he would not be denied access to her carved Chinese bed.

"That was no lamb at all," Lilith replied. But she smiled at him kindly, knowing he had meant well. The startling predictions of doom made by the unlikely punked-out prophet were troubling her far more than her relatively brief immersion in Patrick Kelly's worldview. She had a feeling that he was not a bad man to have on your side, although it would always be difficult to be certain where exactly his loyalties had been placed.

"You love wolfish things," he said softly, taking off the heavy necklace and removing the ornaments from her hair. He massaged her bare arms and shoulders, unzipped the dress. "There is no escaping it for you. Is Patrick Kelly a member of our pack, my alpha femme fatale?"

"No," Lilith said shortly. "He has no one but his boy to pack with, and from now on, they had better hunt on the other side of the river." Compared to the cool Japanese women on the walls of her bedroom, she was a hot and sticky mess.

Ulric put out his hand and almost touched her cheek. She could not help herself—her head inclined toward his hand. As her earlobe and throat brushed his fingertips, she blushed; her cheeks were the same color as her nipples. He put his fingers in her hair and loosened the tresses. As each lock slithered from the top of her head to curl past her shoulders, her breath quickened. He put his hand over her mouth, and she nervously bit at the edge of his palm. Ulric froze. "Changed your mind?" he asked, keeping quite still.

Her blunt mortal teeth instantly released him. "Never," she said curtly. "I could not bear to lose you."

He studied her, still holding one of the ruby-headed hairpins. "Shall we quarrel, then?" he asked, as if it were a polite offer to dance.

She gave him an outraged look. Then looked down. "Please, not tonight," she whispered.

"What, then?" he murmured, standing closer to her, his hands on the four remaining pins that kept her hair from freedom. Lilith inhaled and sampled him, wondering if it was his hunger that made her own stomach suddenly contract. They often had each other's dreams, knew what the other was thinking. Love's gift and curse, this mingling of their perceptions and needs. "Let me fix your headache," he suggested.

"I am in your capable hands," she muttered, giving the carpet a conspiratorial smile.

The rest of her hair was suddenly released, and a great feeling of relief tingled along the edges of her scalp. He bent and picked her up—not as a mortal man would, helping her to rise by offering her a hand or by gripping her upper arms—but the way a shepherd picks up a lamb or a mother cradles her baby. He took her entire weight into his arms, literally sweeping her off her feet, rocking her like a colicky child. She had a perverse flash of putting her mouth to his nipple and finding strange but nourishing milk there, all that she could swallow.

Once he had her undressed and in bed, he ministered to her headache, massaging her scalp as gently and completely as he had tended to her feet. "Mmm," she purred. "That feels so nice." The pain was stubborn, however, taking much longer to abate than usual. Finally she became so concerned about the passage of time that she made him stop and sent him to shelter. He knew that she was lying about feeling better, but gave her a kiss and told her they would have a better day tomorrow.

He was puzzled by what was happening to his own body. Normally, the quantity of blood he had taken from Patrick Kelly and Davy, and the experience of holding each of these men, then watching Lilith whale away on someone, should have made his dick as tall and hard as a flagpole. Instead he was shamefacedly relieved that Lilith was not putting any demands on him for stud service tonight. He went to one of his bolt-holes in the attic, then sealed himself in, just minutes before dawn broke.

Neither one of them noticed that the cats had not greeted them at the bedroom door when they came off the elevator.

Lilith spent a few lazy moments in bed enjoying the warm nest and the luxurious feeling of being able to stretch out diagonally across the king-size mattress. Now that Ulric had taken his hands from her scalp, the headache came back with crushing force. Eventually she couldn't ignore it any longer. The medicine cabinet in the bathroom downstairs was stocked for the comfort of guests. There would be something in there for the pain. Then she would go into the kitchen and make herself a cup of tea or coffee. *A little caffeine ought to help the aspirin along.*

Sighing, she got up and put on Ulric's paisley satin dressing gown, and slid her feet into her favorite shearling wool slippers. She went into the kitchen and switched on the electric kettle. Her vision seemed off, as if she were looking through a fish-eye lens. A cup of Earl Grey tea and a stack of buttered toast was usually delicious. Maybe she would have some breakfast to keep the aspirin from hurting her stomach. She filled a small pan with water and set it on a burner, thinking of comfort food from childhood, a soft-boiled egg chopped up with toast. Before she turned on the stove, she remembered that it was better to take the eggs out of the refrigerator while the water was heating up. Eggs at room temperature were less likely to crack. So she went to that ridiculously large appliance, hoping she wouldn't have to bend over to find a carton of eggs. Her head hurt so bad that she was afraid she might throw up. She would take the eggs out and then go to the bathroom and look for some headache medicine. Something strong.

She opened the refrigerator door and screamed. The cats had been stuffed into the refrigerator. Each of them was arranged on its own shelf. They had not gone happily or quietly into confinement. Even though the vampire sleep held them motionless now, they were frozen in positions of anger and fear, backs arched, claws extended, mouths snarling. Lilith grabbed her head and wailed. Something bad was going to happen. Something bad was already happening. It was too late. *Too late!*

She backed out of the kitchen, knowing she should do something to keep Luna, Charley, Anastasia, and Hecate safe from the rays of the sun, but unable to think of a better place to put them. She could not bring herself to go back to the refrigerator with its gruesome contents. She shuffled toward the living room, forced there by painful waves of terror that felt like a heart attack.

There in her favorite chair the corpse of a woman was sprawled, a slender but middle-aged woman in tattered remnants of moiré silk lingerie the color of champagne. Her long brown hair was caked with blood. Lilith's mind felt like a strobe light, a rapid-firing camera that recorded the artificial highlights in the woman's hair, her tight mouth and freckled shoulders, the dark brown silk stockings and pale pink G-string, her big feet in pink satin slingbacks, and the torn slip.

A hoop of Lilith's embroidery lay in the dead woman's lap. It was clear by the reddish brown runnels of old blood on her ravished neck that she'd been killed by a vampire. Ulric could not be responsible, so that meant some malevolent stranger had done this terrible thing, entered their house, and left the corpse here as a warning. There was a furnace in the garage that she knew Ulric had used to dispose of bodies, but she couldn't carry this poor woman down there. Besides, she didn't even want to touch her. Maybe the killer was still here somewhere, hiding behind their telepathic power, ready to grab her. No, that could not be, it was daylight!

Only one person had a reason to defile their home this way. Too terrified to cry, Lilith ran to the library. Where was Ulric? He had to help her—he could not leave her alone with this dreadful tableau. She screamed his name and beat on the fake wall of books that hid his favorite sleeping place. It was no use. The button that made the wall move would not respond to her touch, and even if she could gain access to his vault, she probably could not awaken him. It was also possible that he had picked another one of his niches for this night's slumber.

Lilith huddled underneath his massive desk and made herself as small as possible. Having such a powerful lover had given her a false sense of security. Now she could do nothing but wait for him to arise, and she did not know who she was more angry with—herself, or Ulric.

She had no watch. There would be no way for her to tell how long she had been under the desk. How would she know it was safe to come out?

That was the wrong thing to worry about.

The house was so well-carpeted that she never heard a warning footstep. She was counting seconds under her breath, having some kind of mad idea about adding up the minutes while she hid. It was winter. Darkness would come early, by 5:30 he should be awake.

Time and her breath stopped when a pair of boots appeared in front of the well of the desk. A highly polished pair of black logging boots, knee-high, with utilitarian goldenrod laces. "Here you are," a voice with a slight German accent said triumphantly, and a hand as strong as Ulric's fastened on her wrist. "My ripe little peach," a blonde woman with a bleak expression said, dragging Lilith to her. Lilith's mind was stuttering. *It couldn't be, it has to be, it couldn't be, it has to be...*

Adulfa.

Her captor nodded, acknowledging the name even though Lilith had not said it aloud. She had gotten both of Lilith's wrists in one hand and her grip was painful, the kind of bad pain that Ulric's careful bondage avoided. Adulfa ran the other hand down the front of her body, lifting each breast with an insulting smile, then stabbing between her thighs. She gasped as she was lifted into the air with a hand inside of her, long fingers indifferent to her pleasure, inserted deeply into both of her holes.

"I see he's used you frequently and well," Adulfa said, lowering her to the ground. She spun Lilith around and investigated her backside, squeezing each cheek of her ass so hard that it brought tears to the smaller woman's eyes. "But there are things that men don't know," she said with a hint of a smile.

Then Lilith was flying through the air, and she landed on Ulric's desk upon her back. Adulfa was there to keep her still and splay her legs apart. "Does he make you use this on yourself?" she asked, showing Lilith one of their sex toys.

"Yes," Lilith found herself saying. "I masturbate with it and beg Daddy to fuck me."

Adulfa's face twisted in disgust. "By the time I'm through with you, you won't have any use for a man's stupid stick," she promised. There was no bragging in her voice, just a calm assurance, a recitation of a fact already proven. Lilith had no time to protest, because Adulfa thrust the implement into her mouth, all the way in, and laughed when she resisted. "Oh, what a shame," she said, bringing the dildo out gleaming with spit. "I'm taking you away from him before you lost your gag reflex."

Then Adulfa took her, with professional skill and quite a bit of distaste. Lilith resisted, but her conditioning from doing such things with Ulric seemed to switch her body on, created involuntary responses that were confusing and humiliating. "Such a little animal," Adulfa reproved. "How can you arch your back like that and make such sounds beneath his roof? Have you no loyalty at all? See what a little thing your 'love' is." Leaving the dildo deep within Lilith's vagina, she put two of her long fingers up her ass and lightly touched her clit with her other hand. Lilith's fingers scrabbled across the top of the desk, looking for something she could grab and use as a weapon. Adulfa stopped touching her long enough to backhand her, cutting the right corner of her mouth. "Stay!" Adulfa bid her, and she could not move at all. Everything froze in place, including the muscles that would have needed to contract to make her come.

"Why, having sex with you is like fucking a corpse!" Adulfa said, and jammed the dildo up her ass. Lilith was not prepared, and her anus tore just as her mouth had broken open. Adulfa fucked her that way until the inside of Ulric's bathrobe was streaked with blood. Lilith couldn't scream. The very tears were frozen within the lower edges of her eyelids, unable to spill freely down her cheeks. "Meat, that's all you are. Just a walking, talking piece of meat," Adulfa told her as if she were a judge issuing a verdict on a petty criminal. "Nobody's consort, nobody's lover, just a thing that I am going to take away from my brother, who is too stupid to know how worthless you are. And then I will show him what it means to be helpless. To be violated."

Lilith somehow mustered the resistance to be able to say, "So far, you've only shown *me* what it means to be raped."

Adulfa's eyebrows went up, but she refused to acknowledge Lilith's words. She pried Lilith off the desk, leaving the bathrobe behind and tossing the used dildo on top of it. "Such a nice little Christmas present for my brother," she said, grabbing Lilith by the hair. "I hope your roots are healthy, my girl, because we have a long way to go, and you'll be dangling like this from my hand, the whole fucking way. But I understand you love to fly."

"I love to fly," Lilith found herself saying.

"And you're so glad I paid you a visit," Adulfa prompted.

".Thanks so much for coming by." *What is this idiocy?* Lilith tried to bite down on her tongue to keep it from obeying her captor.

Adulfa spun her around and made her face a corner of the room. "Tell the security camera about the new love in your life," she instructed.

"I'm in love with someone else and I'm leaving you," Lilith said. She wrenched her face around, clamped her jaws together, tried again and again to escape the compulsion that made her utter Adulfa's script. Each word came out like a piece of broken glass extracted from a wound. *He will know I don't mean it*, she told herself, praying it was true. *The speech is so distorted, he will know she made me do it. But how can I let her control me this way? What's wrong with me? Why can't I fight her off?*

"Your hands are tied at the small of your back. You can't separate your wrists," Adulfa said, and Lilith's body crept into that position and then froze. "Now show him how much you love me," Adulfa said, and jammed her fingers into Lilith's smarting ass. Somehow, she made Lilith experience a potent climax, despite her hatred and fear. That was worse than being made to talk like a demented doll whose string had been pulled. Every cell of her body felt soiled. Adulfa showed the security camera her bloody fingers, licked the torn corner of Lilith's mouth, and then pushed and kicked her gagging prisoner to the backyard deck.

They did indeed have a long way to fly.

CHAPTER 13
The Course of True Love Never Did Run Smooth

Lilith was bound to some kind of wooden structure with a rounded top. There was no padding. Her hands were over the barrel or horse (if that's what it was) and firmly tied with real rope to the base of the device. Her legs had been separated and tied apart as well. She was relatively comfortable, except for the fact that there was no padding beneath her stomach and hips. And there was a bag over her head, a dark sack that admitted no light at all.

Since it was tied firmly around her neck, there was no way to peek under it, the way she sometimes could under a blindfold. She felt very thirsty and light-headed, maybe hungry, if such a vulgar thing was possible in these dire circumstances. It occurred to her that she could perhaps dislodge the sack, so she tried rubbing her neck against the wooden structure. Wrists and ankles were not going to budge, and she could not reach any of the knots. It was no use; she remained a blind, captive girl in the power of a very dangerous creature. Someone who had all the power that Ulric had, and more; but none of his compassion or romance.

Lilith realized, as she forced herself to think about what might happen, that she was afraid of pain, and she was afraid to die.

Unending pain was more frightening than death. But worse than both of these was Ulric's shame, agony, or death. The worst thing about being kidnapped was the fact that she could be used to bring Ulric into Adulfa's sphere of influence, where her no doubt elaborate fantasy of revenge would be enacted. Thus demonstrating for all time that Ulric had indeed been a fool to take a mortal for a consort.

Her heart was plunged into a medieval hatred. This was no ordinary slight of the kind that modern people inflicted on one another—an unpaid loan, a hurtful thing said behind one's back, an affair with the husband of a friend. For only the second time in her life, the word "enemy" had genuine force behind it. Hate, however, was as dangerous as fear. It would dull her senses, give her a grandiosity unmatched by her circumstances, hush the unpleasant voice of sanity that was her only potential road away from harm. Still, she could only shift that red rage a few inches to the side. It colored the darkness over her face a pulsing maroon. *My love is no fool*, Lilith vowed. *He will take no hurt from me.*

She tested each of her bonds and decided that her right hand was perhaps not as snugly lassoed as her other extremities. (In fact, they all felt equally tight, but her right hand would do the most good if it was free.) So she began to wiggle her wrist and tug against the rope, resting only when she felt a cramp coming on that might disable her for longer than a short break. Then she went back to her determined, if futile, campaign to break free.

A door opened, and the air in the room shifted, became slightly cooler. Lilith froze. She could hear footsteps. She thought she detected two different treads. *Adulfa and someone else?* They were arguing. Or rather, one of them, a voice Lilith did not recognize, was trying to argue with Adulfa, who would have none of it.

"What is she doing here? Why do you need her when you have me? She hates you! She'll never give you what I give you. Stop walking away when I'm trying to talk to you. Answer me! What is she doing here? I hate her. Make her go away! Get rid of her. Look at me. Please. Please look at me. God, why do you have her all tied up like that? It looks so indecent. Did you fuck her already? I can't believe you're going to do this right in front of me. You're going to make her give you head while I stand here just two feet away, aren't you? I hate you. No, I didn't mean that. I'm sorry. I'm so sorry. Please forgive me. But I can't stand this. It's killing me. It's tearing me apart!"

The voice was choked off by weeping. There was such a long stretch of silence, Lilith wondered if Adulfa would continue to ignore whoever was spouting off like a jilted lover.

"Stay or go. I don't care," Adulfa said at last. "Your part in this is finished."

"You can't mean that! I know you have to feel something for me. Nobody could look at me so intently when I can't hide any part of myself from them and then take me to the darkest places in my soul, and feel *nothing*. I've given you my pain. Agony. Humiliation! Every time you've called me I've come to you, and you didn't have to force me. I've served you in ways that no one else would tolerate. I—I love you. There will never be anyone other than you in my heart. You've hurt me so much, but I can't help it, I just love you. Why won't you let me love you?"

Lilith was abruptly assaulted. Hands smaller and less forceful than Adulfa's rained blows upon her back, head, arms, and legs. She could not cover herself or move away. She took the only control she had left and refused to cry out. The slaps and punches stopped as abruptly as they had begun. There was a loud thud, the sound of something large falling on the floor or hitting the wall, she could not tell which.

"I've given you life. If you don't value that gift, I will be happy to take it back," Adulfa said.

There were loud tears and more accusations. A door opened and shut. Lilith tried to bring her racing heart and panting breath back to a normal, steady pace. But she was alone with Adulfa, and the tall vampire woman was coming closer, her tread as steady and sure as a night watchman making the midnight rounds in the village of his birth.

Reaching accurately despite the intervening cloth of the hood, Adulfa touched a bump on the back of Lilith's head. Then she untied the strings at the back of her neck and slowly removed the sack, so that it slithered across her face. What she said then took Lilith entirely by surprise.

"You have such pretty hair," her captor said, running her hands through it. "It's amazing how many different shades of blonde there are, isn't it? You and I, we have the same hair color, but it's not the same at all. Yours is...welcoming. Lush. Innocent."

Adulfa sounded almost wistful. Lilith shook her head and tried to steel her heart. Was this some kind of manipulative tactic—bad cop, then good cop? A conscious attempt to trigger Stockholm syndrome? She couldn't empathize with Adulfa; it would weaken her already frail and insufficient defenses. But she had been trained to read a top, to pick up on the vaguest hint of Ulric's moods and whims. She had a knack for flowing into the perfect role to accommodate his needs.

Adulfa walked to the front of her. Lilith's face was level with her hips. She could smell Adulfa's body and sex. How nice it would have been if she smelled putrid, like a ghoul or a hanged man left on the gibbet for a fortnight. Instead, she smelled elegant and enticing. Lilith was surprised to find herself constructing a mental image of Adulfa's cunt and thinking that even though she was a complete bitch, she probably tasted wonderful. She asked herself if she could do a good job of licking Adulfa's cunt. She couldn't help it; she was a sex-slave. Ulric had trained her to use her mouth with intelligence and delicacy.

A clit wasn't like a cock; it wouldn't enjoy the same treatment. But Lilith thought she could be creative. She could slide her tongue along Adulfa's inner lips and shyly explore her clitoris. Move down, lick the opening of her vagina, lick up the other side of her cunt, then make sure her mouth was wet before she moved the clitoral hood back and forth with her pointed tongue. Put her soft lips around it, tug it gently, and see if any of these caresses were rewarded with a movement of Adulfa's hips or a change in her breathing.

Lilith's mouth was open and she was panting. Adulfa was touching her neck and her back, gently, but with a pressure that was possessive. Lilith knew—with a faith that was religious in its intensity—that Adulfa was a wonderful fuck, the best a girl could ever have. But she had saved her worst for her brother's unlucky mortal property, not her best. Would Adulfa do as Ulric had done and take blood from Lilith? And would Lilith enjoy it as much as she did when Ulric penetrated her this way? The thought was horrifying. But Adulfa's hands on her were thrilling. The combination of the sensual caresses with Lilith's terror overwhelmed her; she cursed herself for getting wet and for the way her skin begged for more contact with Adulfa's perceptive hands. She must look like a wanton strumpet strapped to a horse, anybody's ride.

Adulfa touched her face. She was gathering up Lilith's hair. Both of her hands fell upon Lilith's face as she tried to twist the tangled tresses into a single strand she could pin up in a clip. When the palms of Adulfa's hands landed on her cheeks, Lilith spun off into a movie that was as real as the present. Only her prior experience with Ulric's reminiscences allowed her to figure out that she was receiving a piece of Adulfa's past. A piece that Adulfa might not have given her deliberately. A piece that Lilith was not sure she wanted to experience.

But she had no choice. She could only stifle hope, and endure.

Normally, Henri would not bring his fine pair of matched sorrel geldings to this poor part of Paris. He was very choosy about which streets he trusted with his fine coach with the German-milled springs and the seats upholstered in Spanish leather. But he had no choice tonight. He had missed his customary roast beef dinner at the Café Jolie, the trilled flirtatious greeting of Madame Rousseau, his two glasses of red wine, the small salad afterward to cleanse the palate, and to finish, the little cup of espresso with lemon peel and cardamom. Not only was he bringing his unusual passenger to her squalid destination, he was going to wait to take her home once her unspeakable business was concluded.

That passenger was Adulfa, wearing a man's expensive evening suit and a top hat, the apparel she favored during the 1890s. She carried a cane with a ruby knob and wore a fashionable short, black wool cape. Nobody would catch her wearing a man's shirt and suit coat with a long skirt, like the faux-butches who frequented Le Monocle. But then, Adulfa did not have to worry about getting stones thrown at her by angry citizens who disapproved of mannish women. Street toughs and fishwives gave her a wide berth. Adulfa thought with deep satisfaction, *I am a tiger with brass tits, a lioness stalking on two legs through the wilderness of mankind.*

Tonight, she was bound for the Heavenly Golden Palace of Sleeping Dragon Dreams, an upscale opium den *cum* brothel run by the fascinating and dedicated libertine, Monsieur Albert Ching. Last year, Adulfa's passion had been for tubercular poets (*too wheezy*). After a brief fling with absinthe addicts (*too sticky*), she found herself gravitating toward the hazelnut flavor of humans besotted with the exotic, dark gum of the Turkish poppy (*just right*). And Monsieur Ching was as happy to take her money as he was to receive the coin of any other degenerate Caucasian. Unlike many other opium parlors, the Dragon's Palace did not serve any Chinese patrons. Adulfa suspected him of being quite racist, in his own way. But she saw no reason why Monsieur Ching should be any fonder of one part of the human race than she was of the entire species.

The cabdriver waited on his bench, chafing his hands and blowing on them, wondering why his stomach hurt. It was a cold, foggy night. Adulfa had placed enough of a compulsion on him to make him keep to his station, but she had not bothered to erase his awareness that he was doing a dangerous and foolhardy thing. *Let him worry.* She didn't want him in a barmy state of bliss that might result in a heist or an assault that would leave her without normal human transportation. She'd left him her small, pearl-handled derringer, and imprinted the knowledge to use it.

She walked through the carved mahogany doors, handed Monsieur Ching her usual fee (without removing her gloves), and adjusted her monocle before strolling through the corridors. As usual, the palace's beneficiaries ignored her. Given her slim silhouette, Adulfa was often mistaken for a youth, until she opened her mouth to speak. So perhaps the Golden Dragon's habitués were as unaware of her gender as they were of her sinister intentions.

This was the ground floor, where most cubicles were occupied by single men, each attended by a Chinese girl or boy who knew how to load the proper-sized bead of opium into the tiny bowls of the pipes, how high the flame must be turned, at what angle to hold the pipe, when to put the pipestem to the client's mouth so he could inhale heaven. There were also larger rooms where friends could chase the dragon together, and hire female or male companionship if they wished—though this was more for show than actual eroticism. Opium ecstasy apparently superseded the more acrobatic human pleasures.

No one seemed to notice her passing. If the inebriated customers saw her at all, they probably assumed she was on her way to her own cubicle or cubbyhole. Instead Ching's customers sprawled, limbs childishly akimbo, heads full of peaceful and lovely visions, dead to any awareness of the Chinese servants' scorn or the murderous intention of the cross-dressed woman with short blonde hair. The people who worked here were already familiar with Adulfa, and let her know, through their exquisite courtesy and bland smiling faces, how much they detested her mission. It would not have surprised her to learn that they knew she was a vampire.

She idly sorted through the personalities of these besotted people, as if they were fortune-telling cards bearing bright illustrations of many possible futures. What mood, what story, what sort of face and body did she wish to dine upon? She had been overindulging of late, so the hunger was not particularly painful. She could afford to take her time tonight and select someone pleasing, somebody special. The Palace was such an appropriate venue for her quest. All of the people here wanted to die, or at least escape. She was simply a more rapid means to that end than opium or syphilis.

A pipe at Monsieur Ching's did not come cheap, and you had to be brought here by someone who was already in good standing in order to gain membership. So he had taken some trouble with the appearance of his establishment. It was not a hovel of mismatched boards and dirty plaster like some of the more desperate opium dens closer to the docks. There were thick rugs with embossed designs in deep blue, soft red, and tan upon on the floor. The walls had been painted red, with occasional ornamentation in black and gold. Here and there stood lacquered screens with carved designs of birds or flowers. Oversized blue-and-white porcelain vases full of fresh flowers stood on pedestals in alcoves. There was plenty of detail to catch and confuse an intoxicated eye, enough pretty comfort to keep the atmosphere tranquil. Adulfa could not imagine anyone becoming contentious or rowdy after a bowl of opium. It was the perfect drug, except for the part where you got addicted and felt utterly miserable if you could not afford to smoke a little more of it every day, twice a day, three times a day.

Monsieur Ching's attention to appearances extended to his employees. The Chinese attendants wore red or blue brocade jackets embroidered with the golden, sleeping dragon that was his escutcheon. They wore matching round caps and slippers. Their lower limbs were swathed in loose black trousers. The young men were lithe and handsome, the young ladies serene and pretty, and all of them moved as if they were dancing, an everyday grace that charmed Adulfa no end. Their faces were never marred by sadness or anger. The atmosphere of the palace was always calm and measured. No crisis in the outer world had power here.

She yawned. So far, nobody was proving to be as exciting as she had hoped. There was a professional gambler who had lost all of his sponsor's stake. Again. Not even he could pretend to be surprised. A successful businessman with too much money who was angry about his wife's affair with his secretary. What a bore, when he could simply have embarked upon his own adulterous fling. A man in pain from arthritis. Another man in pain from something else, some annoying mortal ailment. A shopkeeper who had acquired the opium habit when he was a young sailor. She almost turned aside for this one, because he had many interesting stories to tell, but his body was past its prime, and she was in no mood to hold a soft, aging body tonight, or look into middle-aged eyes ringed with laugh-wrinkles.

She hesitated before climbing the stairs. Was the second floor going to be more of the same? Unwilling to come up with another hunting ground this late at night, Adulfa sighed and put her cane to the first step. Up she went, remarkably spry for a person of her advanced age. This floor was arranged differently than the one she had just left. There was one large, circular room, with little individual zones of privacy partitioned off by curtains that could easily be pulled back. The floor was littered with huge, brightly colored cushions. There were much smaller, secret rooms around the perimeter, with hidden peepholes, but the women who came here to shed their troubles did not know about that. Tonight Adulfa had paid to be the only spectator at this evening's debauch. (The idea of men spying upon women's ways with one another offended her.) But she did not enter one of the voyeur's stalls. She stood near the fireplace—this room was kept quite a bit hotter than downstairs—and took it all in.

The party had begun at sundown, as soon as enough worshipers of the sweet-breathed dragon had gathered. Already most of the curtains had been withdrawn, so that the women were able to see (and touch) one another. Adulfa watched as two of the female servants approached a reclining woman whose eyes were closed while she savored the twilight state induced by the drug. One of them loosened the brunette's clothing, slowly unbuttoning the top of her dress, and briefly massaging her shoulders before moving down to her breasts. Adulfa felt her breath quicken as the lush brown nipples crinkled and became painfully hard. It didn't take them long to completely open her dress, and her naked olive-skinned body lay against a purple cushion, like a gift for royalty.

Smiling at each other, the attendants continued their mission of seduction. One of them tied an ivory object to the drowsy woman's right heel. It was shaped like a plump duck with a long neck, round head, and fat protruding bill that pointed straight up, as if the bird were trying to retrieve a fish held over its head. The other drizzled oil upon the toy, and then her partner bent the woman's leg at the knee and guided the duck's head into her. She had only to move that leg back and forth a few times before the client took over and penetrated herself of her own accord, moving slowly and sleepily.

Oil fell in a thin stream from the enamel pitcher, directed at the top of the dark-skinned beauty's sex. One attendant put her index finger there and rubbed the oil in, moving in time with the flexing thigh, calf, and foot that were stroking their owner deep inside. The brunette put both of her own hands at the juncture of her thighs and massaged herself, then one hand moved to her breasts, plucking and compressing them. The attendants smoothed her hair away from her face and withdrew, chatting softly in Mandarin about their lucky numbers, in preparation for buying their daily chances in the lottery. One of them asked the other about an herbal remedy for swollen ankles, to take home to her grandmother.

Other servants had lifted another of their guests into a large piece of fabric that hung from the ceiling like a sling or a hammock that one could sit in. While one of them gave her more opium to inhale, the others parted her legs and inserted a pair of fairly large, cloisonné balls. Adulfa knew the balls were hollow, and contained smaller, heavier spheres. As their host was rocked to and fro by her attendants, this device would engender a slowly building sensation of pressure and heat within her.

Other, more adventurous or simply more compliant patrons were being guided to one another, arranged in various tableaux which seemed to be the product of the serving girls' imaginations. Several pairs lay head to foot, pleasuring one another with nimble tongues, occasionally dipping their languid fingers into themselves or the other woman.

Adulfa took a few steps to her left to get a better view of a couple who had perhaps known each other before they arrived. The smaller one reclined with her legs splayed. Her long brown hair was done up in an elaborate coiffure that provided deliciously decadent contrast to her naked body. Her bulkier partner had an unfashionably short haircut that looked awkward rather than attractively masculine. No doubt she had to wear long skirts on the street rather than Adulfa's more comfortable trousers. Adulfa felt an old anger stir, her protest of these times in which women could not arrange their appearance to please themselves. The revolutionary feminist declarations of the Paris Commune had given way to the status quo of *La Belle Époque*.

But what did she care about mortal politics? It was all the same to Adulfa if they helped or harmed one another. She angrily drew her attention back to the here and now and the visual banquet of sapphic skill. The larger woman thrust between her partner's legs, manipulating an artificial phallus that looked as if it was made of ivory or smoothly polished bone. Her strong hands held her lover's shaved sex open, and Adulfa liked the way the bare skin became shiny with her juices. She relished the play of muscles across the active partner's shoulders, the liquid slapping sounds of penetration, the abrupt changes in breath that communicated a desire for a change in pace or depth. The two of them seemed perfectly in synch, and Adulfa wondered how the female stud on her knees obtained her own pleasure.

Eventually she wandered on, loathe to miss any of the fun. There was something that was not easy to arrange—a daisy chain, a small circle of women placed on their sides, each one's pretty mouth aligned with the inner lips of the one who was ahead of her in the circle. This had apparently been one of the first configurations put together this evening, because the participants had roused themselves from their dreams, and were perhaps even a touch frantic in their pursuit of mutual release. Adulfa made herself laugh by going 'round the circle and putting everybody back a pace or two. By the time they each got what they were trying to achieve, perhaps they would value it a little more, having had to work harder for it. Under the incense, Adulfa could smell their sweat and other secretions, and it reminded her of the hunger that had brought her here.

A continuous sobbing sigh came from the women scattered throughout the room, a rising and falling noise that pleaded for just a little more sensation. The attendants moved through the orgy, occasionally replacing a small toy with a larger one, or adding their attentions to bring about the crisis of climax. *No wonder Monsieur Ching's establishment is so very lucrative*, Adulfa thought. Men were so ignorant of women's needs that they were stunned by the simple sight of a girl making herself come, and could not believe it when they learned that each woman has a different way of touching herself. Why the sight of women together should arouse men so much, she could not understand. Amd what an irony that was since the ease and great success of lesbian lovemaking seemed to her to indicate they had no need for male companionship.

Enough of these fruitless speculations about alien psychology. There, curled up like a little lost doggy on a Nile green silk pillow, was Adulfa's pet. She knew it the instant she spotted the girl's Raphaelesque red curls and skin the color of the first slightly blue milk of spring. Not to mention the bruised psyche that oozed out of her, and the remarkably high level of entitlement. Resentment, pride, weakness, indolence, and a desire to be special. A tasty combination. Tabitha (*what an odd name*) was still fully clothed, having resisted the blandishments of her attendant, who now sat back on her heels and kept her narrow eyes on the pipe and lamp. There, at least, was one person who would not be sorry to see someone leave the palace on Adulfa's arm.

Adulfa took the young lady's elbow and helped her to get up. Tabitha did not like being disturbed, but she came upright rather than do something as undignified as fight off Adulfa's hand. She balked, however, at being led toward the staircase, and so Adulfa saw she would have to take the pipe and its contents along. The lamp she had already in her flat. She made a show of pocketing the drugs and paraphernalia, then Miss Cloud of Ruddy Hair was willing to follow her anywhere.

A conspicuous purchase of even more opium from Monsieur Ching by the front door was enough to seal the bargain. The girl patted her hair and bit her lips to pretty herself up when she saw the number of bills that were changing hands. Adulfa was pretty certain that he had no illusions about what happened to the unfortunate inebriates she "helped to find their way home." The only limit he placed upon her was that she must not abduct anyone with a yellow skin. (She had toured Japan five years ago and had her fill of geishas and samurai. It was no sacrifice to abstain from victimizing his Chinese employees.)

Once outside, Adulfa dropped Tabitha's arm, and walked to the coach without looking behind her. The girl ran after what she thought was a young gentleman who could afford costly clothing, somebody who would not be too difficult to manipulate, someone whose embrace, if he should be enough of a boor to insist upon it, would not be aesthetically displeasing.

Adulfa did not help Tabitha into the carriage, which was up a little high for a girl in party shoes. But once the redhead had settled into the seat across from her, the vampire maiden slammed the door with the knob of her cane, and gave her prisoner a conspiratorial chuckle. "Ready for a bit of fun?" she asked, and relished the look of comprehension, the ambivalence on the girl's face as she realized that her companion's sex mirrored her own. *So you smoke opium among the devotees of Sappho,* Adulfa thought, *but you consider yourself high above the cunt-lickers. We'll just see about that. Right now.*

"Show me your breasts," she said crisply.

Tabitha gasped, and kept both of her hands on the cold leather seat.

Adulfa's cane spun through the air and struck her prey across the thighs. It was a crushing pain, and Tabitha cried out from it, and rubbed at the welt.

"I never repeat an order," Adulfa said, clearly prepared to strike again, and derive as much pleasure from it as she would from activities that would be much easier for Tabitha to endure.

The lass reluctantly undid her sheer floral print dress and allowed it to fall to her waist. She had small, perfectly round breasts with coral pink nipples. At first, she thought to cross her arms in front of them, but one look at Adulfa's avid face persuaded her to drop all defenses.

The ruby-headed cane crossed the gulf of space between them once more. Adulfa drew its almost-sharp tip down Tabitha's cleavage, twirled it at the line between white skin and aureole. The nipples responded, and Adulfa smiled triumphantly. Effective stimulation was always more important than a mortal's illusions about their erotic preferences. She firmly believed there was no such thing as a woman she could not seduce and satisfy, even without using her vampiric power to alter the object of her desire.

"Pull up your skirt and spread your legs," she said, putting a mean note into the sentence.

Tabitha grew pale and stammered. But as she dithered, she gathered up the skimpy skirt in both of her hands and crumpled it just below her belly. She wore stockings held up with elastic garters around her thighs.

"Take those off," Adulfa said, pointing to the thin knickers that covered her upper legs and mons veneris.

Tabitha was so frightened, she actually used one hand to keep her skirt up while she awkwardly used the other hand to slip her panties off. Once she had removed them, she did not know what to do with them, and Adulfa said curtly, "Drop that!" The wisp of underwear landed somewhere between their feet. Henri would find a fragrant little surprise in his empty cab, a tawdry flower.

"What a pretty cunt you have," Adulfa said, being vulgar because she knew it would offend her victim. Tabitha's face was flushed, making her look as if she had applied rouge that was too dark. She was one of those women who get large, perfectly round circles of color on their cheeks when they blush.

Knowing Tabitha would study her slightest gesture, Adulfa put the knob of her cane to her lips and delicately licked it all over. "Well-spread now," she reminded the girl, whose thigh joints were already aching, and put the cane between her legs. Its handle was as large as a goose egg, a ruby red oval of hand-blown glass, so carefully mated to the wood of the cane that there were no sharp, protruding edges. It was just the right size to make an impression on a self-centered beauty who disliked having to pay her own way. There was resistance at the entrance, which Adulfa neatly overcame, and soon Tabitha was hissing as her secret passage was filled.

"Let's just sit and be cozy, shall we?" Adulfa purred. The bouncing of the carriage moved the rod within Tabitha. The vampire kept one hand around it to make sure the motions did not cease. She watched Tabitha through slit eyes, interested to see if this cold and calculating person had a sensual side that could be awakened under duress.

It took more than a mile, but eventually Tabitha began to respond to the relentless pressure within her. She bit her lips as her hips moved involuntarily.

"Go ahead," Adulfa said crudely, "moan and groan and fuck yourself. Lick your fingers and finger your clit. You're my whore for this evening. Put on a good show, if you expect me to light the lamp for you later, pretty slut."

This bald statement of the situation seemed to give Tabitha permission to reveal the sensations she was experiencing and the need they evoked. Her narrow hips went back and forth, struggling with the piercing head of the cane, and she ran her hands down her own breasts, scratching them lightly, before placing one hand between her own legs and squeezing her sex. She used the palm of her hand to apply pressure to her clitoris, rather than stroking it with a fingertip. Adulfa watched and remembered.

"Do you want me to fuck you?" she asked, escalating her attack on Tabitha's notions of propriety.

"Oh!" Tabitha said.

"Oh!" Adulfa mocked. "Any whore would know the right answer to that question, my dear. Is my little adventuress less bright than a streetwalker?"

"Yes," Tabitha whispered, her hand going up and down upon her vulva. "Oh, please, I must—I need—put it in me, yes, oh, it's in so deep, it's so big. I—I—"

"You have permission to come," Adulfa said dryly, just before the inevitable storm of weeping and genital contractions took over. It was a good way to plant the idea that Tabitha's sexual response was now under someone else's control. Adulfa yawned. When she was not replete with blood, it was difficult for her to empathize with a human in heat, or to remember what it felt like to crave such an inferior delicacy. La petite mort, *indeed. Let's hear it for* la grande mort.

Withdrawing the cane, Adulfa put the jewel to Tabitha's lips. "Clean it," she insisted. The girl's little pink tongue came and went with surprising rapidity. *So she doesn't mind tasting herself,* Adulfa thought, then said it out loud.

"I wouldn't mind—" Tabitha began, then stopped herself and stared out the coach's bobbing window into the dark, one hand stroking her thigh.

"You wouldn't mind, but you can't say it," Adulfa responded meanly, unwilling to give her any credit. She sponged the cane off with her pocket handkerchief and checked their location out the window. They were getting close to her home. A few moments of silence would be useful for bringing Tabitha's anxiety to a peak.

"Nothing from your old life can remain with you now," she explained, sounding almost kindly, when the carriage halted. "Leave your dress and shoes here in the cab. You can keep your stockings on. Walk ahead of me into the house."

Tabitha hesitated, and Adulfa brought the stem of the pipe out of her coat pocket far enough to remind her of the reward that awaited. She was surprised to realize that Tabitha's picture of her strange hostess' social status had gone up as Adulfa's demands had gotten more outrageous. Eccentricity and decadence were apparently associated in her petty bourgeois imagination with shimmering gold heaps of inherited wealth. This was how Tabitha persuaded herself to obey the latest shocking command. Surely such a wealthy person would not discard her in the morning without replacing her cheap dress with something finer.

Henri had done more than a night of good work for her. Adulfa gave him a generous amount of money and allowed him to remember a brief glimpse of Tabitha's hindquarters. Then she sent him home, and followed Tabitha's slim but nicely rounded buttocks, straight back, and narrow, sloping shoulders down the path that led to the large house where she lived when she was in the mood for a sojourn in Paris.

The path to the house was made of irregularly shaped slabs of slate. It curved between thick stands of night-blooming jasmine. Adulfa was especially fond of this plant, and had it put in around every house she occupied for more than one season. *The stones must be cold beneath her naked feet.* It occurred to Adulfa that she could remove her jacket and drape it over the frightened girl's shivering shoulders. But she dismissed this uncharacteristic, charitable thought with an impatient shrug. Tabitha would know much greater discomfort before she expired. She had been brought here to provide Adulfa with pleasure, and right now, the only pleasure available was the sight of the naked stem of her legs, the pale blossom of her torso, the slight tremble that verified Adulfa's power.

A turquoise light bathed the front door, the illumination of an electric bulb dispersed through a blue-green glass fixture. On either side of the door was a pair of panels made of inlaid ebony, bits of mirror, and mother-of-pearl. Adulfa liked the geometric figures, their impersonal symmetry. Tabitha waited, hugging herself and looking down, as if she were a shy, poor little wench. Adulfa put her key in the door, but before she would let Tabitha into the warm house, she pressed the redhead's naked skin against the cold decorative panels and inflicted a particularly intimate kiss upon her sulky lips. Adulfa's mouth did not ask for a response; she simply went where she wished to be, and forced Tabitha to yield and be sweet about it.

It was particularly enjoyable to know that her prey's thighs smarted from the pressure of Adulfa's body, and to sense her indignation when Adulfa's insolent hands investigated her buttocks. Adulfa stepped back, drew Tabitha away from the wall, and spun her through the door. Would girls never learn that their false modesty simply attracted attention to the very zones they were pretending to defend?

In the hallway, Adulfa hung up her hat and cloak, and doffed the coat of her suit. Now she was clad in snug black wool trousers, a starched white shirt with a pleated front, and a satin bow tie with a subtle black-on-black design woven into the fabric. Her hair had grown a half-inch past her scalp, she noticed as she removed the top hat. Dawn was only three or four hours away, then. Enough time, surely, to have all the fun that was possible to wring out of slender, small-breasted, wary Tabitha.

The girl was standing awkwardly with her weight on one foot, looking off to the side with an unattractive blank expression on her face. Drug addicts were so boring when it came right down to it. Adulfa shoved her toward the drawing room and kept after her like a sheepdog until she was safely behind its doors. The fire had to be fed, and she ordered Tabitha to take care of this task, ignoring her plea that sparks might fly and singe her bare skin. "All to the good, my dear," she said, arranging the lamp, pipe, and opium upon a low table. "Injuries become you." One of Tabitha's hands fluttered toward the welt across her thighs, but hesitated to touch the wound lest it awaken to new pain.

The wallpaper was the color of weak tea, printed with the segmented stalks and thin, long leaves of bamboo, and the floor was covered with a stippled brown-and-cream wool carpet. There was only one chair in the room, a carved wooden throne imported from Malaysia. Tabitha was bright enough to understand that this was not meant for her, and even asked Adulfa's permission to sit on the floor at her feet. Though perhaps her motivation was to get closer to the flame and the pipe it would bring to life.

"You may smoke as much opium as you like," Adulfa said, and handed her an already-loaded stem and bowl. Tabitha hesitated for a moment, not precisely sure of how best to heat the opium, but there was so much of it, she probably would not get into trouble for wasting some. So she attempted to imitate the attendants at Monsieur Ching's, and eventually drew the solace she had been waiting for into her eager lungs. Adulfa relished the smell of a happy mortal and the hazelnut smoke.

They sat there for at least an hour. From time to time, Adulfa would require Tabitha to submit to one sort of vulgar fondling or another. Appeased by the opium, Tabitha moved in a drowsy semblance of enjoyment. But Adulfa was not some rube who could be conned into thinking he had actually driven a courtesan into a state of ecstasy.

There was a mirror with a wrought iron frame in a corner of the room. Behind it was a larger-than-life framed oil painting of the martyrdom of Saint Sebastian. Adulfa had bought it because it was one of the few works of art she'd ever seen that actually captured the correct color of fresh blood. The saint's loins might be swaddled in yards of prudish white cloth, but his hips thrust lewdly forward to receive the pointed shafts of his enemies. His eyes were turned heavenward, and the look on his face evoked the transports of the brothel rather than the quiet pleasures of the cathedral. Adulfa positioned Tabitha so that she faced the mirror and the painting, and was not surprised to see that she had no response to the work of art. If someone was ever stupid enough to give her such a fine thing, she would hock it.

Instructing Tabitha that she must remain standing, Adulfa proceeded to stroke her with the sharp claws that her nails had become. The night passed. More quickly and more quickly still her hands flew across the blue-white flesh, striping and scoring its surface with faint red lines. Tabitha writhed but stood her ground, her terror barely kept at bay by the reassuring fumes of the poppy.

"Look," Adulfa ordered her. "Do not turn away. On penalty of death, do not close your eyes."

Then she took Tabitha's chin in her left hand, twisted her neck a bit, and sank her fangs into the tender skin at its base. Even lost in the joy of feeding, she had enough presence of mind left over to rejoice at Tabitha's response — naked fear, repulsion, pain, disbelief, and still more fear.

Adulfa decided to make things still more difficult for her victim, and forced her legs apart. Her hand sank home, ignoring the dryness created by the narcotic. The combination of sexual penetration with the puncture wounds of the vampire's sharp teeth made Tabitha's eyes go wide with panic and confusion. Adulfa wound her own priorities through and over Tabitha's instinct for self-preservation, so that the girl stopped thinking about the danger of being fucked by someone with razors at the end of her fingers. *Get hot*, Adulfa willed her victim. *Pant for me. You've never had it so good. You can't get enough of it. You don't care what you have to do to get more of it. Yes!*

Hating herself even more than her captor, Tabitha yielded to Adulfa completely. She had no idea that her thoughts and physical sensations were no longer her own. Her orgasm was a catastrophe. It shook her to her foundations and left her wondering if she'd ever really had one before. If not for Adulfa's hand beneath her buttocks, she would have fallen to the floor.

Adulfa withdrew from her feeding place, contented by the lovely texture and savor of Tabitha's blood. She had not drunk hard enough to still the girl's heart, but she was fairly sure she had not left her enough blood to keep it going for many more hours. Dawn was closer than she had estimated. It was long past time to be abed. *Let the wench expire here before the fireplace*, Adulfa thought. She would take out the rubbish tomorrow evening.

"Where are you going?" Tabitha asked, clutching at her ankle.

Adulfa evaded her fingers. "Away from you," she succinctly replied. "Somewhere you cannot go."

"But what about me?" Tabitha cried.

Adulfa shrugged. "What about me?" she mimicked shrilly, and left the room, stopping to take her coat and cape with her. Tabitha might try to steal something valuable or vandalize the house. Who cared? The villa was rented. The only thing Adulfa knew she was unlikely to do was run away, because there was not a stitch of female clothing in the entire place.

When she arose the next evening, Adulfa was a little surprised to see that Tabitha had lived through the night, and furthermore had used up every bit of the opium they'd brought home from Monsieur Ching's. "You don't have any food in this house," Tabitha informed her, sounding cross. "What am I to do for breakfast?"

"It's dinner time," Adulfa said absently, looking at her injured and still-bloody neck.

"So take me out to dinner," Tabitha suggested. She had found a length of fabric that Adulfa recognized as an ice blue damask tablecloth. It took her only a moment to wind it about her body, tuck it here and there, and she looked as if she was wearing a chic evening gown. *French girls! Always stylish.*

"You deserve a reward for such ingenuity," Adulfa said, and went to fetch her coat and hat. She was amused by how quickly Tabitha had accommodated herself to the unique physical requirements of her new patron. Perhaps getting your neck mauled was less unpleasant than being pummeled by some Bordeaux-soaked student of philosophy. Tabitha could gorge herself while Adulfa decided where to go for her own feast. *Perhaps,* Adulfa thought, *I shall slip out without paying for her meal.*

But she did no such thing.

Looking back on their first evening many years later, Adulfa could not say for certain when she had decided to keep Tabitha by her side, and allow her to live. Perhaps it was the great joy of clasping and blooding someone whose shock and fear were expressed with unusual intensity. Certainly she was tasty, exceptionally so, though that had never been enough to engender mercy in the past. In fact, she was really quite an annoying person — petty, whiny, greedy, vain, ungrateful. But nice to look at and charming simply because she would never try to be anything other than herself. Tabitha was content to be a social-climbing parasite with no particular talent other than her youthful beauty, flawless table manners, and ability to waltz with the grace of a swan upon the water. No matter how much she enjoyed the pleasure that Adulfa gave her, she never stopped protesting that she did not like or need these perverse caresses. Contact with the supernatural could not budge her stout French atheism, tinged with a dollop of Roman Catholic guilt. Adulfa supposed people loved their dogs or cats for less good reasons. No matter, she did not love Tabitha. And certainly did not need her. She was simply a convenient amusement that overstayed its welcome by a year or two.

Toward the end, things did get, Adulfa was prepared to concede, a little out of hand. She didn't seem to be able to stop herself from taking blood from the girl too frequently, and taking too much of it each time. She was ambivalent about her decision to allow Tabitha to live, and part of her was curious to see how much hard use she could survive. The girl got more wan, she swooned more often, she became more prone to talking to herself and even had the occasional hallucination. But she went on living, a scion of the durable mercantile class.

Tabitha almost at once developed the irritating habit of trying to run away while Adulfa was asleep. For a while, it was entertaining to pursue and retrieve her. Adulfa would sometimes wait several days before setting out after her, to allow Tabitha to think that this time she really had gotten away. But eventually that was not very much fun. Tabitha could not seem to think of many original ways to run, or new places to hide. So Adulfa kept her chained to the seventeenth-century canopy bed where she preferred to use her.

It's true that Tabitha complained bitterly about this, but why? Adulfa brought her everything she might need—food, books, games, newspapers, art supplies, music, toiletries. She even bathed her. The chains were long enough to allow her to reach the commode and bidet. Adulfa also brought her kittens, puppies, fish, a bird or two, though she had trouble remembering to care for them, so they did not last very long. But Adulfa thought the novelty of having a new sort of creature about the place ought to have made up for that. And the opium was never allowed to run out.

The problem was that Tabitha could not entertain herself. She had inadequate inner resources. She longed for the society of others like herself. She would, Adulfa knew, not last very long in the isolation of the vampire's cursed immortality.

The first saffron hint of sunrise made the thin curtains at Tabitha's windows look as if they'd been dipped in piss. Adulfa had left the room at least a quarter of an hour ago, headed for wherever she'd made her daytime nest. The vampire had a disconcerting habit of hiding in places where you wouldn't think to look for her—beneath the floorboards, in between the walls, behind a rack of bottles in the wine cellar. It was as if she had lost any sense of herself as a human being and relinquished even the pretense of needing the comforts that weaker beings relished. When the sun came up, she put herself away like a dish towel going back into the drawer or a photograph being tucked into an album.

Not that Tabitha had ever been lucky enough to discover her gaoler in a helpless state. She'd tried, ages ago, before she'd been chained to this bed. But she'd been frightened often enough by Adulfa's abrupt rising at a time when Tabitha had assumed she was alone and therefore safe. Adulfa would punch out the plaster and appear, nonchalantly bedecked with dust and cobwebs, or loom suddenly out from under a slab of slate in the garden path, picking moss from her sleeve. You couldn't even compare her to a wild animal, really, because she was completely indifferent to most of the things that attracted or frightened the beasts of the wilderness.

The yellow stain of light continued to seep into the room, making its dinginess and clutter too apparent. Tabitha forced herself to stay awake. It helped to put her fingers into the newest of her wounds. She had to keep moving from throat to thigh to flank, from one side of her body to the other. She was so accustomed to extreme pain that any lesser hurt quickly lost its potency. Adulfa could heal bite marks with her spittle, but she rarely bothered to perform this cursory maintenance for her captive.

The general standard of care had also deteriorated. The pretty dresses, hot food, and other amenities of their early life together were no longer offered. Perhaps it was because Tabitha had been unable to convince Adulfa that she loved or desired her. Tabitha roused her internal defenses against this odd reproach. Why should she love someone who treated her so badly, who mocked her and called her terrible names, who taunted and tortured her? Who could desire the battery that Adulfa called lovemaking? She'd been given nothing to eat for two days but a loaf of bread, which had quickly gone stale, and a few soft brown pears. Adulfa knew the difference between genuine ardor and the manipulative ways of a starving wretch.

If only I were a better actress, Tabitha thought bitterly. If only Adulfa had been a man. Men were so much easier to fool, and what they needed physically was relatively easy to provide, as long as you did not lose your sense of humor or allow them to think they were special.

No cheese, no chicken, no olives, no beef or salad or cooked cabbage, no wine and no hot chocolate. But there was always plenty of opium. Every night, Tabitha lost her struggle to resist its lure. But it no longer dulled the pain. Adulfa's teeth could punch right through the strongest soporific. Tabitha took in the dragon's breath simply to avoid feeling even worse than being bled until she blacked out.

But right now, it was good to suffer. Pain was Tabitha's friend. She did not have the strength to fill and light the ivory-stemmed pipe with its bowl of pure gold, just as she could not spare the effort it would take to get out of bed, dragging an unbearably heavy chain behind her, and wash her nightgown in the sink.

Smoking opium alone, in the light of day, was a possibility only because Adulfa had left the lamp aflame. Tabitha could not quite believe her good fortune. She had not noticed its faint glow until Adulfa left the room, for a wonder, or the vampire would have filched that knowledge from her mind and pinched out the lamp's hot, wavering spirit. Perhaps the open flame was a hallucination. She frequently saw things that were not real. It was as if Adulfa had drained the sanity out of her along with her blood.

Tabitha needed a little time to think about what she intended to do. A chance like this might never come again. Adulfa was intelligent and meticulous. Tabitha was not allowed to have so much as a belt for her robe. On the rare occasions she was fed meat, there were no bones in it. Not even a pencil was left within her reach. Adulfa wore the key to Tabitha's bondage on a silver chain around her neck. It was never left unattended. Even if it was abandoned by chance on a table, Adulfa had demonstrated that that would be no help. She used to love to put the key just inches away from Tabitha's hand, give her a head start, and still snatch it up before Tabitha could touch it. She could also close Tabitha's fingers around the key and then make her forget that it was there, or remove her understanding of what it was for. Adulfa found it amusing to clasp her prisoner and feed while she witlessly clung to the useless tool that would have set her free.

Tabitha felt a wave of sick rage come up the back of her throat. There was a whining sound in her head, the audible aspect of a worsening headache. She quelled the rebellious anger with a great effort. The way Adulfa had stolen her knowledge, her perceptions, upset Tabitha more than being used the way Mongolian nomads used their own horses, opening a vein to drink. But she could not afford to lose the moisture that throwing up would take out of her. She would not think about the times when Adulfa raped her will as well as her body, and laughed at Tabitha for shuddering in ecstasy when things were done to her that she had dreaded before they happened and felt bitterly ashamed of as soon as the pleasure and the amnesia were gone. To be made to beg for what you hated, and to believe in the moment that it heated your loins until you could not hold still, to whimper while you received it and to thank the one who granted you this favor—how could self-respect survive such a thing?

Was she really ready to die? Adulfa had shown her death often enough. Before Tabitha had understood that pleading for mercy was pointless, that there was no mercy in the vampire's imperious and parasitical heart, Adulfa had thought it was amusing to bring another victim home when Tabitha begged her to be left alone, afraid that one more feeding would end her life. Tabitha had seen a dozen men and women terrorized or hypnotized and then drained, left to fall lifeless to the floor. Big strong hearty loud thick men, slender and beautiful young boys, shy maidens and brassy women of the street, old ladies and new mothers and confused shopkeepers in clean white aprons. All of them turning one last pleading glance upon her, Tabitha, as if she could offer them some explanation or salvation. Thinking of their lost faces, she sobbed and dug her fingernails into the palm of her other hand.

Adulfa was then wont to force Tabitha to examine the bodies in great detail, to perhaps express her gratitude to the person who had died in her stead, and sometimes ravished her while she was bent over the corpse or propped up against it. Screaming did not make Adulfa stop, and neither did a stoic silence. She did with you as she willed, though Tabitha never seemed to be able to remember that bitter truth when she struggled with Adulfa, and could not accept it.

Death as one of Adulfa's scarlet suppers was dramatic and prolonged, but short compared to the length of time Tabitha had suffered in this gaol of a bedroom. Still, being burned alive was supposed to hurt a great deal. She was no Jeanne d'Arc to go impassively into the flames, refusing to recant the holiness of her visions. And suppose it did not work? What if she only succeeded in scorching a little of the floor, perhaps the bedroom wall? Tabitha thought the punishment for trying to kill Adulfa would be terrible indeed. But she somehow knew, by the way the slightest movement left her breathless, by the way that breathing hurt and the light seemed unbearably strong, that she was close to the end. Her body was nearly used up. How many times had Tabitha cursed the same vitality that had allowed her to stay up for days at a stretch, going from one party to another? The departure of this stamina was more welcome than the back of a nagging mother-in-law. And even if Adulfa did not intend to kill her, any sort of rough revenge was going to snap the thread of Tabitha's life in two. So perhaps even failure would be a blessing.

A pang between her legs made Tabitha gasp, and she tried to shift her position on the bed without making herself pass out from the effort it took to rearrange her hips and legs. Adulfa was very rough with her, and got more violent every day. Sometimes it seemed to Tabitha that she forgot what she was doing or who she was with. Who was this Ulric that she called upon so often? Tabitha had the strangest feeling that sometimes Adulfa was doing to her prisoner some awful thing that had been done to her. But who would dare attack such a strong and savage creature? What sort of being could even accomplish such a monstrous crime? Whoever might be capable of that, she did not want to meet them.

As she shifted a fraction of an inch on the bed, the sad, sour smell of her own body rose up in Tabitha's face, and perhaps it was that indignity which made the decision final. She could not remember the last time she had been allowed to wash her hair or sponge off her skin. This was no way to live. Perhaps the smoke would be thick enough to smother her, so she would not feel the tongues of fire licking at the thin, dry leather and paltry fat of her mortal shell. Once the conflagration was set in motion, there would be no way to put it out and no way to escape. Even if her agony was intolerable, it would not endure forever. And if Adulfa had secreted herself away in pantry or attic, perhaps she would perish as well. Regardless, Tabitha would never be forced to stare at her lips again and ask, against her will, for a kiss that tasted like it came from a butcher's cleaver.

With a wry smile, she thought about the passage in the novel that had drawn her to Paris and from there to its frenzied nightlife. The naughty book had said that there were private but large dances to which only women were invited. She wanted to see two women waltzing together. Wanted to be dancing among other female couples, the whole room an exclusive picture of feminine beauty, the full skirts of the ball gowns moving gracefully to the music.

Adulfa hadn't really understood Tabitha's sexual identity. Her psychic winnowing of Tabitha's mind had been colored by her own assumption that all humans were false; hypocrites. Tabitha didn't imagine herself to be separate or different from lesbians. It was a word she hadn't known till Adulfa accused her of hiding from that label.

When she first came to Paris, Tabitha had the usual extravagant dreams of a young girl who imagines she will set the world on fire. She did not know if she was fated to be an actress, a model, or a famous singer, but she was sure that some powerful person would discover her unique and fascinating self and elevate her to the status of a star. Then she would be invited to scandalous soirées where women might caress or kiss one another. Instead she found herself working in a shop that sold ladies' hats with several girls her own age, who were, Tabitha was fairly certain, not ever going to waltz with her.

It had taken her months to hear a rumor of lesbian orgies at the Palace of Sleeping Dragon Dreams. As frightened as she was of opium dens and their sinister Chinese masters, she had dared to go there, hoping to at last encounter a woman who might kiss her or show her the kind of bliss that she'd never experienced at a man's hands, no matter how skilled or kind he might be. She had been so dazzled by the spectacle that greeted her that she had not known what to do. Paralyzed by her own excitement, she could only smoke more and more opium, which was insidious, affecting you far more than you realized at the time. Then Adulfa had closed her hand around Tabitha's elbow, and her life was over. Perhaps the encounter with the vampire was a just punishment for all of her perverse thoughts about other women's breasts and bellies.

If Adulfa had not been such a bitch, Tabitha thought, she might have found in her the sort of lover she was looking for. The vampire must have been beautiful when she was a woman. Her body was lean and strong, yet achingly feminine, and she was fearless in pursuit of pleasure. But her disregard for Tabitha's acquiescence or cooperation made her even worse than the first man Tabitha had ever allowed to undress and penetrate her unready flesh.

The thought of holding a gentle, lovely woman in her arms made

Tabitha smile. Perfume. A trace of powder, two sweet lips outlined with color. She could feel a slight sensation of heat warming her aching body. Maybe there would be angels where she was going, and perhaps they would embrace her and offer her comfort for the suffering she had endured. Maybe they would have firm high breasts with nipples that were eager to be touched. Perhaps their Venus mounds would be covered with downy layers of snow-white feathers, instead of the coarse pubic hair worn by the daughters of Eve. Perhaps they would make her an angel as well, with huge wings that were strong enough to take her away from any harm or trouble. You were supposed to be happy in heaven, weren't you? And Tabitha could not think of anything that would make her happier than being able to feel the round, tender arms of a woman around her waist, and two soft breasts pressed to her own. Soft against soft, no strength without tenderness.

She slid out of the bed and shuffled to the windows. Too weak to yank on the curtains, she simply gripped them at the hem and leaned on them until they came down. She fed a corner of one of them to the lamp, and while the little flame gorged and made itself great, she searched for other things that would burn. There were some magazines. She tore pages out of them, tossed them into the blaze, then realized it was strong enough to take them whole. She dug stuffing out of the sofa cushions, then contributed the pillow cases. Eventually the center of the room was an inferno, and she was bathed in sweat from the heat that came off it and from her own exertions. She skirted its edges and took to her bed, exhausted. But before she tucked herself in, she lifted the down coverlet and tossed it toward the fire, so that one corner was in harm's way.

The angels had skin like white satin and eyes as big and blue as the china doll she had carried everywhere when she was a little girl. They caressed each other, but their love was not possessive; they did it only to show her what gifts they wished to bestow upon her much-abused body. And they waltzed, as light on their feet as the fluffy seed balls of dandelions. Their moving hips promised Tabitha a surfeit of unearthly joy. The angels, beautiful sisters of the morning, were calling her in their enticing and compassionate voices, with the celestial music of the spheres all about them. Soon she would be free to go to them and join the dance.

Then the fire laid its fluttering, ardent hands upon her. It hurt more than even Adulfa could imagine.

The vampire was awakened by the unfamiliar sensation of pain. She sat up, disoriented by daylight, so befuddled it took her three seconds to understand that the room around her was in flames. It too would have gone up if not for the fact that it had a steel lining. What providence had guided her to install this metal compartment behind the painting of Saint Sebastian's martyrdom? Adulfa gathered her power, hoping it would be enough in all this cursed glare, and lifted herself away from the danger. She was badly burned escaping, down the left side of her body, which hurt a lot. She knew that the damage could be repaired by a few extra feedings, but that did nothing to improve her temper in the short run.

From outside the villa, she could see that the fire had started in the wing where Tabitha's bedroom was located. Levitating and going closer, she was able to reconstruct the sequence of events. Tabitha had used the opium lamp to set the villa on fire. Her bones had long ago been eaten whole by the roaring red-and-yellow riot of heat. The redheaded girl had hated Adulfa so much that she had been willing to die this terrible death if only both of them would perish.

It was not what Adulfa had expected. Not at all. She found herself filled with betrayal, hurt, rage. How dare she? *Ungrateful bitch!* Shaken by the unexpected pain of loneliness, Adulfa found herself liking mortals rather less than usual. She thought perhaps she might kill more frequently tonight than was absolutely necessary to restore her blistered skin. If only Tabitha had left behind some kin or dear friend that Adulfa could snatch up. But, like the vampire, Tabitha had been a solitary creature. Raised in an orphanage, once she reached the age of majority and left the nuns, she had no one to rely on but herself.

Hissing with shock, offended in body and soul, Adulfa soared away to recoup her losses. Monsieur Albert Ching had perhaps been a bit overweening in his dealings with her, had perhaps been a little too quick to assume that his word was law. The Sleeping Dragon would be very busy tonight. The voyeurs in their hidden cubicles would see spectacles not drawn from their irresolute, pastel dreams. Their fastidiously tended opium lamps could be overturned as easily as the one she had carelessly left ablaze in Tabitha's room. Then the abundant and untidy glare of a volcano would replace the discreet glow of a hundred secretive and habitual visions.

CHAPTER 14
See What You Love

There was a split second when Lilith once more felt gentle hands cupping her face and knew that she was back in Adulfa's lair. Then hard slaps landed on her bowed head. Her cheeks were ringing from the impact. *Hold still*, she told herself, recalling a lesson from Ulric's training. *Don't spoil her aim. Yes, she might hit you on the ear or some other place where you could really be injured. But she's more likely to miss or be provoked if you thrash around.*

Perhaps that wasn't actually the wisest strategy, because Adulfa shrieked, "Move, damn you! Why don't you scream?" She ran behind Lilith and punched her on the buttocks and the sides of her torso. "Thief!" Adulfa cried. "Dream snatcher. Memory robber. Sorcerous bitch!"

This was so clearly not an S/M scene; the lack of a safe word was the least of Lilith's worries. Nevertheless, she was clearly the one who had no power, and the top had voiced her wishes. *Scream.* So Lilith obliged, letting go with the full voice that Ulric had coached her to release, a scream from the pit of her stomach. From the way that it resonated, Lilith got the impression that the room was not terribly large beyond what she could see. It was the size of a big bedroom, not an empty warehouse, even though it had an industrial smell.

"So you're a little empath, is that it?" Adulfa demanded, yanking on Lilith's hair. These locks had already suffered a great deal of mishandling, and so Lilith screamed again, though not as loudly as before. "Well?" she insisted, squatting down in front of Lilith, one hand clamped around her chin so hard that the hinges of Lilith's jaw ached. Adulfa's indignant breath, huffing on her face, smelled like the taste of silver and mint.

"I...don't...know," Lilith managed to say hoarsely.

Was it possible? Before meeting Ulric, she had been a skeptic about all things spiritual or magical, seeing them as the delusions that desperate or dim people relied on for false comfort. She had modified her cynicism, was forced to do so, after proving the reality of his extraordinary condition with all of her material senses. But his vampirism set him so far above the mortal world that it made it seem even more unlikely that she (or any other mortal) could see visions, read minds, foretell the future, or cast a spell. But if Adulfa had not intended to tell her about Tabitha, how had the tragedy been imparted to her in so much visual and emotional detail?

"Well, I know how to fix your psychic shoplifting, you

presumptuous piece of mortal dung. Where are my gloves?" A drawer opened. The room had been prepared, furnished. Lilith wondered how long Adulfa had been constructing this hideaway, dreaming of luring Ulric here and heaping further misery on his already unbearable life. "No more contact with my naked skin, I think," Adulfa said, speaking to Lilith over her shoulder.

When she returned, Lilith could see that Adulfa was wearing long kid gloves. It was absolutely traitorous of her to appreciate what the beautiful Germanic warrior had chosen to wear on the rest of her body to torture her tonight. The black leather catsuit with its scarlet zippers was worthy of Emma Peel. But Lilith's grudging admiration was brief enough to salve her conscience, because Adulfa promptly shoved her head into a bag once more and knotted its strings tightly behind her neck. The gloved hands took Lilith out of bondage, stood her upright, and guided her to another area of the room. Her hands were tied behind her back.

"I've prepared a display stand for my new dolly," Adulfa said. It sounded like she had regained her equanimity — forgotten the involuntary meeting of minds just as she had forgotten her compatriot's tirade and tears. "Get on your knees, find it, and put yourself on it," she instructed in the severe tones of a tutor sent to brush up some scapegrace's Latin.

Lilith wanted to run. She thought she had kept her bearings well enough to know roughly where the door was. But she knew Adulfa would catch her before she could find it. How much physical damage did she want to sustain while she fumbled for a doorknob or latch with her hands tied snugly behind her back? Adulfa seemed to want her to go on living, for now at least. Was it worth it to mount a useless bit of resistance? Would the pain of Adulfa's retaliation be worse than the shame that Lilith would feel if she complied?

She bent her knees before she was aware of making a decision. Was Adulfa compelling her once more? If so, the vampire's melding with her will was seamless. Lilith could find no taste of a foreign power driving her actions. On her knees, she moved to the right. "Cold," Adulfa said. "Colder." So Lilith went to the left. "Warm," Adulfa replied, seeming amused by their game. Eventually Lilith encountered the "doll stand."

As she fumbled to get on it, she deduced it consisted of a large, donut-shaped cushion that she could kneel on. But in the center of the pillow was a slender metal column that contained a spring of some kind. It rotated freely, so getting herself up on it was not easy. Adulfa chuckled each time she failed. She could not use her hands to steady the device, nor could she see or even feel the top of the column to find out what was there. But eventually she mounted it. There was a long, fat dildo that went into her cunt, and an even longer one, though thankfully not quite as thick, which slid into her ass as if it had been custom-made to fit her. She was on her knees, to all outward appearances quite comfortable on her cushion, but the full weight of her torso settled upon the dildos and made them seem immense.

"Next time I'll make you grease them up yourself," Adulfa said. "I like watching girls do that, especially if they have tears in their eyes. Now listen to me, animal in rut. This toy of mine is very special. It's not just a way for lazy slaves to pleasure themselves while I'm out shopping. It's electrified. See?"

A bolt of pain went up Lilith's tender insides. She gasped, and tears did indeed come to her eyes. This was not the tickling, buzzing sensation of Ulric's ultraviolet wand. It was brutal.

"Made in the U.S.A.," Adulfa gloated. "For export to some saber-rattling South American dictatorship. But it got hijacked. Kind of like you, my dirty little dolly." She paused, perhaps for Lilith to beg for mercy, but her prisoner had folded her lips shut and would not speak without being forced to do so. A bit nettled, Adulfa decided the tears she could sense running down Lilith's cheeks were enough, and continued. "But there is a way to escape torment," she continued. "All you have to do is fuck yourself. Slide up and down the lovely big plastic pricks, and keep moving. Or this is what you get."

Again, the electricity struck Lilith's cervix and rectum. She was terrified of being burned internally, injured beyond Ulric's power to heal her.

"Are you deaf as well as blind?" Adulfa said scathingly. She hit the punishment button again, and this time Lilith screamed. "You're not going to get an engraved invitation, slut. Start pumping."

I forgive myself in advance for doing whatever I need to do to survive, Lilith told herself, and obeyed, knowing her thighs would soon be begging for mercy even though they were in condition for the Olympics—if this had been one of the medal-winning events. She should be thankful that Ulric liked to be ridden. But the thought of him was too painful. She had to send it away. For now, she was in Adulfa's power, and must focus only on that. There had been a tender moment. Maybe there was a way to crack open this creature's hard-as-a-diamond heart. Masters competed with each other to try to take Lilith away from Ulric. Mistresses as well. She was a superb slave. She knew how the game was played; the luckless Parisienne opium fiend had not.

The sheer physical presence of the dildos was impossible to ignore. She had been taught to come often and easily, and no one had forbidden an orgasm now. She fought it off nevertheless, strained to keep her body moving without allowing her arousal to overflow, but her cunt and ass were not taking orders from above the waist. There was a vague flutter of a contraction, she slid up and down once more, and then knew more

were on the way.
I forgive myself for doing whatever I must to —

Ulric was relieved when he first woke up. The awful feeling that had haunted him yesterday was gone. Thinking it was a bit odd that none of the cats had slept with him, he sat up and stretched, then extricated himself from his fireproof nest. The desire he had felt for Lilith last night was still present, but with a new night came the necessity to renew his potency with fresh blood. He resolved to go out and feed quickly so he could return to her and banish the miasma of discord that had almost ruined their evening.

When he entered the library, he smelled Lilith's blood. *By the big hairy balls of the Sky Father, what is this doing here?* It was more than a paper cut's worth on the edge of a page. And it wasn't time for the sea and moon to call blood forth from Lilith's womb. Then he saw the mess upon his desk—a soiled bathrobe, the profaned sex toy. A second later, he heard his cats squalling and ran to the kitchen. To get there, he had to pass through the living room, where he barely noticed a corpse in Lilith's favorite chair. The cats were leaping out of the refrigerator, which had apparently been left open. If they had been trapped in there while he ran off to find Lilith, what would have become of them? He sat on the cold kitchen floor and opened one of his veins to feed them. He picked them up and kissed them, despite their protests. They asked him what had happened, and he didn't know. Someone had entered the house while he was sleeping and desecrated it.

Cats placated, he went to the living room and took hold of the corpse. It had Adulfa's smell all over it. Grimly, he carried it to the elevator and down to the basement, where it went into the furnace. It was just the husk of a body and should be reduced to cinders in an hour or so. He had no curiosity about the identity of the person Adulfa had killed. He only hoped his sister had not left careless clues that would guide forensic experts to his home.

While he was in the basement, he unloaded the tapes from the security cameras and took them upstairs to play on his VCR. He already knew who had done this awful thing, but he didn't know where she had gone. His mind and heart were screaming at him to do *something*—go, find Lilith, find her now! Instead, he forced himself to sit and watch what the cameras had to tell him about the crime. Excited by her triumph and by Lilith's luscious vulnerability, Adulfa might have left him some clue about where she was going.

When he came to the library tape and saw and heard Lilith forced to repudiate him, he bent in half and keened like an ancient Greek woman in mourning. The cats came close to him, pressing their fur against his legs, telling him they loved Lilith and hated whoever had taken her; they had the intruder's scent and would help him to find their girlfriend. (In their minds, Lilith was as much their property as she was Ulric's.)

The guilt was what almost undid him. If it had not been for his interference in her life, Lilith never would have attracted Adulfa's attention. It was his fault for loving her. He had put her in harm's way. The shifts in his emotions were compressed into mere moments because of the pressure he felt to take action, guilt rapidly erased by a flood of anger. Yes, he had harmed Adulfa in the past, but the abduction of an innocent was not fit reparation for his own evil deed. Let Adulfa harm him if she could; Lilith had to be retrieved and made safe at all costs.

"Yes, Luna," he said, touching her head. "I know you will help me. Help me. I need somebody to help me. Ah—the family!" Why hadn't he thought of it sooner? The people that Lilith had asked him to bind to them, the kernel of a tribe that it was her dream to restore. She had known them much better than Ulric, talked to them, had their phone numbers and email addresses. But Ulric had a better way to contact them.

He retraced his steps to the place where Adulfa had made Lilith stand, with her poor mouth bleeding and her body violated. The doors to the back deck were still open. Ulric put his hands up to the moon, his patron, and noticed that she was almost full of the souls of the dead. In a few days, she would be perfectly round and ready to send new souls back to earth to be born again. "One of our own has been taken," he told the night air. "My consort, our queen and priestess, she has been taken from us. Come, all of my children. Come to me now. Come quickly and come in force. We must go to her aid. Come!"

Lilith was exhausted, perhaps too exhausted to be frightened anymore. But she could still feel pain, and so she continued to rise and fall upon the merciless device that Adulfa had created to punish her for loving the vampire's half-brother. For a while she had wondered if Adulfa was even in the room to hear her scream when her muscles faltered and she could no longer keep the penalty of shock at bay. But now she heard the hatefully familiar panther-tread and smelled her torturer, just inches away. Adulfa untied and whisked off the hood, but Lilith refused to look at her. She heard a dress slither up, didn't hear any elastic stretch, and wondered if that meant she would be spared additional humiliation.

"Silly thing, I don't wear panties," Adulfa purred, and put Lilith's mouth to her sex. She had timed it perfectly. One of the climaxes that Lilith could not fight off took her just as Adulfa's clitoris was nestled between her lips. The mortal girl wept as Adulfa laughed. "Such a compliment," she whispered in her sultry voice. Then steel took over: "Lick me," she commanded. "Lick me while you fuck yourself to another big noisy come, my bound and helpless sex toy. Oh, you do that so nicely. Much nicer than Rhys. That feels so good I almost wonder if you're worth keeping alive."

It must have been Adulfa who planted the images of eating her cunt in Lilith's mind, because the experience was just as Lilith had envisioned it. Or perhaps it was more pilfered knowledge, an empathic reflex that passed Adulfa's knowledge on to Lilith without her asking to be told. Oh, it was so hard to keep fucking herself while she roused Adulfa and brought her off. All of her attention seemed to flow toward the vampire, so that her hips forgot to keep time. A sudden shock rocketed through Lilith's body and found its way through her lips and onto Adulfa's sex. The vampire chuckled.

"Oh, that felt even nicer," she cooed. "Like a vibrator. Do it again, slave girl. See? I can make you stop whenever I want to. Do you need a rest? No? You're such a whore that you haven't had enough fucking? Then you'd better pick up the pace and lick me with all your skill.

"Ulric is a pussy, but I doubt he showed you how to do this. No, he didn't, did he? But you're learning fast. We can add sucking cunt to your résumé. Tell me you love that big fat dildo that I've got inside your cunt. Persuade me that you mean it, or I'll find something more challenging than what you've got in your ass. How about a nice butt plug with spikes all over it? Like a cat's prick."

Mouth buried in Adulfa's cunt, Lilith took her cues from the vampire's demands, saying whatever was required to keep her happy. But she could not keep herself from crying. Adulfa seemed to find that very exciting, and came several times with her hands wrapped around Lilith's face, pushing her tongue deep inside her cunt. She had no breath to scream when Adulfa's greed took precedence, and she unwittingly paused for a moment upon the cruel pair of steeds. "What a nice finish to a refreshing session of cunt-lapping," Adulfa said, retreating far enough to hold Lilith's face up so she could see her wet mouth. "Is that a little treat you gave me because you love me so? Are you offering me your pain to gain my favor?"

Lilith thought, *No*, but it was "Yes" that came out of her mouth.

"It's a seductive slut," Adulfa said, and switched off the pedestal where Lilith was poised on her knees. "Now that you've licked me, I think it's time I used my mouth on you."

She lifted Lilith up off the dildos with both hands on her waist. She carried her to a leather-covered surface and sat her down upon it. Then she arranged her to her liking, running her hands all over Lilith's naked body, paying special attention to her nipples. "You can't keep all this titty for Daddy," Adulfa said, squeezing her breasts. "I have a special treat for these, for tomorrow night. But it's almost bedtime for me and for you too. We've played hard, and we deserve our rest. But not before we have dinner."

Suddenly realizing that Adulfa was about to feed from her, Lilith was startled and jumped forward. But it only carried her into Adulfa's embrace. She was in the familiar position, held as Ulric would have held her to take blood from her neck. Adulfa licked her throat in the same way that he did, teasing her. "Now, I have a question," Adulfa said. "Is it at all faithful? Does it have the ability to keep something back for its master? Surely if anything at all belongs to him and him alone, it is your blood. The right to breach your skin. And I know you experience supreme ecstasy when he drinks from you. What do you think will happen when the teeth in your neck belong to me?"

The sharp fangs grazed her, and Lilith gasped. "Please don't," she whispered, and realized she was breaking down. "Oh, no, I beg of you, don't make me, please, don't. Don't!"

"You make me so hot," Adulfa said, and her teeth sank through Lilith's skin. As she took the blood, she sent Lilith a sense of longing and devotion that reduced her to the IQ of a mastiff. The stolen girl had a frightening look at what it could mean to be Adulfa's prisoner for life—the full scope of adult consciousness denied to her, allowed to feel only the things that Adulfa chose for her to feel. Sobs racked her as Adulfa hummed against her neck and fed, gulping, one gloved hand holding Lilith's head in place while the other hand roamed across her breasts. "I'll let you alone when you tell me you love me and make me believe it," Adulfa said, withdrawing from her neck. "Tell me you're my freshly minted lesbian lust puppet."

The sense of compulsion also left. Lilith was on her own. Adulfa waited, one eyebrow crooked. "Want some more, then?" she said helpfully. Her mouth was stained with Lilith's blood. Blood that belonged to Ulric! Once again, she was caught in the hostage's dilemma: should she resist, knowing that would get her nothing but more pain and suffering, or should she acquiesce, and come even more under Adulfa's spell?

The same spirit of truth that had led her to notice the handsome stranger at the bottom of the library stairs, and later accept his love and lust, and return it even though he was an immortal, night-walking blood drinker possessed her. Lilith looked up at Adulfa and said, "You have a beautiful body. You're strong and intelligent and cruel. If I had met you before I met Ulric, I very well might have fallen in love with you. It's not the fact that you're a woman that keeps me from desiring you or loving you, Adulfa. It's your hatred. I can't love anyone who is Ulric's enemy."

"Your day," Adulfa said between clenched teeth, "is not going to be very pleasant."

She slammed Lilith onto her back on the bondage table and wrapped bare chain around her wrists and ankles. Lilith could hear padlocks closing. The links of the chain were small enough to make them fit close to her flesh. She would not be able to drag her hands or feet out of their grip.

"I was going to give you a drink of water and a little something to eat," Adulfa said. "But now you'll just get something in your other holes." She coated an apparatus with mentholated ointment. Lilith could smell the harsh chemical. Dread climbed down her throat and crouched like a huge spider in her stomach. She was able to keep herself from pleading verbally for mercy, but when Adulfa approached her and put a hand on her thigh, she did everything she could to get away from her. The effort won her only a few inches, and made Adulfa laugh.

"I had this specially made for you," Adulfa said, parting her labia. "I call it the trident."

Lilith tried to calm down and relax her sphincters. Not being able to see exactly what Adulfa intended to stick in her made that impossible. Ulric's half-sister had already torn her anus and subjected her to gynecological electrical torture. But she knew that tightening up would not stop Adulfa, and would increase any damage. Her terror eased when the size of the ass plug and vaginal dildo were manageable. But then a sharp burning sensation erupted at her urethra. Adulfa had inserted something there as well—a catheter? A sound? An electrode? Lilith couldn't help it, she broke down and cried. She had never been so frightened, never felt so alone and helpless.

All three openings in her body began to burn. The ointment was stimulating her mucous membranes, forcing them to fire off their pain receptors. "But wait," Adulfa said cheerfully, "there's more." Lilith couldn't see what her tormentor was doing. She felt something bulky between her legs and rope around her waist, cinched tight as a corset. Then Adulfa flipped a switch, and a powerful vibrator went into action.

"I just hate those cheap battery-operated things, don't you?" Adulfa said. "How much fun can you have when you know that sooner or later those batteries are going to go dead? But this is going to run all night long, because it's got industrial strength lithium-ion batteries, with a backup power pack. Oh, dear, it looks like you're wetting yourself. Disgusting lack of self-control, but about what I expected. Made your bed. Lie in it. Etcetera, etcetera, etcetera," she said, rotating the wrist of one hand in an amused imitation of Yul Brynner in *The King and I*.

Lilith thought that Adulfa was on her way out of the room when pain struck the top and inside of her parted thighs. A cane had wrapped around her leg and bitten the tender inner surface of her leg, close to her pussy. Adulfa caned her until her thighs were heavily welted. She would give the blows in groups of six, then wait long enough between each one for Lilith to believe once more that she had gone. She was weary, hungry and thirsty, and had no reserve to call upon. All of her strength had been used up. Adulfa would have been able to use the agony and suspense to good advantage if she had wanted Lilith to betray someone or give her the location of the hidden treasure. The fact that there was no escape from this torture, that she could not end it by giving up secret information, was what broke Lilith in the end. She realized, while waiting for blows that never came, that Adulfa could have made her do or say anything to make the pain stop.

But the pain did not stop, and she had no way of keeping track of time, to know when the day was drawing to a close and bringing the torturer back, and perhaps a change in the pain as well. Lilith suffered the pounding triple penetration in silence and fought against it with screams. She could not decide which made her feel worse, and had no ability to control how she responded. Eventually she realized that her own body was showing her mercy and attempting to shut down her mind, so that a part of her would not be there for all of this degradation. Then she let herself go, too embattled to worry about whether her faculties would be able to reassemble themselves if her body were set free. She became an animal, drooling out moisture she could not afford to lose, crying out wordlessly, her pelvis struggling to come to terms with what had been done to it.

And once every hour or so, there was an orgasm that came from the pits of hell and shook all of her convictions about the difference between pleasure and pain. She had no way of knowing that Adulfa had set this time schedule up when she handled Lilith's body. Even animal-Lilith was astonished and confounded by these disasters. She had no experience with this sort of orgasm that is physically intense but devoid of romantic intimacy or even peaceful bliss. Each one left her more afraid, more of a thing, less and less herself.

As she prepared herself for dawn, Adulfa bit her lips raw (which was never very hard to do anyway) in a fury of conflicting emotions. The little hussy was strong, unbelievably strong. It took a surprising amount of Adulfa's energy to control and compel her. She fought almost as well as a lesser vampire would fight for its autonomy and its life. And she was pretty as well, genuinely in love. Adulfa could respect a valiant heart even if she despised the object of its devotion. Masochism baffled her, but it was also attractive. A mortal woman who liked to be hurt, who gasped and got wet when the whips and chains and fangs came out, was quite a bit more fun than one who hated every bit of the experience of being taken.

Speaking of masochists (or thinking of them, anyway), Rhys was cluttering the psychic stratosphere with rain clouds of distress. Her refusal to go away was a genuine surprise. Adulfa thought that any sensible person would have hated her for the terrible things she had done to the skinny dyke musician with the odd and brave haircut. Not to mention the tattoos that made her look like an alien insect's exoskeleton. Granted, Adulfa had not completely erased the link between them. Like a hacker, she preferred to leave back doors wherever she went in case a discreet visit proved necessary in the future. But she had been completely sincere when she had told Rhys that her part in this business was done, and she was free to go.

Mortals. Such messy things.

All their sniveling about love, when the only thing they really cared about was their selfish pleasures. Thoughtless beasts, doing whatever they pleased with no regard for the consequences. That sort of behavior was wise only if you were powerful enough to avoid fallout. If they weren't necessary for her life to continue, Adulfa thought she would be happy to see them all drop dead tomorrow. Why should they live when everyone she loved was gone forever?

The prospect of luring Ulric into this trap should have made her carefree and glad, but Adulfa found that her mood just got worse and worse. Perhaps it was the approach of the sun that made her heart so contrary. She cast about for some escape from disquieting introspection.

When self-examination is uncomfortable, it is often helpful to focus on the faults of others. Rhys thought she was in love. In love with a vampire. Adulfa clucked her tongue in reproof. The foolish girl shared Lilith's vice. It would not be right to seek to expunge this delusion from Lilith and leave Rhys' idiocy to flourish. Adulfa tickled herself by cupping her hand over her mouth, like a well-bred person hiding a yawn, and chuckling instead. Meting out therapeutic persecution was so much better than Wellbutrin.

LET'S SPEND THE NIGHT TOGETHER, Rhys felt/heard like a neon brand upon her brain.

She retraced her steps back to Adulfa's hiding place. A small flame of optimism bloomed, and proved too elusive for Rhys to stifle. She followed Adulfa's mental shouts until she was in her sleeping niche.

LIE DOWN BESIDE ME.

Rhys did not wait to protest the use of mental communication when she was in range of verbal commands. She arranged herself in Adulfa's coffin, where there was scant room for two bodies. Before she could get completely comfortable, Adulfa had her close the lid and lock it down from the inside. The vampire's strong arms went around her, drew her closer still. The satin lining of the coffin was scratchy, and it stank of dead flowers and incense. Rhys nestled her face into the hollow of Adulfa's shoulder and felt utterly happy. Adulfa looked at her indulgently, kissed her on the lips, then said, "See what you love."

A rigidity like rigor mortis stiffened Adulfa's limbs. Rhys was caught in a marble embrace and restrained against a woman carved from the same cold stone. Adulfa's eyes were half-open and her lips still curved into a kiss, but Rhys could not reach her mouth to kiss her again. It occurred to her that if she wanted to, she could wound Adulfa now, even kill her. But it seemed as if Adulfa was already dead. You had to be very patient to follow the slow rising and falling of her chest. Her heart beat was slower than a marathon runner's or a hibernating bear's. The heat had rapidly left her flesh.

Rhys realized that what she really wanted to do was stroke the curve of Adulfa's breast and cup her hand around her cunt. She wanted to explore this magnificent body, even if Adulfa would not respond with a sigh, goosebumps, or a slap. One of her hands was trapped under her body, but her free hand extended itself and hovered over Adulfa's left breast. But was touching Adulfa this way, unbidden, without permission, just another way to wound her?

Rhys tucked her free hand into the waistband of her jeans. "I've slept in worse places, Miss Haunted-House-Redrum-No-Wire-Hangers. Sweet dreams."

The troops were at Ulric's house within the hour. They came with wet hair from an incomplete shower, in full leather from an interrupted date, and in one case in grand black-and-gold pagan regalia for a Winter Solstice ritual. (Who knew that the archetypal dyke-on-a-bike, Pipe, would look so utterly convincing and feel so centered in the flowing robes of a Wiccan priestess?) But all of them were willing, worried about him, and determined to organize a search. It was strange to accept their embraces and condolences. But he sensed genuine concern beneath the come-hither he had laid upon them. So Ulric told himself that Lilith's hugs and kisses had been preparing him for this moment, and tried to relax and let them take care of him.

He took them into the dining room, where Lilith had never found the time to hold her formal dinner party, and rolled a large surveyor's map of the city onto the table. They discussed likely hiding places, divided the city into zones, and themselves into four search teams. Each team was to be accompanied by one of the cats, who could use their vampiric senses to augment human ingenuity. They all agreed that there was only a small chance of Adulfa remaining in the city with her hostage. They would take only one day to comb through San Francisco while Ulric probed other Bay Area locations, seeing if he could pick up the scent.

When the meeting was coming to a close, motherly and gray-haired Janice said to him, "Shall I pack you a bag?" Ulric looked at her with surprise. "You can't stay here after what's happened," she insisted.

So Adulfa was going to chase him out of his beloved mansion, the house that had waited for decades to become a home. It felt as if she was winning, stripping one of the most important signs of his humanity away from him. But Ulric saw the wisdom of what Janice was proposing. "I don't need much," he said.

"I guess not," she replied. Isabeau volunteered to go with her anyway. Ulric told himself that the two of them were perfectly competent to pack his clothing and toiletries. But he sent Janice an order to pack the book by the bed that he had started to read, Patricia Cornwell's *Portrait of a Killer*.

"There's something else you need," Curtis pointed out. "We've got to make sure you are well fed."

"I'll take care of that," Ulric said curtly.

"I beg to differ," the older leatherman retorted. His bristly mustache quivered with strong feeling. "I don't trust your judgment right now. So take what you need from two of us. We'll take turns. We'll just have to make sure we find her soon. Because every time you go out is one more time she can set you up and trap you."

"I've got to go out to look for Lilith," he argued.

"Yes," Moe agreed, "but when you're hungry you aren't as alert." She shoved her girlfriend forward. "Shuck your top, Alice."

"Please," Ulric protested. He couldn't bear to take a woman other than Lilith in his arms right now. "Not Alice. I'm sorry. Maybe in a day or so? But no girls." The lesbian couple seemed to understand.

"Me, then," and "Me!" said Fox and Lynyrd. Curtis just waited, knowing he was first in line. So Ulric found himself being fed by mortals as willing as Lilith. The experience was novel, and he felt threatened by so many changes. Too many people were involved in what should be his private business. What if Adulfa injured some of these fragile well-wishers?

He had little energy to spare on empathy, but the three men took it well. Lynyrd was a stoic and Fox was a whimperer. Curtis got very close to him while the feeding was taking place, and Ulric could feel his cock getting hard. He apologized, but Ulric only squeezed him harder, appreciating the reminder that life goes on despite catastrophe. There was potential to extend his sexual involvement to someone other than Lilith. Any of the family would have served him sexually as well as by donating blood.

That was something he would have to think about later. What he had to think about now was how to acquire enough power to defeat Adulfa. He had no quarrel with the vampire who straddled Oakland and Berkeley and currently worked on an ambulance crew as an EMT. Sacramento was too far away to sense its status, and anyway, he knew a potential killing field that was not all that far away.

He would give the vampire monastery in Marin County one more day of respite from killing. If they had not found Lilith before the night was over, he would sleep and then attack them. He was not looking forward to yet another encounter with Christian fanaticism, even if it had been twisted into a Satanic cult. And he would rather find Lilith without starting a feud with anyone else who shared his and Adulfa's proclivities. But he had a premonition that he would need the strength he could only obtain by killing another vampire. That would allow him to stay up during the day, and enhance the powers he needed to locate Adulfa.

Night fell. Adulfa awoke in Rhys' arms, for a moment forgetting that she was an immortal or that she had forced this woman to answer her call. They made love with the awkward sweetness of two people who were not fully alert. Rhys was an excellent kisser, and her musician's hands were more deft than most women's. Adulfa came sucking on Rhys' tongue while clever fingers coordinated pressure inside of her and upon her clitoris. She reciprocated, and Rhys quickly followed her into languid but complete release. This was the way she was accustomed to saying farewell to her women before the Germanic Knights attacked the Boar People of the Red Springs.

With that thought, memory returned, and so did awareness of the enclosed space. Adulfa broke away to release the catch on the coffin's lid, and stepped from its soiled white satin depths. "Let's have some fun," she said to Rhys, who followed behind in nothing but her damp underwear, a tiny pair of little boys' Spider-Man briefs.

Lilith was where she had left her, but her energy field was banked like a fire that had been reduced to embers. Adulfa shut off the vibrator, took off the harness that had held it in place, and removed the trident. Holding Rhys off with one hand, she bent and licked Lilith's genital and anal injuries, healing them with her potent saliva. The area continued to be sore and puffy, but Adulfa didn't care about that. She just didn't want Lilith bleeding to death before Ulric arrived. This mortal's death had to be carefully timed so it could be charged in full to Ulric's account.

The mortal woman blinked in confusion. She had dark circles under her eyes. "Thirsty?" Adulfa asked, and hoisted Rhys onto the table, knees on either side of Lilith's face. She took a strap off the wall that had a funnel in the middle of it, and buckled it around Lilith's face. The funnel was perfectly shaped to mold itself to a woman's crotch. "Piss," she said briefly to Rhys. There was the usual pause—that pesky human reluctance to openly victimize one another instead of sneaking about. Adulfa's early evening moment of nostalgic closeness with Rhys dissolved into acidic annoyance. She followed the command with a strong bolt of compulsion, and urine shot from Rhys' body into the funnel.

"Drink or drown," she kindly advised Lilith, who had barely come to understand that she was no longer being raped by the battery-operated trident. Her overtaxed psyche quickly resorted to a hallucination. *Ulric has sent me this bitter water to save me from dying of thirst*, Lilith thought, and drank freely, saving herself from choking.

Later, Adulfa removed the funnel and forced her to lick and suck Rhys' cunt until the vampire got tired of watching Rhys struggle to remain indifferent. Once more, she punched Rhys' psyche with a command that tipped her over the edge. Rhys came and Lilith cried. Some more. *Ho hum.*

"Remember what I said about those hot titties of yours?" Adulfa asked, picking Rhys up and setting her on the floor. She unlocked the padlocks and made Lilith sit up, then stand. While Rhys watched, stone-faced, Adulfa roughly fondled Lilith's breasts until both of her nipples were hard. "We both know you're an animal," she said thoughtfully, "but it's been bothering me to decide exactly which one you are. Well, today I believe it's obvious at last. Anyone looking at you could tell. Rhys?"

Startled to be included in the dialogue, Rhys, jealous and clueless, gaped at them both. Adulfa hissed. "A cow, of course!" she cried, shaking her head at the lack of cooperation. Attention was not being paid. *Well, what can you expect from Rhys, the girl voted Least Likely to Work at Hooters?* Adulfa dragged the two of them, Lilith by her hair and Rhys by a noose of thought, back to the horse. There, Lilith was forced to bend forward, and Adulfa secured her carefully, wary of the surprising strength of her resistance the previous night.

She wheeled a cart up to the horse. Adulfa squatted and lifted Lilith's breasts so she could nip and lick each one of them and force them to make an untimely change. Lilith gasped as she felt her breasts become even larger and more swollen. They felt hot and full. Large cups were attached to each of the prisoner's nipples. "We'll just leave this on long enough to get enough milk to put in Rhys' coffee," Adulfa said, confiding the news in Lilith's ear, as she switched on the pump.

"Did you ever think about the fact that your inhuman stud can never give you children?" she accused. "What's happened to your maternal instinct? I don't want to knock you up, but I do think you should at least experience lactation. It's only natural. Unlike the rest of the use that those udders have been put to. Do you think your daddy would get hot if he could see you now?"

Lilith realized that she had been connected to a milking machine, altered to fit human anatomy. She cried out when the first jets of hot milk were drawn rapidly out of her nipple ducts by vacuum pressure. The sensation of having her breasts compressed and emptied was making her womb contract the same way that it did when she came. While Lilith writhed against the horse, begging for mercy (*At last!*), Adulfa took Rhys over to her cabinet full of toys and outfitted her devotee with a harness and dildo of her own. "Every cow needs stud service," Adulfa said, laughing. "We'll turn you into a brave little bull. You've already got the ring in your nose."

"I'm a bottom," Rhys protested.

"So you'll do what you're told," Adulfa replied dryly, and took her back to Lilith's position. There, Rhys was told to grease up her latex prick and embed it within Lilith's cunt. "Fuck her as hard as you love me," was the exact order. Rhys was slow to comply, and when she finally got her dick inside of Lilith, she did not show enough enthusiasm to suit Adulfa's plan—even though her efforts were clearly having an effect on Lilith's hormonally primed body. It took only a modicum of stimulation for her vulva and vagina to supplement the pleasurable sensations that were meant to reinforce breastfeeding a child.

The vampire yawned. "Your love is a paltry and wimpy thing, Rhys," she complained. "I've got an excellent memory. When we finish with this milk cow, I'm going to fuck you. Exactly the way you fuck her. Stroke for stroke."

Artistry and ardor were restored.

Lilith's affirmation had been reduced to one word.

Survive.

A score of humans, four vampire cats, and a vampire master scoured San Francisco. They tracked Adulfa from downtown to a strip club and from there to Ulric's house. But there was no sign of her after that. Ulric put himself to sleep in the penthouse suite of an expensive Japantown hotel. He had two suitcases that fit together into a lightproof box, and before he crawled inside that, he donned a Kevlar sleeping bag. The cats squeezed in with him. The beds were occupied by some of the crew who slept with him as guards, which was very brave of them, Ulric thought, considering how outmatched they would have been if Adulfa had made another daylight appearance. Some of the rest dispersed to their homes to sleep as well, while others called in sick to their employers and kept on searching, albeit without the cats' uncanny assistance.

Ulric's only consolation was that Adulfa was probably unconscious as well and therefore unable to prolong Lilith's ordeal. Hiding her presence from him and then stealing Lilith would have taken, he hoped, whatever strength she had managed to build up before the kidnapping. When evening returned, he would do battle with the whole monastery if need be. He would gladly trade their lives for Lilith's.

And Adulfa's as well.

CHAPTER 15
The Pack Must Stay Together

On the second night of Lilith's absence, Ulric woke up with memories of
a rare dream and a sense of purpose strong enough to glow in the dark.
In the dream, he relived the day when Olav, his mother's brother, a few
other grown men of the village, and the oldest man living there had
taken him far out into the woods and left him there with a blanket, a
knife, sparking flint, some fishhooks, and his bow and arrows. He was
on his own in the wilderness from one new moon to the next, then he
had found his own way home. That had been his first successful attempt
to claim manhood. A second and even more important ordeal was upon
him, and his manhood was at stake once more. A man who could not
protect the ones he loved from harm was a poor excuse for a human
being. He would, he vowed, be ruthless in pursuit of victory.

He had embraced his own immortality for Lilith's sake; loving her
had made him love his own life. And now he was taking that love to a
whole new level. He was thrusting aside the guilt that had discolored
his joy ever since he ran from the fortress of the Germanic Knights with
Adulfa's curse on his heels. Until he met Lilith, he kept himself alive in
part because he believed he deserved to eventually experience Adulfa's
punishment for his unforgivable crime. Rage had replaced that anxiety
and timidity. He no longer felt himself doomed; his half-sister was the
one who was about to find that the scissors of the Fates were closing on
the red cord of her life.

The tortoiseshell kitten that had slept on top of his head was
hanging over his forehead and licking his nose. Her tongue was even
more rough than a regular cat's would be. Thank goodness his skin was
tougher as well. The other cats had awakened and were complaining
about the close confines of the trunk. He worked his arm out of the
Kevlar sleeping bag and threw the latch on the lid. They climbed on top
of him to stretch, digging their front claws into his chest to make sure
they could really loosen up their vertebrae, and then they leapt out,
digging their back claws into him to get traction. He laid there while
Luna, then Anastasia, then Charley repeated this ritual.

"I'm not your damn trampoline, you knife-toed acrobatic sneak
thieves," he complained, and they purred at this endearment, circling
the trunk where he had managed to sit up, lashing him with their tails.

He hated killing other vampires. The blood lust that chased him
from his resting place each darkfall quailed before such a challenge.
Vampirism was not like hemophilia or hepatitis—a genetic mutation or
a viral-borne agent that changed the immune system. It was magical as

well, and it was always difficult to predict which talents another vampire would possess, or how much they would have developed them. Unless they were exceptionally new and weak-minded, other vampires presented much more of a threat than mortals, who were usually no more than blood-bags on two legs.

Even if they were newly changed, with scant blood from their creator, like the pathetic girl he had taken when he first claimed San Francisco as his stalking ground, their deaths were more memorable to him than the run-of-the-mill, fatal taking of *önd* and heart-fuel. The girl in her plastic jacket and vinyl skirt still haunted him—he saw her face occasionally when he was on the prowl, and sometimes forgot she was not real, trying to greet her so he could make some kind of explanation or apology. But there was no restitution. She had bled out clasped to his stronger, much older body; and her naïve wistfulness, her expectation of companionship and mentorship that he could not provide, reinforced his depression and loneliness.

People of one kind ought to be able to gather together, share their stories and make plans together; have friends and lovers and families, games and songs; labor together to mend each other's houses, get the crops in, celebrate the eight sacred days of the year. They should cook food for one another, dance together, carve wood into plates and goblets and braid leather into horse harnesses and dye cloth together.

But vampires were no longer people, and each time he killed another immortal, Ulric was forced to recall that ugly fact.

Adulfa was more powerful than the other immortals he had stalked and slain. She had taken centuries to plot and prepare. She had chosen the place where he must assail her. He did not doubt that she would use Lilith against him. Exactly how she would manage that, he could not predict. A rescue would be harder than simply killing his sister. He would have to be crafty as well as strong to face her and regain custody of the bride of his soul.

The Jäger Family, as they called themselves, taking his own surname, had proved themselves to be hunters indeed. But their rapid and exhaustive search of San Francisco had been fruitless. Even the vampire cats could do no more than trace Adulfa's path from downtown through the Tenderloin and then to his house. If the West Wind knew where Adulfa had taken Lilith, he was not telling. Ulric's search of Oakland, Berkeley, and the rest of the South and East Bay had been frustrating as well. The traces of Adulfa's presence in Walnut Creek were tantalizing, but she had left no maps, journals, diagrams, or gossip to indicate where she would take her hostage.

He would have to increase the range of his senses and supercharge his physical and magical power to go to Lilith's aid. Adulfa could torture Lilith until her injuries were even worse than what he had seen on the home security videotape. She would keep Lilith alive as long as she wanted to torment her.

And Ulric was certain that Adulfa would not kill Lilith immediately. If she had wanted to punish him by murdering his slave, she could have done it in the library of his own home.

No, she wanted Ulric to suffer, and that meant he had to master his fear for his lover's safety so that it did not make him rash or stupid. Lilith was tough. An exceptional masochist, she would find a way to endure physical torture that would break a Navy Seal or a Green Beret. But would she retain her sanity? Up to a point, Ulric could mend broken bones, restore damaged internal organs; putting her psyche back together was a different matter. If Adulfa combined pleasure with mayhem, Lilith would have no more control over her orgasms than she would have over when her skin broke beneath the cracker of a bullwhip. Since Lilith was as submissive as she was masochistic, she would interpret any arousal or sexual gratification as disloyalty to him, and the shame that would cause her to experience might be as harmful to her as broken bones.

There was only one source of additional power that was close enough to allow him to visit it and still use the majority of the night to track Adulfa down. Of course, if he triumphed there, the daylight would be his to walk in as well. He had known for almost five years about the existence of a bizarre cult in Marin County. A vampire overlord was capturing men, torturing them, changing them into vampires like himself, and then compelling them to remain within range of his diabolical influence. Ulric could not imagine the agony his "postulants" endured. Nor could he comprehend the energy it must take to prevent them from escaping or committing suicide.

There he would find a fountain of vampire blood. But drinking it would be as hard as sipping from a mountain river in springtime flood.

He could not take the mortal foot soldiers with him. This job was simply too dangerous. And he could not spare the effort it would take to protect them from harm. He was not, to be honest, going to rescue more than one hostage tonight. For Lilith's sake and the love she bore these people, he would not use them to mount a distraction. Getting them to agree to this would not be easy, and he did not have time to waste arguing with them. So he would have to dissemble.

Trying to keep this concealed from the cats, he sat with them on the eggplant velvet loveseat and gave them each a cuddle and some blood. The love seat was comfortable despite its chrome legs and asymmetrical, modernistic back and armrests. (He had been too tired this morning to really look at the suite he had suborned the night clerk into making available for them. He didn't want to take cash out of the bank or use a credit card to pay for anything until this battle was finished. Adulfa was more likely to track him with her eyes and nose than snoop on his whereabouts electronically, but perhaps she had decided to enter the twenty-first century. There was no reason to be careless.)

Janice and Isabeau were up already. They must have reached an agreeable accommodation with one another during the night, because he could hear them laughing in the shower and occasionally shrieking with erotic glee. Ulric got up, dialed room service to order them a hearty dinner, and then took his own quick shower in a separate bathroom located in the other bedroom of the penthouse suite. There were clean clothes for him to put on when he got out—a comfortable pair of blue jeans, a T-shirt and a warm coat, thick socks and hiking boots. He found a knitted watch cap in the pocket of the coat and some gloves as well. As if he could get cold! But he could have a fashion crisis, and it pained him to think of riding his motorcycle without the leather jacket with the fringed sleeves. It was the kind of thing a practical mother would do, send you off to school with the warm jacket your friends would make fun of rather than the cool windbreaker with the skateboard logo.

Admit it, he told himself, *you love them too.* This little family was all that Lilith had promised—allies and blood-bonded friends. Only false pride would have let him believe that he would have been just fine planning a rescue effort on his own. It was time to dispense with falsehoods and illusions. And old feuds. Blood feuds.

He barely contained himself, sitting on the bed and tapping his toe, waiting for the two women to come out of the shower. When the door opened, they smelled so delicious, it was difficult to keep himself from taking a single jump across the room to attack them. They were wrapped in towels, their skins flushed from the hot water and desire for one another. He opened his arms and they went to him, smiling as they said good morning and drew him into the bed between them. While Isabeau cuddled against his back, he took Janice in his arms and fed from her, sparing her both pain and scars. Even though she was bisexual, she did not, he could tell, find him sexually attractive, but she was willing to offer him blood out of her fealty to him as head of their barely established clan. When he was done, he rolled to the other side, and Janice guarded and cradled him while he feasted from Isabeau's breasts.

The New Orleans beauty spoke with the same Cajun accent that Alain had, and she whispered lewd endearments in French while he worked her hard, black nipples with fangs and his rough file of a tongue. Her large breasts overflowed his hands, and so he could not avoid squeezing and molding them while he fed. Ulric took a little more from her than he intended because she encouraged him to do so, drawing him back to her three times when he would have withdrawn. The smell of her sex impinged more and more upon his inflamed senses, and it was all he could do to avoid allowing himself to get hard and slip between her legs. There was no time; he should not have sex with someone else while Lilith was in peril; and Janice had plans for that pussy and they did not include a cock. What he had done so far was exciting to both of the women, but it would be very rude to compete with the gray-haired woman's expert fist.

Finally Ulric was sated enough to regain self-control. He pressed Isabeau's breasts together and licked her cleavage and nipples, healing the puncture marks, then sat up, enjoying the feeling of vitality that made each feeding seem uniquely refreshing. There was a knock on the door and he went to bring in the room service trolley. He took the time to set it up for them near the bed, so they could also renew their energies. "When you gather the troops tonight," he told them, "please send them north of the city. I will be going over the Golden Gate Bridge."

"Do you think you can cover that much ground on your own?" Janice, who had become the volunteer coordinator, asked.

"Yes," he said shortly. "The cats will stay here to help you, of course." Adulfa had already endangered his pets. He did not want them within arm's reach of her again.

He was startled at the front door by Luna, who was sitting on a table beside it. She had been hidden by the lampshade. When he touched the doorknob, she reached out with one paw and smacked his hand, hard.

"What was that for?" he demanded, rubbing the injured appendage. She whipped around and showed him her little gold tail feathers and a crinkled, roseate asshole. Not deigning to speak to him, she jumped off the table and went back to the room where Janice and Isabeau were rattling cutlery and cutting up roast beef. Ulric hoped they enjoyed the Caesar salads and baked potatoes, and the cheesecake and chocolate-covered strawberries. There was also some champagne. Everybody liked champagne, didn't they? Other than Curtis, who had twelve years of sobriety. Why was Luna being so pissy?

So what if she didn't agree with his plan? He was in charge!

Ulric tried to slam the door, but its pneumatic hinges took over and put it slowly and silently back into place. Shaking his head and muttering complaints he knew were unreasonable and self-pitying, he took big butch stomping steps down the hallway, looking for the elevator to the hotel's garage. He would take his motorcycle to the monastery. He needed to feel like he was doing everything he could, and riding the bike was more demanding than driving Lilith's car. Besides, he could not stand being in it and remembering how it had looked waiting outside Alabama, the biker bar, when she told him they were driving home to San Francisco together. Together. What a wealth of sensuality, laughter, invitation, and healing that simple word concealed. He had not spent a night away from her since then.

Ulric's bike could easily do a hundred and twenty an hour. Despite a strong wind on the Golden Gate Bridge, he did exactly that. There was so little traffic that he didn't have to waste a breath on keeping the highway patrol off his tail.

Once he had passed Sausalito and gone deeper into Marin County, Ulric turned off the freeway and took surface roads toward the more rural sections of this beautiful bit of California. He was looking for a dirt track somewhere between the farms and wilderness areas protected by the state and federal government. It would have been faster to spot the monastery from overhead, but it was surrounded by a thorny hedge of look-not, and the buildings had been thatched with this rare and aromatic plant, rendering them almost completely invisible to mortal eyes.

This thorny stuff was so rare nowadays that it worked even better than it had when Ulric was a boy. When people don't believe in magic, they don't know how to spot it or combat it. But he had known what look-not smelled like, and that was how he had found the monastery in the first place. So he needed to be on the ground where his ability to pick up a scent-trail was strongest. And he did not want to waste energy on defying the power of gravity. Ulric bitterly regretted every moment he spent on travel, but it was the best strategy he had been able to come up with for finding his sweetheart.

After backtracking and getting quite frustrated, Ulric realized he probably had not gone far enough, and took himself back to a main road. He forced himself to slow down and stop periodically to make sure he had thoroughly sampled the air. A man in a pickup truck with a Harley-Davidson logo on the back window pulled over to ask him if he needed help with his bike. Ulric thanked him and explained he was just on vacation and taking in the beauty of the green world. "We need a little more of that," the man said, and shook Ulric's hand before getting back into his truck. Ulric noticed that he was careful to pull back onto the road at a low speed so there would be no spew of gravel directed at Ulric or his metal steed. Perhaps he should have detained the man long enough to take some blood from him, but that would have been churlish.

As if nature was rewarding him for this bit of charity, Ulric caught the first whiff of the look-not. It had been dissipated by running water, so his first job as a tracker was to spot the body of water that lay between him and the monastery. Since he had solved this puzzle once before, he cudgeled his memory and was able to jockey the bike down a series of trails and farmers' tractor paths until he found a little-used gravel access road that was full of spicy but unpleasant herbal notes. Sneezing every few minutes, Ulric took the bike along the hard-packed side of the road, not wanting to have his wheels fouled in the deep gravel. Eventually his body got accustomed to being immersed in the aromatic atmosphere of the hedge and he stopped sneezing. But his sinuses felt as if he had shot them full of Tiger Balm, a treatment he would have enjoyed only if applied externally to portions of his body other than his face.

He left the motorcycle at the entrance to the monastery, where there was a small slice of asphalt marked off into parking spaces. There was no use in being subtle. If the master of the order was here, he probably knew by now that he was outside the walls that guarded this heartless charade of a pious life. Ulric's only hope was to kill quickly and in quantity.

He found the first body just inside the gate. Two men in dark brown habits were arranged head-to-toe in the shape of an arrow. Ulric followed the pointing fingers of the monk at the head of the symbol. He found bodies aplenty to lead him on, but none that contained a single drop of the magic that he so desperately needed. The life-seeking sense in the roof of his mouth had been fouled by the look-not, but he decided with considerable frustration and consternation that he should trust its report that there was no one useful left alive in this virtual warehouse of sorcerous blood. The hours of the night had been whittled down to half their number by this fruitless search. None of the bodies he turned over had the aura of an elder, so the overlord of this cult must have fled. It was such a temptation to fall into despair.

Philosophy is the first retreat of the adherent to a hopeless cause: "Always outnumbered, always outgunned," he said to himself, recalling the title of his favorite Walter Mosley novel. Driven by the protectiveness that is a male essence of love, he did not even think of changing his tactics.

It wasn't hard to figure out who had committed this massacre. If Ulric had needed a definitive clue, he found it by the last body—the fore and aft prints of a tiger's paws in blood-churned mud and a fence post that was shredded eight feet from the ground. When she quit Europe and headed east and south to India, Adulfa had been delighted when she first saw one of these beautiful and efficient predators. Its striped hide had become her trademark four-footed guise. The dead monk had a knife in one fist and a clump of orange fur in the other. She had eaten his screaming face.

Ulric would have to face his sister without bolstering his power, and there was no cavalry to charge over the hill and save him at the last minute. She was here, waiting for him somewhere. Ulric thought she would probably take her ease while she felt him nearby, gradually closing in, rather than ambush him. The passage of time only left her in a more powerful position while he weakened.

Adulfa would not be found in a garden shed or a dormitory, no matter how smart it might be to hide her proceedings in a discreet location. She would want to be in the center of things. Someplace grand. She was a vainglorious jewel that would only settle into an emperor's ransom of a setting. Destroying this order had probably made her unbelievably powerful. From his experience with a lesser order of slaughter, Ulric knew the danger that such power carried with it: a sense of grandiosity that could cloud one's judgment, just as too much alcohol fuddled the common sense of mortals.

He located a tall, square building with a round, gilded roof. It was topped with a Christian cross, reversed. The chapel. Of course.

Lilith and Rhys had been confined in separate cages. Adulfa had been pissed off at both of them. Rhys had not performed with the appropriate degree of nastiness as her surrogate fucker and Lilith had not provided her with an entertaining level of resistance. "You've got a long way to go, the two of you, before anybody casts you as Renfield or Mina Harker," she said. "But never mind. The final act is about to ensue, and the two of you are only props. Not even spear-carriers or members of the chorus."

Then she left. Lilith was ashamed of herself for being so full of hope when the only thing she should feel was guilt or resignation. If this drama was about to reach the climax that Adulfa desired, it could only be because Ulric was near. She had done the damage that Adulfa told her mortals must inevitably do to any vampire weak enough to love them. She would be the death of him. Adulfa's strength of body and will had broken her. She could not believe that Ulric would win, even if his attention was not divided by the need to rescue her. She ought to simply kill herself, because then Ulric might have the impetus he needed to come out of this alive. He could flee, since the reason for fighting Adulfa in the first place would be gone.

Lilith reconsidered. Her death would send him straight for Adulfa's untouchable throat. Even if she had been brave enough to commit suicide, Lilith had no weapons. She might have been able to steel herself enough to chew through one of the veins in her wrist. And knowing that Ulric was about to die because he had loved her made death seem very attractive. It also sounded restful and so much cleaner than living. After what she had done at Adulfa's bidding, Lilith was not sure she could ever look Ulric in the face again, much less presume to love him.

But these arguments were presented in a moot court, because Adulfa had left her in standing bondage, hands far over her head, with duct tape on her mouth and the same ugly stuff wound around her ankles. She had no way to get at herself and tear her own flesh. Before she had left, Adulfa had bled her again, then sprayed most of it over Rhys, who had shrieked and cursed like a Russian sailor. She felt so weak that she kept blacking out. The pain of losing her footing and having the full weight of her body hanging from her wrists woke her up every time. But nothing could keep her in the here and now for long. Her body was giving up of its own accord.

Only the desire to see Ulric one last time before she passed focused her ebbing attention. Lilith wasn't sure where this idea had come from or what its attraction was, but it quite stubbornly took up residence and would not let her go. It was like having a nail thrust through her soul, a nail that kept that unhappy spirit from sailing away to a better place. "You've lasted this long," a voice seemed to say in her ear. "It won't be long now. You can last a little longer. *Survive.*"

What did that last word mean? Without wanting or meaning to, she lost consciousness again.

When she returned, yanked back into her body by the pain in her arms and shoulders, Adulfa was back. She was carrying a heart in both of her hands. It was still beating. While Lilith watched, too stupefied to really understand what she was seeing, Adulfa raised it above her head and squeezed it like an orange. Red juice cascaded into her open mouth. "Last fruits of the harvest," she explained to her two prisoners. Her voice rang in the air as if she were speaking with the tongues of several women—the chorus of Adulfa, a surprisingly harmonious sound, like a trumpet summoning the troops to battle. She tossed the deflated bag of red muscle between the bars of Rhys' cage, and its inhabitant scooted as far away from it as she could get, exclaiming, "Oh, gross!"

Clad all in red, as if she had been dipped in liquid latex, Adulfa sailed through the air to Lilith's cage. Her feet did not touch the ground. The room had enough dim indirect light for Lilith to be able to see sparks of gold shoot through minute cracks and pinpricks in her catsuit of blood. Lilith's long hair was sodden with sweat and her own blood, but the raw power Adulfa emitted made it stand away from her scalp as if she had leapt into a tornado. The cage door was ripped off its hinges. Adulfa was in too much of a hurry and in too good a humor to bother with cumbersome keys and locks.

"No!" Rhys screamed, beating on the bars that separated her from Adulfa. "Bitch! Not her! Why is it always *her* and not me?" She was carelessly damaging the same hands that she had begged Adulfa to preserve. But her jealousy and longing for Adulfa had taken control. As usual, Rhys' instinct for self-preservation was far weaker than her other passions. "Take me! *Take me!*" She pressed herself against the cage door hard enough to bruise herself, and continued to plead with Adulfa at the top of her lungs until she lost her voice. But she remained in place, as if welded to the bars, her mouth working with slurs she could no longer utter.

The rope that held Lilith upright in her confinement was severed with a vicious twist, and Lilith found herself carried along in the same wind that bore Adulfa to the center of the room. She glimpsed the bottom half of several frescoes and a few rows of wooden benches — an odd thing to put in a dungeon. Her human eyes could not see much of the room, which was even bigger than Adulfa had allowed her to understand. The hot storm that surrounded the Amazonian vampire made it difficult to keep her eyes open. But she could smell her. Adulfa had drunk and bathed in so much unnaturally potent blood that she stank like a hyena who has rolled in carrion.

Dangling at the end of a rope, Lilith was spinning through the air, parallel to the ground, buffeted by the storm of Adulfa's power. She spied an enormous pit, then was twirled in another direction, where she could almost make out the epically proportioned mosaic that covered the domed ceiling, as if it was a Byzantine cathedral. Was it a tribute to the strength of her love or merely an accidental firing of some stray neuron that reminded her now how she had wanted to see Ulric one more time before she died? She pried her eyes open and kept them staring as wide as she could. She somehow damped down the nausea and agony that had been her constant companions for two horrible nights and a day. With her bound limbs and gagged mouth, she was of no use to Ulric as an ally in a physical battle, but perhaps she could use the power of her mind to warn him away.

And indeed, when Ulric touched the door of the chapel, the pitiful and altruistic emotions of his beloved smote him from head-to-toe. "I love you," she said to him in a mind-to-mind rush. "Forever. I tried to wait for you, but she is too strong. Run! Do not worry about me, because I am lost to you through no fault of your own. If you love me, run! Someday you will have vengeance for my death, but not today. Please, Ulric, master, lover, my best friend and champion. Save yourself and flee!"

Not for the first time, the thought that today he might actually die chilled Ulric's rage. But he had been trained to fight his way through such fear. It was only the first rank of the enemy's forces. "Today is a good day to die," he retorted, then sent Lilith as much comfort and rueful affection as he could. "If this is to be the last time that we see each other in this world," he whispered to her soul, "you will not look upon a coward."

He threw open the door and had no time to absorb the details of his surroundings. Adulfa was six feet or more off the ground, holding Lilith perpendicular to her own body, also suspended. Below her was a pit. "There will be no fond farewell," she said in the voice of a demonic throng. She threw the echoing, repelling words at him like a weapon. He staggered back, astonished and dismayed by her glory. Adulfa was full of so much energy that she was in danger of disintegrating. But her dedication to her cause held her form together.

Adulfa's clawed hands dove toward Lilith's face, and each came up with a bloody eyeball in the cage of her fingers. The mortal woman's body remained suspended in midair, held there by Adulfa's will alone. Ulric bullied his way forward, fueled by a purpose as intense as his enemy's. But he could not get there in time. Adulfa regarded Lilith's eyes with a shrug, then tossed them into the pit. When he was still a body's length away from her, Adulfa lifted Lilith and broke her body across her knee as casually as someone snapping kindling for a bonfire. He tore toward Adulfa, burning up everything he had in the attempt, and then she dropped her precious cargo.

So much for his determination to be sly and strategic. Ulric didn't waste a second on protest or planning. Without thinking or making a conscious decision, he dove after Lilith, careless of the damage he took from spears that were embedded in the walls of the narrow shaft, angled to point upward. Somehow he got beneath her, just as he heard a massive iron grate being dropped overhead.

He caught Lilith on the tips of his fingers and eased her down, careful not to tread upon her eyes. Her back was broken, and she was hemorrhaging from internal injuries. He popped the first eye into his mouth, wondering whether it was her left or right, and then maneuvered it back into the socket. Lilith inhaled sharply through her nose, regaining consciousness, and he laved and replaced the second eye as precisely as he could. His hands were shaking with shock. He was bleeding badly himself, but he didn't care enough about his own safety to inspect his body for wounds.

As her eyes settled into place and the optic nerve reconnected, Lilith swiveled her gaze to regard him, and he noticed that the brown iris had acquired a sharp crown of red, and her pupils were a dark gold. His beloved mortal companion's eyes no longer resembled those of an ordinary human being. There was a thick piece of duct tape across her mouth. He picked at a corner of it until he could separate the makeshift gag from her face without tearing her delicate lips.

"I knew you'd come," she said, apparently forgetting her earlier plea that he abandon her. "I want to put my arms around you, dear heart, but I can't seem to manage it."

"Don't worry about that now," he said, stretching out beside her and undoing the rope around her wrists. The soles of his boots contacted a solid surface which he hoped was dirt. Dirt could be dug through, if he could figure out a way to keep Lilith alive long enough for him to tunnel out. The floor of the hole was barely large enough for them to lay side by side. He took off his jacket and arranged it on top of her and stroked her face. She had never looked more beautiful.

"Where are we? Is somebody sick?" she asked, looking worried.

"There's been some trouble, but we're okay now," he lied. "Just rest. I'll explain everything later." He sat up and took the tape off her ankles, lifting her feet as little as possible to peel it off. On closer examination, his hope that this oubliette had a dirt floor expired. Beneath a crust of soil was a concrete shell, and when he kicked at it, he could tell it was so thick that he could not punch through it.

He had been gone too long. When he laid down again, Lilith looked alarmed. "I can't shake my head. Ulric, why can't I feel my fingers and toes? Am I paralyzed?"

"Maybe. I'm not sure," he said. Strength was ebbing from him fast and with it the ability to maintain an illusion that all was well. He ran his hands down his sides and found a large ragged slice below his ribs. There was a puncture wound in his left calf. Other than that, and the fact that he was incarcerated with no source of blood, and the only person he cared for in the world was dying, everything was spiffy-grand-bully.

Reality was apparently impinging on Lilith as well. "She got us," she said. "Oh, Ulric, I'm so sorry." Tears gathered in her eyes. "Are you sorry?" she whispered. "I know I'm being selfish, but I just have to know that you're not sorry that you met me."

Since she probably would not be able to feel a hug and it might make her injuries worse, Ulric stroked her cheek and let his finger wander down her neck, to the spot where he had often tasted her essence. She recognized the gesture and gave him a coquettish smile. "Nothing could make me sorry," he swore. "I love you, and nothing can change that or take it away."

They were silent for a moment while she seemed to dream with her eyes open, and Ulric focused within himself, trying to knit his wounds together. It was slow-going. Fighting Adulfa had sucked the strength out of him as easily as an oil rig pumps black gold from beneath the earth. But he wasn't finished yet. His body had been strengthened by more than the blood of the tribe Lilith had gathered. Their love had also buffered him from at least some of her animosity. He would heal in time. It wasn't the wounds he had suffered during the fall that would kill him. It would be the lack of blood.

Lilith inhaled sharply, and he jumped. "What is it?" he asked. "Please, dear, don't upset yourself."

She laughed, but the sound was hampered by pain. Breathing seemed to be ever more difficult for her. "Do you believe in life after death?" she whispered.

"Of course I do," he said, thinking of the elders' teachings about the soul's voyage to the moon. He knew each stop along the way, and the prayers to say when he was challenged.

"Will we recognize each other there?"

He was so moved by her plaintive question that he took her hand and squeezed it. "Oh, yes," he reassured her. "Lovers can be reborn and find each other again and again. I will know you in the world to come, and we will rest together. There is no pain or hunger there, and no discord. In the Land Behind the Moon, we can set sail in a ship that responds to our thoughts and visit each magical island. We can lie on grassy hills in orchards where fruit falls whenever you are hungry and birds bring you sweet warm loaves of bread. We can learn the speech of bears and crows and salmon. You can take your pick from a clutch of dragon's eggs and raise your own fire-breathing scaly skyrider. We won't have to leave until we have sampled every delight and adventure and grown tired of them all. When we are ready to be reborn, I will find you in your next life. And maybe then we will have more time..." He could not go on speaking. The painful sensation of weeping without tears was closing up his throat.

"Ulric Jäger." She sounded like a mother calling her recalcitrant son to her side to be chastised. "I don't have much longer. Kiss me. Then save yourself."

He looked upward. The grill that sealed the throat of the prison was bristling with long knives, pointed downward. "I can't," he said simply.

"Change yourself into a bird and fly away," she insisted.

"I can't," he said again. "Adulfa has many animal forms, but she was a shape-shifter before she became a vampire. I have only one form, the wolf. When I have recovered from my wounds, I will be able to fly to the ceiling, but I will be in human form, and those spikes would cut me to pieces once more. It would be useless. In order to lift that grate, I will have to throw myself on those points and push it out of the way, then wriggle off of the spears before she manages to come up with another way to kill me. Without more blood, I am too weak to survive such an ordeal."

The woman who could not feel her fingers and toes, the woman with a broken spine, grabbed him by the collar and dragged him to her throat. Ulric had the all too rare experience of being frightened of her. "I have blood," she said in a gravelly voice. "It isn't going to do me any good. Take every drop."

"No," he protested, and threads of blood ran down his cheeks from his eyes—tears at last. "I have had enough of bloodshed. You know what it did to me to send Alain away from this life. How long I suffered. I think I would go insane if I had to live on, knowing I had been the one who ended your existence."

"I'm dead already," Lilith said. "And she's the one who killed me. Not you. I need you to live, Ulric. I need you to live so you can waste her wicked ass. Let me die knowing I will be revenged."

"Oh, Lilith," he chided. "You're trying to trick me by making me angry. It won't work. I'm too sad to be angry."

She shook him once, then her hand fell weakly away from him. "Snap out of it!" she said in what was a shout for her failing body. "Stop wringing your hands and *do* something. You're the daddy. You're the master. You're supposed to be the one in charge. So do your fucking job!" She turned her face away from him in a stubborn fit of pique.

"All right," he said slowly. "You're right. I am the one in charge. I own you, don't I?" He diverted energy from healing and sent it into his right hand, sharpening and lengthening his claws.

"Yes." She admitted it with her face still turned away from him, so he grabbed her head and forced her to look at him.

"I refuse to send my property to the Land Behind the Moon," he said, and slashed his throat open with the fingernails of his free hand.

She opened her mouth to protest, and the gout of blood drowned out the sound. She glared at him with a fury akin to Adulfa's. He had broken his solemn vow to never force her to accept immortality.

"Sometimes," he hissed at his lover, "consent is overrated."

Lilith gasped, feeling the strange substance of vampiric immunity begin to alter the bones, tissues, and fluids of her body.

"Now I will drink from you," he said, and took nourishment that he could return to her as quickly as he could cut his own wrist and shove it into her mouth. The balm of her rage quickly healed the wound in his neck.

Above them, a voice pealed out. They barely registered it. Adulfa was taunting them. "Everything is going according to plan," she gloated. "You have broken faith with her just as you violated my trust. Now she will join you in immortality, and the two of you will find each other's company intolerable. While you struggle to get away from each other, all traces of your love melting into thin air, I will keep you and watch you waste away. Perhaps I will even prolong your suffering with an offering of blood now and then. But you will die. At my hands. And at my feet."

A second cover was fitted over the grill, sending them into darkness. Lilith had recovered enough to fight him, and she was feeling the weird pain of transformation. He struggled to contain her and continue the feedings. Just as he had brought Adulfa over, he used his blood like the cock of a rapist to force Lilith to do his will.

Adulfa had not bothered to close the door to the church. She had her back turned to it as she wrestled the lightproof cover of the tomb into place. She was no longer bloated with the full force of the massacred monks, but she still had a full head of steam. Perhaps she would taunt the sun by staying awake after dawn, and entertain herself with Rhys on top of Ulric and Lilith's prison. It was so courteous of the head of this order to furnish her with this blasphemous sort of church where he tortured and incarcerated his raw recruits. She had not been able to find the master vampire who ran this scam, and that was annoying, but she knew he was nowhere within range of her enhanced senses, which now extended for at least two hundred miles in all directions. Amazing. So much to see, and so little of any importance or interest was happening.

She danced in a spiral on the top of the grille, into the center and out again. She was almost back to its rim when every candle in the place lit up and the interior of the church became nearly as bright as day. Then she heard a truly disagreeable noise—the sound of small bells, shaken all together.

A woman in a pleated, transparent linen sheath and an Egyptian wig walked through the double doors. She had one hand out, bidding the candles to burn more brightly, and in her other hand she shook a sistrum, the ancient symbol of Isis. Adulfa threw her hands out in a vain attempt to recapture the power that was leaving her in streams of fading gold.

Behind the Egyptian priestess came a woman wearing an Edwardian dress and a long sable coat. She held the hand of a child who was wearing a smaller version of her mother's dress, only her coat was shorter, and made of blue velvet. The little girl's hair was striped black, orange, and white. This couple went to the left of the priestess and joined with her in throwing a commanding aura in Adulfa's direction. Once they were in place, Adulfa saw a man emerging through the church doors. He was nearly seven feet tall, wore red long johns and a flannel shirt under a pair of overalls, and had a red bandanna tied around his neck. There was a raccoon hat on his head, complete with tail. He strolled over to the cage where Rhys was kept and whacked the lock off with his ax. The girl ran to Adulfa, who was being moved back, away from the iron circle where she had danced in triumph just minutes ago. Then he, too, put up his hands and assisted the others in binding her.

As she felt her arms being forced to her sides, Adulfa reached for Rhys and tucked the musician under her arm before she could no longer control it. Rhys spat at the foursome that faced them. If Adulfa could have moved, she would have shaken her head and rolled her eyes. What was the munchkin thinking? It seemed to her that she should recognize these intruders who were spoiling her plans. But when would she have met...?

Oh.

"Yes," the priestess said. "If a woman can become a tiger, surely a cat can become a woman."

A small crowd of mortals had barreled into the church. Some of them looked around, distracted by the odd furnishings, but their mates urged them to focus on the task ahead. Some of them carried crowbars, and others carried steel cable. Was that an engine block hoist that was being wheeled into her lovely retreat? Adulfa snarled, but the priestess shook the sistrum again, and she was denied the power to even curse at the insolent serfs who gradually succeeded in shifting the heavy lid of the underground prison. It was set aside, and then the grille was tackled.

Adulfa could not go forward to prevent this, so she squeezed Rhys, a frustrated reflex. "Ouch!" said the waif. And Adulfa actually found herself wanting to say, "Sorry." The whole world was being turned upside down.

The two prisoners saw none of this, although they were aware of light returning. From struggling with each other, they had turned to a more familiar activity, and were pounding at one another in a sexual frenzy, venting all the fear and fury they had experienced since they were forcibly separated. Lilith was already naked, and Ulric's clothes had been discarded and demolished. "I hate you" and "I love you" flew back and forth from both of their lips, which then locked together in deep and desperate kisses. Both of them believed it might be the last time they would be able to make love with one another.

When the light hit his face, Ulric looked up at a miracle. The mouth of their prison was open once more. The angle of the sun had changed slightly, and what he saw now was not an impenetrable thicket of spikes on the walls of the pit. Instead, he saw a stairway. But it was not a stairway that a man could climb. There was one point where a great leap would secure a launching pad that could be used to escape in a series of dangerous but doable jumps.

"Lilith," he said, drawing back from a kiss that had made his head reel and his cock jump. "Listen to me. We have to change. We need the strength of the wolf, its cunning and balance. I know it's too soon for you, but I believe you can do it. We're already linked together. Just let yourself go and change with me. You're a woman. You already have more magic in your little finger than I have in my whole body."

He showed her the succession of thick spear shafts that he believed it was possible to balance on for an ascension. Then he called out for the change, and at the same time hung on to all of his links with her, remaining inside her body, the two of them of one blood, their passion for each other knitted together as tightly as their limbs. Adulfa's bane had mysteriously eased, and his body was fit once more. For the moment, Lilith wanted nothing more than to be with him. The only reason she had rejected immortality was the threat of being separated from him. Rather than have him depart into another form, Lilith went with him. Ulric felt cautious optimism when it was clear that the first part of his plan was going to work. They might become the fiercest of enemies once they were free, but at least he would know she was alive.

Lilith shifted in his arms, mercurial as Proteus, skin and fur, two-legged becoming four-footed, her beauty taking a form that was older than *Homo sapiens*. Anyone who was watching would have seen a huge black wolf hunched atop a woman in a shrinking fur coat, and then they would have seen a female wolf, white, with golden tips along the flanks of her pelt, being mounted by the black wolf. She accepted the thrusts of her consort, and when he was done, the two of them nuzzled each other's faces and licked one another's bellies and rumps. When he attempted a second mating, she snarled briefly and leaped atop his back. Then she was gone, leaping several feet into the air and landing on the first precarious foothold. The black wolf followed the fearless, white-gold streak of his mate, blazing a path up and out of their prison, heading for the sky like a meteor in reverse.

How comforting it is to have four feet back on the ground, Lilith thought. Her new body was even healthier than her human form had been, and enriched by a powerful sense of smell that gave her facts human beings would never have been able to gather. At first, she and Ulric were too happy to be free to notice the spectators. They frisked around each other, whining, lunging and then wheeling away, in the ancient game of tag that their kind could play for hours. There was no more hatred or anger in her heart toward him. He had saved her. He was her companion and king.

The abrupt transition to animal form had felt like being turned inside out, but it had taken away the pain of being infused with the catalyst of vampire blood. Ulric, too, was fit and happy once more, so funny, so much fun, and she could not get enough of the smell of him. She had never felt so much joy and strength. Colors were brighter, every detail of the world seemed much more interesting than it had before, and they really should be running. She wanted to hunt with him across land they had marked out as their own.

But a human concern nagged at her, some obligation that must be satisfied before she could be carefree. Lilith broke away from Ulric and trotted over to the humans who had risked so much in their behalf. He followed her, anxious about how well she would be able to control her instincts. He had gone back and forth from the world of man to wolf many times, and it was still hard for him to feel anything but hostility toward mankind. His mate accepted the humans' caresses with rare grace for a feral creature. Judging that it was safe to do so, he advanced to the four in front who still held Adulfa backed up against the pulpit of this unholy church. Lilith was soon at his side, although her hackles had risen at the tingling charge of the magic they wielded. Black and white wolf put their front paws together, lowered the front halves of their bodies, stretched out uttering whining barks, and bowed their heads in thanks.

The pair bounded away out the door of the chapel, interested only in each other. There was no animosity apparent between them, only the strong bond of an alpha wolf to its mate. For the immortals and ordinary people who loved Lilith and Ulric, it was a much too brief reunion. Some of them were weeping from relief and also the pain of separation. They were part of this pack as well, were they not? Lilith had bound them all together with her blood, named them a family. And a pack should stay together.

Adulfa was so incensed, she managed to break through the field of repulsion to scream, "Nooooo. How can it be? They should not be together! They hate each other. He changed her. I saw it! They have to hate each other. How can this be?"

"Before I let you go," Luna said, "there are some things you should know, Adulfa. All is not as you have believed it to be." She wore a collar of turquoise, red, and white beads. Her wig was impeccably styled and perfumed. On each wrist, she had several enamel bracelets in the same colors as her necklace. The starched linen must be scratchy against her nipples and shoulder blades. She had a sandy red complexion, full lips, and slanted golden eyes outlined with kohl. Since she could not look away from her, Adulfa had ample opportunity to take note of all of these details, even the fingertips sheathed in gold and the jewels glued to her toenails, and the incongruous single diamond earring she had worn as a cat.

"I—don't—care—what—you—have—to—say," Adulfa grunted through the magical barrier.

"Ulric did not rape you," the Egyptian aristocrat said. Then she lowered her hands a little, allowing Adulfa to fully regain speech and the movement of her arms.

"I was there," Adulfa said, her indignation as fresh as the day when she had left the crusaders' cell, marked by her brother's semen and fangs, cheated of a warrior's glorious death in battle and her place at the everlasting feast of the one-eyed god of war and his swan maidens. "He did that, and worse."

Luna shook her head. Charley the lumberjack, Anastasia the Russian princess, and her adopted daughter Hecate continued to watch Adulfa with silent wariness. Their mortal friends hovered behind them, suddenly frightened of their foe. They had never seen Ulric in full force, and so the sight of Adulfa in a grand tizzy was very intimidating. Nevertheless, they too stood their ground, trusting that the foursome who had brought them here knew what to do.

"It was the Christian Knight who raped you," Luna explained, speaking slowly. "Hilbert made you believe that Ulric had done it to torture you both."

"No! No! I killed him. I would have seen it in his memory. He's dead these six hundred years, and it is not possible, what you say cannot be true."

"You never killed him," Luna countered. "And he was a vampire long before he killed Rowan Silverhair and swallowed her heart. How else do you think he managed to conquer one of your elders? She was powerful enough to reduce any mortal soldier to a crumbling pile of dust, no matter that he put on his own body-weight in armor and styled himself a general."

Adulfa's mouth opened in shock. All of the pieces of her reality were tumbling down, and she had no idea how to rearrange them.

"He lives," Luna avowed, and repeated it. "He lives. He is full of the power of the Adversary, a power older than you can imagine."

"Then I—all of these centuries—I have wronged—"

"Yes," Luna said, and her tone of voice was kind. "You have tried to kill your brother to punish him for a crime he did not commit. The same evil creature victimized you both."

Adulfa touched her neck. "But he still made me, Ulric changed me, and I didn't want that!"

"No," Luna said, as if she were speaking to a child. She had the full attention of everyone in the room. "Hilbert, whose real name is Lazarus, changed you while he made you think that your brother was forcing himself upon you."

Adulfa was thunderstruck, and even Rhys could not think of one thing to say.

"You have been the hunter all your life," Luna said. "But now you are the hunted. Because Lazarus lives. When you destroyed this monastery, you brought yourself to his attention. Now he will be hunting you. And he won't be alone."

In shock, Adulfa looked at the church door, replaying the sight of Ulric and Lilith, leaping after one another. They had looked happy, frisky, but not human at all. They would be living as wild animals do, looking for territory, forming their pack, seeking game and digging burrows. She knew what it was like to lose herself in the vivid, body-centered energy of an animal, conscious only of the present, free from anxiety or abstract thought. It was often hard to come back to a weak and troubled human body. But wolves were an endangered species. Where would Ulric and Lilith find enough wilderness to support them, and how could they hide from hunters who would shoot from a helicopter, with high-powered rifles that had unerring sights? Then it occurred to her that Ulric did not even know he was innocent; he would still believe that Adulfa was his mortal enemy. She covered her mouth and gasped aloud, a sound that hurt her gut to make. An unaccustomed sensation of pity and remorse was cleaving her in two. The sound of her shock made the candle flames shiver.

"Yes," Luna said in response to her unasked question. "He will be after them as well. And you should pray that they return, Adulfa, the lovers that you tortured and tried to separate. Because without the power of three, you will not be able to defeat the evil that looms over you."

She cast her eyes upward, and everyone, including Adulfa, looked up as well. The mosaic on the ceiling of the chapel depicted an erect lion trampling on a crescent moon, bearing a cross in one of his paws.

Caveat lector! Patrick Califia is the sadistic storyteller *par excellence*. In this erotic tale of love and vengeance, the author of *Macho Sluts* and *Doc and Fluff* sweeps the reader into a world of sinister magic and painfully intense pleasures. When he is not reading other people's vampire stories, Patrick is spoiling his kitty cat or disciplining deserving masochists. He says, "Cats, unlike people, are innocent." For information about Patrick's upcoming appearances and forthcoming work in print, check up on him at www.patrickcalifia.com.